# SUNSHINE
# REPUBLIC

"Together we all write the future!"

Ted Brown

# SUNSHINE REPUBLIC

# REPUBLIC

## THUNDER OVER LAKE WORTH

## TED BROWNSTEIN

ILLUSTRATED BY **JON SIDERIADIS**

New Lands Press

CHICAGO, ILLINOIS

ISBN: 978-0-9832609-0-5

Illustrations by Jon Sideriadis
Backcover flag: iStock©ayzek.
Flag photo manipulation by RD Studio.
Book design by DesignForBooks.com

# HEADS UP TO READERS

As I was writing *Sunshine Republic*, I often started my day with a copy of Shakespeare, Orwell or some other classic author open in front of me. Reading a page or even a few lines helped summon my muse and allowed me to draw inspiration from their distant, echoing voices. Early on, I discovered among Bradbury's Martian Chronicles a story titled *Usher II*, set in a robotic house of horrors, playing whimsically with themes from Edgar Alan Poe's *Fall of the House of Usher*. As my story snaked through a similar robotic landscape, how could I resist trying my hand at *Usher III*? I had a great deal of fun doing so (and similarly tipping the hat to the spirits of other great authors).

*Sunshine* readers may find it equally intriguing to keep an eye out for such ghosts, embodied as allusions to the opening lines of *Julius Caesar* or references to *Fahrenheit 451* or *Alice in Wonderland*. Tidbits, by the dozens, have been buried in the story. The game is hide and seek, if you, dear reader, care to play. (As you go along, you may find things getting "curiouser and curiouser." Wink.)

Thanks needs go to my wife Chris—who tolerated my ongoing Sunshine Republic daydreams, Julie Gilbert—leader of the Kravis Center's Writer's Circle (West Palm Beach) who provided initial inspiration, Karl Monger and Chris Bernard—editors, Jon Sideriadis—illustrator, Taylor Stevens—mystical mentor, Michael Rohani—publishing consultant, as well as the many good people who have read various versions of the story and provided feedback along the way.

I had a wonderful time creating this future Florida of 2130. I hope you enjoy your visit there.

—Ted Brownstein

# JACKPOT AT DAWN

BARELY EIGHT HOURS ago, Lady Luck flashed Inspector Jurat a big, pearly grin, and instantly he found himself in Jackpot Country. For the first time in his uneventful, humdrum career, Solomon Jurat started catching breaks, each one bigger than the last. By noon, he'd tallied twenty-six arrests requiring ten squad car runs to haul in all the perps. The jailhouse was overflowing, not to mention the overstuffed impound warehouse. During the raid on that clandestine cyber factory, thirty contraband robots had been seized along with tons of assembly equipment. Plus, he had leads on co-conspirators from Pensacola to Key West and beyond. There were even implications of international involvement. Gads! He was giddy just thinking about it.

Pudgy hands on his rotund belly, his unfashionably narrow green tie flopped lazily down his chest, he stood in the doorway of his office at the Palm Beach County sheriff's department, scanning the empty building, savoring his sudden good fortune. The long hall might be week-end quiet now. But by Monday morning accolades for the greatest coup ever would be echoing through the soggy, air-conditioned air. By Friday he ought to be sprawled in a corner office suite with high windows overlooking the Intracoastal Waterway and staffed with a personal receptionist, eager, affable—and requisitely cute. By the end of the month he could be holding a new contract, at triple his current pay.

Strangest of all, the whole thing had fallen into his pudgy hands almost without his lifting a finger. Just as the sky was growing light, after a long, uneventful graveyard shift, Jurat had been driving home on what happened to be the right street, at what happened to be the right moment, and he'd seen this kid, a well-known brainy local tekkie, as full of himself as they make 'em, marching a troop of clearly illegal, metal-faced robots down Dixie Highway. Brilliant people sometimes just lacked common sense. The kid might as well have marched directly to the G Street jailhouse and locked himself up.

And now chubby, slack-jowled, balding, little ol' likely-to-snooze-off-during-staff-meetings Jurat, who barely made inspector after thirty years on the force, and who had never caught a break in his stodgy, boring life, was about to become a hero for simply being alert enough to click in the arrest order.

After a brief chase, the kid was apprehended and hauled to the lockup along with two ruffian collaborators and his illegal, toad-ugly buddy bot.

From then on, the inspector had drawn one ace after another. The clandestine factory—a renovated bungalow wired for robotics—turned out to be on M Street, just a few blocks from the scene of the arrest. When the police arrived, they found a score of collaborators swarming the place, destroying documents, hauling off contraband equipment and otherwise removing evidence. It took all morning to finish ID'ing and booking them, but not *NetNews*. The breaking story, complete with photos of a closet stuffed with humanoid robots, hit the web within an hour and quickly spread coast to coast. Jurat was already being praised by the blogcasters, who were crediting him with brilliance, initiative, daring. Daring? Pfff! He shook his head and chuckled. Finally, after the most mediocre of careers, he'd caught one honey of a break. Ah! The sweetness of it filled his soul like a hive at orange blossom time.

But, happy as he was about his easy success, Inspector Jurat wasn't about to let himself get too smug. He'd seen the kid marching at the head of a motley-looking troop of nearly a dozen, but only three humans and one bot from that bunch had been captured. Where had the rest vanished to? And who were those other players they'd picked up and were now questioning? Not to mention the factory. Where had the robot parts and assembly equipment come from? And who was footing the bill? What a big, incredibly complicated case. Just the thought of it was exhausting.

Jurat tossed his hat into the corner and slumped his weary frame into an auto-conform chair. The oversized desk was cluttered with stacks of brain scan disks, remnants of old lunches and a collection of ancient, often reread Ray Bradbury paperbacks. No doubt the smartass kid, pacing frantically in the lockup downstairs, could have saved Jurat days of wading through scan records. But he wasn't talking.

There was more to this than some gang of local amateurs tinkering with illegal robots. The bots were too sophisticated, for one thing. A highly developed research facility had to be behind it. Jurat scowled. Like that place down on the Palm Beach University campus. The Futurist Party Lab . . .

The out-phone buzzed.

"Inspector Jurat," Jurat muttered in his driest police-work voice.

"Justice Pawl here," the caller said. "I understand you're the star of the robot case."

Jurat's eyes bulged. A call from the Chief Justice of the Florida Supreme Court? He pinched himself. Things were moving almost too fast.

"Ye-yes," Jurat said meekly. His knees locked together.

"I hear good things about you: solid reputation, dependable, not a showboat cop, but a steady, level-headed investigator. I'm glad the case is in your capable hands"

Jurat couldn't believe his ears. No one of importance had every described him as anything but a Keystone Cop. "Thank-k you, sir. At this very moment, the robot-builder we caught is locked up in our highest security ten-by-ten. We've already interrogated him, along with two dozen co-conspirators." Jurat hoped the Justice would be impressed with the speed of his investigation.

But instead of offering another compliment, Pawl changed the subject.

"You're located in Lake Worth, in Palm Beach County, right?"

"That's correct, sir."

"And the incident involves a political campaign, is that right?"

Jurat's eyes rolled. He knew nothing about a political connection. "Yes, s-sir!" he lied. "I had hoped to keep that fact hush-hush pending further investigation." He muted the volume on his web interface as he spoke, and browsed to the Lake Worth Web-Times site. The headline of the lead story, posted less than an hour ago, read:

## FUTURISTS FALSELY ARRESTED
### Property Wrongfully Impounded

Jurat's stomach churned. "We're in the process of assessing the involvement of the Futurist Party in this affair. Damn that Times reporter. I gave him orders to hold off," he lied again. "Now he's gone and defended them before we've even accused or charged them. Don't they train journalists to be impartial anymore?"

The Justice growled impatiently. "I don't care about the reporter. I care about the integrity of our electoral process. I'm getting calls from Futurist Party attorneys citing political harassment. I'm told the robots were legally registered to a licensed research facility and that all limitations have been followed to the letter."

"Uh," Jurat hesitated to contradict the Justice. "No, sir, not true. Their metalloid was walking down a public street in broad daylight, and then we found a gang of contraband humanoids, holed up in an unlicensed facility, all clearly in violation, sir."

"And why would they use an unlicensed facility when they have a legal, fully permitted lab just a couple of miles away? Does that make sense to you?"

"Uh, no sir. I have no idea, sir. Our investigation just started this morning."

"You realize the election is just ten days away. I'm trusting you to get to the bottom of this by Tuesday, so we'll have a full week to straighten things out before the vote. The public deserves the truth. We're not going to allow ourselves to be gored or bushwhacked this time, are we?"

Jurat clicked his teeth at the worn-out reference to Palm Beach's role in the disputed presidential election of the year 2000. That controversy was 130 years old yet returned each season like a loggerhead sea turtle to lay a fresh clutch of eggs.

Pawl continued. "I want you to report directly to me. I don't want any more headlines, no more arrests, no more confiscations, until we know what the hell they're up to. Is that clear?"

"Yes, sir, perfectly clear."

"Tell you what I'm going to do to help you out. I'm sending down my personal assistant, Ms. Alice Blain. She'll be my liaison with your investigation. I need to stay on top of developments. In view of the threat to free and fair elections, the reason for this extra precaution should be obvious."

"Yes, sir! Completely obvious."

"Then I can count on your full cooperation with Ms. Blain?"

"Yes, sir. Full cooperation. Tell her I'll have a private office ready for her, one right next to mine."

"Good day, then."

Too agitated to sit, Jurat pulled himself out of his chair and began pacing tight circles around his desk, absent-mindedly picking at crumbled bits from a bucket of day-old conch fritters. His frantic mind searched for a way to wiggle out of this heavy responsibility, with its inevitable micro-scrutiny. But there simply was no escape. Somehow, he'd have to find the self-discipline to get the answers the Justice wanted.

Truth be told, Inspector Jurat had never been exactly a ball of fire at the best of times: he had floated through his years on the force so far by kowtowing to his superiors, keeping a low, comfortable profile, putting in just the necessary effort, and never, ever, rocking the boat. But that strategy wouldn't work in this case. Disappointing the Chief Justice was just not a career option. "Set your butt down," he told himself, "and start wading through the kid's brain scan disks." The entire contents of the kid's mind were stored on those disks. All the answers were right here on his desk. "Sit yourself down," he again ordered himself, "and get busy."

And yet, somehow, it just didn't happen. It was Sunday, for gosh sakes. Heck, after a long week at the office, to say nothing of the greatest triumph of his career, didn't the would-be hero of the month deserve a little down time? Say, a lazy afternoon at the Bryant Park band shell, lounging in his portable hammock, curled up with a novel or lulled to sleep by mellow Cuban jazz, distracted only by the occasional need to get up and buy another beer? . . . Instead, here he was, sitting at his desk, trapped by the call from the Justice and glaring at a huge pile of brain-scan disks. The wall-sized display screen loomed like a gigantic Big-Brother eye; it's highly reflective surface monitoring him, scolding him for procrastinating.

Reluctantly he hit the power button. A text window popped onto the screen.

TO: Inspector Jurat
FROM: Catherine (Kitty) Hescheri – IT Staff
SUBJECT: Futurist Emulation Software
MEMO: Among the materials discovered during our reconnaissance of Futurist Party headquarters was a unique bit of software that translates raw brainwave data into cinematic videos of sight and sound. It has the unique capacity to accurately depict your subject's thoughts and at the same time dress it up in an easy-to-listen-to, fun-to-watch format. Instead of pouring over boring charts of neuron data, you can sit back and enjoy a good story as your computer generates an exciting dramatization on the big screen, just for you. We've set it up in the style of Ray Bradbury, since we know he's one of your favorite authors. To begin, insert the red program disk into Port B.

Jurat grew more intrigued each time he reread the message. IT staff was certainly currying his favor. But he was skeptical. Could any emulation program produce a dramatization on par with so great a writer? Nevertheless, there was no harm in giving it a try. Now, at least, there was hope that today wouldn't be a total drag. He selected the only red disk from the pile and popped it into the installation drive. After a few clicks, the text message morphed into a smiling face, framed in unkempt gray hair.

"Welcome to my new narrative emulation suite," the face said. "For those of you who may not know me, I'm Ray Bradbury, bestselling science-fiction writer from the twentieth century, author of *Fahrenheit 451* and *Martian Chronicles*. The drama you are about to see will be presented in my highly acclaimed storytelling style."

Jurat looked up at the long-dead Bradbury and rolled his eyes. Those IT boys were sure pouring it on thick. With a click of the tongue, he paused the presentation and pressed a worn F3 to bring up the food service menu. From the screen, he ordered up a big bag of well-buttered popcorn with a pint of Cerveza Grande. Thirty seconds later, a little trapdoor opened and the items slid into his desk's built-in food tray. He grabbed a few kernels of corn to be sure they were hot, and sipped the beer to make sure it was cold. Jurat was pleased. He tossed several containers of old food into the recycler to clear space on his desk, then began sorting through the disks.

It took a minute to locate the disks containing the intake records from this morning's arrests. They were labeled cryptically with only the case number and the arrestee's initials. One by one, Jurat loaded the silvery platters into the optical reader. As the computer began to organize the data into a story, its internal instructions ran across the screen in stiff, square letters.

OPEN LIBRARY = CASE (PENDING): ROBOT LIMITATION BOARD v. FUTURIST PARTY OF SOUTH FLORIDA

MODE = DRAMATIZE: (Bradbury Emulation)

SOURCE – DETAINEE BRAIN SCAN FILES

START: (14 July 2130)

The emulator opened to a night scene on the south side of town. The camera panned a row of deeply shadowed townhouses to the accompaniment of a haunting oboe. Jurat kicked off his shoes. The music was too orchestral and melodramatic. Perhaps it could be adjusted. He paused the emulation and quickly located the preference settings menu, killed the oboe music, added a touch of contemporary style and amped to the max the realism setting. From a long list, he chose jazz-singer Ruby Brown's voice for the narrator. Her rich contralto would make for smooth, easy listening. He paged through radio-button–filled screens, wondering at the selection options. He could pick up to three authorial styles, real or imagined, and the program would combine them into a single work. Jurat giggled with mischievous delight. What kind of collaboration would Shakespeare, Stella Street, and Edgar Allan Poe make? Or Thoreau, Donald Duck and Isaac Asimov? After spending too much time staring at the list, he decided to try a wacky combination, clicking the boxes for Bradbury, George Orwell and his own patron sprite, the Cheshire Cat. What voice could the software possibly give to Lewis Carroll's cat? He just had to give it a try and could always change it later if need be.

After reviewing page after page of stylistic options, Jurat was impatient and eager to get started. He accepted most of the remaining defaults. It wouldn't be Bradbury, but a dark, sci-fi drama with touches of parody and fantasy would be much better than boredom. With his shoeless feet on the desk, he settled back and stuffed a fist-full of popcorn into his mouth.

# FILE 001, BRAIN SCAN OF CK:

# A STREET HE OUGHT NOT WALK

A faint half moon hung mid-sky. Blasts of moist, black air intensified as the last red remnants of a scorching day disappeared in the west; the street lamps' green-tinged light cast weak silhouettes of swaying palms on the sidewalk. Down the boulevard, oblivious to the kaleidoscopic dance of light and shadow, Cesar Komenen marched alone, a bulky briefcase in hand, soft-soled boots cushioning his footfalls. He walked carefully, alert to everything around him.

The sound of a heavy landing startled him. A mutant vulture—one of the glow-in-the-dark scavengers that had been irradiated by the Texas dirty nuke—lumbered from one lamppost to the next, slowly making its way toward the corner.

Tattered Republic of Florida pennants, left over from the fifth anniversary of the peninsula's independence, hung from the lamppost crossbars, stiffly flapping, shooing the large bird forward. Thin, pale clouds, slid in from the ocean, obscuring the moon, washing the sky into a uniform, oppressive grey. Cesar's shoulder-length hair tossed from side to side in the muggy wind as he nervously studied the street.

Two years ago he'd been mugged just a few blocks from here by a gang of pill punks. The gangs often haunted shadowy edges of the streetscape, looking for easy marks.

An array of dark-windowed buildings loomed ahead: beach cottages, townhouses, apartment complexes, derelict lots, intermixed as if they'd been dumped at random from an architectural planning guide. Some fenced, some heavily landscaped, some separated by ill-lit passageways; there were too many places to hide. The tightness around Cesar's deep-set eyes radiated down his neck as he scanned the street ahead, eyeing anyplace a body might crouch unseen. He listened for footsteps, but heard nothing except rustling palm fronds and the rhythmic soft slapping of the pennants against the lampposts. There wasn't a living soul out, unusual for this early evening hour. Where was the flow of traffic headed toward the school for tonight's Robot Show or the downtown eateries or over the bridge to the beach clubs? The odd quiet sharpened his hyper-vigilant senses, tightened his stomach, played with his nerves. To calm himself, he focused on his footfalls, forcing one smooth step, then another.

Even when anxious, as he was now, Cesar Komenen moved with a natural rhythm, as if born to dance. His dark eyes and internal music came from his mother's Cuban blood; hips made to merengue. He was 23, of average height and build, but looked older, more settled, with a mature charisma that conveyed a larger presence. Good looks, high spirits, and a radiant joie de vivre attracted plenty of attention from the ladies. Cesar was one of the last guys you'd suspect of being a tekkie.

Despite this, Cesar's inner life was dominated by a confrontational seriousness. Political passion came as naturally to him as breathing, and was another of the traits he'd acquired through his mother's side of the family. His maternal grandfather, Abuelito Carmelo, gave up a lucrative legal career for the privilege of being underpaid by the Futurist Party. Cesar had followed suit. He could have joined his Dad's firm and bathed in ease and comfort. But there were more important things in life than designing pleasure helmets for Drugless Joy Corp. The helmets produced pleasant hallucinations through brain wave resonance, without the use of pharmaceuticals or their side effects; hence the name Drugless Joy. Later models added features to pre-program hallucinations. Overdose risk and bad trips became a thing of the past.

Two steps past the lamppost, Cesar's wrist-implanted phone buzzed. He looked around for a quiet place to take the call. The ruins of a burned-out mosque stood directly ahead. Sidestepping a heap of fallen limestone blocks, he ducked into the mosque's courtyard. In the shadow of the decapitated minaret, he found a corner out of the wind. After reassuring himself again that no one was watching, Cesar set his case down amidst the debris, tossed his tussled mane aside to clear his ear and cricked his thumb to link the call. Jewel's voice piped directly into his ear canal.

"I'm on a mission," he said as his eyes
scanned the streetscape.

"Cesar?" Her voice was shaky.

Cesar held the inside of his wrist to his mouth.

"Hey, Baby! Can you hear me? It's pretty windy out here."

The microphone was set in his forearm, just above the wrist bones: it looked like a hard, white plastic button about the size of a quarter.

"Cesar?" she said again.

"I'm here, baby. Sorry it took me so long to answer."

"Something horrible has happened." Her words were panicky. "Clunk's gonna die unless we get her help quick."

"What's going on?"

Her reply was drowned out by shouting and the slamming of doors at her end.

His eyes deepened with alarm. "What the zag is happening over there? You okay?"

The shouting stopped. "Remember when I trained Clunk to use the toilet?" said Jewel.

Cesar pictured that hulking mass of fur perched awkwardly over the porcelain bowl and stifled a laugh. Toilet training the dog had seemed like a bad idea from the start.

"I remember," he said curtly, his voice echoing around the enclosed courtyard. He looked around at the crumbling stone walls and deep shadows. Staying here too long was another bad idea.

"She slipped off the pot, fell against the sink and tore it off the wall. The sink broke and cut into her. There's blood and glass all over the apartment. She managed to drag herself into the living room and was bleeding by the front door when I got home. She's cut so bad, fading in and out. Can you come over? Come quick!"

"Dios mio! How awful."

"Can you come right away?" she pleaded again.

"I can't. I'm on a deep-cover mission," he said as he assessed alternative ways to exit the courtyard should he have to get out quick.

"Amor, Clunk's bleeding real bad. She's lost too much blood. She's too big to carry down the stairs. What should I do?"

"Call Dr. Suturb. He's a Futurist buddy and a vet. Give him a call and ask him as a favor to me. Lo siento, love. There's no way I can go AWOL on this assignment." He tried to sound sweet. "Call the vet, hurry! He'll take good care of her. The old girl will be fine."

"From your mouth to God's ears," she prayed.

"I adore you."

"Be careful," she said with real affection.

From her tone of voice, he knew she was disappointed but not angry. "I'll give you a call later tonight," he pledged before clicking off.

"Zeez!" he muttered to himself. It was rare for Jewel to ask for help. That she did so now proved how much she loved that big, klutzy dog. Much as he wanted to play Sir Galahad, tonight of all nights he was in no position to do so.

Cesar surveyed the mosque's ruined courtyard. Bits of smashed blue and white Turkish tiles littered the garden. Most of the rose bushes appeared dead, but even in the dim light he could see a few blossoms, as well as the spray-painted graffiti on the surrounding wall, left over from the Naabilat riots, reading, "Rag heads go home" and "Jesus loves you."

Just as Cesar was about to step out of the courtyard, his phone buzzed again. The buzz tone let him know it was his Dad, but he decided not to take the call; there wasn't any time for a chat about his latest idea for some tongue-implanted phone or third-eye enhancer. Cesar's father, like that whole side of the family, loved to tinker with electronic devices. Despite Cesar's frequent eye-rolling over his father's sometimes crazy ideas, he and his dad enjoyed a close relationship. They chalked up their technical abilities to their Finnish blood. Great-grandpa Komenen had worked for Nokia North America until cell phones were phased out in favor of wrist implants in the late 2090s. Drugless Joy was born in the wake of Nokia's collapse. The company quickly grew into a multinational monolith. Both grandfather and father had devoted themselves to advancing escapist technology and made a fortune.

Maybe it was a product of his happy nature, but Cesar didn't want to be rich. Material wealth, for him, represented excess and arrogance. What he wanted was camaraderie and excitement, a sense that he was a member of a team that was shaking up the established order.

Komenen stepped from behind the mosque's crumbling walls and surveyed the street. No one was in sight. Nevertheless, he felt a creepy sensation as if a horde of unseen eyes were watching him. As he resumed his walk through the wafting shadows, his hand half-consciously squeezed the handle of his briefcase. The roar of the wind made it difficult to tell if there were footsteps behind him. Under no conditions could he allow anyone to snatch it from him. Not that anybody would know what to do with the contents. Even so, the fear would not abate.

Without warning Cesar turned, half expecting to see a phantom slipping from shadow to shadow, stalking him. But as the saner side of him knew, there was no one there.

He tried to make his mind wander. He recalled the many previous evenings when he'd walked Lake Worth's streets at night. Jewel likewise enjoyed after-dinner strolls, despite the city's high crime rate. With Jewel at his side, he was stoic about such threats. And she was not easily intimidated. In fact, Jewel seemed to feed off confronting her fears. *Maybe*, Cesar thought, *that's one of the reasons I'm attracted to her.* They would walk hand-in-hand, united in their casual, risk-taking defiance.

But Cesar was not feeling defiant at the moment, and it wasn't just the pill punks that had him worried. He had to be sure he wasn't being followed by Ragers, those shabbily dressed and angry young men who roamed Florida's cities as self-appointed vigilantes and enforcers of the Robot Limitation Laws. Yesterday a robot-hating rowdy had tossed a message wrapped around a brick through a window at Futurist Party headquarters, where Cesar worked. The note, written in a wet, red scrawl, read, "Death will find you, Bot Lover."

Masquerading as a youth movement, the Ragers clearly had someone pulling their strings from the shadows. They recruited from the pill punks and street kids, emboldening them to vandalize symbols of "mutant" technology. Attacks against robot factories, research facilities and average citizens with cyber-implants, even wrist phones, were becoming commonplace. Futurists, as advocates of a robot-infused society, increasingly were the specific object of Rager rage.

Cesar took the threats seriously. No way were these attacks isolated incidents. At the time of the brick episode, several cars in the parking lot had been splattered with red paint; even more ominously, other cars had been planted with tracking devices indicating that future attacks were being planned. Then there'd been the Montag incident, a year ago: Ragers were suspected of strangling Richard Montag, a robot engineer, when he was leaving the Futurist Lab late one Friday night: they found him dead in the parking lot the next morning, his throat stuffed with wads of synth-skin. . . . A war was looming, brutal and secret.

After the brick incident, a general order was given by Braadrik Hayes, the supervisor of Futurist electoral operations: "When on campaign ops, avoid using vehicles of any kind. This compulsory order stands until further notice." Even Cesar's personal hover-car was off limits, although it had been nowhere near the Lab in weeks. Having to walk when on assignment would make it nearly impossible to stick to a mission's time plots. But Hayes loved rules, especially if they inconvenienced someone. What a zagger! The tekkies at the Lab were brimming with nicknames for Hayes: "Braad the Rod," "Out of Phase Hayes," or simply "Bio-Bot." This week's favorite tag was "the Horse." Nevertheless, orders were orders. So he'd stationed his hover-car at the Hotel Hummingbird downtown and legged it.

The briefcase was heavy, more so than it looked. And the weight seemed to grow with each step. His palm sweat so profusely the handle nearly slipped from his hand. Frustrated that he had to stop again, he leaned the case against a tree trunk and rubbed his palms on his pant legs to dispel the moisture.

A worker-bee bot, as carrier and bodyguard, would be jazzy right now. But recent orders from Hayes mandated that a robot must never be seen entering or leaving the Safe House. Reluctantly, Cesar had to admit that this Hayes directive, for once, made sense. After all, robots were still taboo on Florida's streets. The sight of one in a residential neighborhood might incite a panic, and probably call in a Rager or two. The whole purpose of the Safe House was to accomplish in secret what could not be done openly at the Lab.

Nevertheless the restriction rubbed Cesar the wrong way. "We're supposed to be the Futurist Party," he argued with the Hayes in his head. "We own an army of worker-bees. We've got a world class robotic research operation right here in Lake Worth. When will our bots ever be able to show themselves in public and do the work they were designed for?" It was an issue Cesar had raised many times. He shook his head in frustration. "Yeah, yeah! I know I'm not in Cuba anymore."

The Bot Parade on the Lago Cienfuegos pier had been the highlight of the summer he spent in Cuba, how many years ago? That was a happier time. He'd been eight years old, marching proudly down the middle of Marti Boulevard, surrounded by robot servants, without a care who was watching.

The need for vigilance dragged him back to the present. He once again scrutinized the empty doorways on the other side of the street. All clear, but the length of the walk and the weight of the briefcase was getting to him. His arm burned. He focused on the cracks in the sidewalk to distract himself. At the corner of Sixth Avenue South and K Street, he shifted the weight again and exhaled through his teeth in exasperation. "Two more blocks to go."

As he arrived at the next curb, Cesar looked down L Street toward South Grade Elementary. The sidewalks on both sides of the street were filled with parents and kids waiting to get in. Some huddled, chatting away, in small groups under the dim street lamps. Others lined up in front of the brightly lit entrance at the far end of the block. Of course, the prospect of a free robot show would bring out a good-sized crowd, but he was encouraged to see so many show up this early. It was still several hours before the show would begin. The activity and sounds made him feel safer, less conspicuous.

A windowless hover-van, the kind popular these days with growing families, turned off of Sixth and headed toward the parking lot. No one seemed to pay him any attention. He tucked his head down and trudged down the final block. *Perhaps everything will work out*, he told himself.

Just as he started to breathe a bit easier, a car, rumbling, eased up from behind. Its headlights cast Cesar's elongated shadow on the sidewalk. His own off-balance and gawky silhouette startled him. The strain of carrying the heavy briefcase was all too obvious. Cesar loosened his neck, squared his shoulders, tried to act as uninteresting as possible.

The vehicle pulled alongside him and slowed to a crawl. Cesar just kept walking, ignoring it, but the vehicle continued rolling, keeping pace with his stride. It was an older model Habi-Van, the kind nicknamed "cruise 'n' snooze," for people with no other place to sleep: it was used by campers, the young, sometimes the homeless. This one looked especially decrepit. The original metallic black skin had faded to a scoured gray, pock-marked with rust and dents. The motor clanged and wheezed.

Dozens of bumper stickers covered the van from top to bottom. One showed a caricature of a cigar-smoking "suit" looking on with shock as a Rager insisted, "Keep your bot out of my face!" Others read "Segregation Forever," "Machines and People Don't Mix," "Rage Against the Machine." There were New Confederate flags, Texas Lone Star flags, skulls and crossbones, crucifixes. *Why not a swastika, a hammer and sickle, and a tea bag, while you're at it?* Cesar thought, bemused by the range of motley symbols used to mark Rager rebellion.

A sun-bleached map of the Ten-State South was plastered on the passenger-side window over a web of cracks, looking like it was keeping the pane from splintering apart. Originally, the map contained eleven states, each state in a different reddish hue, but with Florida rubbed out to reflect its recent independence. *How does this guy see to drive?*

The driver leaned over and rolled down the window, but it stuck halfway, groaned and popped. The glass split apart and Cesar, caught mid-stride, jumped back as the fragments hit the pavement, sending splinters flying like shrapnel. He jumped again, barely avoided being hit, but kept on walking.

The driver was a gruff, unshaven man, oiled brown hair leaking out from under a broad-brimmed cowboy hat, so scruffy that it looked like it had been laying in a dusty corner of the Alamo since 1836. The angry set of the man's mouth and the squint in his eyes seemed at odds with the white, frilly shirt he wore. The combination gave him the look of a Gilbert and Sullivan pirate. "Hey, there, hold on," the man said.

Cesar stopped and turned toward the driver. The man stuck his head out the busted window and looked back at the glass fragments on the ground. Cesar suppressed his impulse to say something sarcastic.

"Zag, dude, tough break. Anything I can do for you?"

Frilly Shirt glared at Cesar as if the broken window had been his fault. Cesar stared back, wanting to put distance between himself and this dude, yet nervously fighting off laughter, thinking, *What part of his Confederate buggy will fall off next?*

The man looked him up and down. "Don't you call me Dude. My name is Tex."

"Tex?" Cesar suppressed a guffaw of disbelief. The guy was a stereotype in Million-Colorz.

"Yes, sir—you got a problem with that?"

"No, sir."

"See here, Orange Blossom Boy," Frilly snarled, "Ya

want me to wipe that sunshine grin off your face? No Dallas nuke rays never touched me nor my kin." He shook a fist and spat in the gutter.

Cesar choked back his laughter. *Who does this guy think he's kidding?* There was no doubt this dude was a Texas blast survivor but reluctant to admit his gene pool might have been tainted by the dirty bomb that went off in Dallas a decade back. It was common for those who'd been exposed to heavy radiation to fear their kids would be mutants or else branded as mutants, whether true or not.

The driver's glare intensified.

"No offense intended, friend," Cesar said.

"Friend?" the driver yelled. "Where do you get off calling me friend?"

Cesar knew, altogether too clearly, how this might play out. He'd love to be able to tear into this creep. "Let me tell ya somethin', *friend,*" he'd drawl, "Flor'da was first, and I know which Great State is gonna split next. Ten-gallon Texas, so high and mighty. Y'all don't need nobody. Lone Star's revved to screech off on its own. Ain't that so, friend, *ami, amigo?*" That's what he was itching to say.

But he had the sense bite his tongue. With a curt nod, he turned to go. However, Frilly Shirt was not about to let him off the hook quite so easy. "Hey, sport, let me see your wrists. Isn't that one of those mutant phones? And open up that case. What're you hidin' in there? More Robby Robot trash?"

Cesar turned back and examined Tex's face. That sure came out of the blue. Could this guy know anything about his job, or the mission? Tex's eyes were squinty and mean-looking, but his mouth was twisted in a goofy smirk. How sharp was this guy? He looked silly driving around in that rust buggy with two days of stubble, wearing a tuxedo shirt, like Blackbeard trying to pass as Bozo. Maybe he was just an ignorant punk who enjoyed harassing random strangers. Then again, maybe the outlandish clothes and junky van were a cover, and he was up to something genuinely nasty.

In any event, Cesar knew that letting himself be bullied would only invite further abuse. He leaned forward until their noses almost touched. "You must have taken a wrong turn," he whispered. "This is the Republic of Florida. Implants are legal here. Why don't we just go our separate ways before things get ugly?"

The driver withdrew his head from the window. His face soured. "I have someone to meet, but I'm warning you—I'd better not catch you around here with any using mutant technology, or I'll kick your legal Futurist butt into next week," he shouted.

Just as Tex shifted into gear, ready to drive off, Cesar stepped backwards and tripped over the curb. His briefcase slipped from his sweaty hand and slammed on the sidewalk. It popped open. A small metal saucer rolled out, instantly sprouted two big eyes and began spinning around, trying to orient itself. The little bot was an L-3, designed for clandestine information gathering. It spun back and forth to orient itself, then stopped and raised its two eyes with an obedient gaze to Cesar.

*Yikes! These machines need to be reprogged to be more discreet,* flashed through Cesar's mind. He smothered the bot with one hand, tossed it back into the case, snapped the latch shut and hurried off. The saucer rattled against the sides of the case for a few seconds before putting itself back into hibernation mode.

"See ya 'round, *Tex*," Cesar called over his shoulder.

Tex said something in reply, but Cesar couldn't make out the words over the squeal of tires. How much had Frilly seen in the dark? Most likely he wouldn't recognize the L-3 as a minibot. It was only three inches on a side, and Cesar had partially blocked his view of it. Yet it was exactly the kind of fusion organic-mechanical machine that terrified folks of his ignorant ilk. Fortunately the L-3's voice system hadn't activated. The last thing Cesar wanted was to have to give Hayes awkward explanations involving a bot and a Texas Rager.

Cesar watched the van's tail lights disappear around the corner. He was worried. Even before the case had popped open, the dude had called him a Futurist, a sign the encounter might not have been random and his fear of being followed wasn't totally off the wall. Now at least, his adversary had a face. As he walked, Cesar rechecked the latches on his case. They seemed secure. How the blazes had they popped open at the worst possible moment? Talk about bad timing! There was nothing he could do in any event but make doubly sure he wasn't being followed and press on. Instead of using the sidewalk, he walked close to the curb, the grassy swale muffling his footfalls.

Across the street, sprawled across a cracking stucco wall, was a mural of happy kids dancing on the back of a huge, red-coiled snake. Underneath, a caption read,

"Don't Tread On Me. Legalize Child
groaned. The repeal of the labor laws w
of the Micro-Government Party. But many ι..
thirteen-year-olds were already quitting school and getting jobs on water management dikes or at hydroponic
shrimp farms. How many kids would be left in school
if child labor were legalized? All it meant was more
recruits for these zagged-out street gangs.

The wind subsided and the scent of night jasmine
spiced the air. Cesar took a few strides forward and froze
in his tracks. There was a crash overhead. Two 25-story
apartment buildings stood facing each other on opposite sides of the street, towering over a cluster of single-
family homes. Residents derisively tagged the buildings
Twin Sours for their seedy tenants and tangerine color.

Something white and billowy floated out of the sky
and landed at his feet. A girlish giggle interlaced with
the sound of clash drums reverberated overhead. On a
third-floor balcony, a preteen couple was kissing, illuminated by intense red strobes from inside the apartment.
She was undressing and seductively tossing her clothes
over the railing. The boy wore a cobra mask with oversized fangs. They were both bare-chested now, moving
jerkily in the pulsating light. They sported tattoos of
coiled red snakes, typical of sea farm workers. Their
dance was steamy and growing hotter by the second.
Cesar smiled condescendingly. "They'll be making
babies before they're fourteen."

Cesar forced his eyes away from the balcony and
checked the time. His wrist display read 8:29 P.M. He
was a few minutes behind schedule, but he had allowed

himself a cushion. The bot show wouldn't begin until eleven. The late start hour was crucial to the plan. There is a simple truth about taboos: it's easier to break them at midnight than at any other hour of the day.

A familiar squeal of tires arose two blocks ahead as the battered van reappeared. It made a high speed turn at the intersection at Dixie Highway and came to a halt. He could make out little beyond the glare of the headlights, but he thought he saw at least three guys in cowboy hats climb in. Then the van began moving again, headed right toward him.

Cesar clutched the briefcase to his chest, jumped a low picket fence, and darted across several front yards back toward L Street, keeping his head down. He ran and ducked and ran and gasped, his chest heaving in the heavy, humid air. The ornamental bushes and low fencing didn't provide much cover. At the far corner, he stopped and turned to see what his sprint had accomplished. The driver's head stuck out the van window, scrutinizing the houses as the vehicle crept up the street.

Cesar glanced toward the school. Clusters of pedestrians were still milling about. He continued his flight down Sixth Avenue, crossing L and then K Street before slipping behind one of the last houses in the block. It was one of those faddish designs nicknamed bullets, windowless tubes that looked like artillery shells. He stopped near the pointed end to catch his breath. Cesar detested bullets. *Hideous things*, he thought. *Creepy way to live.* When some fear-mongering engineer had proposed them after the 2064 tsunami to counter the ocean's fury, they were an instant hit, but their dank interior and austere exterior made for a short-lived fad.

Frilly Shirt and company stood on the sidewalk two doors down. With a twisting glance up the street, Cesar retreated into the pitch-black shadow of the bullet, feeling his way along its smooth, windowless shell. The glossy touch made him recoil. It reminded him of a coffin. He remembered Montag . . .

Cesar flashed on a picture of himself: he was lying inside a shiny, ebony box, his eyes shut, his head on a silk pillow, his hands folded across his breast, his elbows in silhouette against the white, satiny, diamond-tufted lining.

*You're letting your fears run away with you,* he thought, shaking himself.

At worst they'd beat him up, break a bone or two, leave him a bloody mess. "Hey Futurist!" they'd laugh. "How about some mutant technology now?"

A shrill female voice shouted from across the street. "Riccardo, I can't go out with you tonight. My sister's in town."

The high-pitched voice of the driver whined back, "You dumping me for your *sister?*"

Cesar almost laughed out loud. "Estupido! Frilly Shirt is driving around looking for his date while I'm running away from him, cowering in the shadows, scaring myself to death. Tz! I've got to get myself a new brain."

# RUN TO YOUR HOUSES

The front yard of the Safe House was surprisingly dark, surrounded by an eight-foot hedge and shielded from the street lights. Not a crack of light showed through the two large, round windows. Cesar's heart quickened. Was no one here? The newbee was supposed to be inside, waiting. Had something slipped?

He followed a brick-paved path toward the side entrance. Thorny bougainvillea vines grew on a series of trellises staked along the lot line. Long, unkempt boughs hung over the path, blocking his way as he gingerly worked from one lattice section to the next, carefully pushing aside each prickly limb. The tiny red lights of the security pad indicated the entrance door. He pressed his left palm on the entry pad, then added his left thumbprint. The door clicked twice but remained locked. *Zang!* Holding his breath and fearful the clearance list had become scrambled again, he dug the master e-key out of the briefcase and inserted it into a hidden slot behind the pad. This time the thick, pecky-cyprus door creaked open.

Cesar let himself exhale. With the first step inside, he had gone from a world of peril to one of safety. A grid of sixteen security monitors blinked into life. With a quick glance at the monitors, Cesar confirmed that no one had followed him into the yard. Likewise, the alley and the sidewalks across the street were clear. The heavy wooden door swung closed behind him, but the expected click of the lock never came. He turned around and tugged hard on the doorknob to be sure it has fully shut. Even this failed to produce a rattle. The place was deadly silent, a welcome relief from the low moan of the wind outside.

In the glow of the monitors, Cesar could see that the hallway walls were covered with a strange, fuzzy material. He shouted, "Robots are our future!" The walls momentarily glowed with soft purple pulse in response. His voice sounded muted, as if coming from across the street. *Must be some sort of electro-dynamic sound dampener.*

With briefcase still in hand, Cesar flipped on the light and started down the hallway. The floor was spongy and made his footsteps, already muted by the soft soles on his boots, completely silent. The stillness exuded a womb-like comfort.

At the end of the entry hall, two doors stood across from each other. Both rooms had been bedrooms for this, originally, small private home and had been converted into workshops. Taking up most of the floor space in the room on the right was a newly installed robot-recharging station. Cesar entered to take a closer look. The huge machine had an open tubular chamber and a rolling table that slid in one end and out the other, like an old MRI unit. A machine this large could handle hundreds of robots a day. Yet, as far as he knew, there were only a couple dozen robots in the area. *Was some kinda major project in the works?*

Rolls of leftover wall covering, heaps of spongy floor tile and unopened boxes of equipment were stacked high around the room. Cesar had to move a pile of stuff just to get to the machine's control panel. Even so, there was barely enough room to squeeze by.

Cesar switched on the RRS, and the unit roared to life, throwing him off balance as he grabbed the wall. *Damn, that's ziggy. The power gyro must need recalibrating. It's making the whole room shake. Probably wasn't properly aligned when the unit was installed. From the look of this place, quite a few jobs were left half done.*

A gyro was a poor choice in any case, chronically loud and in need of maintenance. He'd have to get his hands on a QuantP and install it later. QuantP generators were remarkably quiet. They literally pulled energy from the air, leaving behind only frozen cubes of solid nitrogen. He'd seen models so quiet the faint hiss of nitrogen vaporizing from the frozen cubes was audible. Meanwhile he'd have to make do with this antiquated monster.

Once up to speed, the gyro's vibrations subsided. The digital readout blinked three times, then flashed that the station was ready for use. Despite mistreatment from the misaligned gyro, the refueler appeared functional. He flipped the switch off and stepped back into the hallway.

The entrance to the second work room was just a few steps down, on the opposite side of the hall. It too had fuzzy wall covering, here colored hospital white. Cesar stuck his head into this larger room, which had been outfitted as a bot-assembly shop. A headless torso lay on a gurney, its chest cavity open, exposing organic-looking internal organs wired to electronic controllers. Four empty gurneys took up about half the available floor space. An array of fabricating tools, presses and welders and cutters, cluttered most of the rest. The equipment was mounted on wheeled metal skeletons and looked like a troop of hangdog scarecrows, tube-and-cable arms drooping to the white, smooth floor. The room's shelves were stocked with bottles of neatly labeled fluids and powders. Hayes seemed to have done a thorough job, for once.

Suddenly a vial of powder fell from a shelf. The glass tube landed with a sharp smack and shattered, spilling its orange contents over the floor. Two curly-tailed lizards jumped down from the same shelf and began licking up the scattered powder. The work room quickly filled with the strong smell of rotten meat.

Cesar instantly recognized the powder as synth-hemoglobin, an essential component of the robotic circulatory system. He bent down to examine the broken vial's small, square label, which confirmed its contents to be robot blood. *Amazing,* he thought. *Did these reptiles intentionally knock down that container? Lizards normally aren't so smart. Perhaps they were desperate for the salt.* He picked up a broom standing in the corner and shooed away the critters, who scampered off to take refuge under a closet door in the far corner.

Surprised to see three lockpads lined up vertically on the closet's door jamb, Cesar made several attempts to open the closet with various combinations of thumbprints and access codes, but without success. Unlike the thick wooden doors used elsewhere in the Safe House, this one was made of reinforced steel, with a massive frame, and would require either an authorized party or a cutting torch to open. He jiggled the doorknob only to find that it didn't connect to a latch mechanism: the doorknob was purely ornamental. *Hm. Curiouser and curiouser.* Using his code analyzer, Cesar pried into the inner workings of the mechanism and discovered to his surprise that there was only one party authorized to unlock the door, but he couldn't crack the name.

Unfortunately there wasn't time to tinker with the locks. Cesar mentally filed away the problem and turned his attention to the mess on the floor. By hand, he picked out the remnants of glass and used the broom to mix a shaker of pleasure stimulant with the synthblood powder. Next he opened his briefcase, took out the L-3 and verbally instructed it to live-trap the lizards, using the mixture as bait. The diminutive robot, looking like a Christmas ornament arrayed in colored blinking lights, scooted around the floor, vacuuming up the would-be bait, then positioned itself, with its small, gaping trap door open wide, in front of the closet. A dose of feel-good drug was an expensive way to deal with pests, but at least the little creatures would have a pleasant confinement.

The end of the hall opened up into a central salon. Cesar's boots hit the wooden floor, which echoed back

like summer thunder in the mountains. The soundproofing was not yet half done. Perhaps he'd been too quick
to credit Hayes with efficiency.

A lanky, limp body was draped over the corner chair
in the unlit salon, arms flung awkwardly over the sides,
legs sprawled forward. Tuuve's reputation as an eccentric
was well established. After waiting a moment, seeing
no movement other than breathing, Cesar kicked the
exposed sole of his shoe and demanded, "You asleep?"
The feet did a little tap dance on the wood floor. The
eyes snapped open. The lips spoke. "You like my platinum wingtips?"

In response to Tuuve's strange greeting, Cesar
yawned deliberately and shrugged.

"Were you really asleep?"

"No, just resting my lids."

"OK. Nice to see you. Would you please turn on the
light?"

Tuuve jumped to his feet and reached for the lamp
switch.

"By the way," Cesar commented, "those shoes look
awfully uncomfortable."

Tuuve D'Camp was young, maybe 21, a quirky
mechanical engineer out of Palm Beach University, a
kid with a boyish face, sandy hair, large, puppy dog eyes.
His family was well known and wealthy, a Lake Worth
institution. The grandmother, Marge D'Camp, had
been a popular mayor. Tuuve's dad inherited the family
mansion and money and did a good job preserving both
through tough times. The D'Camps were powerful and
vocal opponents of the Futurist Party. Despite coming

from an upper-crust family, Tuuve was something of a black sheep. *Don't bite the guy's head off the first time he screws up,* Cesar cautioned himself. *He's used to soft sheets, he'll need some coddling.* The burden of inefficient workmates taxed him. It was yet another reason he preferred working alone.

A reading pad lay open on the end table. From the look of the masthead, the newbee had been absorbed in reviewing Party operational protocols. *What a do-bee,* Cesar thought, wondering if the guy was a stickler for rules and how easy he'd be to work with. The newbee's blond, almost white, hair fell into his eyes as he stretched forward to shake hands.

Before he had a chance to respond, Cesar's wrist phone buzzed. Up popped a text message from Hayes. Taking a piece of film from his shirt pocket, Cesar rubbed it over the phone's face; a coded message appeared on the film. He took a moment to mentally decode it, then stuck the film back in his pocket. Regardless of Boss-Man's typically frenetic plea, he needed a few minutes to orient the newbee to life in the hive. Making eye contact, he took the offered hand of his new workmate. "Hey! I'm Cesar Komenen."

The newbee introduced himself. "This is my first job out of Central Lab," he said with an enthusiastic grin. His teeth were large and perfectly aligned. "I'm counting on you to show me the ropes. Clandestine ops have been my dream since I joined the Party. Really looking forward to working with you."

*News flash,* Cesar thought with a shudder. *This guy reeks naive.* The atta-boy attitude was no match for the gritty jobs ahead, yet he'd have find a way to work with the guy. "Welcome to the Remp underground," Cesar said.

The Robotic Election Management Program, acronym R.E.M.P., or "Remp" in Party slang, was the secret political action arm of the Futurist Party. It had been founded seven years before by Party hawks who had become impatient with playing by the Confederacy's status quo–favoring rules. But Remp had remained cash-strapped and stagnant until the arrival of international "capital" in the aftermath of Florida's independence.

"Thanks! I've been working at the Lab for over a year, but until a few days ago, I was completely in the dark about Remp. For three years prior, I worked for a private company repairing dry cleaning equipment."

Cesar winced. This seemed to think his repairman experience was somehow relevant. *Better set him straight from the start.*

"Let me tell you a story," Cesar said, giving the newbee a cautioning look. "A couple of years ago, I was confronted by an angry mob of construction workers, waving pipes, clubs, chains. They were afraid of losing their jobs. I had two, three minutes to reprogram my bots to take orders from them—voice recognition, behavior modification, the whole nine yards—or those guys would have ripped my head off. I created a quick demonstration. The robots flipped off the boss, they wouldn't do a thing the man said, but if a worker asked, they'd lick the mud off his boot. The guys were in stitches. Without the humor, the stunt wouldn't have worked. But it did work. And just in the nick of time."

Tuuve gave him a blank look.

"Shadow ops are not for daydreamers, or idealists, or dry cleaning equipment repairers. We need tekkies who can work under pressure. This is a rough business. It needs guts and a fast, clear brain."

Cesar felt a twinge of guilt for leaning so hard on the newbee. On more than one occasion he'd found himself wrestling with his own unsuppressed idealism; those noble, squeaky-clean dreams needed to be buried out of sight and out of mind in the practical soil of reality where openness and honesty didn't always get the job done.

"I want to get my hands dirty. That's why I took the job," the newbee replied.

"And it's my job to get you ready to handle it," Cesar continued. "You'll need to be quick and tough and clever. Your abilities will be tested, honed. Your every fiber will grow tough and sinewy. Best of all, life will be infinitely more exciting than pressing shirts."

Conjuring up his best tough-guy expression, Tuuve's eyes narrowed. "Understood."

*Say good-bye to your sorry, upper-class, dry-cleaned life*, thought Cesar, careful not to let his demeaning attitude show. He patted the newbee on the back. "Glad to have you onboard!"

Cesar pulled Hayes' imprinted film from his shirt pocket. Turning it over, he handed the card to Tuuve. "This message just arrived from Hayes. He's over at the school, preparing for tonight's event. Can you translate and interpret?"

Not wanting to seem overconfident, Tuuve flashed a self-deprecating grin as he took the film from Cesar's hand and studied it methodically, realizing this was the first of many tests to come. The message read:

Lower BPR.
Deact D.
D bots @ 2230.
U Da Man.

"Hayes wants you to lower the bad press risk," said Tuuve. "You're supposed to deactivate the self-defense program for all the robots, then deliver the bots to the school facility by 10:30 P.M. He signs off with 'You're the man.'" Tuuve winked and returned the film.

"Well done," complimented Cesar, who stared at the film and shook his head.

"Can we finish by 10:30?" the newbee asked.

"No problem. The original plan was to march the bots up the front steps into the school just in time for the start of the show. Now Hayes wants them there half an hour earlier. No big deal. They'll have to go directly to a secure holding pen at the school, that's all."

Tuuve stared in puzzlement. "Why?" he asked.

"You've been in the Lab too long. Not everybody loves robots! The folks coming to the show tonight— most of them have never seen a robot, except for old timers who remember the brute, metal-faced machine-cops, who still inspire fear and hate. Too many people think of bots as tools of dictators."

"The Metal Militia," Tuuve remarked.

The newbee at least remembered his history. In 2112, in a last ditch attempt to hold the United States together, the Metal Militia had come south, the robot soldiers marching across the Mason-Dixon line by the thousands, hunting for "traitors," confiscating rebel arms, removing all signs of confederate allegiance. Their presence had the opposite of the intended effect and solidified Southern nationalism. Good ol' boys attacked them on every street corner. Secession came two years later.

Tuuve chuckled. "They were beaten back by a gang of know-nothing rednecks."

"Laugh if you like, but the Metal Militia set us back decades. Our biggest challenge is to convince people robots aren't space aliens or fascist goons. Our response to trouble has to be tempered, quiet and soft as possible. Deactive D means that, if attacked, the bots won't use their martial arts or fight/flight programs to defend themselves. Hayes believes that sympathy for the bots will get up good PR and help our public image."

"Really?" Tuuve looked doubtful. "With Rager punks running around, turning off self-defense sounds awful risky."

"We can't exactly have robots hurting people and at the same time ask the public to trust them." But Hayes' concern about security wasn't what bothered Cesar about the message.

Working in new protocols at the last minute was a bad idea. There would be no time for testing or debugging. This was crazy. And that insincere "U Da Man"— Hayes was no stranger to patronizing sign-offs, but this one was a bit much even for Hayes. "U Da Manipulator," Cesar cracked.

Cesar had no choice but to follow orders, but he refused to conform to Hayes' panic M.O. The boss man was impulsive, even out of control at times. *No way to retrain that guy for artistic work.*

Cesar began to outline to Tuuve the tasks needed to prep for the robot show. Almost immediately, the phone buzzed again. Hayes was extraordinarily hyper today. "When are you . . ."

Before he could finish his sentence, Cesar interjected, "A van has been snooping around." He told Hayes the story of Frilly Shirt and the pockmarked van.

"OK, listen. I want you to drive the bots over to the school. Use the limo. It's parked in the garage."

"Use the limo?" Cesar said, gritting his teeth and forcing himself to speak as mildly as he could manage. "Number one, isn't that stretch buggy just a tad conspicuous? Second, didn't you just ban the use of vehicles in and out of the S.H.?"

"What are you saying? You want to walk them over? You want to risk a confrontation with this guy on a public street?" Cesar shook his head. Hayes earned another of his nicknames, "Horse," by being incredibly temperamental. "Hayes, our original plan was to box up the bots and deliver them in a truck. That way there would be no exposure on the street. The vehicle ban wasn't my idea. What's wrong with using crates and a truck? That way no one will see bots entering the school."

"Look, there's no time, no crates, and no truck. Just take the limo. I don't like how it looks either, a little too

'Lives of the Rich and Famous,' but at the moment, it's the only vehicle available. And where are they being stored anyway?"

Cesar grunted irritably.

"They're in the limo, right?. So get a move on. And keep your eyes peeled. If you spot that van again, report back to me immediately." Without waiting for another reply, Horse was gone.

Cesar looked ready to smack the first thing that moved.

"Hyper Hayes at his finest," Tuuve said, sympathetically.

"Follow me," Cesar said stiffly with a beckoning wave. With Tuuve in tow, he took a quick tour of the rest of the house. Behind the salon, he found the back bedroom, empty except for a small table and a king-size bed covered with a hospital-blue sheet. The far wall was a mass of electronic controls and readouts. "Looks like the programming center," the newbee offered.

Cesar pulled a silver-surfaced touch pad out of its wall socket. The pad was almost a meter long, a few millimeters thick, light-weight, but remarkably rigid. He tapped the surface to create a wireless link and checked its through-put rate. The chartreuse numbers indicated data speeds in the octogig range. "Ay, the mobile link is screaming fast."

"What is it?" Tuuve asked.

"Our new Puppet Master. The software is specifically designed for bot shows, monitoring the audience's emotional reaction and then giving us the interface to adjust the robots' actions on the spot. I still need to install the string links to the bots, but that should only take a few minutes. This'll be the first time it's handling so many bots at once."

"Sounds like the first time you've used a PM. You sure it'll work?"

"We've tested it plenty in development and the field. It'll work, all right!" Cesar gently set the PM pad down on the bed and gestured for Tuuve to follow him out of the room.

The kitchen looked like it hadn't been remodeled in a hundred years. Long, white-ceramic countertops, chipped and coffee stained, lined three walls with stainless steel appliances underneath and scuffed cabinets overhead. The faucet on the double sink dripped in a steady rhythm to the accompaniment of a minifridge's strained buzz. As Cesar turned into the doorway, his surprised laugh reverberated around the tiny room. Standing in front of the glowoven was a Bot Buddy, wearing a tall chef's hat and an apron, with a recipe book in one hand, a rubber chicken in the other. Around its neck hung a sign that read,

Cesar, I'm yours.

Let me cook you up some votes.

My specialties are Gnos and Ekoj.

Signed, Daarb

Cesar saw immediately that "Daarb" was "Braad" spelled backwards. He blinked, flabbergasted. He had never even heard of Braadrik Hayes doing anything remotely light-hearted. The gift itself was even more startling. Cesar had submitted repeated requests for a bot buddy. Now, out of the blue, Hayes had granted the request. The gesture seemed so out of character that Cesar couldn't help wondering what Horse was up to. Was the robot a Trojan? Or did Hayes want some special favor in return? Cesar didn't know what to think but decided to proceed warily.

Tuuve's eager hand reached for the power switch. "Shouldn't we onboot it?" he asked.

"Not now," Cesar said. "We've got to get ready for the Robot Show. Bring in the team."

Without needing to be asked twice, Tuuve jumped out the back door, leaving the door wide open. Cesar watched as the newbee streaked across the lawn. He struggled to keep a straight face at his overly eager workmate. *Better too eager than dull and lazy,* Cesar thought as he followed his partner outside.

Across the thumbnail-sized backyard stood a ramshackle garage, its side door looking like it had blown apart in the last hurricane and been hurriedly nailed back together. The electronic opener was useless. The door knob didn't turn. It took all of Tuuve's strength to muscle open the door far enough to squeeze inside.

Occupying most of the small floor was the classiest stretch limousine Tuuve had ever seen, luminescent black, five opaque windows to a side, and so highly polished Tuuve could use the reflection to comb his hair. Tuuve strolled around the limo, admiring every detail. Even with his hand pressed to the glass, he couldn't make out anything inside.

At the press of a hidden button, door handles popped up. Cesar opened the driver side door and gestured for

Tuuve to have a look. Long bench seats ran along both sides of the interior. The black upholstery glowed in a subdued golden light. Seven metal-faced robots sat life-lessly in place, dressed as everyday laborers, one in bib overalls, others in a diver's gear, waitress uniform or sani-tation suit. They looked like riders on a public bus, ready for a day of sweat and toil. But someone had thought it would be funny to give the metalloids the faces of the famous and rich. There was at least one movie star, one business tycoon, and at least three former presidents. In an evident attempt at satire, Clinton III and Bush VI had their arms around each other like old pals. Most likely the average working Joes in tonight's audience wouldn't have a clue about the attempt at humor.

One of the bots held a scroll e-banner on its lap. Tuuve climbed in and unrolled the banner. It read, *Buddy Bots Create Leisure*.

"We hoped to put this in the Florida Independence Day Parade," Cesar explained. "The authorities were supposed to allow us a chance to advocate robots, but last minute we pulled out. Someone made a threatening phone call, and it was deemed too dangerous."

"Zig, my eyeballs," Tuuve exclaimed. "Extreme snazzy. But why keep all this in a junk-heap of a garage?"

Cesar shrugged. "Hayes' idea of camouflage, I guess. Who'd suspect?"

"That's crazy. There's no security here at all. The garage door doesn't even close properly. A street bum could peek in and decide to bed down for the night with the bots, or some Rager . . ."

"No need to convince me."

"But shouldn't we talk to Hayes? Convince him to put this beauty in a safer space. To leave it here is zag-nut screwy."

"Let's not get into that right now," Cesar pleaded. "We've got to get going. Just take the bots inside and get their batteries charged on the RRS, while I gather up the equipment I need."

One by one Tuuve activated each of the seven robots, lined them up and marched them single-file into the house. Their legs dragged; their heads and arms were cast heavily downward. Tuuve kept an eye on them from the rear, feeling like a chain-gang jailer.

Once the newbee was out of sight, Cesar punched an eight-digit code into the limo's dashboard keypad. A smooth, flat panel appeared on the floor. A thumb and three fingerprints got the panel door open. Inside he found the sealed packet Hayes had left for him, containing a paper-thin optical wafer. "Zig me," muttered Cesar as he felt its incredible lightness in his palm, total weight maybe 10 grams. It bugged him that Hayes would transport such incredibly light components in the limo while Cesar was forced to lug the heavy equipment across town in a hand-held case. The man was as considerate as a mule.

After carefully wiping off several specks of dust with his little finger, he placed the wafer on the face of his wrist phone and pressed it firmly down with his palm. Body heat activated the wafer. Nine digits, making up today's alphanumeric passcode, leapt into the nerves of his palm, up the length of his arm, circled around the back of his ears, and clicked into his brain.

The bio-link process never failed to impress him. To think that thoughts could be fed directly to living memory cells, like uploading data to a computer. Fantastic! If only such technology had existed when he was in school, calculus and Arabic would have been a breeze.

When the transfer validation was finished, he popped the wafer under his tongue and let it dissolve. Neuro-transsealers pulsed through his veins, found the tendrils that lodged the data, and locked the data permanently in his brain.

Cesar blinked and took a couple of deep breaths. Zing! The pleasant afterglow of the transsealers was nice—very nice. He felt simultaneously calm, euphoric, energetic and extraordinarily alert. With the day's passcode now implanted in his head, he hustled himself back toward the house. All he had left to do was finish configuring the Puppet Master, by linking in access codes for each of the robots in tonight's show, upload the deactivation protocols per Hayes' latest instructions—and off to school they'd go.

A rough-running car roared down the alley, stirring up dust. The motor's arrhythmia sounded familiar. Was Frilly Shirt back? Cesar darted around the garage and down the alley. A van stopped under the streetlight long enough for him to recognize the rusty pockmarks and Confederate bumper stickers, then peeled off down Seventh Avenue. If this guy was supposed to be shadowing him, he wasn't doing a very good job of it. Why drive around in a vehicle that's going to draw so much attention? Why dress so outrageously? Cesar smirked as he recalled how the Dude's date stood him up.

Cesar tried to put Frilly Shirt out of his mind, but the van's reappearance was unlikely to be a coincidence. He was a buffoon but still dangerous. If the Rager suspected what was going on in the Safe House, he'd tell his crazy buddies. And then what? Cesar imagined the possible damage: the neural-chem lab ransacked, synth-plasma containers shattered, curly-tailed lizards feasting on the mutation-causing compounds, the Robot Team smashed. Well, he'd warned Hayes. For the time being there was nothing else he could do.

Reluctantly, he went inside to focus on prepping the Puppet Master. Just as he was isolating the files he needed, his wrist phone buzzed. Braad again. This guy was nothing if not persistent. "Where the hellcat hurricane are you?" Braad barked. "We need those bots here now. Laser it."

"Okay, okay, but I need to set this up right. Do you realize the risks? A lot could go wrong." Cesar sat wide-eyed, staring at the Puppet Master screen. Every panel was filled with red-boxed caution and error messages. The system balked at intermixing two unaligned instruction sets. "What if the sub-system crashes? Imagine the scene if the bots lock up."

"Override the safeties. I'll take responsibility."

"But Braad . . ."

"Just do it! Then do yourself a favor and get my bots over here faster than Hurricane Zeta. People are already banging on the door."

Cesar grimaced at Hayes' claim to ownership. "My neck is on the line here too," he insisted. "One more thing . . ." Cesar spoke rapidly, nervously. "We've never allowed our bots to be seen on the street. Are you sure it's a good idea to show their metalloid faces outside? What about the limitation laws? You sure I won't be arrested?"

"You're forgetting the legal work we did trying to put our bots on display in the Independence Day Parade. There's no violation. Our bots are now legally registered, licensed to the research Lab. We're allowed, and I quote, 'public appearances for experimental and demonstration purposes.' Besides, we have a permit for the show." Hayes' voice grew gruff. "All you have to do is to walk the bots across the damn parking lot."

*Yeah, I remember the Parade,* thought Cesar. *I remember all those hours with the lawyers, filling out endless forms, negotiating with the sheriff, just to cancel last minute due to some rather nasty security threats.* "OK, maybe you're right about the legality. But I'm still concerned about security."

"Decompress, kid. Just get my bots here. I've handled everything on this end. The auditorium is ready to go. The crowd has been waiting to get in for hours. They're getting impatient. Showtime in 57 minutes. I'm starting to seat them now. Don't worry about it. Just get my bots over here pronto. Now get moving! U da man. Hey, hey!" Click. And with that, Hayes was gone.

## NARRATIVE PAUSE 001

"ROBOTS REGISTERED for public exhibition?" Jurat groaned with bewilderment. He'd never heard of such a thing, not until Pawl offhandedly mentioned the possibility on the phone just a few minutes ago. He'd better check it out. All his training, all his instincts told him such a thing was abhorrent as well as felonious. Opening a message screen, he dictated:

> TO: Palm Beach County District Attorney:
> CC: Sheriff Norma Braxil
> FROM: Inspector Solomon Jurat
> SUBJECT: Request for Legal Opinion
> MEMO: Inquiry into the legal status of one metal-loid robot, currently in the possession of the PBSO, item number RLL7765. Request for legal opinion on permissibility of presence on public streets in either commercial or residential zones. Owner claims unrestricted exemption to applicable statues based on alleged negotiation with Sheriff Braxil. Please advise. Expedited review requested.

Jurat shuddered to think what it would mean for his case if it turned out the toad-ugly abomination was licensed, registered and legally clean. His case would be blemished if not compromised. Could his luck be fading so quickly, like a capricious smile on the face of the Cheshire Cat? His chest heaved involuntarily. Good thing they'd found those humanoids at the hideout, at least all his eggs weren't in one basket. He closed his eyes and rubbed his temples, trying to ward off an incipient headache.

BEGIN FILE 003, SOURCE CK:

# CLEAN METTLE

**B**raadrik Horace Hayes stood at the entry door to the school's auditorium, slapping foil stickers on the chests of everyone who filed in. The words "Robots Are Our Future" radiated in holographic copper. As the place filled up, deep red glints flashed steadily around the dimly lit auditorium.

Hayes was a small man by any standard, five-foot-two on a good day, with a slim face, long, narrow nose, and deep-set eyes. What he lacked in stature he made up for in quick wit and aggressive attitude. Hayes lived for his job as Director of Electoral Operations for the Futurist Party of South Florida. His mind was already at work on the gubernatorial election of 2132, still two years off.

When Cesar arrived, he poked his head into the auditorium. Hayes was too busy to notice. Party leaders had feared that robo-phobic taboos would keep attendance low, but Hayes, confident that, like a horror movie, fear and morbid curiosity would draw a crowd, had staked his reputation on the success of this Robot Show. So far, it looked like Hayes had been right. Four hundred sea farm workers and tomato pickers crammed into the modest auditorium. Cy-bot Robot Corp. was due to release its latest model, called a worker-bee, and had linked up with the Futurist Party to spread the word and deal with certain "political encumbrances." People had been waiting for hours and were getting impatient. So far, not one robot had shown up.

As the crowd grew larger and louder, Gamma Joiner, the school custodian and a trusted Futurist, ushered Cesar to a back entrance. After checking to be sure no one was watching, Cesar signaled the limo. Four human-oids followed by four metal-faced robots marched up the entrance stairs in lockstep, stopping inside to await instructions. Cesar breathed a sigh of relief. Despite fears of a Rager ambush from the likes of Frilly and Co., the short drive from the Safe House had been uneventful.

With a thumb jab to the keypad, Gamma opened the steel-ribbed door of the security locker. Fireproof lockers had been installed in all the schools a few years back, after a series of arsons; the secure storage spaces had also proved useful places to protect school records and valuables from vandals. Gamma directed the troop of robots to enter the locker. Wordlessly, they filed in squeezing themselves into the narrow spaces between cabinets stuffed with data spheres and paper files. When all eight had managed to get inside, they did an about-face and stood at attention, sixteen glazed eyes star-ing blankly back at him. Grimacing, Gamma looked over his shoulder at Cesar. "You sure you want them in there?" he asked. "There's no ventilation. Won't they suffocate?"

"They don't need air. They're robots. That chest movement is just for effect. Don't worry. They won't be harmed," said Cesar. "Lock the door."

"It feels inhuman to stack them in this vault like so much cordwood, all those eyes looking straight at me. Why not just bring them backstage?"

"We don't expect trouble, but we're taking no chances," Cesar stated flatly. There might even be a riot, but no need to worry the janitor. His hand stretched past Gamma's shoulder and slammed the heavy door closed. A twist of the thumb on the doorjamb-pad secured the lock. Now he'd be the only one who could let the robots out.

Gamma and Cesar walked down the corridor to the auditorium. The place was packed and noisy.

Hayes looked relieved to see Cesar. "All the talent here?" Hayes asked.

"Safe and sound. Ready for their cue."

"Excellent!"

Hayes turned and motioned Gamma inside. "Please join us," he said. The custodian went into the auditorium and found a seat against the side wall. Cesar stayed with Hayes at the entrance.

For thirty minutes the audience listened impatiently as a panel discussed the intricacies of governmental policy toward robots. Ten experts, in high-collared, long-sleeved white shirts, sat behind an unadorned conference table and droned on about the Robot Limitation Laws; why robots were allowed to do certain types of work under blah-blah-blah conditions but not similar jobs under different blah-blah conditions. A short, buxom woman serving as program chair did nothing to enliven the conversation. She sat passively in her drab green suit, vacant-eyed, head drooped to one side, hands folded neatly in her lap, looking incredibly bored. If it had not been for the promise of the upcoming show, half of the audience would have headed home long ago.

Sitting on stage with the panelists, but saying little, was a tall, striking figure. He sat ramrod straight, shoulders thrust back, his radiant eyes systematically scanning the bored crowd. He exuded the air of a perfect politician—handsome, likable, sincere and no-nonsense tough. His six-foot-ten frame overwhelmed his small, cellular chair. Although the chair was designed to conform itself automatically to the body shape of each occupant, he was just too big. He curled his lanky legs up under the chair as best he could and managed a politician's smile to hide what must have been discomfort.

When the Chairwoman thanked and dismissed the panel, the audience immediately perked up. As the others filed off stage, the mayoral hopeful remained. He moved to the back and stood in the shadows, staring at his feet and awaiting his introduction. "And now we come to the high point of our program," the green suit said. "Cy-Bot Corporation in conjunction with our Futurist Party will show us how we can escape from the chains of economic oppression. I now present to you our Futurist candidate for mayor."

The man pulled himself up from his uncomfortable chair and began to wend his way through the maze of furniture that littered the stage up to the diminutive Chairwoman. "He stands as the sturdiest—some might even say the tallest—pillar of our fair city." There were scattered chuckles from the crowd. "And he stands for a new and brighter future for us all. I give you . . . Forrest Newcomb!"

Forrest Newcomb bowed to the crowd and modestly acknowledged the Chairwoman's schmaltzy introduction. He stepped forward, hands folded at his waist.

"Some folks . . .," he said, waiting for the audience to quiet down. "Some folks are afraid of robots. They're scared they're going to take over."

The audience was now watching him attentively.

Quietly he removed a round saucer from his pocket and, lifting it in the palm of his hand, its lid puffed out, forming a dome. The upper half rotated like a doll's head. Two round eyes burst open, along with a diminutive, smiling mouth.

Newcomb held the L-3 minibot out for all to see. "My friends, is this anything to be afraid of?" The bot's big eyes opened wider still and blinked coquettishly at the crowd. "This wondrous piece of modern technology is cute as a button, but it's not a toy. It cleans floors, it filters air, it disinfects bathrooms. It's capable of scanning your food before you eat it and identifying 5,000 different poisonous pollutants. Shouldn't your family be allowed to own one of these?"

On cue, the bot sprouted legs and began hoisting itself up and down as if nodding yes. A chuckle ran through the crowd.

"Or how about one of these?" the mayoral hopeful said, putting the mini-bot back in his pocket and pointing toward the rear of the hall.

A worker-bee Cy-bot entered, strutting theatrically down the aisle. Most in the audience had never set eyes on such an advanced humanoid model. Its long, limber strides and swinging arms made for a completely human gait. The Cy-bot wore an absurd placticene suit: metal head, hands and neck protruding through puffy, electro-fragrance cuffs and an exaggerated collar. The suit looked much too heavy for this humid evening, but no one cared. Robots don't sweat.

When the Cy-bot reached the stage, Newcomb motioned toward the chairs and tables. The robot scurried about, carrying a heavy-looking stack of chairs with ease, clownishly lifting a table with one hand, hurriedly clearing the stage, and finally scrambling to the front and center of the stage.

"Gentlemen and ladies," Forrest Newcomb began, "Lake Worth needs a mayor who understands what we're up against. Bit by bit the door to the future is closing in our faces. Did you know this private academy where we meet tonight used to be a free public school? The wealthy few grab more and more. They float through life on a cloud of privilege, they inherit money, land and businesses, buy superior educations for their children and gain control of the government, using their power to tilt the playing field further in their favor, all the time telling us, the average working folks, that we have equal opportunity, that if we just worked harder, we too could have the wealth that they have." The robot's eyes tracked Newcomb as he paced about the platform, nodding agreement in all the right places, applauding on cue with what appeared to be genuine delight. Its assigned role was twofold: first, to demonstrate its subservience and thereby alleviate any lingering robophobia in the audience, and second, to augment the crowd's emotional link to the speaker.

The speaker made eye contact with a stone-faced woman in the third row and grabbed his throat. "While strangling us with self-serving policies, they look down on us as lazy and foolish, as if we deserve our poverty. The time has come, my friends, to level the playing field!"

Two young females sat in the front row, facing rigidly forward, their faces half-hidden under broad-brimmed hats. They stood up and turned toward the crowd, sweeping their hats from their heads, allowing everyone to see their robot faces. One of the she-bots leaned over to the other and stage-whispered, "What can anyone do about it?"

Newcomb asked her to repeat the question.

The she-bot turned to the stage, cupped her hands and yelled out, "The greedy fat cats—what are you going to do about them?"

Forrest stretched out his arms as if welcoming the question with a bear hug. "Superb! I'm so glad you raised that question. Yes, indeed, the fat cats—what are we going to do about *them*?" He slowly surveyed the audience's faces, allowing time for the question to sink in.

"The answer is straightforward. Imagine, my friend, that you own a worker-bee. Imagine yourself side by side with your own personal, mechanical assistant, helping you throughout the work day. Let it do the heavy lifting. Let it stoop to pick tomatoes while you hold the sack. Let it be your personal secretary, let it stay up late to finish reports and paperwork. What we in the Futurist Party will do—what *I*, Forrest Newcomb, as mayor of Lake Worth, Florida, will do, is give every single worker a second pair of hands. I say all of *you* are the ones who deserve to be rich and happy. My friends, we'll end the corporate monopoly on robot ownership, *that's* what we'll do!"

A brawny man in the third row stood up. "Sir, sir . . . excuse me . . . I have a question."

"Yes?" Newcomb immediately recognized the man as a Futurist plant.

"How do we know that these robots are safe? What if they try to take over?"

"Excellent question. Robots are often portrayed in the movies as if they were people with metal skin, as if they have the heart and mind of a human. But, my friends, that has more to do with entertainment than reality. Robots are machines, with synthetic bones, micro-motors and wires, wrapped in plasticene. They aren't born, they are built. They are no more alive than a light bulb, or a ragdoll, or a radio. They do whatever we program them to do, without thought, without feeling."

The lights in the meeting hall flashed several times. Then the room went dark. Someone shouted, "Thank God for Lake Worth Utilities."

The municipal power company had been a laughingstock for over a century. Newcomb couldn't pass up such an opportunity. "If elected, I promise Cy-bots will run Lake Worth Utilities, and the lights will stay on." he said. The crowd giggled and the lights came back to dim.

Newcomb continued: "Look at this robot, standing before you. It's a tool, like a hammer, a tool we can use to build a brighter future for ourselves and for our children. We command it how to walk, talk, smile. Why, it even tells better jokes than I do!" The look of dismay on Forrest's face made the audience dissolve in laughter. "And you know why? Because it's been programmed by experts, on how to hold its eyes, when to raise an eyebrow, how to time the punch line. When the programmers do their job right, we laugh."

The speaker lifted a finger as if he were pulling a marionette string. The robot giggled contagiously and the audience giggled back.

"You see?" Forrest remarked with a knowing shrug and a smile. "Now, watch closely. How casual, how human this Cy-bot looks standing there. But the seemingly simple act of standing is actually the product of the hundreds of hours of work by cyber engineers. Since a rigid posture looks unnatural, we programmed in a series of tiny muscle glides and weight shifts. Notice how the robot flexes in the knees. Notice how it shuffles its feet from time to time. Notice the fluid head movements." He pressed a button on a hand-held remote, and with exaggerated movements the robot clownishly shifted weight, shuffled its feet, and bobbed its head. The audience laughed. The robot pranced left, then right, and said, "I dance, too!" More laughter. "I also type 500 words a minute . . . clean the snot from your baby's nose and repair hover-cars." The audience roared.

Forrest addressed an assistant at the back of the cafeteria. "Could we see that slide now?" The room darkened. Lines of computer code flashed on the wall.

"Gentleman and ladies, tonight I open the tin man and invite you to inspect its insides. I reveal to you the secrets of the robot builders. Here is the list of instructions we programmed into this Cy-bot for tonight's show." With a laser pointer, he indicated the sequence of actions the audience had just witnessed. "Here we told the robot to stand naturally. Here we put in an exaggerated weight shift, a shuffle and nod. Here we encoded a conditional action. If . . . and only if . . . the audience laughs, perform the dance routine." A woman with a flowered blouse in the front row laughed out loud. The Cy-bot repeated its dance steps. A heavyset gentleman behind her let out a forced guffaw. The same dance step was repeated, left then right. A wave of delight rippled through the crowd. Again the robot danced, this time with an additional step forward and a formal bow.

An older man with long hair and white whiskers stood up. "Ha! Ha! Ha!" he went, with exaggerated phoniness. This time the robot didn't move. Several others let out phony laughs in an attempt to get the robot to respond, but without success.

Forrest drew their attention to the bottom line of the slide. It read, "Activate dance routine. If laugh, dance. Repeat three times. Bow to audience. Deactivate dance routine."

"We programmed the robot to stop after three repetitions. We could have told it two or seven or thirteen. This robot is not a thinking being. It simply follows instructions. Robots cannot rebel. They can't take over. There is nothing to fear." The audience broke into applause. Forrest snapped his fingers, and the auditorium lights came on full.

Cesar sat in the rear of the hall, staring at the Puppet Master screen that monitored the crowd. A series of vertical bars displayed levels for mood fields. He read the crowd's collective state of mind and adjusted the presentation as needed. When the boredom indicator edged up, he signaled Forrest to ratchet up the humor. Overall, things were going better than expected, hitting nearly all their marks. The audience was having a good time, and the readouts indicated their fear of robots was gradually diminishing. Cesar signaled they were ready for the grand robot entrance.

Newcomb readied the crowd. "Cy-bots will be your servants and grunts, doing exactly what you command and nothing more. The important thing in this election is to visualize what your life will be like if we revoke the Robot Limitation Laws. Would you enjoy taking a skilled robot to work with you? Who would do the dull, heavy labor? Who would collect trash? Who would repair the municipal dikes? Who would clean and package shrimp?"

A Futurist plant in the middle of the fifth row shouted, "Cy-bots!"

On cue, Newcomb announced, "I introduce to you J2016."

The crowd turned to watch a human shrimp worker and his steel-faced robot buddy enter the auditorium from the rear. Arm in arm, they marched down the aisle, chanting in unison, "Can the ban! Can the ban!" Both were shirtless, with coiled red cobras tattooed on their chests. The robot's skin glowed in iridescent pewter, black leggings running down to water shoes, an absurdly oversized dive mask tilted up on its forehead. The man was sailor tanned. Over his shoulder he carried a net filled with plastic, oversized shrimp. A stream of play money blew out of a net he was carrying. The unspoken message: robot and human form an inseparable team. The machine does the work while the human reaps the benefits. The jovial worker romped around the hall, like a clown, stumbling, flipping fake shrimp into the air and chasing after them with his net. With each toss, more and more paper money filled the air. The auditorium overflowed with laughter.

On their heels, another robot-human pair entered the auditorium. This robot—a female—wore a sequined, green bikini and carried a large basket of tomatoes. Its owner reached into the basket and began juggling tomatoes, tossing them, one by one, into the crowd as he worked his way down the aisle.

One of the few teenagers in the audience ran between the few rows of empty seats, gathering tomatoes from the floor. Once he'd collected an armful, he started throwing them at the candidate. The kid's aim was good. The first one splattered with a wet thud against the candidate's chest.

In the rear of the auditorium, Cesar jumped up and shouted across to Hayes. "Where is security?" Before anyone could intervene, a second tomato landed at Forrest's feet. He lost his footing, stumbled, slammed

Arm in arm, they chanted, "Can the ban! Can the ban!"

his knee against the podium, twisted awkwardly and lay face up on the floor, clutching his knee.

The kid rushed the stage firing tomato after tomato, hovering over the prone body, pelting his face and neck. Another youth joined in the attack, hoisted a chair over his head and slammed it down on the prostrate Forrest's damaged leg.

"Ragers!" Cesar said through gritted teeth. He slammed his open palm against the wall in frustration. The monitor flashed an urgent warning that the self-defense programs were still offline. The situation was deteriorating fast. *I warned Hayes, but he never listens to me. Got to do something before the bots are damaged beyond repair.* There was no time to plan carefully. He flipped the screen to program entry mode and began zipping orders to the robots.

The shrimper picked up a chair and used it to ward off attacks. Cesar needed to create a distraction. He sent a command to the waitress bot to rush to the stage and use her blouse to clean the pulp from Forrest's face. The blouse slipped off, revealing smooth silver skin and amply filled bra. Someone in the crowd howled, another whistled. "Hey, baby, take it all off." A dozen men and women mounted the stage and circled around her, clapping and hooting. The tomato thrower, feeling ignored, charged headlong through the mob and threw a tomato at the half-exposed she-bot from a few feet away. The plump missile, thrown with great force, hit her foot with a squishy-thud. She slipped, fell to her knees and looked up at the Rager with pleading, bedroom eyes. The boy stood frozen, mouth hung open, breathing rapidly. The she-bot slowly rose to her feet, then wrapped her long, thin arms around the young man and gave him a passionate kiss. The crowd whooped.

Cesar struggled to see through the roiling crowd. He needed a clear view of the boy's face so he could plan the she-bot's next move. He zipped at breakneck speed, issuing command after command. The bot held the boy's gaze, smiling coyly. His eyes widened as her hands slid sensuously up over her shoulders, waist, hips. The tumultuous room grew silent. With a wet splat, the last tomato dropped to the floor as the boy's hands went limp. The she-bot adjusted her bra strap. "If you don't like those tomatoes, I've got riper ones in the back room." The young man's face turned bright red, but his embarrassment didn't stop him from following her swishing tail out of the hall.

The audience erupted with laughter: it had accepted the mayhem—tomato attacks, chair throwing, the young punk's comeuppance, even the collapse on stage of the Futurists' mayoral hope—as all part of the performance.

Cesar flopped back in his chair with relief. In the worst way he wanted to follow the young punk out of the hall and smash him in the face, but he needed to be at the Puppet Master controls to get the program back on track and prepare for the rally's finale. Anyway, Tomato would know what to do once she got the kid alone: she-bots were programmed to handle sexual harassment just fine, thank you.

While the battered podium was removed and the floor cleaned, Forrest pulled himself up and began shaking hands with surrounding supporters. At Cesar's command, the human-robot pairs resumed serving snacks, scattering money, juggling tomatoes, romping up and down the aisles. A group of young women started a conga line behind the prancing bots that grew until it snaked around the entire hall. Another group, mostly composed of Futurist plants, gathered at the foot of the stage, where they cheered and clamored for "Forrest! Forrest!"

Cesar grinned. Cranking up the setting for Robot Clowning was having an effect. Readouts showed the crowd's comfort level with the presence of robots was increasing. The group experience amplified the effect: seeing the favorable reaction of their peers made it easier for folks to break taboos. Maybe too easy: a group of young men hoisted one of the robots over their heads and started tossing him into the air, and Cesar knew it was time to wrap things up.

He flipped on noise dampening, dialed down the hall lights and focused a spotlight on center stage. The crowd quickly grew quiet and focused on Forrest, who stood in the circle of light. Raising two fingers in a V for Victory, he shouted, "For a brighter future, go Cy-bot."

Cesar entered a final command. A chant went up from the robots scattered through the audience. "Go Cy-bot! Go Cy-bot!"

The tall figure motioned for those still seated to join in. "For a brighter future, vote Futurist."

The crowd bellowed back, "Futurist! For-rest! Futurist! For-rest!"

Cesar congratulated himself. Look how well things had turned out. His orchestration of the show had saved the day, after Hayes' reckless risk-taking. The Party

Council would be pleased; hopefully, it might even earn him some freedom from Horse's stifling oversight.

Forrest Newcomb stood in a sea of acclaim, waving and smiling as the demonstration swelled around him. His eyes scanned the crowd as he estimated the number of voters won over in just one evening, extrapolated exponential increases, and calculated the potential. If this performance were any indication . . . the numbers were staggering. With cold planning and dedicated persistence, Futurists would own the future. Someday he might even run for president. Go Cy-bot!

## BEGIN FILE 004, SOURCE AG:

# TROJAN PASSION

The she-bot led the tomato-tossing punk up the hall to the security locker, ushered him inside, pulled the door closed behind them and punched the lights down to ultra dim. She leaned against the marine blue padding that covered the far wall and licked her lips, her come-hither eyes beckoning.

The closet-sized space was featureless, an empty 6x8-foot oblong containing only a light and an air vent on the ceiling and a single pair of handcuffs dangling from a bent nail. The kid stood, with his back pressed against the door, leering, his pupils dilated, sizing her up, allowing the heat of the moment to build slowly.

Provocatively, she kicked a shoe at him and giggled. The kid didn't hesitate. He stepped forward in the tight space, pressed her body against the wall. His hands moved down from her shoulders, under her blouse, searching for her bra hook. The synth-skin felt rubbery and unnatural. Kissing her long and deep, he stuck his tongue into her mouth. It tasted of freshly-molded plastic, and he recoiled.

"Take your clothes off," he demanded.

The bot draped her arms around his neck, studying his face, lips, cheeks, eyes, and winked. "Tell me your name first," she said.

Up until now, the kid had felt completely at ease, but now he was on guard. Maybe she really intended to give him some sugar, or maybe she was only leading him on so she could later finger him to the police. Regardless, he felt trapped and vulnerable, here in a soundproof security locker with a bad-breath she-bot. He knew nothing of her strength. What if she wrapped her fingers around his throat or hauled off and slugged him with superhuman punches? Would he be able to fend her off? Could he even get away if he needed to? Impulsively, he thought of reaching behind to test if the door would open but refrained, not wanting to show any weakness. Instead, he peeled her off his neck and, holding her hands with interlocking fingers, tried to gauge her strength.

Five shoeless toes found the back of his knee and began inching their way up his inner thigh. "What should I call you, hon?"

He stared down at her long horizontal leg, softly moaned, marveling at the skill of her gently massaging toes.

"I'm Tony. How 'bout you?"

"Tony! Tony's a strong name. Tell me, how old are you?"

Annoyed at her continued questioning, he pushed her leg away. "What diff do it make?"

"Okay, Tony-What-Diff, you can call me Tomato #7."

"Take your clothes off," he repeated. "Show me what you've got. I came here for a Robot Show, remember?"

"Right, baby, but let me warn you, you might be disappointed."

Tony smiled and shook his head. "Quit stalling!"

Her outfit slipped off and she tossed it into a corner. A perplexed look descended like a dark cloud over Tony's face. "You're not all there," he said.

"Oh . . . this is all of me," she retorted, emphasizing the *all*.

"But . . ."

"You noticed! I'm anatomically incomplete. Surprised, hon?"

His mouth hung open but no words emerged.

"No sex tonight!" she grinned. "You've had all the fun you're gonna get. Now turn around and run along home."

She was a manikin. The freak didn't even have nipples. Tony's desire quickly dissipated. He wanted to slap her. Then all he wanted to do was get away. He spun around to open the door, but it didn't yield. He pounded it with his fist, punched the thumb pad, kicked.

"The price of exit is another little piece of tongue," she said with a wink.

"Go to hell," he spat.

Tomato #7 laughed. "The price of exit just went up."

An alarmed look spread over his face. "How much do you want?"

"I showed you mine, now you show me yours."

He shook his head. There was no way he wanted to expose himself to this creepoid.

"Guess you like the comforts of this closet. We can wait all night as far as I'm concerned." She gave him a what-are-you-afraid-of shrug. "You no show, you no go."

He stared at her blankly for a couple of long minutes. Then his hands went to his belt, which clanged as it hit the floor.

Tomato stepped back, cast a glance down between his legs, blinked three times. "Now go home and behave yourself. I've recorded every moment of our romantic evening together."

Tony turned pale.

"Listen carefully, my sweet, young man," she continued, "if you ever harass us robots again, your friends will get to see just what kind of a saggy stud you are."

"Saggy stud?" he protested. "Nothing happened and you know it."

"That's the point, isn't it?" she giggled. "Now, promise to behave yourself and I'll let you out. Do we have a deal?"

"Yeah, yeah!"

Unable to assess his sincerity, Tomato stared at him through narrowed eyes.

"You gonna let me out?" he challenged.

When she hesitated, he clinched his fist and belted her, as hard as he could, straight in the chest.

"Ouch!" he shouted, his fist bruised from the blow against her metal-framed chest.

She stiffened slightly, but otherwise betrayed no reaction to his punch. In a flash, the bot sorted through her programming, searching for a defense routine or, lacking that, any sort of instructions for handling a physical attack, but the search returned a null. Her self-protection protocols were still offline. With no other behavioral options available, the she-bot leaned over and tapped the thumb pad. The door sprang open and Tony backed out, rubbing his wounded hand. "Hope you had a lovely evening," she mocked, blowing him a kiss.

Turning on his heels, Tony steamed away, making it clear he'd had enough of her phony games. "There will be hell to pay," he shouted back over his shoulder. "You won't get away with this."

The Rager stormed out of the building but didn't head home. In the parking lot, in the driver's seat of a rusty van sat his good friend Tex. Tony reached in through the glassless window, opened the door and jumped into the passenger seat. He said, still seething, "Up for some action?"

# NEWCOMB'S PARADOX

**P**eter Reid III, a reporter for the *Lake Worth Web-Times*, sat on a stool at Igot's with an untouched mug of beer in front of him and stared out the open window. Through vacant eyes, he half-watched, as a couple of guys helped their drunken buddy into a pre-smashed car. It was well after midnight. The downtown street was emptying out. But he was in no hurry to get home. He liked this public perch. It was where he did his best thinking.

Pete had grown increasingly suspicious during Forrest Newcomb's speech at the South Grade rally. Sure, they called it a "show," but with only a week to go before the election, it had been a campaign rally, plain and simple. The crowd had been gathered by pretext, a common political ploy. But that wasn't what bothered him. There was something about the Futurist candidate he found troubling, but he couldn't quite put his finger on what it was.

Pete felt a friendly hand on his shoulder. He turned and instantly recognized Senator Joe Newcomb, Forrest's dad, martini in hand.

"Speak of the devil," Reid cracked.

"One who knows where to find his minions," the Senator retorted. "What the hell have you been up to?"

"Actually, I've been sitting here quietly, marveling at your son. He's running a good race."

The two men had known each other for decades. Their kids had attended Lake Worth High together. Growing up, Forrest had always been a misfit—slow-witted, awkward, unfocused. His dad had tried repeatedly to get the boy interested in school, sports, friends, anything. By age 25, Forrest had bounced through five or six college campuses, but spent most of his time studying the mixology of margaritas in Key West. With each passing year, Joe found it increasingly difficult to hide the fact that he was disappointed in his eldest son.

Now the son was a totally different person. The new Forrest was bright, sharp, a clear thinker, an engaging speaker. He seemed to love being with people. The change was astonishing.

Pete motioned for Joe to sit down on the stool beside him. It was as good an opportunity as any to pump the Senator on his miraculously changed son. He reached into his pants pocket, where his mini voice recorder should have been. But the recorder wasn't there. Damn! He must have dropped it when pulling out his car keys at the school. "Say, I saw your kid in action tonight. He gave a terrific speech. Really moved the audience. He's changed. He used to be so unambitious. What happened?"

"Well, you know what I think of Futurist policies. Their heads are in the clouds, with their world of all play and no work! A robot-filled society would borrow the form but nothing of the heart of humanity. But they've done wonders for my son. Ever since Forrest joined the Party, his confidence has soared. It looks like he finally found his place in the world."

"I'm surprised you're not more upset; the conservative Senator's son taking up with those radicals and all."

The Senator downed his drink and motioned for the bartender to bring him another. "Well, you know as well as I do change is in the air. For fifty years, global warming took its toll. We've been hit by droughts, flooding, hurricanes, tsunamis, one disaster after another. Most of the coast was underwater. The cities deteriorated into dirty, crowded enclosures walled-in by dikes and levees. Confidence in the future evaporated. But ironically, the dirty nukes that destroyed Dallas and other cities around the world, kicked up massive dust clouds, screened the sun and cooled the planet just enough to counteract the warming. Now the climate's begun to stabilize. The ocean's receded. Coastal areas have reappeared. We've literally got our country back."

Reid grimaced the way he did whenever a pol lapsed into rhetoric and posturing. However, he had no choice but to indulge his friend.

"Now, all things old, even time-tested policies, are being junked. We have no patience for sorting out the real causes. We're tossing out the baby with the bath water. The breakup of the USA is a symptom of our distrust of the past," Newcomb continued pontificating. "We splintered into four sections, North, South, Greater Utah, and Greater California. When economic and social conditions continued to deteriorate, the splinters splintered again. Traditional political parties had no answers except to promote local control and create ever smaller governing units. Now we've got ourselves an independent Republic of Florida."

Reid piped up. "Well, sure, but what has any of that to do with the change in Forrest?"

Newcomb reached deep into his sarcasm bag. "This is the Sunshine Republic. Everybody's happy here!"

"Right! Sunny and bright!"

The Senator shrugged. "You know I'm just kidding. But look, change is in the air, that's all I'm saying. Our kids are not going to be content with the same old hopes and dreams. They want their own dreams, the wilder the better, dreams big enough to absorb their youthful energy."

"So you actually credit Futurism for your son's personal growth?"

"Yes, Pete, I really do," the elder Newcomb said, taking a sip of his drink. "Hope is a powerful thing."

"Nice chatting, Senator. I'd better be heading off, now."

Reid stepped out into the warm night air, energized, hardly ready for sleep. Interesting, what his old friend had said about his son, but he wasn't convinced. "Something's fishy," he muttered. It was more than Forrest's transformation. The meeting at the school had been just a bit too polished. The Futurists seemed to be pulling out all the stops for this small town election. It made no sense. . .

He hopped into his pale blue hover-van and, hoping to find his lost voice recorder, sped back toward his previous parking spot across from the school.

As he neared the school, he slowed the van to a crawl. By light of the street lamps he could make out three figures walking arm in arm, headed up the east side of M Street. The man in the middle was limping, leaning on the other two for support. The injured man was tallest. From the back, the limper looked like the Newcomb kid. On a hunch, Pete pulled over, clicked off his headlights, silenced the motor. He aimed his web antenna at the pair and donned a headset. The parabolic dish had the capacity to double as a snooping device. The reporter had no clear idea why he was playing cloak and dagger games or what he hoped to learn. Newcomb was doing nothing the least bit newsworthy. Apparently, he'd bumped himself during the ruckus at the school, perhaps sprained an ankle, and was being helped to a car. Yet Pete had a prickling hunch, a feeling the Futurists were up to something. *Might as well follow this hunch and see where it takes me. I've got nothing else to do tonight anyway.*

Although the threesome were almost a block away, the antenna quickly picked up their conversation.

"The bots are at risk. They shouldn't drive the limo back alone," said the one on the right, waving his free hand and pointing back toward the school.

"They're better drivers than you or me," said the guy on the left, sounding like the one in charge. "Chill, m' friend."

"And what about the Ragers? Tzz!" Cesar hissed with evident frustration. "Every time you give an order, Braad, you countermand it within the hour. Drive! Don't drive! Supervise the bots at all times! Let them walk around on their own! Next you might be telling me to scrap covert operations entirely and tell the world what goes on inside our hush-hush secret Safe House." He shook his head. "You know, you are one hard hombre to figure out."

"Ah gegah ragat babee bush," said the third. Reid was pretty sure the gibberish came from Newcomb.

"What?" asked the authoritative voice.

"Gegah Ragers ragaat babe eee," came the reply.

"We've got more to worry about than Ragers right now. That blow to the knee damaged critical functions."

With an abrupt turn left, the three entered the front yard of a private residence near the far end of the block. Reid scowled. A blow to the knee damaging critical functions? And now the guy could only talk gibberish? Was Newcomb having some kind of nervous breakdown that would force him to drop out of the race? He rubbed his palms, sensing the potential for a very hot scoop; at the very least to find out what was wrong with the mayoral candidate. He turned the antenna, tracking the Futurists as they turned into the yard. Instantly, his ear was filled with a high pitched squeal. Reid ripped off the headset. It took a full two minutes for his ears to stop ringing. By the time, he was able to hear again, Newcomb and company had disappeared inside the house.

Reid waited another couple of minutes before restarting the van. He drove slowly down M Street, headlights off, and parked in front of the house in question. He repositioned the antenna, but the squeal returned louder than ever. Incrementally, he adjusted his aim until the dish pointed over the roof top. Silence. The interference was coming from the house. Who would set up an anti-eavesdropping perimeter in a residential neighborhood? Only somebody with something to hide.

The reporter reached into the back seat and pulled a pair of night-vision goggles out of a black leather bag. With them, he surveyed the house and its surroundings. An array of security cams, motion detectors and audio drops were strategically placed around the house. Maybe this was the secret hideaway those guys were talking about. He returned his attention to the antenna's controls, adjusting filter bands as he tried to penetrate the barrier. What was going on in there? But each time all he met was the same high-pitched squeal.

# VIGILANTE JUSTICE

**F**our young men crouched behind the jasmine hedge at the far end of the school parking lot. For this special operation, they'd donned matching shirts with the words, "Rage Against the Machine" embossed across the back in lightning-bolt letters. The four watched as the school's double doors swung open and three shadowy figures emerged. Tony, the leader of the Rager Action Team, leaned forward, lead pipe in hand, trying to get a better look. "Nope, three guys, not her," he hissed through clenched teeth. Jasmine thorns hooked his loose-fitting shirt, and he jerked away and pounded his pipe in the dust.

For nearly thirty minutes, the four watched as the crowd exited the school, first in torrents, now trickling out by ones and twos.

Gradually the school's windows went dark as the building emptied. Only the street lamp and one set of exiting red tail lights broke the blackness. Maybe she had slipped out another way. Just as Tony considered giving up, the doors swung open. Out marched eight robots in single file, their steps in silent unison. The hated she-bot held the seventh place in line. Of course he hadn't believed for a second that her name was Tomato. She'd messed with his mind, made a fool of him to the crowd, enticing, disgusting, humiliating him. He tapped the lead pipe against his open palm. How sweet this payback would be!

Tony surveyed the lot one last time. The robo-gang was unaccompanied and headed toward a limo parked against the south fence, some fifty yards away. At the head of the line was one of the shrimp harvester bots. A keychain dangled from his hand. Apparently the bot was assigned to drive the limo. So much the better. No humans in sight.

Tony popped a red pill, puncturing the thin-walled capsule with his front teeth and letting the sticky fluid seep under his tongue. Reds gave courage.

The column of bots was within steps of the limo when Tony rushed forward. "Death to machines!" he cried out. His three buddies raced behind him, shouting and waving two-by-fours and broomsticks. They soon swarmed the robots. Tex aimed the first blow at the shrimper's hand, snatching the limo key from the bot's loosened grip. The first exuberant release of endorphins warmed his blood. Tony hammered the row of bots like xylophone keys, striking methodically from one to the next as he worked down the line. The bots stood passively in place, whacked, battered and bashed, yet neither defending themselves nor fleeing.

He saved an extra measure for the Tomato slut, pushed the other bots out of the way, rhythmically raining blow after blow on her head, neck, shoulders. Other

Ragers joined Tony in pummeling the bitch-bot. But she merely watched with bemused indifference as her left arm fell off, the detached fingers twitching on the ground.

"Geez, this is too easy. They're chicken, chicken in a can, and I'm awful hungry," Tony shouted as he struck Tomato repeatedly across the base of her neck.

Tomato, still indifferent to the blows raining down on her, bent down and picked up her arm. With a sweeping stroke across the knees, Tex knocked her off her feet. Tony stood briefly above her, his legs straddling her shimmering torso. "Who's laughing now, Little Miss Anatomically Incorrect?" and staring down at her with a vicious grin he drove his pipe through her forehead. There was no screaming, no blood. The only sounds were the flapping noise made by loose pieces of synthetic skin and soft electronic clicks.

The Ragers quickly dispatched the remaining bots. Despite their superior physical strength, the robots didn't fight back. They didn't try to run away. They just stood silently, taking blow after blow, watching unperturbed as their bodies were brutally dismantled. Tex wondered why they made no attempt to defend themselves. Maybe that pretty-boy robot engineer wasn't as smart as he thought he was. Tex just laughed and kept swinging his stick. Within three minutes, the area around the limo was littered with severed limbs, pierced chrome skulls and nondescript bits of robotic carnage.

"That was a riot," Tony joked.

"Your jokes are so funny even the robots cracked up," said Tex.

"I'm just getting started," said the nameless third as he jumped around, like a mad caveman waving his club. "Who's next?" He was the tallest of the gang, a big lumbering fellow. The others laughed at his shadow-dueling with unseen opponents.

"I claim this vehicle as a spoil of war," said Tex, happy to have a stretch limo to replace his rusted van. "Let's cruise the beach and look for babes."

"Or more bots to batter," said the fourth.

"Let's take babes or bots, whichever comes first," suggested the third, smacking his lips against his clenched fist and chortling at his own cleverness. "I can play either Romeo or Rocky."

Tex shook his head. What chance did he have of shagging a fishling with these clowns in tow? "Get in the car," he ordered. "We'll cruise the beach, then I'll take you kids home. Your mother made me promise not to keep you out late."

Cracking jokes, the gang began collecting the bot remains and tossing them into a pile in the back of the limo. Tony gave Tomato's mangled frame a penalty kick one last time, for good measure. She lifted off the pavement, landing with a crash a few feet away. The impact caused her head to break loose. Slowly, hauntingly, the head rolled back toward him.

A chill ran up Tony's spine. Impulsively, he grabbed the head by its hair and tossed it unceremoniously into the limo. "Let's get out of here," he shouted. Before leaving, he removed his pocket flash and took a photo of the gruesome heap. Just as he snapped the shutter, Tomato opened her eyes and grinned at him from the

Tony hurriedly tossed her head into the limo . . .
She gave him a one-eyed wink.

top of the debris pile. "Jeez, did you see that?" he said. "Her mouth just moved."

"You're imagining things," Tex said.

The she-bot's eyes widened and fixed on Tex. She gave him a sassy, one-eyed wink. "Mother of Pearl," he cried out as he slammed the limo door shut and began barfing. The other guys turned their backs on him, holding their own guts, half-sick themselves, embarrassed.

Gradually Tex regained his composure, but the guys stood rigid, immobilized. "Let's get going! Everyone into the car," Tex ordered. But they continued to stand, eyeing one another.

"Get in there with those hissing, twitching metal corpses?" Tony cried out. "You nuts?"

"Damn machines!" cursed Tex.

Tex opened the door, knocked Tomato's head out of the vehicle onto the pavement, took his stick and beat it flat into an unrecognizable platter. He picked it up, inspected both sides, top and bottom, and smiled. Not a sign of facial features remained, it was just a lumpy metal disc. He leaned back and with a mighty heave sailed it like a Frisbee across the parking lot. It skidded along the pavement, clattering like a bouncing tin can until stopping against the hedge at the opposite end of the lot.

"Now, climb in," Tex repeated.

Jumping to, they all squeezed into the front seat, with Tony behind the steering wheel. He drove over to where the flattened head had landed. "Somebody pick her up. We mustn't leave a lady alone at night in this dangerous neighborhood," he quipped as he gestured for Tex to get out and retrieve it.

They all laughed as the limo pulled out of the lot. Tony defiantly drove the wrong way up L Street, feeling elated. The night had been a great success. Mr. D'Camp was sure to be generous.

## NARRATIVE PAUSE 002

A TEXT REPLY to Jurat's message beeped in. Must be the most expedited review in the history of the department, he thought. But it wasn't from the DA. It was from Sheriff Braxil.

> TO: Inspector Solomon Jurat
> CC: PBCDA
> SUBJECT: Re: RLL7765 Request for Legal Opinion
> MEMO: Owner's claim of exemption for presence on public streets of metalloid robot named above is without merit. Negotiated exemption restricted to invitation-only events in controlled meeting facilities with prior notice to PBSO. Application for general, unrestricted, non-noticed or outdoor appearance at first granted then withdrawn earlier this year due to threats of public disorder.

When Jurat finished reading the message, he exhaled and ordered himself a celebratory beer. Without knowing all the ins and outs, he'd been right to put the collar on Komenen. The Lady, it seemed, was still with him after all.

# SPORTING NEW EYES

For Cesar's sixth birthday, Papi and Dad took him to Miami to see his first professional baseball game. The Palm Beach Sharks were playing the Miami Marlins for the league championship. It was the boy's first trip out of the Palm Beach enclave. The long snake-like train wound along the tops of the levees that had protected the cities through the Crisis Years. Despite the receding of the seas, an extensive flood control system was still maintained. The island enclosures stretched like a string of pearls along the once, and now rapidly re-emerging, Atlantic coast: Jupiter, Palm Beach, Boca Raton, Fort Lauderdale, Sunrise, Miami, Coconut Creek.

Rowdy Shark fans, wearing rubber fins on their heads, shouted, cheered and, with bared teeth, hissed the "predator's hiss." More fans packed into the train at each stop. Cesar enjoyed the hoopla. He took a window seat, his nose squashed against the glass as he gazed out at mile after mile of sawgrass-covered floodplain to the west.

The ballpark was colossal. Never before had Cesarito seen 50,000 people in one place. Shuffling through the crowd, seeing only legs at trouser-pocket height, fearful he might get lost, he clung to his dad's pant leg until they found their seats behind first base.

Papi's billfold bulged with cash. He indulged his grandson with an autographed ball, a shark fin cap, and a Chomp 'Em pennant. The game was a high-scoring affair, full of hits and scampering base runners, punctuated with home runs; a kid's delight. All afternoon, Cesar stuffed himself with hot dogs, peanuts and Coconut Cokes. The Sharks won the game 17–15, and the Komenens went home happy, singing "Chomp, Sharks, Chomp" on the train with the celebrating crowd. From that day on, Cesar dreamed of becoming a pro-baseball player.

Cesar's first trip to Cuba came in the wake of The Accident. He was a month shy of 10 years old. Papi had a work shed behind their house, a place to putter on weekend afternoons. There was always some DJ helmet project or electronic gizmo spread out on the work tables. Cesar loved to hang around, eager to help. One day the boy was left alone to hand-polish a helmet shell. Somehow a jar of caustic solvent fell off an upper shelf, broke, and splashed his face. Cesarito was rushed to JFK Hospital's emergency room. The doctors worked a miracle to keep his face from scarring, but his left eye was chemically scorched beyond repair, and the other eye never completely healed.

Unable to play baseball, or even run with the other kids, Cesar moped around the house for months, depressed and dispirited. Fortunately Papi had connections with a Cuban robotics lab and was able to arrange for both of Cesar's damaged eyes to be replaced with cyber implants.

In his youth, Cesar's grandfather had first been inflamed with a desire to change the world when he learned about a Cuban group that was experimenting with different types of governments in the wake of the collapse of state socialism. The Utopian Communities District was founded in 2076, taking over several impoverished provinces along Cuba's southwest coast. Philosophers, economists and political scientists from across the world came to participate in controlled scientific experiments in how to create happy, prosperous communities, in the process transforming political science from an observational to an experimental discipline. In these impoverished areas, they would try out various forms of government: social democracy, laissez-faire capitalism, communal collectivism, theocracy, etc. An oversight board provided an allotment of land and technical assistance. The happiness of the people living under these different types of governance would be measured, compared and published each year.

Papi spent a year after college visiting various communities to learn how they functioned. He ended up in the Robot Republic Experimental Community, working as a gopher at a research lab. It was there that he met Dr. Zy Futano. The two had formed a bond with their dreams of a utopian world where robots would serve every human need.

As Cesar and Papi boarded the Super-Hover at the Lantana Dock for the trip to Cuba, Cesar was nervous about his surgery, and Papi tried to set him at ease. "You know, hijo, Cuban replacement eyes are the best in the world. And as far as medicos go, Dr. Futano is the best of the best. When I was your age," Papi explained, "the basic idea that brains and cyber-components could be linked together was brand new. Dr. Futano and I spent a lot of evenings sitting around after work, drinking cervesas and dreaming about a language that nerve cells and microchips could both understand. He's brilliant. The ideas behind DJ helmets really came from him."

"Did he invent cybereyes, like the ones I'm going to get?" Cesar asked.

"Many scientists worked together. It was what you'd call a collaborative effort, but yes, he had a lot to do with it. The way your new eyes will help your brain see works a lot like a helmet does."

The ocean cruise to Cuba was pure adventure for a boy who had never been far from home. As soon as they were underway, his fear of the upcoming operation faded away. The hovercraft flew across the waves, leaving almost no wake. Cesar sat on the bow deck watching the flying fish leap out of their way. He stuffed himself with corn arepas and shrimp. As the craft slowed near the harbor, a pod of dolphins escorted them in. It was late afternoon by the time they landed at Cienfuegos, the port of entry for the Experimental Zone.

An open-air tram took them along the scenic waterfront. A broad bay and a busy commercial harbor lay cradled within a rib of coastal mountains. Fishing boats, of all shapes and sizes, plied the waters, tooting greetings to each other at every opportunity. The whine of the tram's engine drowned out the boat whistles as the train began to slowly zig-zag up the steep slope inland. At the top, everyone got out to admire the view: the ocean on one side, a deep blue freshwater lake on the other. Windsurfers sporting orange and green sails zoomed across the surface of the lake, periodically leaping acrobatically into the air. Cesar gazed over the landscape, mesmerized. This is paradise, he said to himself.

"My Papi and I are going to the Robot Republic. Can you let us off there?" Cesar asked the conductor as they re-boarded.

"Republica Robotica, proxima," shouted the conductor, with his hands cupped over his mouth, just like in the movies.

After a breezy downhill ride, the tram deposited them and their luggage on the steps of the Welcome Center for the Robot Republic. The Center was shaped like a wire harness with huge hollow connectors for entrance portals. Above the entry were etched the words, "Plug In To The Future."

Once inside, Cesar and Papi received visitor visas and were each paired with an attendant robot. Cesar was assigned to a kid-sized model named Chatter, who stood just a little taller than Cesar but was a lot more talkative. Its body had a hard, burnished surface with an iridescent finish; in contrast, its pliant hands and animated face seemed completely human. When it leaned over to shake hands, Cesar was surprised at how skin-like its hands felt.

In rapid-fire Spanish, Chatter explained what the Robot Republic was all about. "Everyone here owns at least one personal robot. For us, this is the most important and exciting idea for the advancement of human happiness since the domestication of the horse. It means people can have a better life without working too hard."

"Can you talk slower?" Cesar asked. "My Papi never españols so fast."

Chatter slowed down and spoke with great fanfare. "I am here to be your servant, guide, friend. I will do anything you ask."

"Anything?" Cesar's face lit up.

"*Almost* anything." Chat's friendly smile showed a hint of demurrer. "As long as it's not illegal and doesn't hurt anyone."

"Cool! Get me a popsicle, red mango flavor."

The robot opened a compartment in its side and drew out the requested item with a smirk. "That's a surprisingly common request," it explained. "Red mango is very popular this month."

"That's so cool!" Cesar said as he took the popsicle, gleaming pale orangey pink in the hot Cuban sun, and then took a cold, sweet bite. His eyes got big as he tried to imagine what else might be inside the robot. "Can I get a three-foot-long hot dog with cheese and chili?" he said between mouthfuls.

"Maybe another day." Chat winked as he watched his human charge savor his treat. A pile of napkins was at the ready.

*This is going to be a ton of fun,* Cesar thought. He looked around to see whether Papi was in ear shot. Once he was sure he wouldn't be overheard, he turned back to Chatter with a mischievous look. "I order you to kiss my ass."

The robot, fully programmed with parenting skills, scowled deeply. "That, young man, is not an appropriate request," it admonished. "Don't ever try anything like that again."

"Okay, okay! I was just kidding."

During his six-month stay in Cuba, Cesar lived with the Futano family in Robot Republic Territory, just east of Cienfuegos. Dr. Futano was a big man with big hands, a big gut and a gentle smile. Now retired, he lived with his son and three grandchildren in a sprawling villa bustling with robot servants. Robots did the laundry and house cleaning, prepared meals, performed whatever household chores were asked of them. Each day the doctor's wife would give the robot cook a menu for the day's meals. His oldest grandson, Freddie, ordered pretzels and chocolate snacks whenever he wanted as long as the items were on a pre-approved list. At ten each morning, the bots would walk the six blocks to the store and carry their purchases home without the slightest grumble or fatigue.

A few days after Cesar's arrival, Dr. Futano drove him to the clinic. A young surgeon with bulging cyber-eyes patiently explained the replacement procedure, step by step.

"Will my eyes be *that* big?" the boy asked, staring at the surgeon, evident worry on his face.

"Not unless you want something larger," the doctor grinned holding his eyelids open as far as possible.

Cesar giggled nervously.

"I recommend average-size eyes for you," the doctor reassured him. "That way no one will know you've got new cybers instead of birth eyes. And you'll be able to see better than you ever dreamed. You'll love them."

Phase one of Cesar's procedure involved inserting bio-cyber interfaces to convert digital images into neural signals that his brain could process. Cesar was strapped into a large, metal chair, his head held perfectly still in a vice, and watched in a mirror with his one good eye as the doctor implanted long thin tubes through his scalp. He was fascinated by the procedure, which was neither frightening nor painful.

Phase two was the scary part. Cesar checked into the clinic the day before the procedure. He sat on a low stool before a big wooden desk as the doctor opened a box and showed him two round orbs that were to become part of him. Pairing new cybereyes was vital to correct functioning. Cesar's good eye would need to be removed along with his damaged one.

"The fibers we inserted last time replace the optic nerves. They run down through your brain to your new eyes and clip in here," the doc explained, pointing to the snap fitting where the synthetic optic nerve would connect to each eye.

Cesar stiffly nodded his head.

"The muscles that move your eyes so you can look up, down, or side to side are in good shape. We won't have to replace any musculature at all. The tendons attach to these hooks and are balanced with these micro tab adjustments over here."

Cesar didn't fully understand but nodded again anyway.

"Something wrong, today?" the doc asked. "Last time I saw you, you were fascinated by the technology."

The doc checked the remote detection gauges on his desk and noticed that Cesar's pulse was severely elevated. Clearly the boy was very frightened of something.

"Are you worried about tomorrow?"

"Uh . . . yeah," Cesar reluctantly admitted.

"What are you afraid might happen? Are you worried it will hurt?"

"No, nothing like that." He stirred in his seat.

"What then?"

Cesar pointed to the orbs. "Will they work? Will I be able to see after the operation?"

"Of course," the doctor said with a reassuring smile.

"Are you sure? I mean really, really sure? I mean once you gouge out my real eye, the one I can see with now . . . well . . . if something goes wrong, you can't put it back, can you? . . ."

"Have you been worrying about this a lot?"

"Yeah!" Cesar bit his lower lip.

The doctor paused and looked tranquilly at Cesar. "I'm absolutely sure," he said in a careful voice. "I've done this millions of times."

Cesar just sat there looking glumly at him.

The doctor shrugged slightly.

"Tell you what . . . just so you feel better about it," he continued, "let's just do only one eye tomorrow. What do you think? Let's replace just the bad one, the one you can't see out of at all. Then once that heals, and when you are ready, we can do the other one. You may have a bit of trouble focusing at distance, telling how far away things are until we fix both, but I can do one at a time if it makes you feel better. What do you say?"

Cesar's face immediately brightened.

A month later, Papi came down from Florida to see how Cesar was getting along. The new eye was working perfectly.

There was a story that Papi told repeatedly to show how Cesar's visual acuity was sharper than ever. M&M Candy was running a series of promotional contests at the time for the Robot Republic Founders' Day. Special packages were marketed with each piece colored a slightly different shade. Cesar won the contest by sorting out forty-eight shades of red in the correct sequence from deep maroon to baby's breath pink in less than three minutes. Lucky for him, having a cybereye hadn't been a disqualifying factor.

After that, Cesar didn't hesitate to undergo the next procedure. His second eye was replaced the following week.

Recuperation from the second operation took less time than the first. Within a week, the bandages were off, and Cesar was outside playing as if nothing had happened.

Since the school term was only partly done, it was decided that he should finish the year in Cuba. Freddie Futanos was a friendly kid who made Cesar glad to be staying. The two of them were in the same fourth-grade class at Nuevo Fuego Middle School where they sat next to each other, conspired to cheat on math tests and, after school, would pal around together, playing béisbol and riding bicicletas over the town's hills of fire. Even though they weren't blood relations, they called each other "primo."

Cesar was delighted to have his vision back. Gradually he learned how to get the best use from his new cybereyes. The eyes were in some ways better than natural ones. Besides distinguishing fine shades of colors, Cesar could see in pitch blackness and focus on tiny items almost as well as a microscope.

However, his use of his special abilities was not always on the up-and-up. One day, when playing baseball, Freddie spoke with him in the dugout while their team was up at bat.

"You're in centerfield, right?" Freddie asked rhetorically.

"Uh, yeah," replied Cesar, wondering what his friend and teammate was getting at.

"Last time a fly ball came your way, you lost it in the sun, right? And dropped it, right?"

"Yeah?"

"I heard my Grandpa talking about a trick you can do with your eyes. You wanna hear it?"

"Sure!"

"Check this out. Squeeze your eyes shut, hold them, then blink quickly a few times and then stare at the ball."

"Do what?"

"Stand facing right at the pitcher. On the next pitch, squeeze your eyes then blink and stare at the ball."

"Why?"

"Your eyes will lock in on the ball, they'll track it, they'll focus on it."

"Really?" said Cesar. "That's click cool."

"Quiet," chided Freddie. "Let's keep it a secret, between us two."

"Uh, okay," said Cesar, looking around to see if anyone had been close enough to overhear. "You sure it'll work?"

Freddie gave him a deep nod, crown to chin. "Just try it."

Next inning, with two outs and a runner on third, there was a loud crack of the bat. A long fly ball was coming Cesar's way, out over his head. He followed Freddie's advice—squeezed his eyes shut, held them, then blinked fast a few times and stared at the ball— then turned heel and made a mad dash for the outfield fence. Somehow he just knew where to go. The computer chip in his eye must have calculated the trajectory and sent the flight path to his brain. At the base of the fence, Cesar made a spectacular over-the-shoulder catch to end the inning. All his teammates expected Cesar to miss and were ready to razz and boo. Instead, he trotted to the dugout to a chorus of cheers: "nice one, way to haul 'em in!" Cesar felt happy, happier than he had felt at any time since the accident.

Batting was even more fun. He stood in the batter's box and realized he could pick up the ball's spin. Even when he was thrown a fast ball, his eyes would track and refocus quickly. The red stitching seemed to jump right off the ball. His batting average rose to .580, and he was in line for Chico League batting champion, when the cat wriggled out of the bag.

It happened during the final game of the season. Cesar was up for the third time, already he had two extra base-hits in previous at-bats. The opposing pitcher was a tall, lanky guy with a good fast ball and mean enough to throw at batters. Sure enough, the first pitch was a fast ball high and inside, forcing Cesar to jump out of the way. He took his time straightening his belt, adjusting his socks, making the pitcher wait. Irritated, the pitcher waved both arms in the air. Finally Cesar dug his cleats into the batter's box, crowding the plate, making sure the pitcher knew he was not about to be intimidated. The pitcher was just as tough. The second pitch was fired straight at Cesar's head. Cesar had to hit the dirt to avoid being beaned.

Then, as he scrambled back to his feet and dusted himself off, he glared at the pitcher and inadvertently reset his eyes. The next pitch came over the heart of the plate, but Cesar couldn't pick up the curve. He swung and missed the ball with an embarrassing whoosh.

With the count at two balls, one strike, Cesar tried to fix his eyes on the ball, but the pitcher kept nervously moving it from glove to free hand, never holding it still long enough for him to get a good look at it. Cesar took the third pitch for strike two.

Now it was Cesar's turn to get nervous. He paced around the batter's box, refusing to get in, waiting for a chance to stare at the ball and reset his vision. Finally the ump ordered him to step up to the plate. In a last moment of desperation, Cesar got an idea. He asked the ump to inspect the ball.

"That pitcher's throwing spitters," Cesar claimed although he knew better.

When the ball was lobbed in for the ump to look at, Cesar stared at it long and hard in the catcher's glove.

In his desperation, he forgot the need for secrecy. The pitcher came storming off the mound.

"Hey, aren't you that kid that had his eyes replaced. Do you have trick eyes?"

In the heat of the moment, Cesar yelled back, "Yeah, what if I do?"

Everyone in the ball park froze. The ump scowled. "Do you have machine vision?"

"Yeah, so what?"

The opposing team started to yell, "Cheat, cheat, cheat!"

The umpire pointed to the dugout. "Sorry, son, I can't allow you to play."

His coach and all his teammates ran out from the dugout and mobbed the umpire. Everyone was yelling at the same time.

"You can't toss him out of the game," the coach insisted. "He's worked hard to be this year's batting champ. He deserves it."

The boys on the opposing team continued to shout, "Cheat, cheat, toss him out!"

Eventually things calmed down enough for Cesar to explain. He had to admit to his coach and the team that his replacement eyes gave him super-focus. When it was all sorted out, it was plain that there were rules against that sort of thing.

The ump was sympathetic, but there was nothing else he could do. "Hijo, robotic enhancement is against the rules. It's unfair to the other kids."

Cesar spent the rest of the game on the bench. After an extended protest meeting he was kicked out of the league and had to turn in his uniform. What was worse, he couldn't play on any sports team after that. No béisbol, no basketbol, no futbol. Gradually he stopped running around with Freddie and the other kids and became more and more of a loner, spending his time shut up in his room reading.

Although it passed quickly, Cesar's time in Cuba made a lasting impression in another way. From day one, he was fascinated by the Futurist vision of a world filled with robots performing life's drudgery. He loved to watch Chatter clean his room, scurry to get him snacks, scrape mud from his shoes. If he only could bring Chat back to Florida—then his mom would never have to nag him again about making his bed, picking up dirty clothes or doing house chores. Daydreaming of a work-free life gave birth to an obsession with learning all he could about robotics.

During a class field trip to the robot congress that year, Cesar became a diehard Futurist. Señora Rogas, dressed in a white linen pants suit and Cuban flag cravat, led her students onto the helicopter that was to carry them to the capital at La Placenta. "You're in for a treat today," she said, as they approached. "La Casa del Congreso is beautiful from the air, surrounded with fountains and pools on every side. Look out your windows."

Cesar pressed his nose against the glareless, blue-tinged glass. The reflective chrome edifice was surrounded by rings of burnished steps that led up to a circle of majestic, tapered columns supporting a vaulted, obsidian dome. All the kids were ooh-ing and ah-ing.

"Señora Rogas," Cesar said, "the Casa has pillars and a dome and looks like pictures of other capital buildings from other countries that we've studied. I don't see what the big deal is."

"That's very observant of you, Cesar. You're right," the teacher said carefully; as a committed Futurist, she saw her duty to convey the maximum enthusiasm about robot government to her pupils. "It was built that way for a special reason, to show that our Robot Senate abides by the same principles of democracy as any other legislature in the world. What we have done is to perfect the traditional ideals of government in a way that no human legislature could. So this architecture, the design you see out of window, represents the continuity of tradition. Do you understand?"

"I guess so," Cesar shrugged. "But wouldn't it be cool if the whole building was a gigantic robot that could get up and walk around?"

"That, indeed," the señora said, with gentle irony, "would be unique."

The transport landed on the lawn. Senator Segundo Ocho was there to greet them and shake every student's hand. The senator looked like a bigger version of Chatter with an expressive human face and a metalloid frame, but he spoke slowly and with a deeper, more authoritative voice. "Cesar," he said when it was the young Floridian's turn, "How are you enjoying your time in our beloved community? How are your new eyes working out?"

"Fine," he said through tight lips.

The senator kneeled on the grass and looked Cesar in the eye. "I bet you're wondering how I know so much about you, right?" he asked kindly.

"Uh, yeah!"

"It's my job as a representative of the people to know the people I represent. I need to know their names, their jobs, what problems they have, and what the government can do to help them in their pursuit of happiness. I'm a Cy-bot, manufactured right here in the Robot Republic. I can remember a lot more about my constituents and their needs than any human senator could. You've studied about the pursuit of happiness in class, right? The more I know about what people want, the more I can help them."

"Yeah! My eyes see great, only I can't play béisbol," Cesar explained.

"Yes, I know. You used to play in the Chico League but were kicked out because of your enhanced eyes. I'll see what I can do about that," he winked as he stood up. "It's time to head inside. Follow me."

From the gallery, the class looked down at the wide oval of the main legislative chamber. Rows of wooden desks occupied most of the floor where the senate conducted business, supervised by stern portraits of the founders of the Republic looking on in stiff poses. Robot senators were milling around in small groups, chatting with visitors and constituents.

Cesar scratched his ear. "That's the Legislature?"

"That's it!" said the teacher. "It's just like the Florida Senate in your home state, except that our representatives are Cy-bots. When they are in full session, hundreds of their mechanical colleagues fill the room, listening to each speaker, nodding or shaking their heads, with approval or disapproval."

Cesar conjured a silly picture in his head. "And I bet members of the speaker's party nod and those of the opposing parties shake," he said.

"You're probably right. Each robot follows a script and nods or shakes his head according to the policies chosen by the voters."

Several of the kids, bored with the tour, took the comment as an excuse to run wildly around the Congressional corridor, jiggle their bodies and shout, "I'm shakin' all over."

Cesar, however, was full of questions. "So why do our robot politicians bother having debates when everyone knows they're going to disagree before they open their mouths?"

"That's another good question but a tough one. Maybe we could have Senator Ocho explain that to the class." She motioned for her scattered pupils to quit running and re-gather.

The senator, who had been conversing with a staffer, turned at the mention of his name. "Sir," Señora Rogas repeated, "could you explain to our students why our Robot Senate bothers with public debate when everybody knows their position beforehand? It seems so wasteful, so divisive, so human. Why program our robots to go through empty theatrics?"

"Ah, Señora Rogas, your young students are asking some very mature questions today. Well, yes, the reason has to do with political science, something you kids will study when you're older, in university. But let me give you an easy-to-understand example. When we go to watch a ball game, we don't go just to learn the final score, do we?"

The kids all shook their heads.

"Of course not, we go to cheer for our team, to hope they'll win. It's all about personal involvement. We want to feel part of it. Government is the same. Feeling that the government represents your opinion is important. So we have a full debate, put all the facts and the arguments on the table, play out the entire script, so to speak. When the final vote is taken, at least everyone feels they had some part in the decision. It's important not to short-circuit the process."

"But how's that so different from humans." Cesar objected. "If they're all made to act exactly like humans, why bother with robot senators?"

"Well, chico, there are some important differences. First of all, our Cy-bot officials do not engage in personal attacks. They don't avoid the real issue with fake distractions. They cannot lie, twist or spin. Unlike human politics in your country, debates are fair and factual. Second, after the debate, we always come to a decision. There is no gridlock or stalling. Government works. Whereas humans have ego and cannot stand to let the other side win, robots are egoless. And there are many other advantages of a robot congress that you'll learn later in school."

A boy ran by and cracked, "Advantages like stealing from the public and smoking big cigars?"

"No," said Señora Rogas, with her characteristic idealism. "This is the Robot Republic. Our representatives are always honest. Their behavior is completely controlled by their programming. There are no bribes, no closed door meetings, no secret deals."

Cesar looked doubtful. "But how would anyone know if the robots' programming was changed in secret? Couldn't a real sharp hacker break in and craze them up?"

The teacher smiled patiently. "Every jot of program is public and transparent," she explained. "If anyone doesn't trust the results of a congressional vote, they can double check the source code. Since people are always grumbling about one issue or another, hundreds of examiners, all with different political points of view, are on guard all the time. If something dishonest happened, they'd find it pretty quickly."

"Who fixes the congress when it breaks down?" Cesar asked hurriedly, hoping he wasn't talking too much.

The senator stepped up. "Our repairmen are certified graduates of one of our local training institutes. They do an excellent job. So far, there have been small-scale glitches but no system-wide emergencies. Thousands of people inspect the system every day. They are especially on the lookout for any sign of hackers. Someday, you might take a course in robot programming. Then you'll be able to see for yourself how every action of our congressmen can be traced back to the directives of the voters. It's an amazing process, unique in all the world. Our Cy-bots represent the true will of the people."

"Cool!"

"In a few short years of our existence the Robot Republic has done very well on the annual Happiness Survey. We're always in the top two or three. While our community is not perfect, we have proven that robots can govern efficiently. The impossibility of corruption means that people can trust their leaders. And, while there are always a few eternal skeptics, most people do. Our courts have robot judges who never take bribes, something the world has never seen before."

"Is this utopia?" Señora Rogas asked for the benefit of the class.

"Oh, no," the senator chuckled. "We're far from perfect. There is still occasional crime on our streets. Too much leisure has led to drug abuse and other problems, especially among our youth. And on economic issues, a few rich families still control most of the businesses, making it hard for new, bright entrepreneurs to break in. On the positive side, however, we have full employment. No one is poor. The economy expands due to export of our Cy-bots all around the world. And robots do much of the work while most people make good use their leisure time to lead creative and enjoyable lives. Our citizens are pretty happy." The senator leaned over, winked, and whispered conspiratorially, "And between you and me, I wouldn't live anywhere else!"

"Will robots ever come to Florida?" Cesar wondered out loud.

Señora Rogas shook her head. "I don't know much about your country," she said. "You can ask your teacher when you get home."

"I don't think there are any Futurists in Florida," Cesar said sadly.

"There will be at least one—you."

Cesar joined the other boys, who were running around the halls of the robot congress, chanting, "Viva, viva, viva! We are the Republica Robotica."

About a week later, Cesar had a visit from his old béisbol coach. The coach knocked on the door in the early evening after dinner. "I can't come in, but I have some good news for you. If you'll let the League's medicos reset your eyes to work like the average kid's during the games, they are willing to reinstate you. You can play béisbol again. And you'll still be able to use enhancements off the field."

"Really?" said Cesar, not believing his ears.

"Yep, the League got a call from a senator's office. You must have a friend in high places."

"That's great! Senator Ocho must have tried to help me," he said slowly. "But there's one problem. I'm going back to Florida before next season."

"Oh!" said the coach. "Then best of luck to you, wherever you play."

But Cesar's heart wasn't in it anymore. He never did play baseball again.

# REAL POLI SCI

One stormy Sunday afternoon, when it was impossible to play outside, Chatter offered to take Cesar and Freddie to the Museum of Experimental Communities, near the Cienfuegos Harbor. As they stood across the street, Chat pointed out the building's modular architecture, which resembled cubes piled askew.

"The museum's design," the robot said, "represents the diversity of communities on exhibit inside. Each one is separate and distinct, a box unto itself."

They entered the first hall through a gate in the largest of the cubes and stood gazing up at a large video map of the exhibits. Around the perimeter of the hall were twenty-four portal gates, each corresponding to one of the experimental communities in the Zone. The portals opened into winding tunnels that led to the galleries. The ceiling soared two hundred feet above and echoed with the sounds of hundreds of visitors moving from portal to portal.

Chat motioned Freddie and Cesar in the direction the entrance marked "Prisoner Rehabilitation Experimental Community." "The exhibit is set up like a real high-security area," Chat said, pointing to the iron bars blocking their way. "Put your palm under this DNA checker. We've got be to ID'd and cleared before we can enter."

"What's so secret in there?" Cesar asked.

"You'll see," said Chat.

Once they had each been scanned, a mechanical hand reached out and stamped ID codes on their wrists.

Cesar looked at Chat. "What's the stamp for?"

"Let's imagine we're all criminals," Chat explained, "tried, convicted and sentenced for our crimes, and entering this facility for the first time. It's a bit scary, isn't it?"

Before Cesar could respond, an iron gate swung open and a series of mechanical hands ushered them inside.

"Creepy, yes!" Cesar said, as the gate clanged shut behind them. A red neon sign flashed, "Exit Only at Far End. Proper Authorization Required."

As they rode an escalator upward, Chat explained the concept behind this community.

"People living there are either prisoners or professionals who work to reform prisoners."

"Are there murderers here?" Freddie wanted to know.

"Not here, this is just an exhibit. The actual prisoners are located in the rehab area, on the eastern end of the Zone."

"Do they ever escape and get into the RR at night?" Freddie pressed.

"From time to time someone escapes, but they don't get far. The prisoners all have heart tags to trace their whereabouts day and night. The tags cannot be removed without killing them."

"How about if they have a heart transplant?"

"That answer is not in my database." Chat said flatly.

At the top of the escalator was a theatre where the boys watched a presentation about the penal colony. The hardest core prisoners were sent from all over the world. Governments paid a lot of money to get these troublemakers off their hands. As a result the community had become quite wealthy. Additionally, the colony had an excellent record in making productive citizens out of even the worst of the criminals.

Cesar was most excited to learn that DJ helmets were used in the rehabilitation process. Helmet programs re-created crimes and allowed criminals to relive their crimes through their victim's eyes. They saw what the victim saw, felt what the victim felt, the pain, the panic, the post-traumatic stress, the angry aftermath. Ongoing repetitions trained perpetrators to avoid bad behavior, just as a mouse could be trained to avoid cheese by repeated electrical shocks.

"What if the criminals don't want to put on their helmets? Are they forced to?" Freddie wanted to know.

"No one is forced. That would be against the ethical standards for human experiments."

"Then why do they do it?"

"Examining their past behavior, taking moral inventory, is part of the healing process. Unless they go through that step, they have little chance of ever getting out. And the most effective means of self-examination, it turns out, just happens to be the DJ helmet."

As they wandered the halls, glancing at the exhibits, the boys continued to ply Chat with questions.

"Are the criminals ever released?"

"Do they commit more crimes once they are out?"

"Are there kids in the community? Are the kids of the criminals treated like criminals? Do they use DJ helmets to play games? Can they get red mango popsicles? Do they go to school? Can we visit them?"

Without complaint, the robot answered the incessant questions as best he could. When necessary he networked into the museum's database, but even then, not all of the boy's questions were answerable.

"Kids go to special boarding schools and have supervised visits with their parents every evening. There are lots of planned activities, parent and child sports teams, that sort of thing. No information is available on popsicle consumption in the PREC," Chat said, "but most likely the kids get the same kinds of treats as everyone else."

As they approached the exit, they were scanned to confirm their identity, just as would happen in a real prison, and allowed to leave through another iron gate.

Once they had regrouped in the main hall, Chat asked, "Where should we go next?"

"I want to see the egg unbreak," said Cesar.

"That old Humpty-Dumpty trick?" smirked Freddie.

"It's not a trick, it's real time-travel."

"Well—it's not exactly time travel, but it does involve time running backward," explained Chatter.

At the lecture hall, the presentation Cesar wanted to see, the one with egg time-travel, was not on the schedule. Instead there was something on the history of the Cienfuegos region.

"Sounds boring." said Freddie.

"Talk, talk, talk." said Cesar.

"What, then, do you want to do next?" Chatter asked.

Neither answered. The boys just stood there looking tired.

"Why don't we get lunch and bring it to the lecture?" suggested the ever-practical bot.

After a quick trip to the cafeteria down the hall, they joined the line outside the auditorium and were soon seated in the front row of the crowded theater, sandwiches in one hand and Zingade soft drinks in the other.

An empty, transparent cube, made entirely of glass, occupied the center of the otherwise vacant stage. As the theater lights dimmed, there was a loud pop, a cloud of smoke, and an elderly man materialized in the glass cube. He brushed off his drab green military uniform and shook the dust from his cap while scrutinizing the audience.

Whether he had been waiting there all along, hidden by the reflections of the auditorium lights on the surface of the cube, or had popped up through a trap door in the floor, was hard to tell. His salt and pepper beard and wavy hair stood straight out as if he had been zapped by static electricity.

With a deliberate professorial gesture, the man raised a finger: the cube's glass wall opened up like the two sides of a gate, and, wearing a thin smile, he walked up to the edge of the stage. "Ladies and gentlemen, boys and girls, my name . . . is Fidel Castro. You recognize my name? Almost two hundred years ago, we Cubans fought a Revolution to make a better life for our people and I'm here today to start again, to recruit you into my army. Who will be the first to join our fight?" He furled his brow and squinted ferociously.

The audience, already bemused by his dramatic entrance, stared in stunned silence; some looked like they had just seen a ghost. After pausing to gauge the effect of his introduction, and now certain he had the room's full attention, he smiled mischievously and went on. "No, no, actually it was my great grandfather who was the soldier." He bowed modestly. "My name is Dr. Fidel Castro IV. I do hope you find me a peaceful and funny guy. Welcome to our theater."

A wave of relieved applause swept the hall.

Dramatic entrances had been a Castro trademark since his rise to fame several decades before as a moderate leader, responsible for the creation of the Experimental Zone. It had been a family trait going back several generations, even before the still-notorious first Fidel.

"Today I'm going to be talking about a very important development in the history of our small country. Throughout the modern era, governments, whether of the left, center or right, have been notably inefficient at best and, at worst, corrupt and dictatorial. Every country experienced periods when the strong grabbed control by force or trickery and used the reins of government merely to increase their power and wealth. Should we let that continue?"

The crowd booed.

"It was over forty years ago, when we brought together a group of social scientists who created a plan to put government on an objective, scientific footing. Imagine an ordinary medical laboratory filled with dozens of rat cages. Now imagine a lab large enough to house a large sample of governments. That's exactly what the Cuban Experimental Zone is; a representative sampling of communities, each with its distinct political philosophy and economic model, functioning side by side in a thousand-square kilometer laboratory.

"Think about what a truly scientific experiment requires. You kids have learned in school that rigorous standards are necessary. One important standard is to have a variable and a control or benchmark to compare your results against. Every good experiment requires something like that. And so we would need something similar when experimenting with governments, too."

Castro paused, staring long and hard at the crowd.

"Consider the twentieth century. That period, two centuries ago, was dominated by conflict between two great economic systems: capitalism and socialism. In their pure forms, capitalism advocated competition and private enterprise, while socialism pushed for enterprises that were cooperative and state-run. Historically speaking, state socialism in its extreme form, with its centralized control, became oppressive and dictatorial. It stifled innovation and failed in its promise of a just and vibrant economic life for its peoples. Socialism stagnated and faded away. Capitalism came off victorious. Despite cycles of boom and bust, personal stress, rampant nervous disorders, insecurity, greed and elitism, it produced greater technological innovation, motivated personal initiative and produced greater wealth, not only for the upper crust, but also for a large middle class.

"As a result of that historic experience, are we to conclude that capitalism is, under all conditions and circumstances, a better system than socialism? Consider the facts in greater detail. By the time of the fall of the Soviet Union at the end of the twentieth century, capitalism had borrowed many socialist ideas, ceded a measure of power to organized labor, established a vast network of well-funded public schools and universities, offered unemployment benefits, provided retirement benefits, abolished child labor, improved working conditions in mines and factories, and regularly intervened in markets to moderate the cycles of boom and bust that had plagued earlier, purer forms of laissez-faire capitalism.

"After the Cold War ended, social protections that had made capitalism more humane came to be viewed as appendages of a now discredited socialism and were systematically dismantled. Universal education disappeared in favor of private schooling, labor unions were weakened, retirement income programs scrapped. The result was a radical shrinking of the middle class and the virtual end to upward mobility.

"Clearly, my friends, it was a very specific form of state socialism, a centralized, dictatorial socialism, that 'lost' the Cold War. And it was a very specific form of welfare capitalism that 'won.'

"Do you see the analogy, my friends? The natural laboratory of history compared socialism to capitalism but left many forms of both untested and many questions unanswered.

"Historians wonder: Would socialism have fared better if it had varied its form, if it had been more liberal, allowed freedom of the press, promoted rather than oppressed religious life, granted more autonomy to workers in place of centralized control?

"Similarly, we'd like to know what form of capitalism is best. Would markets run better with less government interference? How much should personal initiative, hard work and innovation be rewarded? How much disparity in income between the richest and the poorest results in the greatest good to society as a whole?

"Fundamentally, the question for us as scientists is: How can we test the entire array of variants of socialism and capitalism, as well as other types of governance? How can we put political science on a sound, scientific footing, conduct rigorous experiments that isolate each variable, test against appropriate controls, step by step discover the optimal mix of elements and thereby optimize the performance of our political and economic institutions?

"In order to study these important questions, we established the Experimental Zone of Cuba. This is the place where many of us now live and work. This whole region of the country is one gigantic laboratory for testing and measuring the success of various forms of government, an environment where controls are established and distinct factors varied one at a time in measured doses.

"We are greatly aided by brain science in being able to measure psychological well being and societal happiness. Do you see?"

Fidel IV was now energetically pacing the stage, his voice growing more intense. "Do you see why our work here is so vital and exciting? Our Happiness Index allows us to objectively analyze every attempt at improvement.

"Now we can find out how much education is best, how much is too much and how much not enough; what kind of education does a garbage collector need as compared with a carpenter, a factory manager, an engineer?

"Likewise, we can now learn how to best regulate business cycles, how much boom to allow without creating speculative bubbles or rewarding inefficiency. And how about economic downturns? We know that periodic recessions help prune dead wood from the economic system and over the long term strengthen the economy, but how deep should they be? What, if anything, should governments do about unemployment, business failures, investment loss, inflation? We Cubans have long believed that full protection against such stresses was best, but we are discovering that a certain element of risk actually increases happiness. The spice of danger, fear, risk, even loss, in fact makes people happier as long as they exist in the right measure. Our task is to figure out how best to manage risk and to construct a society that produces the greatest happiness for the greatest number of people.

"This is a very exciting place, my friends. This is a very exciting time. We are discovering the best, most effective and most humane way to integrate public and private enterprise. We can now resolve age-old conflicts over the best form of government, not with war and bloodshed, not with strife and hate, but with evidence and rational science. What a great privilege it is to live and work in the Experimental Zone of Cuba!"

Castro bowed graciously. The crowd rose to their feet in applause. Many of them didn't fully comprehend everything the doctor had said, but they were swept away by his enthusiasm.

As they exited the theater, people were chanting "Zonies, Zonies, Zonies!" Cesar too was caught up in the excitement. "Glad to be a Zonie!" he shouted.

Chat pointed toward the left. "Let's head over to the Robot Republic cube." he said as he strode off. "There's something I want to show you."

The lighted sign ahead of the robot and the two boys read "Robot Republic Experimental Utopia."

Cesar asked, "What's an Experimental Utopia?"

Freddie piped up. "We learned about that in school. Utopia is paradise, a perfect world."

"And because no one knows yet how to create a perfect society," Chat interjected, "we keep experimenting with different ideas, and we keep improving."

Cesar nodded. "So people in the RR are getting happier all the time?"

"That's right," Chat confirmed. "The Robot Senate is elected after the happiness census each year. People vote on what new idea they want to try next to increase the Robot Republic's happiness score for the following year. We are allowed only one idea per year in order to comply with the oversight board's experimental design."

"I'd vote for more chocolate," said Freddie.

"Me too," said Cesar.

"That sounds like a very good idea," agreed Chat, "but how much more? Too much of anything is not good. There is a perfect daily allowance of chocolate, for example, that gives you the greatest happiness. More will actually decrease your pleasure and can even make you sick. Understand?"

"Oh, yeah. There was that one time at carnival when we got sick as dogs from eating too many goodies," the boys agreed.

They reached the RR gate. There was a long line waiting to get in. "That's where the scientific measurement of happiness comes in. By monitoring nerve impulses and body chemistry, we can determine the right amount of any sort of pleasure: chocolate, winning ball games, riding rollercoasters, anything. Sometimes the results are unexpected. Let me show you."

Chat led them to a table where they each put happiness monitors on their wrists. Cesar's digital readout showed an 81. He looked over at Freddie's. It said 85. Immediately Cesar's dipped to 79.

"Why is he happier than me? And why did mine go down when I saw his was higher?"

"There could be many reasons. One is the Choplin effect: the drop could be caused by a bit of jealousy that Freddie got a higher score."

Freddie stuck out his tongue, and Cesar's score dropped another point.

"Also . . . are you thirsty? Tired?" Cesar's meter held steady. Chat continued to probe. "Are you still upset about the baseball league?"

"I hate that ump," Cesar grumped. His meter dipped two more points to 76.

"Sulking about past wounds decreases happiness, as does watching the meter and comparing your score with others'. That's why we only wear happiness meters on special occasions. Now, follow me. I want to show you something."

Chat led them to the front of the line and flashed a preference pass. The guard let them in ahead of the line, and they continued down the corridor toward the main robot exhibit. Cesar glanced at his wrist. "Hey, it's down to 62."

Freddie's had also fallen dramatically.

"Now watch this," Chat turned on his heel and marched back to the gate. They took their place at the end of the line. Immediately their readouts began to rise.

"You're not babies anymore," Chat explained. "You've been taught it's wrong to jump the queue. You may think that putting yourself first and getting an advantage over others would make you happier, but actually it's the reverse." By the time they reached the front of the line, their happiness quotient was back in the seventies.

As they walked down the corridor for the second time, this time entering at their proper turn in the line, Cesar said, "You tricked us, didn't you?"

"I sure did," Chat responded, with a wink. "And it worked pretty well, didn't it?"

Cesar gave Chatter a look. "Are you really a robot? Sometimes you seem human."

"Yes, I'm just a robot, but I had a very smart programmer."

"Was that what you wanted to show us?" Freddie asked, referring to the recent lesson in happiness and line etiquette.

"Yes, but there's one more thing."

They walked past a lot of exhibits. Chatter gave a running narration.

"The Robot Senate," he explained. "is elected every year when citizens vote for the programs that run the robot senators. The system will not work, however, if there are tricks or hidden agendas in the programs. To prevent trickery, the source code is open to public inspection. That way, our robot politicians are completely honest. They cannot be bribed, flip-flop or go back on their promises."

As they turned a corner, Cesar saw a glass case containing a row of robots that looked the same but were different sizes, from toddler to adult.

Cesar examined them closely, then looked back at Chatter. "Hey, they all look like you!"

Chat smiled smugly.

"Cool. But what are they for?"

"One of the early experiments in the RR was to give everybody a personal robot at birth, one that was their own size, a small one for toddlers, teenage-size for teens, and so forth."

Freddie looked puzzled. "How come I don't have a personal robot? None of the other kids do either."

"We found out that kids are actually happier when they learn to do things for themselves. Now everyone earns their robot in school. You'll get one when you graduate."

"So how come I get you?" asked Cesar.

"Because you're a visitor here and because of your eye operations," Chatter explained. "I'm one of only a few kid-sized robots left in operation."

Cesar looked sad. He felt guilty about receiving preferential treatment. He didn't dare look at his wrist meter. Then it dawned on him that one day soon he'd have to say good-bye to Chatter and go home to Florida. . . .

Freddie put his arm around Cesar. "I'm glad you came to Cuba to get your eyes fixed, and I'm glad you got Chatter to help you out."

Cesar and Freddie's wrist meters started pinging: they both topped 95.

# FREEDOM

At the end of the school year, Cesar returned to Lake Worth. He'd been sorry to say good-bye to Cuba and the Experimental Zone and Freddie and Chatter. But when he got back home, he quickly adjusted to being back.

Cesar had been gone less than two years, but there were a lot of changes in the works. The flood control dikes that had been erected on Palm Beach Island to fend off rising sea levels were coming down. Cranes had brought in huge piles of sand and recreated the swimming beach.

The historic beachside casino was reopened and swarmed with well-dressed gamblers day and night. Elderly Carib men in dreadlocks sat on the boardwalk, smoking funky weed and playing dominoes.

The old fishing pier was widened and transformed into a night spot with restaurants, art galleries, dance clubs. Almost every night there was live music at the band shell. Lake Worth had always been a magnet for artists and nonconformists. Once more it was becoming an exciting place to live.

During that summer, Cesar became more and more of a loner. Although the baseball controversy had been successfully resolved, he knew that he'd never live it down if anything like what happened in Cuba ever repeated itself here in Florida. He had nightmares of opposing teams jumping all over him, clutching his face, clawing his cybereyes out of their sockets, boys cheering at his disfigurement. For a time his implants made him feel like a freak, and he never tried to play sports again.

Instead, he'd occasionally go over to Memorial Park and sit on his bike at the edge of the outfield, mournfully watching the games. The most contact he ever had with the other kids was to throw an occasional foul ball back onto the field. But more often his days were spent alone, biking in the newly opened areas outside the dikes, exploring further and further afield, expanding his horizons. New roads were being laid; new communities of brightly colored houses were popping up like spring flowers. Bike lanes and trails went everywhere. And Cesar especially enjoyed the large expanses of undeveloped land, grass-covered dunes, rolling like waves one after the other. The open vistas gave him an exhilarating sense of freedom.

On the wall above his bed Cesar taped up a set of aerial maps of Lake Worth. Starting from 2063, they showed the accumulating effects of the series of natural disasters that had led to the construction of the dikes enclosing the city.

The first map showed old Palm Beach with its historic mansions, grand gardens and beautiful sandy beaches, both ocean and lakeside. The next map showed the devastation of the First Wave, the Tsunami of 2064. All of Palm Beach and most of Lake Worth had been ravaged by floods. The caption read, "No one had believed that tsunamis were possible in South Florida. Increased water weight from global warming caused stress on Caribbean tectonic faults, leading to an intense series of earthquakes and tsunamis."

The impact of the flood had been staggering, and Cesar wished he had a similar map of the Second Wave. In its place he had a printout of a web article describing the catastrophe. "The Tsunami of 2071 proved to be a knockout punch for the economy. Anyone who could move north did so. Even the rapid construction of improved flood control dikes around cities from West Palm Beach to Miami failed to stem the flooding. The beaches were gone. South Florida was left to stagnate."

The most recent map showed the latest changes to the landscape. In 2079, Hurricane Zeta came ashore packing 235 MPH winds and a ninety-foot tidal surge once again submerged most of Palm Beach County. The storm swept away a half-mile stretch of the barrier island, opened up the Lantana inlet and, further west, drilled a channel to Lake Osborne that went right past Cesar's home.

Little by little, Cesar emerged from his self-imposed isolation. After school, he'd hang out with Papi at the lab building, enjoying rubbing shoulders with the scientists who worked there. High school years were littered with girlfriends, music, and fun, playing bass guitar, bopping around teen dance clubs. Cesar graduated from Lake Worth High third in the Class of 2123. On the wings of a three-year scholarship he finally engineered a practical plan for getting inside the lab. He would return to Cuba and take a degree in robotics at the Poly-Cyborg Institute in Cienfuegos, then apply for a job.

His implants, which could magnify up to a hundredfold and functioned exceedingly well in low light, proved a real boon in his courses on robo-maintenance and repair. Enhanced eyesight gave him the edge over classmates in locating problems in the confined interior of a robot's arm or leg. His ability to spot a crack in a greenboard or a frayed ligament amidst the tangle of synth-tendons and muscle put him at the top of his class.

After graduation, Cesar briefly considered settling permanently in the RR, but when he heard about the establishment of the Florida Futurist Lab, coincidentally located not only in his hometown but in the same building as the Cy-bot Lab, he couldn't resist. The thought of expanding the RR movement fired his ambition to do something significant with his life.

Two years of absence saw another one of those dramatic population shifts that were so endemic to South Florida. In addition to tempering global warming, the Dallas dirty nuke led to anti-Muslim riots all over the former USA. The ripples were felt in far away Lake Worth, which had become a haven for Turkish and Afghani workers in decades past. The rioters destroyed shops, homes and places of worship. Thousands were forced to flee. Many took refuge on uninhabited islands in the Bahamas, leaving the local economy without the cheap labor it had always relied on. Jamaicans, Cubans and Puerto Ricans were brought in to fill the void, and Lake Worth again pulsed with island rhythms, just as it had a hundred years before.

Cesar's first assignment at his new job was a joint project between the Futurist Lab and Lantana Sea Farms, which used robots to tend shrimp and oyster beds. It was there he met Jewel, who worked as secretary for the owner. She shared his social conscience, often lamenting the mistreatment of human workers, knowing that the boss skimped on safety precautions and paid them as little as he could get away with.

Jewel had joined the Futurist Party at Cesar's urging and for a while worked doggedly, day and night, for the repeal of Robot Limitation Laws. After a couple of years, however, the reality of the situation began to sink in. The world was an inertial system and slow to change. The political upheaval in the wake of the dissolution of the USA and the subsequent tyranny of the Confederacy left Florida out on a limb. Independence was inevitable, but had incubated for years before the final break occurred. The economy was still dire, with most of the wealth in the hands of a few oligarchic families and the masses left to struggle. Ordinary people were too distracted by everyday pressures to give serious consideration to new proposals for change. The Futurist message fell on deaf, or cynical, ears.

As time passed, Jewel was drawn toward spiritual interests as she discovered her "sixth sense" and a gift for visions and premonitions. More and more of her time was spent meditating or attending classes at the Cloister Retreat Center. Occasionally Cesar would tag along. He loved the technical aspects of his Remp job but often questioned his effectiveness. Thoughts of giving up on Florida and heading back to the RR were ever-present.

Cesar viewed himself as essentially a light-hearted guy—optimistic, fun-loving. Yet somehow—he could not recall precisely how or when it happened—he had one day found himself, as a result of his work with the Party, in a shadowy world of political intrigue and dubious legality, immersed in a state of constant anxiety, continually looking over his shoulder. "Every political movement is inherently two-faced," he had thought. "The public sees the light-of-day façade but not the dark underbelly. At least I'm accomplishing something for the little guy. I hope."

Nevertheless, he started to brood about returning to Cuba for good. He'd take Jewel along with him . . . and they'd settle down. He mulled over ways to convince her to go. The Cloister was affiliated with GEMS, the God-Encounter Meditation Society. They ran a large retreat center and utopian experimental community right in Cienfuegos, just down the road from La Placenta. She might be easier to convince if he agreed to live at GEMS and commute. GEMS was nice and quiet. He could get used to living around those ever-smiling meditation junkies. And another thing: Cuban authorities were encouraging population growth in the utopian corridor. Jewel could have as many babies there as her heart desired.

Not that he wanted to get married. None of the couples in their social circle had tied the knot. Yet, when it came to having a family, Jewel made it clear she was an old-fashioned girl. She wanted a commitment that Cesar would be her full partner in parenting.

Marriage suited Jewel in another way, too. She was intensely possessive of Cesar and liked the idea of having exclusive rights to him. Last Saturday night they had been out dancing at a crowded beach club. Jewel's jealousy was provoked by all the women buzzing around her man. She "accidentally" elbowed one honey in the chin during a particularly vigorous salsa number. The women had shouted accusations at each other above the music while Cesar cheerfully looked on, grinning from ear to ear, until the contender viciously attacked, clawing at Jewel's face. Only then did he intervene to protect her. Jewel had shrugged off the incident, but clearly she was feeling insecure about Cesar's commitment. Maybe it was time to go shopping for a ring.

Jewel lived on the nineteenth floor of a tower at J Street and Eighth, practically around the corner from South Grade Elementary School. After a couple of years their relationship had settled into a comfortable routine: dinner on Tuesday and Thursday and a night out at the dance clubs on Friday or Saturday. Occasionally they would eat dinner at Bizarre Avenue Café or Rotelli's, but most days of the week she would cook. Few homes had kitchens anymore, and those that did featured glowovens, which cooked with radiant heat, captured from the air, and required neither fire nor electricity. To most people, using actual flames to prepare food seemed crude, a throwback to the pre–global warming days when people burned fossil fuels with no thought of the future. Cooking on a stovetop was now a lost art. But

Jewel had cultivated a serious hobby of retro food prep. She had somehow managed to find an old gas range as well as a source for bottled fuel. Jewel's fondness for traditional ways stood in stark contrast to Cesar's Futurism.

During their walks, Jewel mused about the large families with four or five kids who lived in their eclectic neighborhood, crowded into small well-groomed cottages surrounded by white picket fences, yards filled with perfumed jasmine, chameleon hibiscus and the shimmer of bi-breed bougainvillea. These folks were content to work six days a week, putter in the yard on Sunday mornings and picnic at the beach on Sunday afternoons. Jewel made no secret of her dream to live like that: get married, move out of Mama's apartment, buy a house, tend a yard garden, make babies. Her idea of paradise was a quiet life on the ground floor.

The laborious climb up nineteen stories had become an exhausting daily burden, often two or three times a day, a burden she had never agreed to or got used to. A year or so after she had moved in, the anti-grav lift in her tower building broke when it lost its repulsion generators between the third and fourth floors. The thing plummeted to the ground with a half dozen riders inside. Luckily the fall was only three and not fifteen stories. No one had been seriously hurt. But, despite numerous promises, the lift had yet to be repaired. She longed for a normal life, which to her meant living in a house, streets filled with mobs of kids on scootboards en route to Bryant Park and chatting with the neighbors across the fence. But money was tight, and she couldn't make her dreams happen without help.

Their playful debate about lifestyle was ongoing. Jewel, true to her name, saw herself as strong and beautiful. Cesar, on the other hand, was not content to dream small dreams. He ached for world-embracing challenges. He was determined to leave his mark, leave the world a better place than he found it. His dream was to re-engineer society based on a scientific model he had learned during his two stays in the Cuban Robot Republic at Cienfuegos.

## NARRATIVE PAUSE 003

JURAT PUSHED his chair back and stared at his dreary-eyed reflection in the looking-glass screen. This was all helpful, even entertaining (the robot bust-up in the parking lot had been a kicker), but he needed better information, solid data on those Cuban entities. After draining the last drop of his beer, he heard footsteps in the hall. It was probably Pawl's records clerk arriving. He stood up, tucked in his shirt, combed his hair and tried to brighten his saggy face. It was a good idea to make her feel welcome, despite his misgivings about having the Justice's spy underfoot. He found her seated at the desk in the adjacent empty office unpacking her things. She was dressed entirely in black, an attractive woman, if a little severe, with efficient black-rimmed glasses and her hair, also black, with a few strands of gray, drawn back in a tight bun. Fortyish. The spitting image of a Chief Justice's assistant.

"I see you made it," Jurat said pleasantly. "Is the office space to your liking?"

"How can I help you?" Ms. Blain responded in a flat, officious tone.

"Well, Alice—mind if I call you Alice?"

"Not at all," Alice replied dryly.

"Hmm, well then, er, Ms., er, I mean, Alice . . ." He stopped, blushing furiously.

"Ye-es?" Ms. Blain said, the trace of a smile at his consternation on her lips.

"Well." The inspector paused, then continued, mustering up a professional tone. "Could you check on a couple of things for me? First, find out what you can about a Cuban zone called the Robot Republic? It's located in the Utopian Communities District along the south coast."

"U-to-pian Com-muni-ties," Alice Blain said slowly as she wrote down the name.

"Second, see what you can find on the God-Encounter Meditation Society, both in Cuba and Florida. Our info system should be the same as yours in Tallahassee. Pull whatever records we have."

"Any names of leaders or Florida affiliates?"

"Nope, just check the public records."

"Very well. I'll see what I can dig up."

Jurat sighed and returned to his desk. There wasn't much chance in that department! He plumped down in his chair and began sorting through the brain scan disks. Surprisingly, the name Jewel Ruth Jensen was scrawled across one. Nice to see someone in the department had been on the ball enough to call her in for questioning. He inserted the disk into the player and searched for the earliest available entries. Unfortunately, the disk contained nothing that could be called deep background. The oldest file date coincided with Cesar's visit to the Futurist Safe House, just a couple of days ago.

A dimly lit stairway peppered with peeling paint flakes popped onto the monitor as the emulation restarted.

# THINGS THAT GO CLUNK IN THE NIGHT

**A**fter a long walk home from work, Jewel began the climb up the flights of grungy stairs to her apartment. When she reached the seventh floor landing, she stopped to catch her breath. Only a dozen more to go! And once again she cursed the broken elevator.

Jewel worked as a dispatcher at Lantana Sea Farms, where they raised seafood, mostly macroshrimp and oysters, but also a new shellfish hybrid called Kamilchi clams, in a series of underwater domes that stretched for miles along the reef line. Each day hundreds of minisubs would ferry workers and product back and forth between the harbor warehouse and the various sea domes. Jewel had worked there since high school and liked her job. The day she was hired she introduced herself to her prospective boss as Jewel Angelina Jensen.

"Are you always an angel?" he had gibed, as he stood back seductively examining her figure.

Jewel had turned beet red from embarrassment, but after a few months on the job, she grew accustomed to the sexually charged banter of the rough-edged seaworkers and eventually learned how to use it to her advantage. Nowadays, she could get an oyster sweeper turned around in half the time of her male co-workers with playful taunts, "Hey, stud, move it! Or the oysters'll be in menopause before you get them unloaded." The banter made the men and the workday fly.

As she wearily continued her climb, she heard the kids from her floor running down to greet her, their excited voices echoing down the stairwell. Petri reached her first. He stood breathless, unable to get the words out. Pongolisa ran up behind. "Clunk's in trouble! She's been yelping through the door all day." A dozen children, ranging in age from three to eight, crowded around. "We tried to call someone to open the door." "She sounds like she's hurt." "My mom's at work." "We couldn't find nobody to help." "Clunk is hurt bad." "Really, really bad!"

They were speaking of Jewel's good-natured, 200-pound St. Bernard. Kids adored her, despite the fact she was constantly bumping into walls, furniture and people. What could she have done to herself this time?

"Jeez, let's go have a look," she said with a nonchalant wave of her hand. Jewel wasn't worried. Petri and Pongo often got themselves worked up over nothing. Nevertheless, a tingle of apprehension went down her arm as she pressed her palm into her apartment's keypad. The lock clicked open, and Jewel heard a pained whimper as she stepped inside. Her heart quickened. Clunk lay motionless on the living room floor, her fur matted with dried blood, her chest heaving. She kneeled down and softly stroked Clunk behind the ears. Clunk rolled her head without lifting it, closed her glazed eyes and moaned.

A smeared red trail led to the bathroom just off the living room, where Jewel could see a towel rack ripped from the wall, jars and bottles broken and scattered across the floor. Blood pooled in thick puddles on the floor tiles. One of the sink's chrome legs, near the toilet, had been knocked out of place, and the sink dangled precipitously from the wall mount. Apparently Clunk had fallen off the toilet, knocking trays and tubes from the sink, ripping open her side on the sharp end of the towel bar, landing awkwardly, causing internal injuries that could only be guessed at.

"Poor baby!" Jewel crooned over the injured St. Bernard as the big dog nuzzled against her torso.

The kids pressed in. "Wow! What a mess!" "We told you she was in trouble." "Is Clunk going to die?"

"I don't know, kids. Quiet! Please! Give me a moment to think."

That damn lift! How could they get a 200-pound animal down nineteen stories and to a vet without a working lift? None of the kids' parents were around. Jewel's mother was the only one in the building with a working wrist phone, a gift from Cesar. Jewel had received one as well, but it had been damaged some weeks earlier in a scuffle with a drunken chick on the third floor of the beach parking ramp. She could kick herself for not getting it fixed. *Where was Mama? Damn! Mama should be home by now.*

Combing gently through the dog's long, clotted fur, she saw the bleeding had stopped. Still Clunk had lost a lot of blood. The mob of noisy kids was creating havoc in the apartment, their shoes tracking blood into every corner. One of the younger kids tripped and fell squarely on top of Clunk's injured body, making the dog squeal in pain.

Jewel was about to give these out-of-control kids a piece of her mind when the stairwell door slammed shut and the kids ran to see who had arrived. Mama and Jewel's three sisters entered the apartment, breathless from the climb and dragging bags of groceries. When they saw the blood, they gasped in unison. Without bothering to explain, Jewel grabbed her mother's arm. "Mama, call Cesar!" The voice-activated wrist phone dialed automatically.

The phone rang once, twice, six times, followed by the sound of wind. It was impossible to hear if Cesar had picked up, there was no voice at the other end, just dead air. As Mama was very short, she had to hold her hand on top of her head to align her wrist with Jewel's mouth.

In a shaky voice Jewel said, "Cesar?"

He finally answered. "Hey, Baby! Can you hear me? It's pretty windy out here."

She feared losing the phone link and so blurted out, "Clunk's gonna die unless we do something quick."

"Aw, Jewel! What's happened?"

Jewel's sister Dii looked into the bathroom to check things out and quickly retreated, screaming, "There's blood everywhere! That poor dog. I can't take all that blood."

Cesar heard the racket but could make no sense of it. "What the zag is going on over there? Are you okay?"

Jewel held Mama's forearm and leaned into the phone as she explained what had happened. "There's blood all over the bathroom floor. Clunk's cut real bad, she's barely conscious. What should I do?"

"Call my friend, Dr. Suturb, the vet," Cesar replied. "Ask him to make a house call as a special favor to me."

"Can't you come over, right away?"

"Oh," he groaned. "I can't right now, I'm on a mission. But hurry, call the vet right away. I'll call you back later," he pledged before ending the call.

Clunk started to wheeze. Jewel slipped to the floor, cradling the limp hulk. "Call the vet, Mama! Tell him to get here fast."

While her mother placed the call, Jewel's panic spurred her sisters to action. Dii herded the neighbors' kids out of the apartment and started sorting through the debris on the bathroom floor while Emerald wiped up the blood. Starr, the youngest, knelt down beside Jewel, trying to comfort both the animal and her sister. Clunk recoiled, moaning. Starr looked over at Jewel. "What happened?" Jewel made no reply. She stood up and gazed out the window, blinking as if trying to clear something from her eyes. A flock of mutant night vultures swooped and circled around distant streetlights.

This was all her fault. Having tired of climbing up and down the stairs so many times a day to walk the dog, she had had a brilliant idea: toilet-train the animal. The effort had met with immediate success. How Cesar laughed the first time he saw Clunk's enormous mass perched on the porcelain throne. Now, however, there was nothing funny about it. Clunk's fall brought Jewel's brilliant plan crashing down. Sheer laziness had got the best of her. Clunk had been clumsy and accident-prone from birth. How could she have been so stupid?

Jewel paced aimlessly as her mother waited for the vet to return her call. Mama's phone was unreliable. Jewel imagined the vet not being able to get through. A nauseous dread welled up in the pit of her stomach.

A photograph of her guru, Enrico Einalli, hanging on the wall above the stricken Clunk, caught her attention. He was standing in front of Lake Worth's Cloister Retreat Center, where Jewel went for classes, and his kindly eyes gently chastised her: she was forgetting her prayer training. With a long, deep breath, she thought about the teachings of the Cloister movement and desperately searched her frazzled mind for a technique to calm herself. With one finger she traced a circle around the stigmata tattoo on the palm of one hand and prayed, "O Lord Jesus, heal!" over and over again. Synchronizing the repetitions with her breath, she recited the names of the Divine Voices, "O Allah, the merciful, heal. O Prince of Peace, shower down Thy peace." Within moments, her pulse slowed and her panic subsided.

When the vet finally called, the fear had returned. Mama talked to him on her wrist phone as Jewel's eyes bulged bigger and bigger.

"Please, come! Please, please, come!" she shouted into the air, hoping he could hear her.

Jewel realized she was asking a lot. The vet, who had evening office hours, would have to leave a waiting room full of animals, drive over, find her building and then scale what she had dubbed the Stairway to

Heaven. If he proved unwilling or unable, Clunk might not survive.

Mama carefully described the situation to the vet. Jewel felt another wave of panic. She clutched her waist with both arms, leaned in toward the phone and yelled, "Hurry! Please hurry! My 200-pound St. Bernard is bleeding badly, and we can't get her down the stairs."

Mama gestured for Jewel to be still, her eyes signaling reassurance. "Yes, dear, he'll come."

"God is good," Jewel shouted as she plopped down next to her stricken pet. Starr, who had been vainly trying to comfort the injured animal, gave Jewel a quick hug and left her alone with Clunk.

Einalli's photo hovered above. It had been taken on a weekend retreat at the Cloister, her first time meeting the Master and gazing into his wise eyes. She stared up gratefully at his face while stroking the dog's head—it radiated a peace Jewel sorely lacked right now, just when she needed it to think clearly though the crisis.

Jewel put her hand over Clunk's heart and gazed into Einalli's eyes. She felt a reassuring warmth pass over her. The photo was one of her most prized possessions. The Master was an extraordinary spiritual guide: in his bushy unkempt hair, smirky grin and deep serene eyes, she saw a complex man who was comfortable with paradox. A cross, a Buddha and other interfaith symbols were interlaced on the front of his robe. The image of spiritual unity was typical of Einalli's universalist teachings. She felt her breathing slow as she gazed at the portrait. She began to chant softly under her breath.

Jewel felt her breathing slow as she gazed at the
portrait of the Master.

Clunk whimpered and pressed the tip of her nose against Jewel's folded leg. "Hang on, girl, the vet's on his way." Clunk nuzzled closer as Jewel stroked the matted fur on her head. Jewel took another deep breath, closed her eyes and resumed chanting until the vet arrived.

# THE CLOISTER

Jewel stood in the apartment doorway, clutching her dog-eared copy of *Universal Skills of the Spirit* to her chest. The bandaged Clunk tried pulling herself up to a stand but immediately fell back to the cushion where they had moved her with the vet's help; she thumped the cushion weakly with her tail.

"Don't stand there like a deer in the headlights," Mama said. "Get going, the girls and I will look after your wounded princess."

Jewel hesitated.

"And don't worry about what the vet's helper said. It'll be all right."

"OK," Jewel said, doubtfully.

"The vet did say Clunk will be fine in a couple days," Mama continued. "Hovering over her every minute won't make her recover any faster. Now get going, or you'll be late."

As usual Mama was right. Although Jewel dreaded descending the stairs for the umpteenth time, tonight of all nights she needed the succor of her weekly Healing

Circle. The Cloister was located on the inner beach, a pleasant fifteen-minute walk from her apartment. The fresh air would do her good.

Every Wednesday evening the women gathered at the Cloister Temple for prayer, meditation, sharing personal news, and mutual support. Jewel would invariably feel calm and grounded after her prayer meeting, especially on nights like tonight, when she started out with jumbled nerves and a migraine. And she always relished the relaxing murmur of surf on sand during their barefoot meditation walk afterward. She hadn't missed a circle in years.

Willing her exhausted body down the stairs and out into the street, Jewel tried to perk herself up. She took quick, crisp steps and, in sync with the rhythms of her footfalls, began to recite, "Shema Hallelu Allah."

Over the years Jewel had studied hard to advance in the Universal Skills, a toolkit for building a serene inner life. But, in the midst of her upset about Clunk's injury, the vet's helper had rattled her serenity with his hate-filled slander against her beloved Einalli. She'd never in her life seen such visceral venom and was unable, unwilling, to Kindly Eye it gratuitously. Kindly Eye was a skill Jewel worked hard to cultivate. The idea was to see others, and herself, through the lens of compassion so that people's frailties and unseemly attributes were seen without judgment, irritation or condemnation. As one of the prophets had said, "Do not hate the hurtful. For their malevolent acts are as the sting of a bee against a hand that would steal honey." And the vet's helper, like the honey bee, no doubt, simply intended to protect himself and his cherished ones from a perceived enemy.

But the more she thought about what the man had said, the hotter her resentment grew. She had let Sutty into her home as a friend of Cesar. The vet had brought along a husky, young assistant, carrying a canvas stretcher, on the chance they'd need to take the large dog to the animal clinic. Fortunately, the difficult move down the many-flighted stairwell hadn't been necessary. The vet patched up Clunk, stopped the bleeding, then bandaged and medicated her, behaving with perfect cool professionalism. He helped the big, bulky invalid to a soft cushion where she could sleep off her trauma and take as much time as she needed to recuperate. But, while the vet attended to his patient, the helper had nosed around Jewel's apartment. As the bill was paid and the two prepared to go, the helper turned to Jewel with a cold look and a gesture toward the photograph of Einalli.

"I see you love your dog, but you also admire terrorists," he said darkly. Jewel looked bewilderedly up at the photo, wondering what had upset him: an Islamic Crescent stood out prominently among the symbols on the guru's robe—some ignorant people still equated Islam with terrorism; could that have been it? The assistant was wearing a long, white medical coat and grasped a stretcher pole in one massive hand and planted the pole-end like a staff at his feet, making him look like a would-be a Moses about to shepherd his people into the wilderness. "Beware of evil men who sneak into our country in spiritual guise but are terrorists through and through. I have seen the picture of this man in the homes of the enemies of Christ," he had said. "Now, you may be naïve, or you may be a traitor, but either way you are allowing this evil to gain a foothold in our nation. I am morally bound to report you. The Reverend Rebolt shall hear of this."

"Report me?" Jewel asked, perplexed.

He stalked out of the apartment, with a roar: "Righteousness shall prevail!"

Jewel had no idea who this Reverend Rebolt was, but even his name sounded a bit revolting. Shocked and upset by the threat of him appearing uninvited at her door, she had a sinking feeling she wouldn't find much comfort in his particular version of righteousness.

What right did this stranger, this guy who came to her house solely as a medical assistant on a strictly professional mission—what right did he have to censure her? Who had appointed him judge and jury—this Reverend Rebolt? And what had given *him* such authority?

It was against Jewel's nature to see malice in anyone, and her religious training encouraged heartfelt forgiveness and the gracious overlooking of faults. But this man had pushed all her buttons, deliberately insulted, even threatened, her most profound beliefs. Weakly, she tried to enumerate his good traits. Apparently he loved animals; why else work for a vet? But then again, he really hadn't done much for Clunk. The vet had been busy assisting her injured dog while the helper had snooped around her apartment. Also, the helper had hauled that enormously heavy stretcher up her seventeen flights of stairs. But that only showed he had strong arms and a good set of lungs. She could think of nothing about the man that began to excuse his bigotry. The kindness gig wasn't working.

She'd have to try another tactic to relieve the knot in her stomach. Ebb and flow . . . breathe in, breathe out, align her breath with her steps, imagine kicking and juggling a ball of white light off her shoe tops, the ball bouncing from one foot to the other in sync with each footfall. When this trick was not enough to distract her, she added a second ball, then a third, each ball rising to eye-height. Eventually, concentrating on complex motions saturated her mind and forced out her anxiety.

If left unchecked, worry for Jewel had always been like a gravity well that drew her in and trapped her soul. She had spent much of her time in the past climbing out of emotional black holes. For her, these techniques to soothe away worry were indeed a godsend.

The GEMS Sisters, however, believed that climbing was the wrong metaphor, that transcending one's baser instincts required, not a climb, but a leap. However, taking leaps of faith did not come easily to Jewel. Her mind continually poked and prodded, anxiously searching to sort the certain from the questionable. Jewel had learned that much about herself—wariness, distrust, even skepticism, often came more naturally to her than immediate, trusting belief.

Rather than experiencing the freedom of total surrender to a group conscience, as many of her friends at GEMS managed to do, she often found her mind held captive by one dubious assertion or another. Some of the Cloister's concepts struck her as hokey: Fifth Dimension of Awareness? Nine Dimensions of God?

The Sisters often encouraged her to disregard the chattering of what they call "the monkey mind," but she knew in her heart that thought avoidance was no path for her. Doubt was not always an enemy: sometimes, indeed, it was a savior. There must be a route to serenity that didn't involve disowning her questions.

At the same time, paradoxically enough, she found that even the most fanciful ideas helped her feel closer to God. The Sisters had taught her to soothe her anxious nature, forgive frailty in herself, embrace the ups and downs of life and escape the limitations of time and space by connecting with something larger than herself. It was those moments of connectedness that Jewel valued and kept her going back.

When the shoe-top juggling grew tiresome, she switched to another image in her repertoire of mental soothers. Jewel's retro food-prep hobby was her private fiefdom, a place she could escape to without fear of interruption. Since cooking had become a lost art, none of the women in the circle could relate: oh, they enjoyed her food whenever she prepared a luncheon, but they were bewildered by her fondness for the labor-intensive cooking process. It was the one joy in her life, maybe the only one, that she could not share with them.

As she moved through the darkening evening streets, Jewel pictured herself in the kitchen, preparing a dish step by step. Simmer a skillet of sweet cream on a low flame. Spoon in bitter dark cocoa. Add cane syrup. Gently stir. Remove skillet from fire. Roll in raisins and cashew bits. Allow to cool, then eat. Amplify each sensory sensation, the taste, the aroma, the feel of smooth and sweet on the tongue.

Images of chocolate could always take the edge off her anxiety. Maybe thoughts of food just made her hungry, so the primal desire to eat trumped nervous anxiety. Regardless of the reason, it worked, especially when she could reinforce the mental images with a tangible sensation. She reached into a pocket, unwrapped a shiny brown cube and popped it into her mouth with a mischievous smile. The food meditation was supposed to be entirely mental, but sometimes there was no substitute for the real thing.

As Jewel crossed the intersection at Sixth and M Street, she was gripped by a premonition. Maybe it was just the ominous shadows of the circling night vultures. Maybe it was her imagination—her nerves had been fraught after Clunk's accident and the assistant's warning—but there had been something in Cesar's voice when she talked to him over the phone that only now registered.

What in the world was this "secret mission" he was on? It was the first she'd heard of it; Cesar was usually completely open with her about his whereabouts. Was the Party pulling him into something over his head? What harebrained risks was he taking in his vain attempt to remake the world? She kissed the air with chocolate on her lips, sending it to find Cesar wherever he might be. Jewel now had three things to worry about and pray for: Clunk's recovery, escape from the assistant's bigotry and Cesar's safety.

On the next block stood the Naabilat Patriot Church. As Jewel approached, she heard strains of music sung by a chorus of children's voices, coming out the front door: "A mighty fortress is our God . . ." Jewel stood for a moment outside the open doors, listening to Luther's famous hymn.

A lifelike projection of the crucified Jesus rose up spontaneously from the sidewalk, startling her. Jewel had walked past the church many times, but she'd never seen this before. The figure was vivid, grotesque, naked except for a loin cloth and a crown of thorns, its wounds running with blood. The figure writhed in pain. Fixing its gaze on Jewel, the Lord cried out, "Why have you forsaken me?"

The hymn had just ended when a small, golden-haired preteen boy wearing a blue choir robe darted from the dark church, shouting, "Let me go! Let me go!"; a big, burly, determined-looking middle-aged man in a black suit was in hot pursuit. A gang of kids of various ages, also dressed in choir robes, appeared under the door's archway and, transfixed, watched the unfolding scene.

With an acrobatic flourish, the boy ran up to the light sculpture and aimed a kick at the phantom's groin. His foot struck nothing but air, and he fell flat on his back. Stunned and wailing, he began banging his fists, then his head, against the ground. "Sin is how we hurt ourselves!" the burly man cried out. He caught the boy's head and shoulders in his hands, clasping the boy firmly as he wrestled to get out of his grip. "But Jesus protects us even at the cost of his own suffering!" A luminous stream of blood seemed to pour across the pavement.

The boy, yanking himself free, jumped to his feet. Eyes wide with amazement, he turned to Jewel standing only a few feet away. "Is that my blood or yours?"

"It is neither." The image of Jesus spoke. "It is my blood that I shed for the salvation of you both." A spear emerged from the figure's side where the blood spurted from the wound. The boy, astonished, threw himself into the open arms of the brilliant image of Jesus as his choir robe was sprinkled with blood. The burly man looked at the boy, then slowly opened his arms and raised his eyes to the night sky. "Hallelujah," he intoned. The boy stared at the man for a moment, then cried out: "I'm saved! The blood of the Lord has saved me!" He broke into a run around the churchyard, raising both arms in victory, shouting, "I'm saved! I'm saved!" then ran back toward the Church.

The other kids mobbed him at the Church door. "Jesus loves you! Jesus loves you! We love you! We love you!" they chanted in unison.

Seeing Jewel, they swarmed across the sidewalk, surrounding her and trying to herd her into the church. But Jewel planted her feet and refused to budge. They shouted and jeered: "What's wrong? Are you too good for Jesus?"

"Stop it! Leave me alone!" Jewel shouted back. "I have to get to *my* church."

"And what church is that?" one of the kids demanded.

"Cloister Church."

"Cloister Church!" another sneered. "Is that a real church?"

"I need to be going," Jewel said firmly. "Please get out of my way."

A circle of boys surrounded her, refusing to move. "The Cloister isn't a real Church, it's an Arab front," an older boy shouted.

"Shame on you for betraying our Christian Republic," another scolded.

"Are you a liberal terrorist?" asked the youngest of the lot.

"Someday soon we're gonna purge all the dirty liberals," an older youth with a scruffy Naabi beard proclaimed. "You must either repent or be purged."

The kids chanted, "Repent or purge! Repent or purge! Repent or purge!"

The boys continued to chant and cheer as they tried to shove Jewel toward the church. Jewel, resisting, stuck out her hands to them, showing the round, red markings on the center of each palm. "Do you boys know what these marks are?"

The boys turned stony silent. "Is that blood?" a small voice asked.

"They look like blood because they're stigmata. They represent the nail holes in the hands of the Lord on the Cross. Do you know why I had signs of the suffering of Jesus tattooed on my body?" she asked.

"Suppose you tell us," a tall one cracked.

"These marks show that I love Jesus—love him just as much as you do. And I forgive you for the disrespectful way you've treated me. I forgive you freely." She smiled. "I forgive you liberally."

At the hated word "liberal," the kids stuck their fingers in their ears. The big burly man in black, who had been watching and listening throughout, began to usher the kids back to the safety of the Naabilat Church. He raised an angry fist at her. "Liberals are cursed to eternal hellfire," he thundered.

"You know," Jewel's blood boiled at his arrogance. "there's nothing Christian about you. Why don't you hypocrites just fuck off?" she exploded.

He gave her a razor-edged glare and studied her up and down, memorizing her appearance before turning to re-enter the church.

Jewel heart was beating rapidly as she hurried across Dixie Highway and entered the Palmway Garden Zone. The walks were lined with every sort of flowering plant. After the ordeal with the Naabilats, she needed some time to compose herself, needed it badly. Stopping at a night jasmine bush, she leaned in and inhaled deeply, hoping its sweet fragrance would brighten her mood. "Stay in inner peace," she told herself. "Don't let the crazies get under your skin." The Kyzy oranges were also in bloom, their scent mingling with that of the hybrid cinnamon that grew in florid rings around each trunk. Her staccato walk gradually softened into what Cesar teasingly called her gazelle glide.

Jewel eased down the two short blocks to where Sixth Avenue ended, then turned left. Through the silhouettes of massive banyan trees in Cloister Garden, she could make out the breaking surf, parallel waves of rollers shining under the city's ambient light. Just ahead, silhouetted against the night sky, was the octagonal Cloister tower. Her anxiety and fatigue began to evaporate the moment she stepped into its familiar shadow.

A flowered archway marked the Cloister entrance. The intense sweet smell of night jasmine opened her nostrils. Pulling one of the four-petaled blossoms from its thorny host, she crushed it and held the fragrance under her nose, inhaling deeply. *Thank you, dear God, I'm so glad I'm here*, she thought.

The heavy wooden double doors led to a long, glow-lit hallway. Rough stone walls formed an ancient entrance to the fortified temple, narrow passages bending to right and left. After passing through several arched doors and a labyrinth of corridors and galleries, Jewel arrived at the gateway to the Hall of Peace. The passage before her opened up into a vacant inner chamber. Flowing banners flanking the entryway proclaimed, "City of Peace" and "Enter in Peace." Jewel had expected to find other group members gathering in the courtyard. She pressed on alone.

To her left, on the eastern wall of the courtyard, spanned a mural, a view of a moonrise above stone battlements. Straight ahead was an old, medieval-looking wooden door, reinforced horizontally with decorative iron bands. With her fingertips, Jewel tapped the horns of the crescent-shaped door pad, twice each. A half-height door swung open to her right. A Persian carpet stretched across the threshold. Kneeling down, she crawled through.

On the other side, Sister Suyapa, smiling in the dim light and murmuring a greeting, extended a hand, helping Jewel back to her feet. "Please sit, beloved," she said, pointing toward the dark center of the room.

A few yards ahead, candles formed a star pattern on the floor. The flickering light barely reached the domed ceiling, twenty feet up, at its highest point. As she approached, Jewel could see that two of the circle women were already seated, one twentysomething, one white-haired.

"Greetings, beloved," they said.

Jewel took her seat in one of nine intricately carved chairs. The hidden door opened and closed several times as others crawled in and filled the remaining spots. The chairs were throne-like, upholstered in maroon velvet, with thick wooden arms and high backs, symbolizing each occupant's sense of nobility. As they entered, each woman gave the customary greeting and sat in silence. When the last of the nine had entered, the door was shut and secured with a thick timber. The elaborate entrance procedure, the ancient setting, the circle of women in flickering light, combined to create an enclosed space, womblike, fluid and warm.

A sweet soprano voice announced, "Welcome, ladies, to the Circle of Healing. You may, if you wish, set aside your cares and concerns. Now is a good time to be here. Only here." Jewel closed her eyes and counted her breaths. At the familiarity of the ritual words, her shoulders drooped and the muscles of her cheeks softened as she plunged her mind into the soothing sounds. "Feel the solid floor under your feet, the solid seat supporting your weight. Allow your burdens to float away. Focus on the moment's breath. Slowly, in awareness, breathe out and in. Out, then in. Breathe out the outside world. Breath in the presence of our time together." By the time Jewel had counted twenty breaths, the rhythm was hypnotic. By fifty, she was approaching an altered state: the room seemed to expand and contract with each breath. After one hundred, she lost count as the spirit-soaked darkness lifted Jewel out of her body, stretching her spirit across the vaulted ceiling.

A disembodied whisper rose . . .

"I call on Thee, O Creator of Life, O Sovereign of Health. . . . Heal us."

Voices high and low cycled clockwise around the room.

"O Creator of the Heavens, lead us from our outer dark to your inner light."

"O Maker of Mind, bring us into the arena of consciousness, the Heights of the Fifth Dimension."

"O Viceroy of the Void, fill our empty souls with Thy Presence in the Seventh Dimension."

"O Self-Existent One, open anew the gates of heaven. Bring us into the Ninth Dimension.

Enfold us in Thyself."

Around the circle in the dark, the voices seemed to move in orbit, going from one seat to the next, chanting the Calls of Divine Encounter.

Before they had a chance to complete the circuit, an abrupt pounding on the door broke the stillness.

"Sister Suyapa, please forgive me for disturbing the Circle. But men are here from the Naabilat Guard. They insist on seeing you immediately."

Suyapa approached the door and removed the brace. Opening the door half-way, a kneeling, nervous-looking receptionist said, "Sorry, so sorry. There are four men in the lobby, demanding to search the premises. They claim we are harboring terrorists."

"I see," the Sister answered. "Dear one, set aside your fears. Treat them like any other guest. Please welcome them to the Cloister."

"Yes, Sister."

"Please guide them here."

The receptionist looked doubtfully at the Sister.

"Are you sure that's a good idea? Won't the sight of the murals anger them?"

"Anything outside their narrow view of God may upset them, true. But we can't very well hide who we are. It's too well known that we honor the prophets of every faith. We must hope, dear one, that they'll be reasonable and see we pose no threat. May the peace of all prophets protect us. Just bring them to me."

"Yes, Sister," the receptionist acquiesced, then hurried away, her light footfalls echoing down the hall.

Suyapa kneeled placidly at the entrance; the circle of women gazed at each other nervously in the following silence. Jewel felt a stab of remorse. *Why did I lose my cool? Why oh why did I say I was coming here?*

A few minutes later the sound of heavy feet came thundering toward them.

Jewel fought to retain her composure as four broad-shouldered Guards crawled through the half-gate. The scruffy appearance of most of them startled her:

unshaved, wearing badly wrinkled uniforms, their greasy hair pressed flat against the scalp.

How she hated this invasion of this, her sacred space. Their presence would mar the Cloister's serene atmosphere; they might be seeking a way to shut the sanctuary down. Then she had a shock. One of Guards she recognized: it was the burly middle-aged man in the black suit she had cursed outside the church. He gave her an unpleasant look of recognition.

"In Jesus' name, welcome to the Mecca Room, my friend . . ."

"Reverend. Reverend Rebolt." He towered over the diminutive Suyapa, a big man, with an outsized head, broad shoulders, a bulky barrel chest, massive thick forearms.

"Reverend, is this your first time visiting us? You are most welcome. We have two main sanctuaries, the Jerusalem Room, down the hall, and the Mecca Room, where you now stand. We consider you friends and fellow worshippers of the universal God. Please feel free to make yourselves comfortable. Won't you join us for prayers? Afterwards, I'd be happy to show you around."

"Thank you, ma'am," Rebolt drawled sarcastically. "But our time is limited. We're looking for a Muslim terrorist who goes by the alias Ahmed Rajul Khalid. There are reports you may be hiding him in your facility."

Suyapa restrained her outrage. *Hiding terrorists?* The real reason for the visit was more likely to be a chance to harass them: how had they found out they were meeting at just this time? The meetings of the Healing Circle, though not a secret, were generally only known to the members.

"Rajul Khalid, the Church bomber? Here? We are peaceful servants of the Lord. Why would he seek refuge here? And even if he did, why do you think we would be grant it?" Suyapa briefly closed her eyes, praying for a mustard grain–sized bit of reasonableness from this man.

"Where else would he go?" retorted Rebolt. "Your Cloister is the most Muslim-friendly place in Lake Worth."

"I assure you, Reverend, no anti-Christian terrorist would be tolerated here, in fact no terrorists or bombers of any kind."

"That's what everyone who harbors terrorists says, ma'am."

Suyapa smiled serenely in return. "Won't you gentlemen join us while we finish our prayers?"

"No, ma'am, we'd rather have a look around and be on our way."

These men were deadly serious underneath the barely controlled attempts at courtesy. Suyapa could ask them to leave; after all, they lacked a warrant or any legal authority whatsoever. And though they would hardly be charmed by being ejected, they were not likely to do them serious injury, now. But that was no guarantee for the future. They were capable of harassing the Sisterhood in subtle and not-so-subtle ways. Better to be compliant. She apologized to the circle of women and gently raised the intensity of the room's lighting.

As soon as it was bright enough to see the surrounding walls, a howl erupted from one of the Guards. The others stood frozen, gazing in horror and disgust. "There is all the proof we need." The howler gestured at the murals. "That's just evil, it's pure evil."

"Sir, I beg your indulgence." Suyapa spoke with a slight, apprehensive quiver in her voice. "Look, sir, these are signs of the love of God. There's no evil here. Please step closer. Let's examine the painting together."

She walked toward the east wall. Its entire surface, floor to ceiling, was covered with an elaborate fresco. At its center stood the Kaaba, the sanctuary of Mecca. The black jute-covered cube towered over worshipping throngs. Thousands of worshippers, dressed in long robes, were kneeling, foreheads to the ground in traditional salat prayer. "These people believe in Abraham, Moses and Jesus, and in the same prophets and apostles as the Church," she said. "Is there anything wrong with that?"

None of the Guards responded.

"Please," she gestured. "Come take a closer look," she said. "Here, notice what he's wearing around his neck." She pointed at a large, blackbearded figure in the foreground. "There's a cross, hanging from a chain, that has fallen out of his shirt as he prostrates himself."

The howler stepped forward, shaking his head. "Yeah, lady, but that's the stronghold of Mecca. Are you folks nuts? Muslims don't wear crosses."

"These Muslims do. And something else—" She pointed to the upper right-hand portion of the mural where a flowing green banner painted with white letters in Arabic-looking script read, "First Women's Hajj—2092." "Doesn't God work in mysterious ways?

Rebolt frowned. "I know all about this."

"Yes, if you look closely at the painting you'll see that under their head coverings, there are women mixed in the crowd. Tradition banned women from the sacred precincts of Mecca," said Suyapa. "Hajj—or pilgrimage— was for men only. It is one of the five pillars of Islam, and yet women were forbidden. Then something happened. During Ramadan in 2091, when Mecca was full of pilgrims from all over the world, a vision of Fatima, the first wife of the Prophet Muhammad, appeared above the Kaaba. She wore a crown adorned with a circle of crosses, stars of David, emblems of OM . . . with symbols from all religions. We call that interfaith symbol the sign of Fatima. She announced that hordes of women from all over the world would soon join the men in circumambulating the Kaaba. Thousands of pilgrims were present. The witnesses came away buzzing with excitement, and soon the word spread. The following year saw the first Women's Hajj. Most of those who went were Muslim, but there were Jews, Buddhists and Christians too. They wear the sign of Fatima as a sign of solidarity."

The howler gave her a thoughtful look, muttering "Muslims wearing crosses. Well, praise the Lord . . . !"

"You aren't buying this slop, are you?" Rebolt asked brutally.

The others cast him stony looks as the target of the rebuke looked shame-faced at his feet.

Suyapa held up her palms, appealing to their better nature. "There's nothing wrong with praying to Jesus in Mecca, is there?"

"That is your belief? These Muslims are saved?"

"The universal spirit of God can be found in all faiths. Yes, that is our belief."

Rebolt glared at the gentle Suyapa. "Universalism is insidious, a temptation, a perversion."

"But is it a crime?"

"No, ma'am."

"It ought to be," said the fearful one.

Suyapa turned to him. "Didn't we just form an independent Florida to safeguard our religious liberties?"

"Soon we'll take the liberty of getting rid of stench like you," cried the man.

The other Guards stared down the outspoken one. Jewel thought: *He let something slip out.*

"Good sir," said Suyapa, addressing Rebolt, "The heart of faith of the Lord Jesus Christ is forgiveness and tolerance. Didn't the Lord, while hanging on the cross, dying, say, 'Father, forgive them for they know not what they do'?"

The reverend's eyes narrowed with impatience.

"Christ kindly forgave those who murdered him. But the Church did the opposite. Instead of forgiving the guilty, it persecuted the innocent—Jews of later generations, who never lifted a finger against the Lord, calling them Christ killers. Can you imagine a more unchristian a thing to do?" She paused. "You, my friend, are doing us a similar injustice."

The howler started to speak, but Rebolt cut him off. "If we give her enough rope, she'll hang herself," he grunted.

Without a blink, Suyapa softly tilted her head inquisitively and continued, "Now, tell me, Reverend, why do you reject the kindness of the Lord? Why do you deal harshly with us? Why do you persecute us for honoring both the Christian and Muslim paths? We are not enemies of the cross. We love the same God as you do," she said with her disarming smile. "So why trouble and threaten us?"

But the Reverend and company were not about to be distracted from their mission by any sweet-talking, scripture-misquoting anti-Christ. "We've heard more than enough from you." Rebolt glared. "Just quiet down while we conduct our search."

Without further instructions, the men spread across the room. Using hand-held sensors, they scanned every nook, pounded and kicked the walls, stood on chairs to examine the ceiling, stomped around the floor in search of hidden panels or hiding places. Half an hour of thorough searching, and searching again, brought up nothing. Rebolt gave his searchers a disdainful look.

"Reverend, where else should we look?" they asked.

Suyapa gestured toward the door. "Would you like to see the Jerusalem Room now?"

"No, ma'am." Rebolt shuffled his feet. "We've seen and heard quite enough."

"Please feel free to visit us any time. Our hearts are always open to you."

He gave her a *Who-are-you-kidding* look. "We'll be on our way now, but we're watching you. Terrorist sympathizers will not be tolerated in this town," he threatened. The resentful, angry determination on the faces of the Guards, which had intensified rather than softened by the failure of their search, left little doubt of what they were capable. As he waited for the others to crawl back out through the half-gate, Rebolt flashed Jewel an especially intimidating glare.

After the Guards were gone, the air hung with a heavy silence. The women sat and looked at each other, their faces reflecting their common fear that they had not seen the last of Rebolt or his Guards. The latch made a soft click as Suyapa gently closed the door. Moving with slow, quiet steps, she returned to her seat and rejoined the circle.

"We've always said we rest in God's hands," Suyapa observed. "Now it seems we really are."

Something deep, determined, resigned and bittersweet welled up in Jewel's heart. Remembering the beauty of the song she'd earlier heard coming from the Naabilat Church and mindful of the overcoming power of forgiveness, she prayed,

"A mighty fortress is our God,
A bulwark never failing.
Our ancient foe still seeks our woe,
But you're the one prevailing."

Everyone exhaled.

———————

To close the meeting, it was customary for the women to take turns sharing something personal from their week. But in the wake of the Naabilat intimidation, they simply sat together in beatific silence, breathing in unison as the candles burned down. With a trembling heart, Jewel spoke. "I may be responsible for the arrival of these Guards here in our sanctuary. They accosted me on the street. I got mad, told them off, cursed them, then told them I was a member here."

"You're not responsible for their actions," Suyapa reassured her gently, "though cursing them may not have been completely necessary. They do what they do because they are who they are. Our job is to find the strength to love them despite their fanaticism and intolerance."

Just before the last candle flickered out, the women filed out of the room in a slow procession, gliding out the temple's backdoor onto the narrow, private beach, removing their shoes, treading the line between the world of water and the world of land as inch-deep waves washed their feet and filled the trail of footprints. A warm sea breeze danced above the rhythms of wave and walk. This was the highlight of Jewel's week. She had done what needed doing. She had said what needed saying. Surrounded by friends and natural beauty, events would unfold as they should. She allowed her spirit the freedom to be absorbed in the rhythms of life, rising and falling like the ocean waves across her bare feet.

When they reached the stand of coco-palms at the edge of the Cloister Garden, the procession wove its way through the trees, then turned and retraced their steps. Jewel made a point of casually sauntering, avoiding walking in a straight line, rocking right, then left, with each footfall. She couldn't remember where she had learned to do this, or what it originally meant, but it came to represent her awareness that life would always require course corrections.

At the opposite end of the garden, they stopped and grouped together. Suyapa gave the dismissal, "Good night, ladies. Go in peace. See you next week in Jerusalem," by which she meant the Jerusalem Room, where their meetings alternated with the Mecca Room. It was an old joke, but they all found it amusing nonetheless. The laughter melted yet another knot in Jewel's neck, a knot she hadn't realized was there. Instead of walking away with the others, she plunked herself down in the cool, damp sand, not wanting the moment to end, and remained at the water's edge as the voices of the others faded into the night.

# OMENS

Jewel felt the spirit descend like a hail of lightning enveloping her in ice. Through a curtain of frozen fog, her mind soared over a plain of dark thunderheads, wind howling through her hair to all horizons until she somersaulted down, head over heels, to a foreign time and place. Her disembodied feet found themselves in warm, wet sand. When the sun burned away the fog, her eyes took in a broad, unfamiliar beach. To her left a tall-masted catamaran lay anchored, nestled in a grove of coconut palms, and beyond that swelled an endless, turquoise ocean. She had no clue where on earth this place might be.

Rows of stubby mangrove trees lined both sides of a road made of sand and rock leading inland. Less than a kilometer away, the top of a minaret stood above the trees. Without warning or will, she started walking forward as if someone else had taken control of her body. With each step down the long-abandoned track, the sights and sounds grew more vibrant. The stones crunched loudly beneath her feet. The sky was bluer than any real sky could ever be, as if poured from a jar of pigment.

The road snaked through grassy dunes, following the general contour of the shoreline for about half a kilometer. Then her feet left the road and plunged into coarse, tall, high grass, heading directly for the minaret. A stone wall, towering several meters overhead, blocked her way. Stones fallen from the upper tier lay scattered at the wall's base, and to her right a section had collapsed completely. Over the shoulder-high piles of rubble, she was able to peer into the ruins of an Old World town. A cobbled, curving street lined with two-storey stucco buildings meandered toward a central plaza. Passionflower vines clung to crumbling stone and plaster. The bluish purple blooms were huge, some of them nearly a foot across. She looked carefully at the wall, wondering if it were safe to step across. The wall was thick, massive, as if its builders had expected an invasion from the sea.

Other than this collapsed section, there was no readily visible means of entry. Rather than scramble over the fallen stones and risk turning an ankle, she circled around to the left, looking for a gate. The ground was lumpy, uneven, with waist-high grass hiding her feet from view. She had to pick her way through clods of broken earth, carefully placing each step. Her decision to search for a better way in had been a mistake; creeping over the fallen stones would have been easier than this. She circled around half the town, and still no entry gate. The sun was hot. She felt woozy, ready to faint, but staggered on against her will, fearful of falling with each step.

On the north side, on a raised hillock, she finally located the main entry. A series of limestone columns, forming a corridor, ran through the outer city wall and down into the town. Doorposts and lintels framed the opening where, apparently, a pair of wooden stockade fences had once secured the entrance. From this high vantage point, she could see the curious layout of the town. Three ring-streets ran in concentric circles, parallel to the outer wall, intersected by radials, like spokes of a wheel, that ran toward the minaret.

She entered the ruined city and, continuing around to her left, began walking along the outer ring lane. Every structure was heavily damaged, shops, homes, public buildings. The interiors were scattered with the battered remains of furniture and market goods. Most of the roofs had collapsed, but here and there an intact structure could still be found. At one point, she came to a massive breach in the city wall, cleared of rubble, as if punched through by raging waters.

She wandered the streets at random, turning left here, right there, getting a tour of the ruined town, once vibrant, now an empty shell. It looked like the sort of place where one would expect to see hyenas or packs of wild dogs. But there were neither people nor beasts anywhere in sight.

Wherever she went, the upper balcony of the minaret smiled down at her like a toothless giant over the house tops. Inevitably, she was drawn toward it. At the town center, the public square was large and spacious, flanked by monumental buildings. The entire area was littered with tumbled boulders, broken pieces of white styrofoam, multicolored chips of sea glass by the thousands, remnants of plastic flower pots, automobile tires and piles of unrecognizable debris.

The mosque stood on the eastern side of the square, its minaret vaulting a hundred feet toward the sky, like a gigantic conch stood on end. Crumbled sections of its pink stucco surface revealed the white limestone and coral-rock blocks of its walls. Patches of black, sun-dried barnacles ran three-quarters of the way up its height, right up to the parapet wall of a circling balcony, showing how much of the tower had been underwater during the peak of the Warming. Half of the domed metal roof had been dislodged and lay twisted against the side wall of an adjacent building, its ornamental crescent moon also barnacled but still intact. All in all, the structure appeared flood-washed but remarkably undamaged.

Along the outside of the parapet wall, remnants of a mosaic were still visible, depicting the Women's Hajj of 2092. The patterns were similar to the mural in the Mecca Room of the Cloister. When Jewel saw it, she felt welcomed. "We are one in the spirit," it sang to her. "We are one in the Lord." Instantly she felt compelled to climb the tower.

At ground level, an arched door allowed access to the inside of the minaret. Jewel poked her head inside. A steep stone stairway wound upward, leading to the balcony. Suddenly Jewel found a prayer mat in her hand and knew it was time for evening prayers. Like a Chagall angel, she floated up the stairs. Chunks of pink stucco littered the balcony floor. She used the mat to sweep clear a spot, then sat down on it cross-legged. The encircling balcony wall was low enough to let her see clearly the ruined town below and the ocean beyond.

The panorama was breathtaking, with vibrant, sur-real colors. She could see the tawny road from the city gate leading down to a tree-nestled harbor. Azure waves pounded the black off-shore boulders as the last rays of the setting sun bathed the land in deep yellow.

Jewel prayed. The special energy of this place made her scalp tingle. Her neck seemed to lengthen. She felt as if each hair on her head was reaching out, seeking the Master of the Universe.

In her deepening trance, she saw herself floating on a sea of cosmic mind. The waters sparkled, crystalline and fragile beneath a sky of deep darkness. Bubbles the size of fists floated by, untethered by earthly forces. Her hand reached out and briefly touched a bubble with one finger. It convulsed in pain. She touched it again. She could hear cries for help like echoes reverberating down a long empty corridor. It sounded like a soul, drowning.

The voice became more and more distinct. It was a young boy. He was in trouble. She felt an urgent need to rescue him, without the slightest idea what the problem was or how to help. The voice disappeared. Another bubble bumped the back of her hand. A different voice spoke, a soft, sweet voice reciting poetry, as if in the dark. It was beautiful, but she had no time for that now. Sliding her hand forward, she managed to regain con-tact with the first bubble.

The call for help intensified. A boy stared at her from inside the pulsing sphere, his straight black hair waving like seaweed in turbulent surf. The water inside the bubble inside the ocean of mind that carried her was a reflection of Jewel's vision within a vision. She felt overwhelmed, grateful, content, awed and perplexed, all in the same moment.

Her finger moved along the bubble's surface. It was not entirely smooth. There was a deep grove running around the circumference, separating the bubble into two hemispheres. Of its own accord, the bubble stretched, the elongated halves now connected only by a thin waist. Twisting and looping like a living thing, it molded itself into a moebius curve. Jewel recognized the shape from her encounters with Einalli. There were tiny, parallel grooves etched into it. Irresistibly, it drew her finger beneath its surface, squeezing and pulsing. The boy inside the bubble spoke.

"I am Ali," he said.

"I'm Jewel," she replied and waited.

"I am Ali," it repeated.

Jewel wondered if perhaps the voice were some kind of long dead echo.

There was a long quiet, then the face in the bubble asked, "Are you alive?"

"Yes, I'm alive."

"I used to be alive, but now I am dead."

"Oh?"

"I was swimming on New Sheba Beach. The surf was wild. Strong water grabbed me. I tried to get free, but I couldn't."

"And since then you've been floating inside this bubble?"

"Yes . . . I've been here a long time. My father wrapped my body in white silk and buried it under a tree. Then I came here. There were prayers here, and I

"I'm Ali. I used to be alive."

was drawn to them. Now the prayers have stopped. No one ever speaks to me anymore. It's always very quiet."

"How old are you?"

"Nine."

"Are you alone?"

"Yes. I'm glad you came to visit me."

"No one else is with you? Not your mother or father?"

Ali shook his head dejectedly. Then his face brightened. "Sh! Listen! A prayer message is coming now."

The inky blackness of the night intensified. Above the almost invisible watery horizon a crescent moon rose, detached itself from its heavenly course and flew directly toward Jewel. The moon expanded until it filled the view from the minaret just a few meters in front of her. Everything was bathed in its white pearly light.

"In the name of the Most Merciful, this word now descends from on high. You and your beloved are in grave danger. Look for The Cat. The Cat will rescue you. Do not wait. Do not hesitate. Take Cesar and flee."

"Where are we to go?" Jewel asked.

"When the time arrives, your destiny will be made known."

"What is The Cat?"

The moon made no reply. It faded, quickly disappearing in the dark waters of the sea. The face of Ali smiled at her through the wall of the bubble. He bowed his head and followed the crescent moon into the waves.

Gently the vision faded, layer by layer, until she could feel the stone flooring beneath her once more. Jewel opened her eyes and gazed over the parapet wall across the dark city. The sky was littered with stars. The constellation Leo arched overhead, its curled tail wagging at her. It whispered. "Don't you recognize me?" Jewel felt more puzzled than ever.

Although her eyes were already open, she felt them open again, as if she had a second pair of eyelids covering the first. She found herself removed from the stone city and sitting in the cool sand at the shoreline of the Cloister Garden, looking over the Intracoastal at the Lake Worth bridge.

For a second, Jewel questioned whether she was now really back in her body. She tugged an ear lobe and wiggled her toes. *Feels real*, she thought as a sense of normalcy slowly returned. She tried to make sense of the prayer message, but had no clue what it meant. Cat? What cat? Flee? Flee where? There was one clear thing at least. Her earlier premonition about Cesar had been right. He seemed to be in some kind of trouble—why else that urgent message? But what was it? How was she to help him? What in the world was she supposed to do?

## NARRATIVE PAUSE 004

JURAT TURNED TO FACE the doorway with a start. "How long have you been standing there?" he asked.

Ms. Blain rapped the file folder against the door jamb. "Only a couple of minutes. I didn't want to disturb you."

Jurat waved her in with a sigh. Under that all-business black suit, she had a nice figure, trim waist, curvaceous hips, long legs.

"So Alice, did you find a place to stay?" he asked, wanting to make conversation.

"I'm set," she replied. "I found a cute little place downtown. Just one problem," she hesitated. "They won't allow my kitten. I was hoping I could let her stay here."

Jurat looked dubious. He'd always been a dog person himself.

"She's really cute. And she's already completely house-trained."

Ms. Blain gave the inspector her most winning smile.

"Not exactly by the book," he grunted, "but I have no objection. After all, this office needs a mascot. As long as no one else in the office objects and you maintain the cat box, of course."

"Yes, sir."

He pointed at the folder in her hand. "So what have you got for me?"

"It's the info on the Cuban robots you requested. I couldn't find much, just a couple of paper files, nothing in digital. But at least they're recent."

Inside was a news clipping and some kind of official-looking report. Fortunately, everything was in English. The inventory also listed a map of something called "the Utopian Zone," apparently lost.

He opened the file folder and began leafing through the papers.

"Call me if you need me," Ms Blain said as she turned on her spiked heel to go.

Jurat hesitated, then, trying to be nonchalant, called over his shoulder, "Say . . . how about a drink after work?"

If she was surprised, she didn't show it. "Maybe another time, boss," Ms. Blain said with a clipped voice as she firmly closed the door behind her.

So that's all the reward I get for giving her kitten a home! Jurat sighed and settled into his review.

FILE FOLDER FOR:
CEZRR CONSTITUTION (CAPITALIST, EGALITARIAN, ZONAL ROBOTIC REPUBLIC)
CIENFUEGOS, CUBA
FOUNDED: 2083

Information rating: thin

### Contents of CEZRR Archive

**Document #1** — WebCast article, Lackluster Happiness Convo . . . Convo . . . Celebrates Itself Again

**Document #2** — La Sociedad de las Communidades Experimentales Oversight Board, Annual Report 2130

**Document #3** — Seven-Point Program of Floridian Futurist Party

**Document #4** — Map of Utopian Zone (Missing)

# Lackluster Happiness Convo ...
# Celebrates Itself Again

## An Opinion by Jessica Marti

Lago Cienfuegos, Cuba, (SouthFlorida WebCast Blast). Since Fidel Castro IV assumed the Chair of La Sociedad de los Communidades Experimentales (SCE) from his father, twenty-three years ago, he has addressed the plenary session of the Annual Convention each year without distinction. His speeches are backward-looking, celebrating the establishment of La SCE but lacking a vision for the future. Although he bears the external trademarks— the beard and green fatigues and military cap of Fidel Castro I—the passion and charisma are painfully missing. Fidel IV is an innovative scientist and undisputed expert in sociological experimentation, but in the opinion of this writer, he is better suited to research and is a fish out of water in his current leadership position. La Sociedad must have a new public face.

The need for change has never been more evident than at this year's Happiness Convo now underway at the Cienfuegos Forum. Yesterday evening, Fidel IV rose to give the keynote address in what should have been the climax of an exuberant opening session. Despite the significant accomplishments of the past year, after reciting once again the story of the birth of the SCE, his presentation settled into a dull recitation of statistics. As is his habit, he used the occasion to read, in a monotone, endless columns of data from the statistician's annual report. The chair could muster no emotion. The experience was painful to all present, it being apparent that Fidel IV was simply performing a hated duty as Chair of La Sociedad's Oversight Board.

This marks the fiftieth annual convention of the SCE and should have been an extraordinary cause for celebration. Utopian Hall was filled to capacity with sociologists and political scientists from around the world. The ten thousand present for the address played their assigned role as extras in a B-grade cinema extravaganza. Their cheering and applause startled the nerve-shattered Fidel, whose eyes were glued to his z-pad from which he droned in heavily accented Island English.

When asked about the incongruity between the speech and the crowd's response, Dr. Viktor Pada of the University of Trinidad remarked, "These cheers are genuine. Our Society is on the verge of a breakthrough, thanks to the brilliance of this awkward little man."

Dr. Pada pointed to the content of the report as the basis for the crowd's enthusiasm. Certain facts cannot be denied. Happiness Testing is now on a solid footing and accurately reflects the felicity of the inhabitants in the various utopian communities under the Board's administration. Long-entrenched biases have been removed from the testing system. For the first time since the inception of the SCE, neither of the old guard communities—neither the Communists nor the anti-Communists—placed in the top five spots. In fact, two communities received with the highest Happiness Quotient this year: the hitech Robot Republic and the Israeli kibbutz, Leche y Miel.

After reading the report, Fidel returned to his seat without lifting his eyes or acknowledging the crowd. Nevertheless, the audience broke into thunderous shouts of "Viva La Sociedad" and "Viva Fidel." Although a non sequitur to a dry presentation, noisy demonstrations after every speech given by Fidel have become traditional, even when tinged with a bit of self-mockery. Scientific gatherings rarely indulge in celebration. Yet celebration is a long-standing Cuban custom, and the crowd seemed to enjoy hamming it up.

This public display, however, merely disguises a failure of leadership. The heritage of Fidel I deserves better. Perhaps the Oversight Board should excuse Fidel IV from this annual chore and invite a robot to give the keynote next year.

La Sociedad de las Communidades Experimentales
Oversight Board's Annual Report 2130
Lago Cienfuegos, Cuba

**Chairperson's Summary:** 2129 was a successful year on several key fronts. Total population in our utopian communities grew by 8%. Economic output rose by 12.5%. Most importantly, it is clear that our participating communities are learning how to increase the well-being of their citizens based on recent Collective Happiness Index (CHI) results.

The Happiest Community Award this year went to two communities due to a tie in their CHI scores. Our largest community, the CEZRR Robot Republic, and one of our newest communities, KLM Kibbutz Leche y Miel, both achieved record-breaking scores of 139/100. Despite its smaller presence here in Cuba, the innovations of the KLM model have widespread influence around the world, due perhaps to KLM's affiliation with existing Jewish organizations in Russia, California and Israel. By contrast, CEZRR requires extensive and expensive infrastructure due to its heavy reliance on robot technology. As a result, Robot Republic advocates have struggled to export its high-tech Futurist vision to the continental North America and elsewhere.

**Community Development Statistics**

Two new utopian communities were inaugurated this year; DNA Project and Ayn's Anarchists.

One existing community requested and was granted additional lands; Amish Coalition.
Three communities were dissolved; Post-Gender Union, Earthatarians and Mensa 200.

Total communities at year end: 26
Zonal Republics: 8
Registered Societies: 16
Informal Groups: 2
Lands under grants: 29,500 square kilometers (37%)
Lands available for future grants: 50,300 square kilometers (63%)

**Average Happiness Quotient (HQ)**

This year: 127
Last year: 124
Ten years ago (in 2119): 118
Baseline at program inception fifty-two years ago: 100

**Happiest Community Award for 2129**

Utopian Community #012-50
CEZRR Constitution (Capitalist, Egalitarian, Zonal Robotic Republic)
Category: Fusion Economic
Community Members: 114,000
Land Area Utilized: 1,850 square kilometers near Valle de la Placenta, Cuba
Happiness Score: 139

Utopian Community #077-07
Kibbutz Leche y Miel (Milk and Honey Cooperative)
Category: Spiritual Commune
Community Members: 500
Land Area Utilized: 14 square kilometers in Districto
Boca de Vaca
Happiness Score: 139

**Goals for 2130**

Our focus for the coming year will be to reverse two
declining trends: the number of experimental communities and the utilization of land resources.

Background: Recruitment has been limited by
the political history of Cuba. La Sociedad de las
Communidades Experimentales was formed, in the
wake of the failure of state socialism, for the purpose
of experimenting with alternative, community-based
forms of democratic socialism. Since that time our
mission has expanded to include social designs with
capitalistic, monarchistic and religious foci. We continue to seek further diversification. The Community
Development subcommittee has been given the task
of establishing contacts with a wider range of political
organizations in order to invite their participation in
the unique opportunities for testing social and political theories here at Lago Cienfuegos.

Signed: Fidel Castro IV

## Seven-Point Program
## of Floridian Futurist Party

- End of corporate monopolies on robot ownership by repeal of Robot Limitation Laws.

- Provision of free robots to all workers.

- Guaranteed employment at living wage.

- Free robo-doc health clinics.

- Free education in robot ownership and leisure retraining.

- Twenty-hour work week.

- Full pension retirement at age 40.

# COBBLER

The figure known to his Futurist Party handlers as "Forrest Newcomb" sat doubled over on the edge of the bed, lifeless, head hanging limply between its knees, fingers brushing the floor. Hayes stood impatiently at the Lab door, staring at his disabled candidate. "How much longer will this take?"

"You're not thinking of taking our future mayor out in public again tonight?" Tuuve asked incredulously. "It's almost one in the morning."

"Hey, Tuuve. It's Friday night, we only have another week before the vote. A little wee-hour bar hopping is just what this campaign needs—to have Forrest accepted as an ordinary guy with a neighborly image."

Turning towards Cesar, Tuuve blinked wearily. "What are the chances of reactivating Forrest tonight?"

"About the same as a dinosaur egg hatching in my hip pocket," Cesar cracked without looking up.

The Horse, irritated by Cesar's sarcasm, tapped his fingernails on the door jamb as he glared at Cesar. "Dinosaur eggs notwithstanding, how long?"

Cesar nonchalantly slid a straight-backed chair up to the diagnostic monitor and leaned in intently, studying the readouts.

"A lot depends on how much the speech and memory circuits have degraded. You heard the gibberish. That indicates significant damage. And I'm especially concerned about the VMP and MOP."

Hayes hated techno-babble, as Cesar well knew. Predictably, the Horse started to click his teeth. "I'm waiting for an intelligible explanation."

"Let me figure out what repairs are needed, then I'll explain to your heart's content, okay?"

"How long's this going to take? I told Sheriff Braxil we'd meet her for coffee at the Jahva House at two sharp."

"You're meeting the Chief at 2 A.M.?"

"She's always downtown late on Friday nights, likes to keep an eye on the partiers. I told her I'd meet her with our future mayor."

"Better count on going alone."

"It's tough to sell toothpaste with a picture of the tube. Need to sell the white, bright smile." Hayes grinned.

"Not happening tonight. It could take me a few hours just to figure out how bad the damage is—that is, if you quit hovering over me and interrupting. Why not call it a night? We'll discuss the repair plan in the morning. Go. Go!"

"We're too close to the election, I want a plan before I head home," he said, as he stepped toward the doorway. "I'll leave you to it. Pull an all-nighter if you have to."

They could hear his heels pounding like mallets against the antique pine floor as he started pacing up and down the length of the salon outside.

Tuuve looked at Cesar quizzically, wondering if he should also leave.

"I could use your help disassembling the bot's knee joint. And don't worry about hurrying. I never allow the Horse to panic me. He's not my boss."

Tuuve's face contorted. Braadrik was, in fact, his boss, so he wasn't exactly comfortable irritating him. But what he said was, "So, where do we start?"

After a silent thirty seconds, Cesar began tapping screen commands. Forrest's upper torso snapped to a sitting position. It took off its left shoe and sock. With both hands, it grabbed the bare, faux-veined foot and gave it a hard counterclockwise twist. A round data port popped open under the arch, then, gently, the robot lowered itself onto the bed and stretched out, face up. With a series of soft clicks, Forrest's lanky body gradually stiffened. In sync, Cesar unconsciously clicked his teeth as the bot slowly executed the repair-prep version of its shut-down routine. "There are tons of configuration and subsystem links that are in process of being analyzed," he explained. "It'll be a good five minutes before it's safe to start disassembly."

Tuuve stood out of the way with his back against the wall, watching Forrest's face whiten eerily. Despite his previous experiences with humanoid robots, he found the deactivation unnerving. Forrest was the best simulation of human behavior he had yet seen. "He's so pale, he already looks dead," the newbee said.

"It's neither dead nor alive, and it never was," Cesar corrected him.

"Kinda creepy. Like watching a suicide."

"Try to remember that bots are just machines, clock-works, bells, wires and whistles. What you're watching is a fancy toaster, sucking in a slice of bread, heating it, popping it out when done, then turning off the heater."

"But the movements and mannerisms are so human, it's natural to think of it as a real person."

"There's no higher compliment you could pay the builders: to know and yet be fooled. That's our goal, to create a perfect mimic of humanity. Zang, man! Even expert roboticists, who know what to look for, are often fooled. You wouldn't believe the depth of the effort to hide any hint of artificiality. The electronics are shielded. Skin texture, heartbeat, breathing, body temperature, even bladder function, all simulated. In older male humanoids, we even simulate a little prostate trouble. It's an amazing illusion, it can fool even the most experienced observer."

"Amazing? Okay, but also eerie, it gives me the creeps. Life and death—at the flick of a switch." He stared at the lifeless "corpse" on the bed.

Hayes, who had momentarily stopped pacing, shouted from the other room, "Gentlemen, quit talking and get to work!"

"If we open the bot up before all the subsystem microcharges are cleared, we could do permanent damage," Cesar shouted back, rolling his eyes and chuckling under his breath.

"Talk about creepy, look at this," he whispered to Tuuve, pulling up Forrest's pant leg to expose the damaged limb. The shin casing was broken, forming a gaping wound. Squashed synth-muscle the color of raw hamburger bulged through a long crack running down to the ankle.

Finally, three beeps sounded from Forrest's nostrils, indicating total shut down. Cesar strapped a metallic band around Forrest's calf to hold it together while he disassembled the leg. The Smart Key hummed as it executed the unlocking routine, groaning like a wounded bear as it strained to open the damaged mechanism. Pressurized gas hissed out when the lock snapped open, revealing a set of snuggly packed green component boards lined up inside the leg.

"Like to try your hand at surgically removing the damaged modules?" Cesar said. "Meanwhile, I'll check out the memory circuits."

"You bet."

Cesar wired up a cable to the open data port under Forrest's heel, then attached a set of optical cables. Starting with a dim, barely perceivable blue light, the backup sphere gradually brightened as several octogigs of data were copied from Forrest's damaged leg.

Cesar retook his seat at the monitor. Tuuve knelt and began meticulously studying the component array inside the robot's damaged leg-shell and muscle. He carefully extracted one slotted board, then another. A long, thin board, covered with square yellowish chips, had been twisted out of its proper place, its upper end buried in mangled synth-muscle. Tuuve winced at the thought of a similar item jammed into his own thigh, then reprimanded himself for once again thinking of bots as human.

Reaching into the stump with a light touch, Tuuve scraped off as much robot protoplasm as he could from either side. Carefully grasping the board with a micro-puller, he began jockeying the assembly back and forth in an attempt to work it free. Aside from a slight wiggle, the thing refused to move. Breathing deeply to control his frustration, he leaned over until his nose nearly touched the inner workings of the robot's leg. But with the parts so tightly packed and the light inside the leg so dim, he couldn't see what kept the board from sliding out. With wrinkled brow, he stewed over it for a few minutes. Working his fingers around the lower, sliding edge, he tried once again to figure out what was causing the jam but couldn't make head or tail of it.

After several more failed attempts, Tuuve gave up with a hang-dog grimace and asked Cesar to take over.

When it came to field work, Cesar's cybereyes gave him an unmatchable advantage. The delicate work within the narrow confines of the robot's leg sometimes required visual acuity beyond that of Tuuve's or indeed anyone else's natural eyes. Not only could Cesar function in near-darkness, but his cybereyes could magnify components till he could see in perfect detail objects as small as the dust particles on Tuuve's platinum wingtips.

It turned out that the upper end of the assembly board, still well inside the leg, had shattered along the top edge and was twisted out of square at the bottom. In Tuuve's attempt to remove it, slivers of green plastic had wedged into the ejection track. Within seconds, Cesar located the cluster of burrs and gently pried out the assembly.

"There's your problem," Cesar explained, pointing to the green burrs wedged into a slight ding in the rail.

Tuuve shook his head in amazement. "Nice job. I would have had to disassemble the leg from the hip down and then still might not have found the problem. That was incredible. Maybe I should get myself at least one cyber-eye."

"It come in handy in our line of work."

Tuuve unconsciously squinted as he tried to imagine how much better he would be able to see with implants. "Your eyes came from Cuba?"

"Yeah. Unlike this." Cesar held up the damaged board by the tail, like a trophy fish. "Here's the nefarious MOP—the More Options Protocol, a local product designed to sidestep standard safeguards to prevent robots from spin, stretch and deception—in other words, lying. The Cuban component, the Veracity Monitoring Protocol, VMP, is supposed to have the final say on verbal quality control, making sure a robot always tells the truth. The Futurist Lab saw fit to tack on the MOP for the politician bots, from a conviction that telling the plain truth is not always practical in Florida politics."

Cesar held the MOP board under a table lamp to inspect the damage. Three parallel cracks ran along its length, shorting out who knows how many circuits. Several rows of chips had wiggled loose, like a prize-fighter's smashed teeth. The whole thing would need to be replaced. Murphy's Law mandated that this, of all the robot's components, would be the one to take the brunt of Forrest's fall. It was the only item in the entire design manufactured exclusively by the Florida Futurist Lab. Only a handful had ever been made. Who knows how long it might take to get a replacement, unless the Lab happened to have an extra one lying (no pun intended) around. Not a likely prospect.

Cesar turned to Tuuve. "Do me a favor. Go smooth talk Braadrik. Ease him into a calm mood if you can. I've got to deliver some bad news."

The newbee's eyes widened.

"You sure like to give the new guy a challenge," he said on his way out.

Cesar procrastinated, listening to Hayes and Tuuve mumbling through the wall for a couple of minutes (Tuuve said something that seemed meant to get a laugh, Hayes paused and then said something that sounded like "Ha. Ha"). So much for softening Hayes up. Cesar gritted his teeth and walked into the salon.

Tuuve sat in his customary armchair, staring with a meek look at his platinum wingtips. He shrugged at Cesar as he came in. Hayes stood, glaring skeptically at Komenen.

"Here's the dope," Cesar said without any preliminaries. "There's been damage to a number of systems. The knee joint with the supporting musculature is in rough shape, but it's repairable. Under ordinary circumstances, I'd prefer to replace the cracked leg casing, but for the sake of time, and until after the election, a temporary patch should work."

Hayes nodded curtly.

"The good news is, I was able to stop the digital cascade in the speech centers. His babbling during the walk back here came from a damaged component that dominoed through his system. Luckily, I've nearly finished undoing the effects of the downstream cascade. The VMP looks good, but it needs live-testing to know for sure. The bad news is the worst damage is to the MOP. It will be next to impossible to fix in time." Cesar paused. "Till he's fixed, he'll only be able to tell the truth."

Hayes gave Cesar an if-looks-could-kill gape. "What do you mean, next to impossible to fix?" he snarled. "Sincardo heads the team that builds all our MOPs. Hell, she invented them! Getting a replacement shouldn't be a problem." He shook his head impatiently. "What else are we dealing with?"

"The knee, the muscle and the leg casing. With the MOP, that's it."

"And how long will all this take?"

"With a little luck, a day or two."

Hayes stared at him for a second, his face turning red and expanding slightly.

"A *day*, as in twenty-four *hours?*" he shouted. "Two days as in forty-eight? Are you nuts? We're eleven days before the election. We can't afford that much downtime." Hayes paused, braced himself then pulled himself together with a couple of manatee-like exhalations. "Can't you patch the bot up so I can walk him through his remaining campaign schedule? He wouldn't have to say much. Maybe you could give him laryngitis—I'll just have him glad hand and rasp for votes." He smiled wanly.

"Nope," Cesar drawled, secretly enjoying the Horse's meltdown. "Won't work."

Hayes pivoted, fumed and resumed pacing. "And what if I gave you a direct order? Get him running the best you can, and I'll decide if he's up to the task."

"Look, Hayes, without a functioning MOP, your candidate will tell the truth, without limits, without restraint, on any subject, and without warning. Including the fact that he's a robot. That's fine with me, but I feel pretty sure you don't want that, and if anything goes wrong, I'm not allowing anyone to blame *me* for it."

Hayes's impatience simmered. He rubbed his tongue roughly over the bottom edges of his front teeth, and then the lid flew off the pot. "And you're the great know-it-all who's so busy protecting his own butt? You're going to tell me what you're not going to allow? You zero, you little, wet-behind-the-ears pipsqueak! You can't even fix a minor bot bruise! What the shit are you good for!"

Cesar's face went red in its turn. "Pipsqueak?" he yelled. "I can't fix shit, huh? How can you blame me when you don't keep spare parts on hand? What am I supposed to work with? Your good looks? Where's the new knee? Where's the stem muscle protoplasm? And for crying out loud, how quickly do you think Sincardo can build a custom MOP?" His eyes blazed with the heat of a hundred fires. "You expect me to work instantly under these conditions? You're the crazy one. Totally loco! I don't need this. If you're asking for my resignation, you can have it. Fix your canned candidate yourself. Screw you to the blue! Coño!"

Hayes's jaw softened. He turned toward Cesar, rubbing his hands together slowly. "I'm sorry, I'm sorry, Cesar. Truly. I apologize. Look. Slow down. Let's talk this through. I can't have you resigning at a time like this." He had just remembered that, at this moment, he needed Cesar more than Cesar needed him.

He gave Cesar a sincere, pleading look.

*There'll be time for payback later.*

Cesar angrily flipped his hair out of his eyes. "You still want me to finish this job?".

"Yes. Yes, of course I do. We've worked on this too long and too hard to throw it away now." Hayes gestured magnanimously. "Just state your terms."

Cesar looked doubtful. The two stood facing each other wordlessly, Cesar tapping his teeth, Hayes rubbing his hands.

"OK," Cesar finally broke the silence. "You supply me the MOP. Tuuve and I'll do the rest. And it's not just a matter of swapping parts, his entire neural matrix needs to be verified and patched. I'll need three to six hours just for integration work after you get me the part. Is that clear? I'll have Tuuve call you when I'm finished. That's what I can do. Yes or no?"

Tuuve, who had been sitting quietly in the overstuffed corner chair, indicated his willingness with an affirmative nod. "Repairing synth-muscle is my specialty," the newbee said.

"OK," Braadrik said. "OK."

Cesar smiled. "Done. Now go home. Get some sleep."

"No time for sleep," Hayes said as he headed for the street. "I'm already late for my coffee date with Braxil.

Sincardo's on the night shift—I'll call her to get started on it right away. If I send you the MOP first thing in the morning, you'll have our next mayor ready to go by mid-afternoon, right?"

"Right." Cesar shrugged, not believing for a second that such a schedule was practical. He glanced at the time. It was 3 A.M. He wondered briefly how a chief of police would react to being stood up on a date by a political handler. Probably not well.

Once the door closed behind Hayes, Tuuve's face got serious. "Hey, I thought you were really going to quit there for a minute."

"I don't like the guy and I never have. But he's got his talents. And if a small group of us can't work together, what hope is there for our cause, leisure retraining or honest robot governance?"

"For what it's worth, I'm glad you're staying." Tuuve yawned. "And do you mind if I go home? We can tackle the knee repair first thing in the morning."

"No problem, my friend," Cesar nodded. "Go get a good sleep, and no schedule, just come back when you're ready. I'll start processing Forrest's memory data in prep for the new MOP, sack out on a gurney and let it run while I snooze. Soon M. Forrest Newcomb will be right as rain. Or, to be perfectly precise, Machine Forrest Newcomb."

# BEING MECHANICAL

**C**esar awoke with a start and a dizzy, disoriented sense of foreboding. It took him a few seconds to remember where he was. The only source of light was a crack under the door, casting long shadows of gurney bars across wall and ceiling. Safe House. Robot injured. The limo . . .

The limo . . . Where the hell was the limo? And the show bots?

He waited for his drowsy brain to clear, assuming he'd shortly remember what happened after the robot show. But the answer didn't come.

His impetuous jump to the floor made the unlocked gurney roll out from under him, slam against the wall and toss him unceremoniously against another free-wheeling gurney. He stumbled out the Safe House door into the flower-vine surrounded yard. The morning air was cool and bright but with enough humidity to promise the coming day would be a South Florida summer scorcher.

As soon as he stepped into the back yard, he noticed that the garage door was half open. Cesar walked over and peeked inside, half expecting to find that the bots had returned themselves per plan and that he was worrying over nothing. But the garage was empty. No limo. No robots. What the hell? How could the whole night have passed by and no one had noticed that the bots had never returned. *Madre de Dios* . . . .

"Hayes?" he shouted into his wrist phone as he stepped back inside the Safe House. "Do you know where the show bots are?"

"They're not with *you?*"

Cesar launched in rapid fire. "No hay *nada* aca. El carro no esta, los machinas no estan. Que cosa . . ."

"Speak English, Cesar, or shut your trap," Hayes cut him off, followed by a simmering silence.

Finally Cesar spoke up. "The bots are missing, unless, of course, they decided to take the night off to visit their mothers. What a mess! Our whole operation is at risk."

"What do you mean, missing?"

"They never returned to the Safe House. Neither them nor the limo."

"You sure?"

"Listen to me. The garage is as empty as the Liberty Bell. No car. No robots. They're not in the house. They're not in the kitchen. They're not hiding under the couch. There's no sign of burial in the yard. My best guess is—they went for a stroll in South Palm Park."

There was silence on the other side of the line.

"OK, hot head," Hayes said calmly. "Now you listen to *me*. You just do your job. Fix M. Forrest. Get him back on his feet and back on the campaign trail. I'll handle this. Everything will turn out okay."

"Tzz," Cesar hissed like a tea kettle letting off steam. "And where is my replacement MOP?"

"You'll have it by noon."

"Noon? For real?"

"Noon!"

They hung up.

Cesar lumbered back into the house, feeling befuddled. His eyes darted nervously from one security monitor to the next. The entire team of show bots was missing. What the zeet could have happened to them? He remembered the kid who had followed the tomato bot out of the auditorium. Where had they gone off to? Even so, that would only account for one of the bots. Or what if that Tex dude had somehow caught up with them? What if that Tex dude caught up with them? The whole underground operation could be at risk.

Cesar wandered aimlessly into the kitchen. In the refrigerator he found a moldy container of egg salad, sniffed at the contents, returned it to the bottom shelf and closed the door. Then he ambled out the front door, crossed the lawn, feeling the crisp dryness of the brown summer grass under his shoes, re-entered the empty garage, walked around the parking spot where the limo should have been, exited and marched back to the house. Slamming the heavy front door, he pounded his fist against it.

"Madre Santa," he muttered. He stood there for what seemed an eternity, feet together, shoulders against the door, eyes shut, hands limp at his sides, listening to his heart race. With everyone gone, the Safe House was exceedingly quiet. Finally, the shrill blood buzz in his ears began to subside.

Work. That was what he could do now.

He stepped down the hall into the rear repair room. M Forrest was still stretched out, one leg disassembled, the monitor flashing as it continued to reprocess the bot's immense databases. The only sound was the rush of air from the overhead A/C vent.

Cesar sat down, stared at the mind-numbing digital readout.

Certain oddities he had noticed but forced to the back of his mind were coming to the fore. As entertainers, the show bots were legal. There was no need to house them or service them at a secret facility. They should have been kept at the Lab, serviced by the Lab, supervised by the Lab. Only the robot candidates needed a Safe House.

Keeping M. Forrest's identity secret was risky enough. One mechanical glitch could blow the whole operation and mean jail terms for election fraud and Limitation Law violations. Failure was not an option, yet Cesar was starting to wonder how long it would be possible to keep up the ruse. So much could go wrong. Every campaign event, every interaction with the public carried the risk of exposure. Then, even if the robot won the election, there would be two years of service as mayor; a steady stream of city commission meetings, workshops, travel to conferences, coordination with city staff, and after that presumably a re-election campaign, and on and on. "Tzz," Cesar hissed again. It was a miracle they'd gotten this far. And what about the other robot politicians? Although he wasn't privy to the details, Cesar knew there were at least two others. How long could they keep all these balls in the air before the inevitable fall?

It seemed ages ago when the seeds of the risk they were now taking had been sown at one decisive meeting of the Futurist Governing Council. Although only a tekkie, as assistant chief of robot maintenance and repair, Cesar had been privy to the sessions in which Remp had been born.

From the start, Chairwoman Reina Malcato insisted on the involvement of all department heads to ensure that the operation would be executed with the utmost efficiency. The sixteen council members sat around a large, square metalloid table set in the center of the room, with the staff chiefs crowded along the walls.

Georgia Sugimoto, the leader of the young ideologue wing of the Party, had wanted the Remp campaign to be out in the open. As she stood up to speak, her usual, easygoing manner was replaced by a pained look. She leaned forward, her arms locked on the table top, her long black hair hanging to her elbows. "Why don't we seek to change the Constitution so robots can be legally elected?" she asked. "The case to be made is simple and straightforward: We humans need to accept our own limitations: our historically proven inability to govern ourselves effectively." Her surprisingly husky voice and evident struggle to hold back tears hushed the room. She slapped the table with an open palm and repeated: "Historically proven corruption, historically proven inefficiency and waste, historically proven wars for pride and profit." She now had everyone's attention. "Our robot candidates are able, honest, immune to bribes, inspiring and without ego. For good reason, we call them 'Mr. *Clean*'. They make perfect politicians, a campaign manger's dream; no scandals, no gaffs, no off-message rants. God knows how we've searched for bright, charismatic, capable people to lead our country, and we just can't find them, at least not in sufficient numbers." Sugimoto paused. The others in the room leaned forward, waiting for her next words. "We can say that the logical solution is to manufacture our own robots and program them with the leadership qualities we need. The Futurist Party will be able to offer the voting public perfect candidates—literally custom-ordered. There's no need to hide or disguise a robot's superiority. Let's take this case for automated government directly to the people. After all, we can point to the successes of the Robot Republic in Cuba as an example of something we can do in Florida with perhaps even greater success. By changing the Constitution openly, legally, we will have a much stronger likelihood of future success."

Most of the other council members in the room simply shook their heads. No one needed cybereyes to detect the body language of collective disapproval.

Dr. Optima Sincardo, the brightest roboticist at the table, stood up to speak. Her straight red hair was cut no-nonsense short with a long, thin pheasant tail hanging down to the middle of her back. "Though much of what Ms. Sugimoto said is true, the people are not yet ready to relinquish control over the country to robots. We all remember the resistance to robot-controlled aircraft. The first attempts conjured fear, panic, boycotts. Bots had to occupy pilot seats on the

QT. Only after accident rates declined drastically was the public informed.

"Robot politicians are sure to receive even greater resistance," Optima paused, her eyes circling the table. "There's a deep psychological factor at work here. The link between a leader and the people is primal, tribal. Voters choose, not just the most competent, but someone likeable, someone they can rally behind, someone they feel a personal bond with. Only by experiencing the benefits of robot governance first, and later learning that robots were behind the improvements, will they ever accommodate themselves to the switch. It is true there are legal issues involved, but once we have a sufficient number of robots in office, and once the benefits are obvious for everyone to see, the legal issues will evaporate: our robot politicians will have changed the laws that made them illegal in the first place. We have delayed too long. I call for a vote tonight. It's time to move forward expeditiously with a robot candidate."

A chorus of approvals filled the room. Malcato mouthed "well done" to her assistant. Apparently the two of them had coordinated on strategy. "The obvious also needs to be stated," the chairwoman explained. "Robots are not citizens and cannot legally be elected. If we want to run robot candidates now, we'll have to do it in secret with an underground support structure."

Sugimoto gasped and looked around the table, searching face to face, wondering why there was no opposition to this ghastly idea. "But think of the ramifications of running a clandestine operation. Picture the legal consequences, if we were found out. We could jeopardize our movement, and set us back politically for a generation . . . ."

But her warnings were to no avail. Nods, shrugs and a few downcast eyes indicated that Malcato had rounded up her support before the meeting. Not a single person spoke in favor of an open campaign. Sugimoto bowed out, despite seeming deeply troubled. The Governing Council was polled, and the path of illegality and sub-terfuge was chosen.

Sincardo's star rose from that moment forward. Drs. Malcato and Sincardo, previously close, grew into an inseparable team, both personally and professionally. They frequently talked on the phone, ate most meals together. Rumor had it they slept together as well. They supervised the research and construction of an experi-mental team of robots that could be passed off as human, bypassing the Veracity Protocol.

At the next month's Council meeting, it was decided to create a new, independent entity, which would become Remp, to distance the Party in case the project was exposed. Optima resigned from the Council and became head of the Robotic Election Management Program, in charge of setting up separate, secret research and operations facilities.

However, the separation was never fully realized in practice. As before, Sincardo maintained her office at the open lab on Palm Beach University campus and continued to serve as Malcato's assistant. When it came to undercover operations, Reina called the shots.

Remp's budget was ample, thanks to overseas sup-port, but its task was formidable. Improved robot hardware and software would have to be developed. A secret facility, a safe house, would be needed, where robots could be assembled and sent for recharging and repair. Support staff would have to be found to keep the robots in top condition at all times.

Cesar was assigned to Remp from the outset and, despite his reservations about the project (he had been impressed by Sugimoto's warnings), he soon drowned his doubts in his fascination with the technical challenges. He was hurt and disappointed when for some unexplained reason he was excluded from the initial planning for and renovation of the Safe House. Malcato, Sincardo and Hayes treated it as their private fiefdom and kept their imported Cuban collaborators out of sight.

Unencumbered by the supposed separation between the Party and Remp, Sincardo's research team quickly got to work. Housed in adjacent offices, ideas, personnel and parts were, more often than not, shared indiscriminately between the organizations. No one seemed concerned.

The big break came when Dr. Charles Witherspoon, a local guy on the research staff, discovered a brilliant technique for translating neural brain patterns into computer code. Now it was possible to implant human memory, personality traits and talents directly into a robot brain.

Reina and Optima made an efficient team. Their joint efforts quickly paid off. Within two years, Remp succeeded in fabricating a robot that could consistently pass for human. Within another year, the first potential candidates had been placed in society. Thus far, their subterfuge had been flawless. None of their placements had malfunctioned, slipped or been outed. The next challenge was to get a machine elected.

## NARRATIVE PAUSE 005

IT WAS SUNDAY evening, a bad time to call, but Jurat felt he needed to cover his tush.

"Justice Pawl? Palm Beach Inspector Jurat here. Sorry to ring at this late hour, but there's been a development in the case I think you'd want to know about. . . . Yes, I can hold."

He nervously tapped his foot while waiting for the judge to return.

"OK to speak freely now? . . . Yes, I'll get right to the point. You wanted me to find out why the Futurists maintain a secret facility in addition to their licensed research lab, right? . . .Well, yes, I have an answer for you, a rather remarkable answer. It turns out that their candidates, well, at least one candidate, is not human. . . . That's right. They've built a robot, one that can pass for Senator Newcomb's son, and they're running him for mayor."

Jurat held the phone away from his ear and waited for the Justice to finish.

"What I'd like to do, sir, with your permission, is to bring in those involved for questioning, top to bottom: the Newcomb boy, the technicians, the Futurist County chairwoman, the whole lot. . . .Yes, sir, I realize how explosive this news would be if it ever got out. . . . Yes, sir, I realize that disputed elections are nothing but trouble. . . . I don't know anything about the Supervisor of Elections office, sir. Couldn't say how Newcomb's name got on the ballot. . . . Sorry, I don't know who was involved in the fraud. . . No, I have no idea where the Senator's son would be, sir. . . Twenty-six. Yes, twenty-six individuals arrested. . . . Absolutely, every one of them has been interrogated. . . . No, I haven't had the time to review all the interview logs, sir. It took all afternoon to process. . . . It's quite possible the information you want is in those logs. . . . By Tuesday noon?" Jurat's brow went tight as a prune. "That's only a day and a half away."

His eyes rolled up to the ceiling. "I'll do my best, sir, to have answers by then."

After he managed to get off the phone, Jurat rummaged through the mass of paperwork in his inbox and located the arrest blotter. It was a single sheet, a list of the names of everyone caught in the raid on the secret cyber-factory. Actually three had been arrested at the Cloister and twenty-three at M Street. Besides the two Rager punks, none of these folks had priors. While scrutinizing the list, he got a hunch. Sure enough. There were the names: Hayes, Malcato, Sincardo, Witherspoon; current status: booked, questioned, released on bail. Double checking, he made sure that Newcomb wasn't on the list. Still—a big break. Luck, be a Lady tonight! Hopefully everything he needed would be on the interview brain scan disks.

The more he thought about it, the more sense it made. As soon as they heard the news of Cesar's arrest, the staff of the Futurist Lab must have panicked. Even though it was Sunday morning, everyone from supervisor to janitor would have gotten an emergency call and rushed down to the converted house on M Street in a vain attempt to remove incriminating evidence. With all those folks running around that tiny place, it must have been a madhouse. He had been very lucky to nab them. With a crew of that size, it would have taken them less than an hour to pick the place clean.

"Blain," Jurat called on the intercom (he used "Blain" to show slight disapproval, "Ms. Blain" to show serious disapproval; he'd call her "Alice" again once she let him buy her a drink). "I want the interrogation disks from this morning's raid for the following Futurist conspirators, pronto. Here are the names: Reina Malcato, Braadrik Hayes, Optima Sincardo, Charles Witherspoon."

"Can it wait till tomorrow morning? I was about to call it a night."

"Would you call down to the jail before you go—start the ball rolling?"

"OK." She gave a little sigh. "The names again?"

"Sorry, but I really do need this. Malcato. Hayes. Sincardo. Witherspoon." He spoke the names slowly. "Got it?"

"Yes."

"Thanks . . ."

A kitten's hungry meow came over Blain's intercom just before she signed off.

———————

After a restless night full of dreams of robot cats and hounding calls from irate Futurist supporters, Jurat was back at work by 5:30 A.M. There was already a small horde of colleagues present, hovering around the halls, waiting to hear the inside scoop on his coup. He just winked and joked, glowing as he strolled down the hall to his office, enraptured by the choruses of "Way to go," "Great work" and "Can I help?" all of which he translated to mean, "How can I get a piece of the action?" It was sweet to prolong and savor his little moment of glory.

He found a long queue of phone messages on his desk. Eight reporters wanted interviews, from Miami, Orlando, Jacksonville and Havana. Pawl had called three times to explain the importance of having answers about the "robot candidate" by Monday afternoon.

Grossly disappointed at the need to isolate himself, Jurat hung a Do Not Disturb sign on his door knob (he noted that the zealous Blain wasn't zealous enough to be at her desk before 6 A.M.) and closed his office door. He'd have to forego his colleagues and the press in favor of the demands of justice. He sat back with a grunt and a double-mocha latte from his desk snack-dispenser and slipped the next disk into the side slot of the looking-glass monitor.

# A MENDER OF BAD SOLES

It was well past noon when Tuuve entered the repair room.

"Heard from Hayes yet about the new MOP?"

"Not a word."

Tuuve dug into his bag, offered Cesar a kale and carrot ring. "I stopped at the beach Green Market, thought we'd need something healthy for breakfast."

"Sure! But is kale all they had?"

"They were out of pineapple."

"Ouch!"

Tuuve took a seat opposite Cesar, and soon the two of them had devoured the entire sackful.

"Everything go smoothly after I left?" the newbee asked wiping his mouth with a brown paper napkin.

"Smooth as the skin of a moray eel," Cesar cracked.

"Meaning you had a rough night?"

"The bots never returned from the show last night."

"What the hell could have happened? The school is only two blocks away."

"They vanished. Hayes says he'll look into it, but I haven't heard a damn thing. The janitor says they were the last ones to leave the school. All seven of them wouldn't malfunction at once. Somebody must have grabbed them off the street."

"Ragers?"

"Perhaps." Cesar looked at the newbee. "Or it could have been a Cy-bot competitor, or maybe someone who wanted a houseful of servants . . . or the cops. In a way I hope it's the punks. The bots would end up crushed like beer cans, but at least we won't end up in jail."

"My dad's friends like to joke about organizing a robot demolition derby. Maybe they stole them." Tuuve grinned.

"Yeah, I can picture a gang of rich geezers roaming the streets at one in the morning, wearing their silk, monogrammed night shirts, looking to make the pinch."

"My old man wouldn't be caught dead without his silk on."

Cesar threw up his hands. "There's nothing we can do about it at this point. But we can fix the bot we have."

"Right." Tuuve gathered his tools for the procedure: synth-muscle stretcher, acid surface prep, artificial tendons, adhesives. "I'd like to remove the muscle, clean up the smashed chips, patch the leg casing, fix the knee joint, then realign the muscle fibers and insert the muscle. Make sense?"

Both men worked in silence. Cesar had looked forward to these moments of camaraderie to dig into the underling's mind. He was still not sure about Tuuve and his loyalties: it wouldn't hurt to get to know better what he was dealing with. He planned a little DJ trip for his new helper, but it would be necessary to loosen him up first.

"So Tuuve. Have I ever asked you why you became a Futurist?"

Tuuve wiped his forehead and sat up straight, like a schoolboy about to recite a lesson.

"I joined because the Futurists are transforming politics from an art of self-promotion into a true science." He paused as if remembering the next part of the lesson. "Someday South Florida will be a Robot Republic. We need robot administration, honest leaders free from ego. Under the Robot Republic, we can eradicate corruption. Robots will run the government with optimal integrity and efficiency."

"A-plus." Cesar grinned.

"Thanks!" Tuuve returned to removing debris from inside the robot's knee assembly.

The soft finger taps on the monitor and the short scrapping noises were all that could be heard for several minutes.

"Right. But what I was really asking was why you joined the Party. I mean you personally. How did you join?"

This time the newbee took his time responding.

"You know, my family is big in the Micro-Government Party. My parents are both prominent MGPers, or Micro-Brewers, as they like to call themselves, big supporters of the breakup of the USA, big fans of the Florida Republic. When I was a kid, my folks were always busy with some kind of political function. There were endless meetings at our house, people chatting it up all night long. Either that or mom and dad were off to some fundraiser. I went to Happy Limits Pre-School Camp. These people were obsessed with the word 'limited.' Everything good was called limited.

"But as I grew older there were a couple of incidents in school that hit me like a hurricane. One hot summer afternoon, my mom took the three of us kids to South Grade Private to register for the fall term. I believe it was a year or two after the the Florida MGP won a key election and privatized the public schools. I was eleven.

"The school had two entrances. On the left side, a banner read, 'Equal Opportunity Day.' Under it a long, slow-moving line of parents and kids had formed, mostly Jamaicans, Nigerians, Afghanis, waiting to get in. We marched past them through the door on the right, registered all three of us in five minutes, and marched back out. As we were leaving, a boy my age turned to his mother and asked, 'Can't we go in that other door like they did? I'm hot.' The mother answered, 'No, dear, we have to go through Equal Opportunity.'

"When I asked my mom about it, she got mad and explained how she had worked hard all her life and deserved special privileges. Yet I knew that those other moms scrubbed floors, worked in farm fields out in the hot sun, while my mom hosted tea-tastings for her Micro friends. You know who that kid was? Mark Witherspoon. His older brother is Charles Witherspoon, the head researcher at the Lab. In the fourth grade, Mark was one of my best friends. In fifth grade, he had to quit school and get a job."

"Witherspoon?" Cesar said with surprise. "Charley and I were tight all through school. The two of us virtually ran the Futurist Club at Lake Worth High."

"Charles was a Futurist way back then?"

"Oh, yeah. The whole family. His dad was a leader in the African-American community and one of the pioneer Futurists in Lake Worth. His chief aim in life was for his son to become a roboticist, as a way to help the chronic underclass. But the Witherspoons were not far above the poverty line themselves. Spoon was the smart one, so his dad kept him in school. All the other kids went to work illegally when they were twelve to help pay his tuition, his older sisters too."

"Yep, it really bothered me. While I sat in school, Mark stood at a table, up to his elbows in fish guts at the processing plant."

"Not exactly a fun job for a kid."

"It made me mad. I saw how unfair it was. My folks and their MGP friends wanted to make child labor legal, but I couldn't go along with that anymore. I quit wearing my dorky MGP Youth Pin and started wearing a Futurist arm band."

"I had one of those—yellow with a gold robot emblem," Cesar said. "They were cool."

"That's the one."

"So your joining had nothing to do with robots?"

"Not really. I wanted to see my friend get a fair break."

Tuuve kept on talking, revealing his background, getting more excited as he went along. "My dad is trying to revive granddad's firm, the Alliance Group. With other well-connected developers, he's dredging up the long-forgotten Archipelago Project, hugely upscale, villas and mansions attracting a whole new generation of Trumps, Kennedys, Flaglers to Palm Beach. They want to make it a playground for the rich and famous again.

With all the debris extracted from M Forrest's leg, Tuuve articulated the joints, ankle, knee, hip to be sure they were working correctly. "There's a bit of a stick in the knee movement."

Cesar got up from his chair, lifted the robot leg, flexed the knee a few times. "There's a flat spot in the joint alright, but we'll have to live with it. Anyway, what were you saying?"

"Talking about my dad. He's always hobnobbing with Palm Beachers, loves to rub shoulders with important people who own lots of stuff." Tuuve chuckled ironically.

"So how does your father feel about you being a Futurist?" Cesar asked, then added, without waiting for an answer to his first question. "Do you think he'd allow his workers to use their own Cy-bots on the job?"

"Well, he wasn't exactly enthusiastic when I joined. I keep telling him his developer buddies should back us on the Limitation Law revocation. Worker-bee bots could save him a bundle in construction costs. But he's been scared off by web flash reports about riots and workers vandalizing robots."

"Doesn't he understand how personal ownership changes all that?"

"Nope. I don't think he gets the importance of having workers benefit from—rather than compete with—robot workers." A look of disappointment showed in Tuuve's eyes.

It was time to dig a little deeper into the newbee's psyche. "I sometimes have my doubts about shadow ops. How about you?"

"No way!" The newbee's eyes widened with surprise. "We know people aren't ready to accept robot leaders, so we promote No Worker Left Behind: that's our public face. Meanwhile shadow ops works in the background to prepare people for bot leadership."

Cesar shook his head. Tuuve was on automatic again. Maybe a provocative question would get him out of his rut. "You consider No Worker Left Behind just a front?"

Tuuve cracked a smile. "Say, is this some kind of test? Hayes warned me about you."

"If you want your A, you'd better answer the question." Cesar chuckled.

"Well then, it's not a front—it's a step forward. Once robots become part of everyday life, people will become as comfortable with them as they are with radios. Eventually the average guy will see how much easier his life would be with a robot slave serving him hand and foot."

"Slave?" Cesar asked, in a slightly irritated tone.

"It's very appealing to own a slave. They're good for the ego. I master, you slave. They do what they're told. No questions, no back talk. What does it matter if we call them 'worker-bees,' 'beasts of burden' or 'slaves'? It's all the same."

"That's not exactly the most diplomatic way to phrase it."

"We advocate justice for people, not for machines. Reward each child with ownership of a robot when they graduate from school. Guarantee the kid and his robot slave a job and a guy's got a chance at the good life. All the benefits of slave labor without mistreating anybody. That's No Worker Left Behind."

"Why are you so stuck on calling it 'slavery'?"

"Geez!" The newbee glared. "That's what Hayes calls it. Do you always give Remp novices such a rough initiation?"

"Uh-huh, especially those who try to shock me by using hot-button terms like 'slave,'" Cesar winked smugly. "Just one more question. Explain leisure retraining."

Tuuve cocked his head and started reeling off the Party boilerplate: "Buddy bots create leisure," "Freedom is a twenty-hour work week," "Retraining is ga—"

Cesar groaned. "Please, in your own words."

"I'm big on retraining. It'll help us manage the upheaval caused by robots taking over so much of society's work. Hobbies, art, music, sports—all this has been lost while working sixty-plus hours every week. We've grown accustomed to our cage. Going from sixty to twenty hours a week working requires quite a readjustment. Leisure retaining helps us adjust to freedom."

Cesar bent close to his screen to hide his smirk. "Some of us enjoy being buried in our work," he said.

"People have the right to work themselves to death if they want to," the newbee retorted. "But you sure could use some retraining. You're wound up tighter than a spring."

Cesar's mind drifted to an often-repeated fantasy, a sunlit spot in the Caribbean. He liked to imagine himself rich enough to afford a team of robots who'd create for him a private island from ocean floor silt. A big open-windowed house captured and circulated the tropical breeze, bikini-clad babes lazed on the beach, his own deep-diving submarine was tied to a dock. He'd need no help enjoying a life of leisure. "Consider me retrained," he said.

Tuuve raised a stiff arm. "Viva la Robot Republic!"

Cesar didn't respond. There was just so much rah-rah he could take.

"I'm done with the knee," Tuuve said after a few minutes.

When Cesar inspected his work, the newbee looked worried.

"The joint reconstruction looks good," Cesar said. "M. Forrest will limp a bit, but it's better than I'd have thought possible."

Tuuve looked flattered. Maybe he couldn't please his dad, but he was able to please his difficult boss.

Cesar was pleased for another reason too. While working side by side and chatting, Tuuve had loosened up. Cesar felt he had a better read on him: the newbee had a weakness for flattery.

The readout panel flashed the progress of the data transfer. It still had a way to go; there was plenty of time to send the newbee on that little trip Cesar had been planning for him. With his enthusiasm for all things Futurist Party, Tuuve would probably enjoy every minute of it.

Cesar turned to the contented-looking greenhorn and gave him a big, fat, approving smile.

# TRIPPING

**"I**'ve got something to show you."

Cesar reached into his case and pulled out a soft, foldable helmet with the words "Drugless Joy" imprinted on the faceplate.

This, however, was much more than Papi's helmet. Papi's original design had been able to alter moods or induce an altered state of consciousness by mimicking drugs. A user could dial in cocaine, meth or LSD and get an experience indistinguishable from the real thing without any medical risks. Over time, the helmet's capacities expanded. A whole array of new sensations could be created, sensations previously unknown to human experience, new colors, new fragrances, the fancy of flying through four, five, even seven-dimensional space. Best of all, the supply of drugless-joy trips was inexhaustible. Nothing to buy. Just put the helmet on, and off you went to the bliss of your own choosing.

But Cesar saw more in the helmets than recreational potential. As a personal hobby, he continued to tinker with improvements on his own, on nights and weekends, just as Papi had done. Eventually he'd had a breakthrough when he discovered how to transmit video and audio images directly to the visual and aural centers of the brain, bypassing eyes and ears. At his urging, the Futurist Lab had invested time and money in perfecting the process and writing software. A well-programmed helmet could carry you away, mentally, to any distant time or place. By delivering just the right pulse to each neuron in the body, it created vivid experiences that could hardly be distinguished from authentic events.

The potential for constructive use, as well as for abuse, was vast. It could spin reality into exuberant dreams or, with equal ease, produce nightmares of bone-crushing intensity. The one thing that prevented the helmets from being used on unsuspecting victims was that it worked only at ranges of a few centimeters, surrounding and concentrating on the brain, and thus affected only the wearer.

Despite the innovations, however, there were still limits on what DJ helmets could do. For one thing, helmets could simulate traumatic experiences, but they could not remove or alter already preexisting feelings. Similar to the limitations on hypnotic suggestion, attempts to induce acts or attitudes that violated the wearer's moral values systematically failed. The Lab was actively working on techniques to transcend these limitations with the hope that, eventually, the human brain would be as easy to reprogram as a machine. Even within existing limits, the helmets were extremely useful devices for training newbees. Though Cesar sometimes found the implications of reprogramming minds troubling, in this and elsewhere in his work for the Party, he had managed to bury his doubts in the excitement of research and his certainty that the Party was working in the interests of his fellow Floridians, even of humanity at large.

Cesar punched a five-digit code into the keypad on the helmet's crown and then slid the soft, white helmet over Tuuve's head, pulling it down over his eyes and ears. Blackness engulfed Tuuve, with just the slightest touch of yellow and green fairy lights dancing against a dark infinity. "It's the latest model," Cesar said. "The sensations are so real, you'll think you've left your body."

With apprehension in his voice, Tuuve said, "You're sure this is a good idea? Don't send me on a bad trip, now."

"It's perfectly safe. I programmed it myself. These helmets are so advanced they can hardly be called helmets anymore."

Cesar flipped the "on" switch.

Tuuve felt a warm finger touch the crown of his scalp and begin scanning inside his skull, moving in a spiral, around and down toward the base of his neck. His breath quickened as a finger of energy swept over pleasure points, activating remembered sensations. A taste like mango liqueur, distilled to its sweetest essence, popped into a spot just above his left ear and was followed in quick succession by the vibrant green of young spring leaves, the thrilling sweetness of a first kiss, the soft comfort of a thick sweater on a chilly morning. Sensation followed sensation, played like piano keys, one after the other, creating sweet music. The feelings continued to intensify. His tongue prickled with the savory sting of cinnamon, then was soothed by something flatly delicious with an unrecognizable flavor. A cozy velvet blackness enveloped him. Momentary interludes of freezing cold heightened the pleasure of returning warmth. Every nerve tingled with unsullied sensation captured in pulse after pulse of joy, laughter, serenity, euphoria. Tuuve gasped.

After this sensory introduction to the helmet's capabilities, there was a black, motionless pause. A tiny image appeared, distant at first, enlarging until he could see a dozen figures of the Futurist Supreme Council seated on an imposing dais. The huge meeting hall was filled to capacity. Two figures stood on the platform, surveying the crowd. To the right of the podium stood Braadrik Hayes, wearing a broad smile.

Chairwoman Malcato was at the podium. "Remp is the future of the Futurist Party," she said. "Remp is our path to power."

The crowd roared approval. A tactile pleasure gripped Tuuve, at once exciting and consuming. A second wave of pleasure hit him stronger than the first. He was glad he was seated, otherwise the intensity of the sensation might have knocked his feet from under him. A third wave came as a tease, a pulse that slowly drew itself away, urging him to chase after it. Stillness followed, but he knew more waves were coming. The expectation made his skin tighten.

Malcato continued. "Our program calls for the election of 1,000 robots to local offices within its first twelve years. These machine candidates are a political strategist's dream. A robot never forgets a supporter's name, knows how to make people laugh and most importantly never goes off message. Each voter's highest concerns, their deepest motivations, knowledge of what fires them up and what turns them off, as well as dozens of other handles, are instantly accessible online from our voter profile database. An election campaign can tailor every word and every gesture to its audience, whether a single face or a crowd of faces. The key is to have a campaign manager who understands the subtleties of the process. Let me introduce the best: my most trusted advisor and technical expert on robotic elections, Braadrik Hayes."

At the mention of Hayes's name, the helmet sent a signal to the hypothalamus, and Tuuve's brain flooded with ecstasy-producing hormones. Tuuve had never known he had had such feelings for Hayes. And he hadn't had them before this moment.

Reina stepped back and Braadrik moved to the podium. In his typically blunt manner, he began without preliminaries. "Robo-Polling is a vast improvement over traditional techniques. Our advanced robots pass for human beings. They collect polling data discreetly while eliminating observer bias. They detect beliefs and biases that voters themselves are not aware of. Their eyes see in broad spectrums, from infrared to ultraviolet and beyond, and register responses that otherwise go unnoticed. The poll questions are posed by simply raising a topic in conversation or in a stump speech. The voter's response is ascertained from verbal and nonverbal reactions. A half-degree increase in facial skin temperature produced by tightening buccal muscles may reveal mental resistance to something just stated. A widening of the pupils or the slightest lean forward would indicate roused interest. A micro-nod can be interpreted as approval. All of this body language is recorded and sent to the Party's clandestine lab for Deep Scan Analysis, and results are digitized into a voter profile. From the database of profiles, we can choose the most voter-sensitive issues, identify the most effective tactics and thus engineer winning campaigns."

Braadrik's presentation was crisp and dispassionate. Nevertheless Tuuve felt a pulsating, energizing euphoria. Every sentence was punctuated with an exciting taste, neurologically induced by the pleasure helmet. The intensity rose and fell. Each lull provided a period of regeneration between emotional peaks and left him aching for more.

Reina returned to the podium. "Now I'd like to introduce two other important members of our team. Here is the brilliant Ms. Georgia Sugimoto, our incomparable head of research." A lanky, six-foot-two gazelle of a woman with straight black hair stepped up to the left of Hayes. She was the tallest woman Tuuve had ever seen and seemed embarrassed by the accolades. "Under her able leadership, the Cy-Bot Lab has done more to move robot technology forward than all the other robotics laboratories in the world combined." Georgia acknowledged the compliment with a half-hearted wave to the crowd and a coy blush.

"Last, but certainly not least, I'd like to introduce you to Mr. Cesar Komenen, head of Robotic Maintenance. He's our wizard of construction and repair. Without Komenen's herculean efforts, our army of mechanical men would soon grind to a halt." Cesar mounted the platform and stood on Hayes's left.

The three stood shoulder to shoulder and linked arms. Reina looked at the three and pronounced, "Behold! The Futurist Triumvirate. Gradually over time, with your hard work and the help of this able trio, our humanoids will run for higher and higher offices. The Florida National Congress will be targeted in 2136 and the presidency as soon as feasible thereafter."

The convention leapt to its feet and cheered wildly. The demonstration went on for several enthralled minutes. Malcato clapped encouragement, smiled, waved, basking in the moment. She allowed the crowd's enthusiasm to run its course before bringing the meeting to its climax. "Will you pledge to support your party? Will you labor to create a laborless future? Will you sacrifice leisure and comfort in order that we may build ultimate leisure and ultimate comfort? The task is yours. The time is now. Shall we become the Future?"

The multitude roared approval, shouting itself hoarse. Arms in the air, the convention chanted, "We-are-the-Fu-ture! We-are-the-Fu-ture!" The helmet did its work. An inexpressible sweetness welled up in Tuuve's chest. He felt the warm arms of the Party embrace him.

Beneath the helmet time was compressed. What seemed like hours in fact took only minutes. This program's run time had been under ninety seconds. Cesar kept an eye on Tuuve's body language and the helmet readouts. He needed to determine exactly when the emotional climax had been reached. Cesar lacked a robot's skill at reading body language, but some things were obvious even without infrared scanners. Tuuve was fully absorbed in his helmet experience, as if his mind had separated from his body. Suddenly, although sitting alone, separated by time and distance from the crowd, he tossed his head back and began clapping wildly.

Cesar pushed the Save button. At that peak moment, an unbreakable loyalty to the Party was seared into Tuuve's brain—if all went according to plan, that is. Cesar had seen more than one case where the attempt backfired; thereafter the subject had rebelled against taking orders of any sort and had to be removed from the program. Tuuve, however, was a more pliable subject than most.

Cesar sat in silence and watched as the newbee emerged from his helmet trip, looking for indications of an adverse reaction. He saw none. Tuuve was smiling ecstatically from ear to ear, and gradually his clapping slowed. Then the body under the helmet twitched twice and fell into a stupor. After the requisite five minutes, Cesar removed the helmet. Tuuve came to, blinked rapidly as he tried to re-orient himself to the real world, all the while repeatedly muttering, "Stupendous!"

Cesar wanted to clue him in on a couple of things while the newbee was still lapped in euphoria. "You realize the convention images you just saw were a CG enhancement, right? The reality was a small local meeting in a secret Malelucca location, shot before an audience that was more like twenty than 20,000. The entire Party's South Florida membership is a few hundred. So we dubbed in expanded crowd scenes."

"Amazing. Where you really part of the program?"

"Yep, I was new on staff at the time and still got along with Hayes. And Malcato laid it on thick with that triumvirate thing, but then again hype is what political conventions are made of. Did the CG fool you? The technology has come a long way. Could you tell that the crowd scenes, the roaring, the cheering, were CG effects? How could we have such a large gathering where Remp was discussed so openly? Too dangerous, too big a risk of leaks."

Cesar slapped Tuuve on the back. "Congratulations. Only a handful of people are allowed to experience the inner workings of the Party. You will, of course, as previously instructed, keep every scrap of this information under your hat."

"Until death." Tuuve's puppy face gleamed.

# BUDDY BOT

**C**esar walked into the white-tiled kitchen, kneeled to open the minibar fridge and took out a couple of Zephyr-brand beers. As yet Tuuve had shown no signs of reactionary doubt, but better to be safe than sorry; anyway, in the aftermath of an intensive brain entrainment session, alcohol and distraction were standard operating procedure. Over the course of the next hour or so, the impact of the helmet trip would soak into Tuuve's subconscious . . . that is, as long as his conscious mind didn't balk.

When he got the chance, Cesar would review the data logs to see how specific regions of Tuuve's brain had reacted to the treatment. The logs would reveal hints of resistance to reconditioning as well as lingering doubts Tuuve might have about Remp's more questionable methods. But the likelihood of resistance was small. Tuuve's mind showed all the signs of being unusually susceptible to suggestion.

Ironically, it wasn't the newbee but the veteran who was having pangs of conscience. Whenever Cesar had been assigned to an "entrainment," as they called it,

he'd had misgivings—those disembodied, raspy wings in
the pit of the stomach that would neither go down nor
settle down. Ever since the time, a few years back, when
a single helmet session turned a sarcastic loudmouth
into a spineless lap dog, his unease had been growing. The process felt perverse, like extracting a living,
vibrant mentality from a skull and replacing it with
a black-and-white caricature of itself. Was it right to
infuse Tuuve with prepackaged Party loyalty (not that,
already zealous to a fault, he seemed in any need of it) by
destroying his capacity to think for himself, to dissent?
The end result would be an automaton; mechanical,
obedient, effectively lobotomized. Was that the way to
create a better future? Why not simply get rid of human
brains and replace them with switches? Why not just get
rid of all human beings and replace them with robots?

This was an old internal debate, circular, endless,
unresolvable. *Hey, snap out of it*, he scolded himself.
Now was not the time to stew about the ugly underbelly
of party politics. Returning to the bedroom, he slapped
a cold beer into Tuuve's hand.

"There's plenty more."

"Cheers." Tuuve took a swig. "Thank our lucky
stars."

Cesar didn't especially like the sudsy ZH beer. "Just
our starry Zephyr luck, I guess."

"This reminds me," Tuuve said. "Should we onboot
your new bot now? The one in the kitchen."

"Anxious to play with my new toy?" Cesar grinned.

An old-fashioned kitty clock wagged its pendulum
tail on the wall above the kitchen sink. The worker-

bee stood frozen at the service island, dressed in chef's hat and apron, a bottle of rum in hand, silently offering them a drink. "Beer and booze, not a good combination." Tuuve took the bottle and set it on the countertop.

Cesar examined the bot, head to toe, looking for the hidden pilot pad. Probing the silvery skin, he brushed his fingertips over the chest, neck, arms. Eventually he located the pad under the synth-skin on the left palm and entered standard activation codes. The bot gave off a sudden, windy pop, like a belch, shuffled its feet, opened its mouth and in a slow, dull voice carefully enunciated,, "Cy-bot, Bot Buddy, activated July 15, 2130, 2:32 P.M."

"Scaazz, that flat monotone is annoying." Unlike some of his colleagues, Cesar was not amused by igno-rant-acting worker-bees. "Switch to inflected speech mode."

The dry voice droned. "Command not accepted. Initiation pending. Awaiting thumbprint and voice ID verification of Master." The bot popped and whis-tled several times, then said, "Name of Master: Cesar Komenen" and stopped.

A surprised look crossed Cesar's face. He glanced at Tuuve, who looked disappointed, then back at the robot. Amazingly, Hayes had registered the bot in Cesar's name and granted him Master status. This was a pleasant surprise. It meant that Cesar could take Buddy home and have it perform personal as well as job-related tasks. Such generosity seemed radically uncharacteris-tic. Cesar's suspicions were instantly aroused. What was Hayes up to? Maybe it was an attempt to spy on him.

Cesar promised himself to inspect the bot for Trojans as soon as he got the chance. In the meantime he'd assign it to Safe House security duty.

"Give it your data," Tuuve asked impatiently.

Cesar leaned into the bot's ear and entered his voice ID, then aligned his fingertips with five smooth indentations on the bot's palm. Buddy grabbed his wrists, and instantly Cesar felt a warm energy cloud engulf him, like a thousand steamy droplets covering his entire body. The robot hands slid slowly up his forearms, shoulders, neck. Long fingers cradled his scalp and dug into his hair. The sensations felt deliciously familiar, tactile, comforting, layered with the soothing emotions of a popular Helmet relaxation program called "Cleansing Rain." Cesar felt his knotted neck loosen. He didn't know such signals were possible without a helmet. This was no ordinary worker-bee. Buddy's hands had transcranial properties.

Suddenly, without warning, the easy, liquid sensation produced by the robot's hands turned edgy. Cesar stiffened. The metal hands crept down along the length of his skeleton, surveying his body from cranium to metatarsal and back again. On the second pass, the tingling intensified, focusing at the base of his skull. Cesar knew all the bonding scenarios well enough to recognize something strange was going on. The bot was making a complete electronic copy of his neural system, micro-mapping his pain and pleasure centers. He didn't like this one bit. What was Hayes up to?

Intent on interrupting the invasive scan, Cesar raised his arms, grasped the robot by both wrists and firmly removed the metallic fingers from his scalp.

Buddy readily complied. It rested its hands on its navel, making no attempt to restart the scan. In an overly singsong baritone it reported, "ID Cesar Komenen verified. Inflected speech mode initiated." Its eyes flashed, brightly.

"This buddy's programmed to be a tease." Cesar grinned nervously. "It's overplaying my instructions, it acts like it enjoys yanking my chain."

"Maybe Buddy's programmer liked smoking Jamaican weed," replied Tuuve.

"Or it's one of Sugi's humor experiments."

The bot smiled a goofy, exaggerated smile and immediately began to croon.

"Let's take a spin through our history.

America was perfect from its infancy,

Columbus sailed Old Glory to our country young,

Grateful Indians gave him gold and spoke the English Tongue.

Yo, ho, ho, they dug gold for free,

The Queen had the right to more money.

Jeff Davis was a captain, great upon the sea,

He sailed to Africa to set the Black Man free,

Instead they wanted beatings, to see stars and stripes,

So they swam to America to make handy wipes.

Yo, ho, ho, they picked cotton for free,

A planter's got the right to more, more money.

Now today I slave for peanuts, serve the man on bended knee,

Corporation is my boss to eternity.

My plate may be empty, my roof may leak,

But company profits just hit a new peak.

Yo, ho, ho, I work for free.

Shareholders' got the right to more, more, more money."

Tuuve laughed till he nearly cried.

"Not exactly the history I learned in school!"

Those lyrics embodied the spirit of his dad to a 't': money-hungry, insatiable, elitist, oblivious to the lives he'd crushed on his way to ever greater wealth. With the enthusiasm of a five-year-old, Tuuve marched around the kitchen, chanting, "Yo, ho, ho, I work for free. Shareholders' got the right to more, more, more, more, more, more money." He waved his arms, goose-stepped, carried on like a chimp in a zoo, thoroughly enjoying his one-man parade.

Cesar moved out of the way, annoyed by the new-bee's antics.

"Hey, calm down."

But Tuuve wasn't about to be bullied: he held his ground. Standing straight and tall, he recited in a shrill voice, back again on automatic: "The USA was born of one tax revolt and strangled itself to death in another! The history of America is the story of greedy abuse of workers, slavery, child labor, perpetual immigration to keep the labor pool flooded and wages low!"

"Hey, man, you sound like a robot. Can the canned speech, you're preaching to the choir."

But Tuuve was too revved up to wind down. "Yo, ho, ho! We'll never have real democracy until the poor have as much power as the rich, those greedy, power-hungry bastards."

"Hey, profit isn't all bad," Cesar said. "It gets people out of bed in the morning, gets them to work hard, lets them reap the rewards of their efforts."

"Yeah, and makes them hogs who believe fatter is better."

"Give me a system that channels selfishness into productivity instead of oppression. Give every worker a buddy bot, and the workers will benefit from cheap labor along with the capitalists."

Tuuve smiled. "Man, you're starting to sound like me. Robots will do the grunt work, and everybody'll be rich."

Taking its cue, the robot chimed in again. "Yo, ho, ho, I work for free. The boss has his right to more money."

Buddy repeated the refrain over and over in his affected new inflections. Cesar rolled his eyes. "We've got to do something about that voice." Grabbing the robot's data entry hand, Cesar began tapping in commands.

"Decrease inflection by twenty percent, Constrict larynx and reduce lip spread by ten percent."

"Yo-oo . . . ho-oo . . . ho . . ." the bot repeated with increasing flatness until Cesar was satisfied.

Cesar looked at Tuuve. "How does that sound?"

Tuuve laughed. "Yo-oo, ho, ho! I liked the previous setting just fine."

Buddy sang, "Yo, ho, ho! I work for free . . ."

"Deactivate music," Cesar ordered.

# LOOPY

E inalli's office sat at the southern end of a long, airy pavilion high above Cienfuegos Harbor. The room's open Bahamian windows looked out over lush, palm-covered mountains, speckled with red tile roofs and encircling the bay. The office space was exceptionally large and, like Einalli's head of unkempt white hair, in a state of perpetual disarray. Desk, cabinets and most of the floor were covered with data printouts, half-read research papers, piles of book pads ridden with silver-voiced sticky notes and a rubber-banded stack of photo portraits of the guru similar to the one that hung on Jewel's apartment wall. In the corner was a bin of empty coconut shells, dumped on its side, leaking sticky, white milk onto the adobe floor. Tiny sugar ants, crawling in a meandering line toward the milk, seemed thoroughly grateful.

On the office wall behind Einalli's desk hung two black-and-white posters side by side. One showed a middle-aged Einstein peering into a telescope at Yerkes Observatory. An apocryphal quote, which few read and fewer understood, stated, "Moments of time, past and future, do not line up like fence posts but spin, stretch and warp, dancing around each other like the interwoven melodies of a Bach fugue." The second poster showed a wizened Einalli—hair, sweater, smile, pose, lighting, as similar to Einstein's as the photographer's skill could conjure—peering into the crack of a cloven egg shell; the would-be genius parroting the master, with the quote, in this case genuine: "Moments of consciousness, past and future, fold and twist through seven dimensions like the curly hairs of Einsteinian curved space." Einalli was enthralled by the parallels.

The utopian communities of Cienfuegos, Cuba had long attracted unorthodox thinkers from around the world. It was here that Einalli established the Institute for the Observation of God late in his career. That was after his bitter falling out with the academic world, having struggled for more than a decade to build a career.

His appointment to a chair in the Department of Cognitive Science at Princeton came when he was only twenty-six years old, a prodigy. The university had encouraged him to pursue research in both natural and synthetic mental processes. At first, his work meandered through a stream of esoteric topics: loop logic, religious intuition, the biological basis for altered states. But it was Einalli's theorizing on how to generate artificial consciousness that ultimately led to his singular accomplishment: understanding how the human mind generates self-awareness.

It had long been known that physical dimensions of height, width and depth formed three-dimensional space and that time was a fourth dimension. According to Einalli, consciousness turned out to be a special kind of fold in the fabric of time. Like a ribbon, consciousness flowed out, twisted and looped back to its point of departure. Einalli proved mathematically that consciousness requires a folding of space-time so that two adjacent moments fuse into a single entity, a simultaneous existence of past and present.

As difficult as these concepts were, Einalli took great pains to explain them to lay audiences. When he visited schools, he'd show the kids how to make a moebius curve. "Take a narrow strip of paper," he would instruct the children during these talks, "and form a loop by attaching its ends. You get a simple curve. Separate the ends, give one side a half twist and reattach, and you get a moebius curve. Although the loop appears to have two surfaces, an inside and an outside, the two are actually one continuous surface. If you run your finger along the inside of the loop, the twist will lead your finger to the outside. Keep going, and once you have passed the twist a second time, your finger will be back on the inside."

And he would watch with satisfaction as the children followed his instructions using a paper strip and saw the loop's surprising properties for themselves.

Einalli's revolutionary discovery was that moebius-like twists in time create human consciousness. According to Einalli's theory, such twists were a logical necessity. Since ancient times, eastern thinkers had pointed out that self-awareness requires an Observer Self and an Observed Self, co-existing in the same moment. The only way two versions of the same person could exist at the same moment was through a time-loop. Self-awareness was the mind folding back through a twist in the fabric of time to a previous instant and observing itself. That insight was Dr. Einalli's great gift to the world, equivalent in his mind to Einstein's E = mc$^2$.

One of the most exciting implications of his theory was the possibility of harnessing these folds to slide back and forth between present and past moments. If Einalli could demonstrate this slippage in a tangible way, his theory, he was certain, would be accepted and his reputation in the scientific community assured. This became the basis of his Humpty Dumpty Experiment that later proved to have such a profound effect on his career.

But Einalli's gift was spurned, his theory greeted with skepticism, even derision. He was ridiculed as a clown, a pseudo-scientific crank and charlatan. At one conference, a sarcastic colleague had presented him with a long, hand-knitted Dr. Whenever scarf, a prop from the famous futuristic farce, emblazoned with the movie's title, "Chronoton Tales." Einalli had played along in good humor, wrapping the striped scarf around his neck and dragging its tail on the floor behind him for the remainder of the conference.

Things changed dramatically when the doctor succeeded in building his time chamber, forcing even his most diehard critics to drop their opposition. At the next annual conference, just one year after the "scarf incident," Einalli prepared his coup de grace. To a packed house, he showed off a newsprint headline that read *"Einalli's Loopy Theory: Truth or Farce?"* then invited an antagonist to set it afire and place the burning paper into a glass box. Hundreds witnessed the headline, brown and crinkle in the flames, unburn and then burn again. Thereafter, the experiment was quickly replicated throughout the world and the Time-Loop Theory of Consciousness became the new orthodoxy.

Within months, practical applications began to emerge. It was discovered that schizophrenia was often the result of disruptions in the foldings of time within individual consciousness, distorting a sufferer's perceptions of reality. When pharmaceutical treatments for schizophrenia were combined with exposure to dimensional shifting fields, people who had been severely impaired for years showed dramatic improvement.

Despite these successes, Einalli had never managed to earn the sincere respect of his academic colleagues. They showered him with vague, showy praises in public, yet their attitude was patronizing, even grudging, and they downplayed his contribution at every turn. Seldom did first-rate universities invite Einalli to speak, and his grant proposals were largely rejected. He was damned with faint praise, called "lucky," never heard what he yearned to hear: that he had been right. He consoled himself with the thought that he was simply too far ahead of his time. No doubt his unabashed self-promotion—which grew more fervent with his increasing frustration—was partly to blame.

During this bleak period of his career, one bright spot had been a young grad student named Reina Malcato. He hired her as a research assistant in the fall of 2102 to help him organize his sundry projects. She turned out to be a loyal confidante and ceaseless cheerleader. Whenever he received a rare favorable review in an academic journal, she would eagerly appear in his doorway, waving the printout, the first to celebrate every little success. Her support and fierce determination helped him through that dark period.

Worldwide fame eventually came to him as a result of the Humpty Dumpty Experiment, or HDE, as it came to be called. It was sheer dumb luck that the Nova Science Channel chose to webcast the demonstration in prime time. One of his students had been dating an intern at the channel. Somehow the big wigs got wind of it and decided to pick up what they thought would be a cute story about a wacky professor.

With cameras rolling, Dr. Einalli walked onstage at UC Berkeley, wearing a starched lab smock, his white hair even more chaotic than usual. He briefly lectured the university audience on time loops and the significance of the experiment they were about to witness. As souvenirs, he handed out small plastic models of moebius curves. Most inappropriately, considering the academic setting, the centerline of each curve was etched with a self-advertisement: "Einalli's Time Curve Theorem of Consciousness, Mind = $TC^5$. Both of me were there. September 9, 2104."

"Understand," he explained, "that consciousness entails being Observer and Observed, having two distinct existences that shadow each other across a micro-temporal gap."

After he finished his introductory remarks, Einalli strutted, like a carnival showman, into the small, windowed time chamber onstage, an old-fashioned cast iron skillet in one hand and a large goose egg in the other.

Over the chamber flashed a red neon arrow of time pointing to the right. With a magician's flourish, he threw several oversized levers to activate the machine. The device took precisely 6.86 seconds to warm up. During that brief interval, just before the time loop began, he cracked the egg and dropped both egg and shell, shattered into several pieces, into the skillet. The neon arrow flipped to point left, and a worldwide audience saw the broken egg reassemble itself in the skillet: the egg yolk and whites slipped back into the shell, the shell pieces came neatly back together and the splits were sealed up, resulting in a smooth, round, white egg. Einalli had proved to the world that, albeit briefly, time could be made to run backward. His popular reputation soared into the stratosphere.

Thereafter, HDEs (the meaning of which eventually expanded to include all experiments involving brief time reversals) became a topic of intense discussion and study at most major universities. Respectable scholars even began to speculate about the possibilities of time travel for human beings. Einalli predicted that commercial time machines would be on the market within a few years. But those claims proved ill-founded. Studies showed there were tight constraints on how far back in time one could go. Normal, everyday consciousness utilized a time loop of a fraction of a nanosecond. With expensive equipment and terawatts of energy, Einalli's time chamber could achieve a backloop of pi, or just over 3.14, seconds. Under ideal conditions and access to infinite energy resources, the maximum temporal displacement was calculated at pi squared, or less than ten, seconds. He was disappointed, but his discovery conclusively proved that time travel beyond that point into the past, and at any point into the future, was impossible. Unlike the protagonist in H.G. Wells' novel, no one would be riding a time machine into the distant future.

Einalli's second disappointment followed on the heels of the first. His theorem left a major question unanswered: Why did HDE fail when automated or performed by remote control? For some reason, the close proximity of a living being—human or animal—was necessary for the time chamber to function. This dilemma came to be called Einalli's Paradox. Was a time loop required to produce consciousness, or was consciousness required to produce a time loop? Wherever this topic was broached the-chicken-or-egg jokes were not far behind.

While attempting to resolve the paradox, Einalli made an absolute fool of himself. At a conference in Miami, he proclaimed to the world that he had solved the problem. Interlaced memory was the key. Once the number of cross-connections between memory specks was increased to equal the number of synapses in the human brain, consciousness resulted. An enhanced robot with an exabyte ($10^{18}$) of cross-links had effectively catalyzed the HDE process just as well as organic memory.

In the months that followed, scientists from around the world announced that their repeated efforts to replicate Einalli's results had failed. Einalli checked and double-checked his results with uniform success. He could not imagine why others were having a problem. In his lab, a broken HDE egg reassembled itself in the hands of enhanced robots as well as humans. To answer the growing chorus of critics, he promised a dramatic demonstration. The plan was to have a specially designed humanoid robot perform an HDE live on the Nova Science Channel.

After months of anticipation, the critical moment arrived. With the entire world watching the live webcast, the robot walked on stage, dressed in Einalli's white lab coat, its metallic face glowing under the stage lights like a polished mirror, and attempted to re-enact the HDE. But this time, time failed to loop. The cracked egg stayed cracked. The demonstration was an abysmal failure.

Panic ensued in Einalli's lab. Upon investigation, it was learned that, during previous tests, a family of mice had made a nest under the floor of the time chamber. The mere presence of mice brains inside the chamber had apparently produced enough consciousness for the HDE to work. While cleaning the chamber in preparation for the webcast, an assistant had removed the mice. Einalli cursed the confluence of coincidences that caused him so much embarrassment and ridicule. The demonstration had flopped . . . due to mice! Einalli's academic credibility, never very secure, was now shattered beyond repair.

Tempted by his celebrity, and disappointed with his research prospects, Einalli had become increasingly hungry for publicity, granting media interviews, re-enacting HDEs for large crowds, becoming more of a showman than an academic, more magician than scientist. It wasn't long before he resigned his chair at the university to travel the world in an attempt to recapture a rapidly disappearing sense of heroic accomplishment. The loneliness of life on the road led to a series of destructive addictions. Escapist pharmaceuticals became his constant companions. His life went into a downward spiral that threatened to rob him of the last vestiges of hope.

Ironically, the time chamber proved both his nemesis and his savior. While performing re-enactments, Einalli discovered that his problem-solving skills were enhanced, especially during the few seconds that time's arrow ran backwards. If he entered the time chamber with a specific problem in mind, he often emerged with a solution.

He began experimenting on himself, subjecting his mind each day to hundreds of nanosecond-long time slips. Then, during one such session, it happened—the event he would call, in the future, his conversion.

Just minutes before a demonstration at Career Day at St. Ann's High School in West Palm Beach, Florida, he sat in the time chamber with the stage curtains drawn, testing his much-traveled, battered equipment. Just at the moment when the yoke was hopping back into its shell, a local Catholic priest named Father Muro knocked at the open chamber door. Einalli turned and saw, in a beatific flash, the priest blossom into the Eternal Elijah, standing in his horse-drawn chariot, robed in light, a dry, dusty desert wind swirling around him. The apparition said, "Seek Me in Sinai." As quickly as it had burst open, the apparition had dwindled back again to the priest, standing in the doorway with a puzzled look at the ecstatic scientist.

From that moment, Einalli became convinced that the world's mystics had tapped into a time-loop phenomenon. His own encounter exploited theories of high-energy physics and high-tech gadgetry, but perhaps mystics had learned to access loops using the mind alone. The St. Ann's demonstration proved to be his last and effectively ended his career as a traveling magician. He abandoned his former life, moved to Egypt and joined the Kabalistic Hermit Cloister in the wilderness of Sinai, taking with him few possessions, one of them his time chamber.

The subsequent years were filled with mystical study. Frequent HDE sessions continued to sharpen his mental focus. Out of sight of a contemptuous world, Einalli mellowed. He came to understand his own foibles, his obsessive sense of his own importance, his depression over research failures, his desperate attempts at fame; even his eccentricities had been ego-driven. For the first time he learned to genuinely laugh at himself. Out of sight of the world, his world view expanded. He became a universalist, seeing the world as a unified whole. To the Jewish mysticism of his Kabalistic studies, he added Christian love, Buddhist compassion, Taoist detachment. He learned to enjoy simple food and took long treks in nature. His cloister companions marveled at the earnestness his transformation.

The self-acknowledged flaw in Einalli's personal Nirvana was his obsession with Reina Malcato. Einalli he held onto this portion of his past like a hungry boa constrictor. He read and reread Dr. Malcato's papers. A candle and her photo were the only objects on his nightstand. During his days at Princeton, Reina had been one of his star pupils. She had gone on to a brilliant career in academia by applying an innovative macrocalculus of loop-space to political science. As she entered midlife, like so many other scholars, Malcato left the university for a second career in the "real" world.

Einalli tracked Reina's rise in the Futurist Party with fanatical pride, worshipping in her the dream of his unfulfilled aspirations. In the solitude of his cell, he would lay awake at night, the desert wind howling through the stark craggy landscape, and imagine himself back at the university again, working on the challenges of consciousness in robots. This he wanted, not for himself, but as a gift to lay unselfishly at humanity's feet. Yet, for all the progress in mimicking human behavior, robots remained machines, non-sentient automatons, pure and simple.

In the depth of his soul, Einalli believed that robots could become conscious beings with an awareness of their own existence. The potential was there, if only interlaced memory and time-loop mechanics could be rightly aligned. Einalli had forsaken that investigation, but Reina was his surrogate, now the head of one of the most accomplished robotics labs in the world. He prayed incessantly for her to succeed where he had failed.

For ten years, Einalli's only statements to the outside world were the yearly release of a new book. In sync with his growing monkly diffidence, the series of titles gradually shed their grandiosity: *Create Your Own*

*Universe and Move In—In Just Seven Days* was followed by *Outing Your Inner Golden Calf*, followed by *Noiseless Living*.

Einalli's re-emergence from the wilderness accompanied the unveiling of a new time-loop–generating machine that he claimed could put the soul in contact with God in the Seventh Dimension. He returned to the lecture circuit, renewed old academic contacts, subjected his theories to scientific scrutiny. But in repeated tests on impartial subjects his new machine failed to produce measurable mental or spiritual effects. The treatments worked only for those devotees who "had faith." With the controversies of HDE still indelibly attached to his reputation, the public scoffed that Einalli was the cracked egg needing a visit to his time chamber. Notwithstanding these new failures, Einalli maintained a modest demeanor.

Perhaps it was his very failures that attracted adherents. Remnants of Pure Spirit Universalist, Mystic Consciousness and Seventh-Day Meditation movements began to study his books. Eventually he gained a scattered, devoted following. A loose network of Einalli-inspired Cloister Temples spontaneously arose, without plan or ambition. After another five years, the professor-turned-guru felt respected once again, at least as long as he remained behind Cloister walls.

### END OF FILE LIST - INSERT NEW DISK

## NARRATIVE PAUSE 006

BLAIN SLIPPED into Jurat's office. The room was dark. The only light in the room came from an image of a robed guru displayed on the wall-sized monitor. Jurat's body was slumped over, snoring. Rather than disturb him, Blain quietly slipped four disks onto the desk and tiptoed out of the room.

## BEGIN FILE 019, SOURCE RAM:

# QUEEN OF CLUBS

Reina Malcato's shoulder bag landed on the steel lab table with a thud. A tall, ebony-skinned man in a white, floor-length lab coat continued to sleep, stretched out on a makeshift cot, breathing noisily. Formaldehyde or acetone or some similar liquid dripped through a maze of glass tubes, flasks and beakers, filling the lab with its pungent smell. Malcato chided herself for not being more knowledgeable in organic chemistry. A second thud failed to get the man's attention. *Fine! Ignore me*, she thought. *It just makes my job easier.*

She opened the bag. The L-3 inside sprang to life. From its flat underside, it sprouted six short, padded feet, crawled cautiously out of the bag, surveyed its new environs, bobbed up and down twice as if saying farewell to Malcato, and disappeared beneath the shadowy underside of the table. Impatiently, she drummed her red fingernails on the metal surface and was about to begin shaking the sleeping man when he woke with a start.

"Oh . . . Dr. Malcato! I must have drifted off. Optima woke me at home, said she needed my help on an urgent project for Hayes." He sat up on the edge of the cot and stretched. "We worked straight through till dawn, didn't even stop to eat—man, I'm hungry. What time is it now?"

Malcato looked unimpressed as if such long hours were to be expected and catnapping on the job an inexcusable luxury. "It's four in the afternoon."

"Optima left around noon. I must have been sleeping—what, three, four hours?"

He tossed the blanket and pillow underneath the cot, then gestured toward a low-backed chair in the opposite corner of the room. "Have a seat," he said.

With three abrupt strides, she reached the chair, rolled it toward the cot and straddled it backwards, scrutinizing his unshaven face. She came straight to the point. "I wouldn't be here unless there was an emergency."

"Same as Hayes's? The injured robo-candidate? I think it's been taken care of. Optima and I worked out the specs for a replacement MOP. She left here to fabricate and deliver the board." He rubbed his eyes, suppressing a yawn.

Malcato glared at him. "Why weren't you at the school? A Rager got into the show and damaged one of our best bots. Your job is to control the crowd. Your so-called Puppet Master gadget failed, didn't *master* a thing. You weren't even there to monitor the show."

Six petite spider monkeys crept across the room and sat in a perfect line on the floor directly in front of her. The largest scampered over and rubbed the top of its head against her leg.

The young neurologist's name was Charley Witherspoon. He'd arrived at Futurist Lab four years ago to considerable fanfare and with high expectations.

"With all due respect, let me I point out that Hayes didn't want me there. He said he could handle it."

Reina pressed. "You should have insisted. No one knows the brain-to-chip interface like you do."

Witherspoon took the flattery with a grain of salt. "Yeah, seeing it was my invention." It had been a major coup for the Lab: the interface allowed for the transfer of memory data back and forth between organic brains and silicon chips. Only the Futurist Lab possessed Witherspoon's technology; the breakthrough led to the Lab's unique capacity to build Puppet Masters and human-duplicate robots. "When it comes to B2C," Malcato said, dismissively, "Hayes doesn't know a knee from a noodle."

Witherspoon gave a slight nod and said with light mockery, "But he's good at slapping holographic stickers on people's shirts."

"Sarcasm won't get you off the hook this time, Charles. It was your responsibility to be at the school."

"Oh." His eyes narrowed. Dr. Malcato only called him Charles when she was genuinely displeased with him. "I thought my job was to design robot hardware. I'm working odd hours to fix problems caused by accidents out of my control. Fine. And I'm even willing to put up with a certain lack of appreciation for my contributions around here. You didn't like the industry-standard VMP." His voice grew louder. "I gave you more options. I gave you the MOP. Fine. I've done whatever you asked, and I'll continue to. But if you want me to help out on the campaign trail, you and Hayes had better get on the same damn page."

"Please lower your voice." Malcato aimed an index finger at the open door. "Most of the staff doesn't know about the MOP."

He smiled with a half-hearted apology, got up from the cot, brushed the wrinkles from his slacks and rolled a desk chair up to hers.

"Okay, then" she went on. "Past accomplishments notwithstanding, our current need is to protect our candidate from attack. We don't want to surround him with a brutal-looking security force. Your Puppet Master was supposed to project a mental field over the crowd to make an attack psychologically impossible."

Witherspoon sighed. "I know. We've been over this before. The Puppet Master works on most people but not the hardcore cases. What makes you think 100% effectiveness is even possible?" He paused, open eyed, silently asking her to be reasonable.

"Look here," she demanded. "The mind is just a collection of neurons. Destroy the old pattern, implant a new pattern. There's nothing to stop you from reprogramming your average robo-phobic personality, even your hostile Rager, just as easily as we reprogram a robot."

"It's not that easy. If it were, everybody would be doing it." In fact, Witherspoon knew perfectly well that the problem was solvable; he even had the solution in sight. But he wanted Malcato first to acknowledge the near-miracles he was continually asked to perform. He wanted her to quit treating him like a flunky, show him some respect, treat him like he knew how to do his job.

Reina leaned forward and thrust her chest at him. "Are you telling me you're not up to the job?"

*She's so arrogant,* Witherspoon thought as he prepared to spring his surprise. "Look. The hitch is like the restrictions on what a hypnotized person will do. When it comes to lifelong behavioral patterns, and especially where deep convictions are involved, we've discovered that the brain auto-reverses any attempt at reprogramming."

"Auto-reverses? I find that hard to believe," casting him an impatient look.

Witherspoon shrugged. "This is a bit complicated. Are you sure you want to get into it now?"

"Just get on with it," she said with a touch of exasperation, crossing her long legs and settling back in her chair.

Witherspoon spoke slowly. "It's a matter of figuring out, step by little step, how thoughts and actions sync. When we program a robot to pick up a hammer, the robot is told to stretch out its arm, grasp the handle, lift the hammer, and so on. But what happens if we send that same instruction to an adult human brain?"

He leaned forward in his chair to emphasize his point. "There we get into a complex self-monitoring process. If the person has been taught from childhood not to steal, as most of us have, the brain asks, 'Do I own this hammer?' If the answer is yes, the person goes on to pick up the hammer. If not, the question follows, 'Who does own this hammer?' If it belongs to someone who has not granted permission, the hammer will not be picked up."

Malcato tossed her hair with irritation. "Yes, I know about self-monitoring, conscience and all that, but it's your job to find a solution to breaking it. We need it done, and done soon."

Trying hard to withhold a sneer, Witherspoon wiped his mouth. He'd heard the Reina Rant too many times before. *Soon, quick, hurry, hurry.* It was her way of motivating underlings to greater productivity, regardless of any real urgency. Again he ignored her impatience and pressed ahead with his methodical explanation. "While investigating the self-monitoring process, we discovered something that was a complete shock. The brain anticipated our attempts to re-map central personality traits, and especially morality-based behaviors, then began duplicating and hiding multiple copies of the brain patterns before we even began to destroy them."

Malcato's eyes widened. "How could that be?"

"There's only one possible explanation. Time loop."

"You mean an Einalli time loop generates these blockages?"

"According to his theory, essential traits of each personality are etched into a non-temporal dimension, on the opposite side of the time loop, what some call the 'soul,' where they become permanent, impossible to erase."

"I knew the professor in grad school," she interjected, a wistful expression briefly troubling her eyes as she flashed on her days of youthful adoration of the eccentric scientist. "You're not telling me anything I don't know."

"Then you know these memories are said to survive the destruction of the corresponding memory cells, even destruction of the body. I've never believed in an afterlife myself, but could it be pure coincidence that these essentials that Einalli calls immortal are the same brain patterns we can't destroy?" Witherspoon smiled.

"You were hired explicitly to solve the reprogramming problem. You're spending too much time on hocus-pocus theorizing. I was very fond Einalli. He was my mentor. But he's a goofball."

"Madam Chair, we're not off track at all. Now that we've defined the problem," Witherspoon said, "the solution should be obvious."

Reina raised her thin, tattooed eyebrows. "How so?"

"Sever the link between the time loop and the brain. In such a state the person becomes a sort of automaton walking through life without awareness. Then we can reprogram minds without blocks of any kind."

"You believe this is possible?"

He pointed toward the maze of glass tubes on the lab table. "Do you see the pink liquid in those flasks? The molecules are encoded in two time-dimensions. The fumes go up a person's nostrils and are directly absorbed by the brain. They affect both sides of a time loop, sets them out of phase. The immortal side of the time loop can't talk to the mortal side."

Malcato leaned forward, intent on following Witherspoon's explanation closely.

"In other words," he continued, "the conscience is neutralized so there is nothing to stand in the way of the subject committing the most heinous crime." He grinned with a look of profound self-satisfaction. "I call it the Pink."

For the first time in the conversation, a smile emerged on Reina's face.

"Spoon, that's beautiful! And what an irony you found the solution in Einalli's crazy theories."

*She called me Spoon!* Witherspoon thought. *Wonders never cease.*

"Actually I've been collaborating with his people. There are some pretty sharp psycho-chemists on his staff. With their help, I've made amazing progress."

Malcato looked at him suspiciously.

"You didn't tell them what it was *for*, did you?"

"Of course not." He gave her a shocked look. "I told them I needed a better way to control my lab monkeys."

Two monkeys ran across the floor screeching, one chasing the other. Spoon wheeled his chair over to his desk, reached into an upper drawer and pulled out a bag of peanuts, then held one out to the monkeys without interrupting his explanation. "After I treated these little guys, their behavior changed immediately. I thought they'd turn out dull and stupid, but instead they're hyperactive, chatter constantly. Most important, they're incredibly easy to train."

Spoon drew a circle in the air with his index finger. Both monkeys did a full flip, landing on their feet. Each time he repeated the motion, they turned a flip. "The other day," he recounted, "they did this over a hundred times until they were exhausted, falling on their faces, actually hurting themselves. But even then they didn't stop trying. How's that for obedience?"

Reina giggled with glee. "Why haven't you told me about this before, Witherspoon? How long have you been sitting on this?"

A third monkey came up and nudged Spoon's hand, requesting a peanut. "Not long. I'll be ready to test the Pink on human subjects any day now."

"Excellent. I need agents who obey without question. We can't have brains walking about, freely disregarding orders to lie, cheat, steal, or kill, now, can we?"

Her smile, which had hitherto, in Witherspoon's experience, been disdainful and cold now turned positively malevolent.

He gave her a steady look. There was a glint in her eyes—a sharp, sadistic, triumphant look he had never seen before. It came and went in a flash, but he was certain he had seen it. The woman had always made him uneasy: she was brilliant, manipulative, a little uncanny. And now, for the first time he felt he had truly seen her— seen the real Dr. Reina Malcato. Not just his demanding, willful, difficult, incredibly sexy boss. But something else.

She wasn't joking. No, Reina Malcato was not joking at all.

He also made a decision in that moment, a decision that would affect the rest of his career, if not his life. Under no circumstances would he give this woman exclusive control of his discovery. Yet what could he do? She had ordered it from him—there was little he could do but play along. He forced a laugh.

Malcato stood to go. "I have a request. I'd like you to zing over to the Safe House and speak with Cesar about last night's disaster. I need to know what went wrong and have it cleaned up before the next show."

Witherspoon looked at the time. It was 5 P.M. He was still exhausted from the all-nighter and needed more sleep. The woman was relentless. "Okay, sure," he said with pursed lips.

"And one more thing, I'll expect a status report on your Pink vapor first thing in the morning. And I want the formula." Malcato waited for his affirming nod. He didn't move, just stared seriously at her.

"I want that formula," she flushed, "no ifs, ands or butts."

Slowly he shook his head.

"Are you telling me 'no'?" she flared, flushing red with fury. "I'll have it by tomorrow, sir, or you will never work in your field again."

Her reaction took Witherspoon by surprise. Malcato was not one to make idle threats. He felt his blood run cold: what was this woman capable of? He seemed to back pedal. "What I mean," he explained, "is that there's no formula to give. The secret is in the time-dimensional processing. It's tricky, and the process doesn't work every time. In fact, it only works about five percent of the time. I need to refine and routinize the technique."

Her look flamed with contempt. He was lying through his teeth. The egomaniac thought he could keep his discovery to himself. But right now there was nothing she could do but play for time. "Okay," she said, "but let's make one thing perfectly clear. Don't ever tell me 'no.' For now, please do what you can to get Komenen on track."

"Right."

He was keenly aware he had just dodged a bullet.

The click of her heels reverberated down the narrow hallway as she returned to her office. She closed the door and fumed. If she could just get her hands around his long, lean throat—but more importantly, she needed the formula. It was the perfect weapon. Optima would help her make the stuff. Then she'd deal with her enemies, of which she had many, both in and outside the Party. Beginning, naturally, with the inventor of the stuff. How sweet to make him the first human victim. Spoon! Her lip arched with disdain.

She was pleased with the way she'd handled him. She'd been appropriately irritable, demanding, flatteringly interested and then surprised when he told her about the Pink. He had such an ego, he had no idea she'd been watching, crouched like a cat ready to pounce on an unsuspecting mouse. What a fool! Typical male: there was nothing like a bit of tail-swishing bitchiness to blind them. Optima had already given her a head's up about the vapor of slaves. On two previous occasions, they'd even sneaked into Witherspoon's room, after hours, careful not to stir up the ever-chattering monkeys, and "borrowed" some ready-mixed Pink. Unfortunately, the first test went badly when a bright, young operative named Tuuve D'Camp accidentally got a whiff of the stuff and turned into a silly, manic child. Good thing he hadn't breathed in more. At least he was still employable.

Her second round of experiments proved more encouraging. Thanks to Optima, she'd successfully snagged four Pinkee converts with no Tuuve-like casualties. Convinced of the power of the Pink, she now desperately wanted full control.

Dropping into her chair, she flipped on the L-3 channel of her desktop computer and tuned into the signal of the newly placed spybot. Via her monitor, Malcato watched Witherspoon measure out colored fluids into a set of clear glass bottles. With a doubled latex band, he strapped together a bottle of red, another of white, and a small bottle of indigo. The L-3 images were crystal clear. The digital readouts were easy to make out, showing the quantities of each. She jotted them down on her z-pad, double-checking for accuracy. Her alarm grew as he took not just one, but five sets of bottles, using up the supply.

Witherspoon took out a key and, kneeling, opened a lower cabinet. From the back, he extracted a softball-sized device; heavy, requiring both hands to lift.

He set the load into his briefcase, added the strapped bottles, closed the latch and walked out of the room. Although the door to his section of the Lab was usually kept open, he softly closed it behind him. Unseen by the L-3, Charley Witherspoon quietly slipped down the five flights of stairs and out into the evening air.

Malcato turned off her monitor and paced the dark room. Her fist slammed against the wall. The sleazeball had taken every Pink-related thing with him. He wouldn't get away with this. She opened a desk drawer, took out a pack of cigarettes, lit one and stared out the window, half blind with vexation. Below, in the Lab's parking lot, she saw Witherspoon, carrying a briefcase crammed with *her* precious fluid, get into his car and start the engine. She silently cursed him plotting her next move, the tip of her cigarette glowing as she took a long drag, then exhaled angrily. Slowly, her fingernails scratched at the window pane, like a frustrated cat, determined to outsmart the getaway mouse next time. "What a tasty morsel you'll be," she hissed as his car drove out the lot.

# YOUNG AMBITION'S LADDER

//**T**ell Mr. D'Camp we've got a nice surprise for him," Tony instructed the security guard at the entry gate of Surfside Manor. The guard stuck his head through the limo window to look the two guys over— shaggy hair, faded T-shirt, slept-in trousers—and shook his head. He was reluctant to disturb the boss for these punks, but relented when Tony insisted D'Camp knew how urgent the matter was.

"Wait here," the guard said curtly.

The house, a monolith only a few decades old, cast an elongated shadow in the late afternoon sun. Built in typical tropical-colonial style, the square main house was wrapped with broad balconies on all three floors. The north and south wings, equally tall, connected to the main building by roofed, open-air colonnades. White-railed widow's walks topped the three matching mansards. The axis of the structure was aligned parallel to the Intracoastal to create broad views of the waterfront.

After an interminable ten minutes, the senior D'Camp, wearing a dripping bathing suit and a loosely tied robe, ambled down the driveway, making little effort to suppress his irritation. He was taller than his son Tuuve, with a full head of neatly cut, white hair. He looked thoroughly annoyed.

"My grandkids are visiting. What the blazes do you want??"

"*I've* got something to show *you*, Mr. D'Camp," Tony said as he got out of the car.

"*We,*" Tex, sitting in the passenger seat eating pork rinds, reminded the over-enthusiastic Tony.

Tony grinned, then made D'Camp stand facing the limo's rear door before opening it with a flourish, revealing the floorboard and seats covered with wrecked robot body parts. It was difficult to tell how many robots had been demolished, but whatever the number, it looked impressive. Tony smiled from ear to ear, but D'Camp did not seem amused.

"What kind of a zonked-out fool *are* you? Are you drunk? Or just high on spikeweed?" D'Camp roared. "I told you to disrupt the robot show, not ransack it like a bunch of vandals! What in the name of Zeta happened at the school? And where in the world did you get this vehicle?"

Tony stood stuttering. "Uh, she . . . she . . . she . . ."

It took some time, and more than one round of oaths from D'Camp, but he finally pulled the full story from the shaken kid.

"So you stood out in an open, arc-lit parking lot, a camera on every lamp post, the whole world watching, busted up seven robots, stuck them into your very own, freshly stolen limousine and drove off without a care in the world. Didn't you think anybody might miss them?

Didn't you think that anyone would try to find them? Have you never heard of *locator chips?*"

After each question, Tony grew more and more sub-dued. "Sorry, boss," he said, in a quiet voice. "I thought you hated robots."

"Of course I hate robots. Almost as much as I hate idiots! You're out of your mind if you think I'm going to pay you now."

At the mention of not getting the money, Tex stepped out of the car, pork rinds spilling from his lap. He stood beside Tony and glared above his frilly shirt. "You gonna stiff us, Mr. D'Camp—me, Tony and our two buddies who was in on the deal? You think a haul like this comes along every day?"

D'Camp scowled so as not to break into laughter at the sight of these two losers. He thumped Tony on the chest with his index finger. "Did you at least disconnect the locator chips?"

With unusual slowness it dawned on the young Rager: the police would be able to track the damaged bots everywhere they went, including here, D'Camp's home.

He looked at Tex. Tex looked at him.

In a whirlwind of action, impressive even by D'Camp's standards, they climbed into the limo, combed through the wreckage, opened the back of each robot skull, pried out the chips, then smashed them on the driveway cement until they were powder. Tomato's platter-head took the longest. The Ragers were still freaked out, reluctant to touch it; being smashed, it took twice as long to open as the others.

In less than a quarter of an hour they were done. "So much for the police," Tony said to D'Camp with a satisfied shrug, panting lightly from the effort.

The older man peered at him skeptically. "How can you be so sure they haven't been tracked?"

"Only three of them bots are legal. The others weren't even registered; no locator chips. And believe me, these Futurists are up to all kinds of undercover, sneaky, illegal stuff. They ain't gonna call no police."

"And you're so sure, you're willing to bet my reputation on it."

Tony knew he had seriously messed up, but he liked working for D'Camp. The money was good, and the work was one thrill after another. As long as he got paid. And this was not likely to happen if either he or D'Camp ended up in jail. "Okay, okay, you're right." Tony put on his meek, apologetic look. "Just tell me what to do."

"Yes, but will you do exactly what I tell you? No more null-brained foolish stunts?"

It was now time to be contrite, so Tony looked contrite.

D'Camp glared at the two of them, then studied the ground. "Let me think."

Tex had taken as much the abuse as he could stand. He clenched both fists behind his back, ready to take a swing at the boss. Tony gestured with his eyes, motioning his partner to take it easy.

"Here's what you do," said D'Camp, looking up. "Bring this mess over to the Futurist Lab. Then go in and confess. I'll get you a transmitting camera to insert in one of the damaged heads."

Tony looked dumbfounded for a moment, then brightened.

"Oh, I get it. You're still out to lasso the bot fix-it man. When they send the bots to him for repairs, you'll get him."

"My purpose is my affair. Just do as I say. All right?"

Tex broke in. "But—I already know where that guy hangs out."

"You do?" D'Camp, for the first time, turned his full attention to the flamboyantly dressed Texan.

"There's this place over on M Street, looks like a regular house. These Futurist dudes come and go at all hours, day and night. They think it's a big secret, but I was sharp enough to follow 'em there—more than once," Tex boasted.

"Then take the limo there and make your confession. And get a good look inside if you can. See if my boy's there."

Tony shook his head. "I don't know about all this, Mr. D'Camp. You Micro-Government guys took away our juvenile protections, remember? They'll skewer me."

"Don't get fresh now. You should never have brought those busted up bots here. The last thing I need is the police coming around, asking questions. Turn yourself in now and there will be no investigation, understand?" He thought, *And it'll take the heat off me.*

"Uh, yeah . . . but . . ."

"Don't worry, I'll make it worth your while. Just say that you and your friends got a little carried away after the she-bot enticed you and then didn't put out. Say you're real sorry and don't want any more trouble. Ask them not to involve the police. Say you'll never do it again. Cry, sob, moan, put on a good show. Say you'll disband the local Rager gang permanently if they give you a break. If you pull it off and the police don't implicate me, I'll buy you the latest model Habi-Van and pay you the 5,000 credits over and above the 3,000 I promised." D'Camp gave each of them a conciliatory look. "How does that sound?"

Tony squinted as if he just thought of something.

"And what if the Futurists want me to pay for the bots I destroyed, at least the legal ones?"

"Don't worry your pretty little head about that. I'll cover you as long as you keep my name out of it."

Tony's face pruned with thought.

"Give me the 5,000 now," he said craftily, "and I'll do it."

"Listen closely. I'll give you a thousand now, and a thousand when the job is done." D'Camp's cheeks hollowed like an empty bag of blood. "But if you double-cross me, or even think of double-crossing me, you will be shark bait before the next sunrise." D'Camp then assumed a grandfatherly manner. "Boys, are we clear on that?"

Tony nodded.

"Good. Stay here."

D'Camp came back a few minutes later, carrying a wad of bills, peeled off several and handed them to Tony, who gave half to Tex and stuffed his own share into his pocket. Tony then thanked the old man, said good-bye and waved as he drove out the security gate. He was humming a tune, looking like he didn't have a worry in the world.

Tex looked at him as though he thought Tony had just lost it.

"Did you *hear* what the *garch* just *said?*"

"I heard it," Tony said with blasé indifference. "He's more bark than bite."

Tony had no intention of turning himself in. He felt too euphoric. The job had been a blast, and the stash of cash in his pocket meant more than all the threats in the world.

"You know what?" he said to Tex.

"What?" Tex looked at him skeptically.

"Let's go bust up some more robots!"

Tex laughed like a hyena.

# COMPOUND INFRACTION

The tall figure smoothly entered the room and stood by the bed looking down at Forrest's injured leg.

The two old friends nodded greetings to each other.

"Thanks for coming, Spoon" Cesar said from where he sat hunched over the prone robot, his feet tucked beneath him, looking awkwardly over his shoulder at Witherspoon's awkward smile.

"I'll try not to get in your way. Malcato insisted you need my help."

Cesar quickly summed up the situation. ". . . and we're waiting for Optima to send over the new MOP board you worked on." Cesar pointed at the still dismantled leg. "I was just about to wake it up. I could use your help testing baseline memory functions."

Witherspoon shrugged assent and Cesar powered up the unit. M. Forrest's eyes popped open. It looked around the room, then at its foot, then up at Cesar. "What's the prognosis, doc?"

"Bad, son. You'll never play pro football again."

The robot stared at its leg, then averted its eyes. Its face turned beet red.

"It flushes! It blushes!" an enthusiastic voice spoke behind them.

Tuuve was standing, back against the wall, looking on with amazement.

"Now, *that's* an embarrassment subroutine!" he continued. "And one fantastic job of face programming. Congrats, Charley. Even with its leg busted open, wires and chips exposed, it's hard to believe it's a robot."

Witherspoon smiled. "Thanks, but no, my friend, I had very little to do with it. Mimic processes are Sugimoto's department. She makes robots act human. I make humans act like robots."

Tuuve's cheeks paled. "You working on an obedience pill?"

Witherspoon covered his mouth with his palm to conceal a laugh at the simpleminded earnestness of wide-eyed Tuuve, the do-bee of the century. "Not a pill, exactly. It's an inhalant, a pink vapor that lets me restructure a person's thought patterns."

Tuuve looked as if he vaguely remembered something. Then he shook the thought from his head, and his mouth twisted into a stiff grin. "That young Rager punk, the one who attacked our bot here, I'd like to give his thoughts a little restructuring."

"You pick 'em, I'll Pink 'em."

M. Forrest chimed in, "You would have the gratitude of robots everywhere." Then turning to Tuuve it added smugly, "See, I'm a Cy-bot model x4-706, the ultimate human mimic with the full range of emotions. You can buy me on the installment plan for an arm and a leg per month."

Cesar groaned at the pre-programmed comic script that Forrest recited, but laughed in spite of himself. "You really should delete those old jokes before your circuits clog with corn," he said.

"Corn? Me?" said M. Forrest with mock offence. "Never touch the stuff."

After studying the data monitor for several minutes, Cesar continued, "Okay, phase one looks good. Next I'm giving Forrest access to the reconstructed memory files and VMP. We'll test the MOP later." He glanced at Tuuve to be sure the newbee was paying attention.

"I'm following you," Tuuve reassured him. "The Veracity Monitoring Protocol and More Options Protocol."

Cesar triple-tapped a button. A flood of recorded events, things the robot had said and done over the last few months, poured through his VMP circuits for the first time, having been previously rerouted by the MOP.

The smile on M Forrest's face drained into a scowl.

"You made a liar out of me," it announced. "I was designed to bring honesty and integrity to the political process, and you stuck a piece of crap into my circuits and turned me into a liar, a walking deception, a low-down fraud, a sneaky sham, a misinformation machine, a cheating—. . . ."

"Enough," Cesar shouted as he switched Forrest off. "Well, *that* was a mistake."

The three humans looked at each other silently.

"Well, I'll be," Witherspoon said, thoughtfully. "It acted betrayed, hurt, angry. A robot with a conscience."

Cesar's face filled with pride. "Spectacular programming, huh, Spoon? Kudos to Sugi,"

Witherspoon looked puzzled. "I don't mean the human-like emotions. I mean the objection to the MOP. It called it a piece of crap and then blamed us."

Cesar shrugged. "That's what happens when the VMP is allowed to do its job unhindered. We should have waited for the MOP."

Tuuve looked puzzled. "Why would a robot politician balk at doing what it needs to do to get elected? Deception comes with the territory."

"Not in Cuba," Cesar explained. "Not where the VMP comes from."

Cesar lifted his wrist to his mouth and called Hayes. "Say Braad, can you give us a time estimate on the MOP? We're ready on this end."

"It'll be a couple of hours yet," Braad said. "I'll run it over to you personally as soon as we have it. Off."

"All right, then," Cesar said, after hanging up, to Tuuve and his old friend. "Back to work. I'll dump the show data reports. We might as well go over them while we wait."

Spoon picked up the pages of the report one by one as they fell into the printer's output bin. The material was dense and required concentration. Lost in his own world, he stood in a corner, holding the pages inches from his face. Soon he was chuckling to himself, then puffing, chortling, then laughing out loud.

Tuuve gave Cesar one puzzled glance after another as the laughter grew louder. When Witherspoon started pounding the wall with his fist, and repeating, "I knew it, I knew it," the newbee couldn't contain himself any longer.

"You going to let us in on the joke any time soon?" Tuuve said with evident irritation.

"Clamp it, D'Camp," Witherspoon responded without looking up.

Cesar finished the re-sectioning and initiated the final verification process. Wiping his hands together, he walked over behind his old buddy, looked at the paper over his shoulder and said, "I'd also like to know what's so funny."

Witherspoon sat down on the edge of the bed and motioned for Cesar and Tuuve to sit beside him.

"Look at these numbers," he said. "Out of 410 humans present at the school, the Puppet Master got a read on 406, that is, everyone except for four individuals."

"Not bad," commented Cesar. "Four grannies with machine guns can't do too much harm," he said with deliberate sarcasm, intending to get a rise out of Spoon.

It was an old game between them, and Witherspoon refused to take the bait. "For these 406, we could follow their reactions at every stage of the show; they had a steadily diminishing fear of robots. The robot humor helped, the programming demonstration helped, the coupling of human workers with robot buddies helped. And Forrest is a likeable candidate, he seems on the side of the average working guy. So, none of the tests pulled a negative."

"A ninety-eight percent success rate," Tuuve exclaimed. "Pretty amazing! How'd you pull it off?"

Cesar did the explaining. "We planted a thin neural pickup node on every attendee, disguised as a foil admission sticker. Hayes stood at the door and personally attached them to everyone's clothing as they entered the auditorium. This, coupled with the body language data collected by M. Forrest during his speech, got us the data."

"Nice to see Hayes can be useful at times," Cesar interjected.

"As long as he sticks to his task," Tuuve cracked.

Spoon forced a grin and went on. "The patches provided us with a continuous data flow all evening. We used the feedback to tell us how well the show improved the audience's comfort level with robots. As you can see from these statistics, fear went down by fifty-seven percent. Naturally, older folks clung to their old ways more, and younger people were more malleable."

"What does fifty-seven percent mean, exactly?" Tuuve asked.

Cesar took a turn answering. "Simplified, fifty-seven percent represents the decrease in adrenaline when exposed to the same robot behavior a second time. It's a way of getting at the intensity of the fight-or-flight response. It means these folks are now that much less likely to avoid robots."

"What about the other four? And what about the Rager punk? Why wasn't he made more robot friendly?" Tuuve persisted.

"You've put your finger on the problem. He was one of the four oddities. On them we failed to establish any lock at all. We got zilch; no feedback and no decreased robo-phobia from any of those guys."

"This is the very problem I've been working on," Witherspoon said. "And the solution is incredibly obvious. That's what tickled my funny bone. The kid who attacked Tomato #7 clearly holds strong anti-robot beliefs—in fact, they're so strong we couldn't countermand them. The only way we're certain to break that barrier is to physically destroy nerve cells, but that risks major brain damage."

Tuuve snorted. "That guy'd never know the difference."

Spoon grinned and put a hand on Cesar's shoulder as he stood scrutinizing the screen. "What do we know about the other three?"

Cesar got up from the bed and walked over to the Puppet Master monitor. He tapped its screen until the screen showed an array of photos. "Here are the facial scans of the group who sat in the same row as our Rager." Cesar pointed to a man in a frilly shirt. "I didn't know this guy was in the audience that night. He followed me around the neighborhood in a rusty old Habi-Van earlier the same evening. He's a flag-waving Johnny Reb from Texas. Other than that we know nothing more about him and nothing at all about the other two."

Tuuve perked up. "My money says they're all Ragers."

"More than likely. And since their anti-robot convictions are so strong," Spoon said, with a gleam in his eye, "those guys would make outstanding guinea pigs for my next round of testing. The perfect revenge—sweet, cold and pink. Don't you find it hysterical?"

But Spoon was the only one laughing.

# FLYING OBJECTS

"Hey, Tony, my palms are itching." Tex sat in the passenger seat, rubbing his hands.

"Mine, too. I want me some more bots to bust." Tony said, pounding the steering wheel with his open palms.

"And I know where we can git us some more, too." Tex jabbed the air, left, left, then uppercut the windshield with a right. A startled look crept over his face as he rubbed his reddened knuckles.

"You know where more bots're holed up?"

"M Street, like I told the old dude in the fairy robe." They both snickered. "That's where those schoolly bots came from. I'd bet you a Lone Star Hundred there's more stored up over there."

"Now, what you say we do what old Mr. D'Camp said? What say we just pay our friend a little visit and return his robots to him, nice and neighborly, like?"

Tex's curt nod signaled his agreement. "Turn this stretch around. There's a certain alleyway that leads to a certain garage that this buggy calls home. What you say we return it to its rightful owner?"

Ten minutes later, the limo was crawling down the sandy alley as Tex pointed out the way.

"That's the place," he said, gesturing the Safe House and adjusting the brim of his hat. But instead of stopping in front of the garage, Tony stomped on the accelerator.

"Hey, what gives?" Tex protested.

To the grinding sound of tires spinning in the sand, Tony suddenly cranked the wheel to the right, scraping the driver's door against the corner of the garage and crashing through the tall hibiscus hedge into the pint-size back yard. After bouncing off the side of the garage, they went barreling over the lawn toward the house. The pile of dismembered robots shifted back and forth at the back of the limo until the limo smashed into the rear wall of the Safe House and came to a stop. Tex shrieked as the pancake-flat disc that used to be Tomato's head landed in his lap amid a snow of glass from the shattered windshield.

Tex was more freaked out by the head than the glass. "What the hell ya do that for?" he yelled as he tossed Tomato back on the pile.

"My mama taught me to always give back what I borrow," Tony said with a grin.

"Hey, what's happening out there?" Tuuve demanded.

Cesar stood at the security monitors in the entry hall of the Safe House, the newbee and Witherspoon at his side. The third monitor in the upper row showed the crumbled front of the limo, covered with hibiscus branches and flowers, crunched against the house wall. Two figures were easily recognizable despite the dim light.

"Que barbaridad," Cesar muttered. "Our Rager friends have found us." He pointed at the screen. "It's the same dude who followed me before the show last night, with the tomato kid."

Forrest's youthful assailant from the school ran back and forth, pulling odd-shaped objects from the vehicle and dumping them in a heap on the lawn. The frilly-shirted Texan stood by, yowling encouragement.

Tuuve's voice was high-pitched, shrill. "What are those things?"

Once the limo was emptied, the men began to fling the objects against the windows at the rear of the house. The hurricane-proofed glass shook with one dull thud after another.

Tuuve broke into a sweat. "They're gonna break in!"

Cesar coolly adjusted the monitor to zoom in on the pile. They could make out mechanical legs, arms, torsos, also a shrimp harvester's mask, and the tomato picker's battered head.

"They're our Cy-bots," Witherspoon stated with bemused puzzlement. "Looks like they had a rough time."

"They finally made it home" Cesar said, "a little worse for wear."

The figures disappeared from the monitor. A moment later another thump shook the building on the south side, then another and another and another against the round windows at the front.

"They're circling around," said Cesar, "tossing robot parts in their wake."

"Why the HAL are they doing that?" Spoon asked rhetorically.

Tuuve's nerves were giving out. He shouted, "We're screwed!"

"Quiet down," Cesar snapped at the excitable newbee. "I'll handle this." He went into the workroom and grabbed a high voltage battery charger from the shelf, polishing the electrodes with his shirttails.

Another crash indicated the punks were working their way around for a second pass, hurling robot parts at each window. The windows were hurricane-safe and shatterproof; the missiles bounced off the glass.

Cesar returned to the monitor screens.

"Stay here," Cesar ordered Tuuve. At one point the two Ragers appeared again; they were back on the front lawn. Cesar ran toward the front door, battery charger in hand and Buddy at his heels.

He dashed out the door. Tex was almost immediately in front of him; Cesar tackled him, driving him to the ground, jabbing an electrode into the Texan's neck. But before he could stun him, Tex landed a blow on Cesar's chest, knocking the wind out of him.

Buddy leaned over Cesar and grabbed Frilly, twisting the front of his shirt till it choked him. The redneck gasped for air as the bot dragged him to his feet, squirming and pounding his fists against the metal hand at his neck. Tony, running up from behind, tried to free Tex, but Buddy grabbed his throat with the other hand, lifted him off the ground and flipped him over his shoulder.

Buddy hauled the two thrashing, screaming Ragers to the side door. Tex managed to land his boot against Buddy's flank but paid a price when Buddy's tightened grip cut off his air flow.

Buddy threw his master a grin over his shoulder. The two Ragers were already drained with exhaustion. Cesar hurried behind, still holding his battery charger, the electrodes hanging uselessly at his side. Robot 2, Human 0. So much for that brilliant idea.

"This was too easy, boss."

"Way to go, Buddy," Cesar said with a weak smile.

Buddy carried the two Ragers into the assembly room, where Cesar, Tuuve and Spoon strapped them down onto gurneys. Tex groaned, shaking his head, half-asphyxiated. Tony lay still, wide-eyed, frozen in stark terror. Buddy retreated to a corner where he stood stiff and silent, docilely returned to stand-by mode.

Witherspoon went to the supply cabinet and found a canister of spray anesthesia. Within seconds, the two bodies went limp. At last the room was still. Spoon and Tuuve and Cesar stood overlooking the gurneys, assessing the situation.

"We've got big trouble," Cesar said.

"Duh!" Tuuve responded, using a crack that had been popular for the last 140 years.

Cesar ignored him and began giving orders. "Tuuve, take Buddy and go collect the bot debris from the lawn. Pile everything back into the limo for now. Be quick and be quiet. Clean up every last sliver. Make everything look as if nothing at all happened. Then push the limo back into the garage. Let's hope the neighbors didn't recognize the debris as robot parts. Now get moving!"

Buddy broke out of stand-by and headed off with Tuuve to start the cleanup.

Cesar turned to Spoon, pointing at the limp forms on the gurneys. "What do we do with these two? Obviously we can't turn them into the police."

His old friend's eyes lit up. "I thought you'd never ask. Maybe it's time for a little Pink experimentation?"

The two friends shared a grin.

"If this works," Spoon continued, "we'll have ourselves two new, and very loyal, Futurist voters."

"Duh!" Cesar cracked.

Witherspoon quickly adopted the assembly room, with its gurneys and hospital atmosphere, as his Pink Center. He and Cesar rolled the Ragers off to one side, cleared counter space and began to set up the equipment for generating the obedience vapor, then Cesar left to check on Tuuve and Buddy's progress with the cleanup.

Carefully opening the security locks on his black case, Witherspoon peeked under the padded lid, checking the strapped-together vials of red, white and indigo liquids. They were nestled like a clutch of eggs, unbroken.

The lower part of the case had a remarkable carrying capacity. One by one, an atomic scale, then a box of lipstick-sized micro-release vaporizers, then a collection of tools and instruments Witherspoon removed and set on the countertop. Gingerly, as if handling an explosive, he reached in with two hands and lifted out the transmoebius encoder. Though barely the size of a grapefruit, the device weighed twenty kilos. The encoder was shaped like a two-tiered figure eight, with vertical connecting rods along the inner and outer edges. The top surface of the eight was flat with a small door at one end, allowing access to a hollow particle track inside. What looked like a carrying handle protruded from where the tracks crossed at the center.

A button-covered control pad, trailing a tangle of op-wires and cables, was the next rabbit to be pulled from Witherspoon's magic hat. He distanced the controller ten feet from the encoder and began hooking cables to each of the rod ends.

Two pairs of silvery surfaced gloves were placed neatly on the countertop, one atop the other, fingers aligned. With very slow movements, Witherspoon removed the colored vials from their padded nest and placed them in an out-of-the-way corner of the counter, where they were less likely to be accidentally bumped or knocked over.

Cesar had re-entered the room, but he stood back watching, intrigued by Spoon's studied preparations. "Those fluids aren't explosive, are they?"

"Dang, no. I wouldn't be carrying them around if they were. But motion-generated heat can vaporize them prematurely.

"Here, before we get started,"—Spoon waved for Cesar to stand closer—"let me show you a simple demonstration I worked out to impress the Party big wigs." Taking the vials one by one, he poured a small amount of liquid from each into a flat bowl. After stirring, the red, white and indigo liquids turned a dark pink. He attached connector cables to the mixing bowl and tapped instructions into the encoder.

"Don't worry," Spoon said. "There's no transtemporal encoding at this point. Breathing these vapors won't affect you."

The fluids began to swirl in the bowl, forming slippery threads. Strand by strand they wove themselves into the skeleton of something resembling a figure eight, continuing to twist and stretch, melding into one continuous flat, looping surface until a bright pink moebius knot, ten centimeters long, formed on the surface of the darker, wine-colored fluid.

Cesar gave his old schoolmate an impressed look. "Incredible. How is that possible?"

"It's based on programming kinetic movements. The random vibration of molecules is rechanneled with the right sort of subatomic signals to build orchestrated shapes."

Cesar touched the outside of the bowl with two fingers. A perplexed look remained on his face. "How is that possible?" he repeated. When he tried to pull away, his fingers stuck momentarily to the frost that had formed on the outside of the bowl. "Zang, it's literally freezing."

Witherspoon smiled knowingly. "The encoding instructs the liquid to chill itself by draining off kinetic motion until it reaches the right viscosity for strand-weaving."

"Very impressive. But how does it help us deal with our two Rager friends?"

"The accelerator induces a set of vibratory codes into the nucleus of the atoms using energy transformed from the diminished kinetic motion. The atoms are then bombarded with one-dimensional chronotons, time particles that spontaneously line themselves up in long strings. When these cool babies get into the blood stream, they seek out the only one-dimensional object in the human brain, the Einalli Consciousness Loop, and as best we understand, sort of clog it up, interfering with the ability to be self-aware. Once their ECL is clogged, they become spineless sponges, doing precisely whatever they're told."

Witherspoon poured the contents of the bowl into the figure-eight–shaped encoder, then flipped on the power switch. A shrill, almost unbearable shriek of pure acceleration rose from the machine. He held his ears and looked around the room. Several rolls of leftover wall-covering stood in the corner. He cut off four large sections of the quilted sound-dampening material and layered them over the encoder. Now able to hear himself think once again, he turned to Cesar. "The Pink will be ready to use in a couple of hours."

"Anything else to do before getting our Ragers ready for the Future?"

"One thing." Witherspoon removed the lid from the bottle of indigo fluid and dipped his index finger into the liquid. "Stick out your tongue."

"Huh?" A quizzical grimace washed over Cesar's face.

"Consider this an inoculation. A dab of blue on the tip of your tongue, and you're immune to pink for the next 120 hours."

"You know this for sure?"

"Yes, my friend, I am sure. I'm a scientist, remember? I don't make things up. Anyway, how do you think I've been shielding myself?" He gave Cesar an ironic look. "Now, open!"

Spoon put a drop of the fluid on Cesar's tongue, then a second. "Breathe through your nose," he instructed. "Don't swallow. Let the fluid absorb slowly."

Cesar stood awkwardly, feeling foolish, half wondering if Spoon was pulling a prank. "Dis really woiks?" he croaked, his tongue still hanging out.

"Yep." Spoon gave him another dab. "Now be quiet and count to a hundred."

When the time was up, Cesar felt his hair stiffen, and he shivered as if trying to dislodge a chill from his scalp.

"You feel it already?"

"There's a tremor at the base of my skull."

"Oh, that's nothing, probably your KMA69699 receptor being deactivated." When Spoon laughed Cesar knew he was joking.

"No. I'm sure it's not the 69699, probably my 69701."

"It's all in your head," Spoon rejoined.

"Maybe. But then I'm not a scientist," Cesar returned, ribbing his friend. "What would happen to Tuuve if he waltzed in here and got a snootful of your pink vapors?"

"That depends on what you tell him while under he's the influence. If he breathes enough of the stuff, you can tell him he's a chicken and he'll believe he's a chicken—for the rest of his fine-feathered life."

"Seriously, should we inoculate him?"

"No, not necessary. But we'd better keep this door locked so that he or Hayes or somebody unexpected doesn't wander in when the obedience vapor is in the air."

"Now, there's a beautiful thought. Pink Hayes." And Cesar began to imagine the thrill of having an obedient Hayes on a leash.

Before they had a chance to set the room's lockpad, the door crept open. Buddy entered, looked at Cesar, hesitant to speak. The robot's prioritizing subsystem performed several calculations, trying to determine whether the news should be told or withheld. At the end of a few seconds, its jaw opened and a shrill, anxious voice emerged. "There is something I need to tell you. A van just pulled up. Somebody is sitting outside with a listening device pointed at the Safe House."

"Did it see the Ragers?" Cesar asked.

"No. And we were done clearing the debris when he rolled up. But he saw me. What if he got me on cam?"

"You're legally registered, just like the show bots. But we can't let him see or hear anything about . . ." Cesar cut himself short, unsure what the intruder's device might be picking up through the house's sound screen.

Cesar walked over to the security monitors, Spoon and Tuuve joining him, their eyes skipping from one monitor to the other, examining the scene. Witherspoon's car was parked in front of the house. A pale blue van was on the opposite side of the street. Someone was sitting in the front seat. Cesar used his cyberyes to blow up the image for his own benefit; he could see a lean, disheveled-looking middle-aged man aiming a crude, hand-held, parabolic dish toward the Safe House.

"It's Peter Reid, a reporter from the *Lake Worth Web-Times*," said Cesar, waving off any concern. "I wouldn't worry about him. His amateurish gizmos can't penetrate our screen."

Two young guys, wearing matching "Rage Against the Machine" shirts, suddenly appeared on the monitor, running down the sidewalk from the north. In a few seconds, using some sort of a wand Cesar was unfamiliar with, they had jimmied open the front door of Spoon's car.

"What the . . .?" Spoon said with a gasp. There was no time to act; the three men and the bot stood watching helplessly.

Within moments, the two thieves slammed on the gas and were speeding south, out of sight on M Street. The four figures ran outside as Reid's van pulled a U-turn right in front of them and, with a screaming skid, drove after the thieves.

Cesar's face dropped. Everything had happened so fast, and now the street was quiet once again. "Tzz," he hissed. "Let's hope Reid doesn't catch them or the vid will be on WebFlashNews within the hour."

Upset and forgetting where he was, Spoon spat on the floor. "Dang it all! It's one thing to bust up a bunch of robots. But that was my car!"

He caught Buddy looking at him.

"Sorry, didn't meant that like it sounded."

Buddy merely gave him a blank look. After all, it had no feelings to hurt.

"Score one for the Horse," said Cesar as he spat on the same spot as his friend. "He warned us against driving. He won't have the least sympathy."

"That'll be a new one," Spoon retorted.

# GAPS

**C**esar walked into the kitchen, his footfalls reverberating on the planked floor, and helped himself to his first of many cups of coffee. The Safe House had suddenly gone quiet, but it didn't feel quiet.

Hayes had arrived breathlessly not an hour before, delivered Optima's replacement MOP, was told about the stolen vehicles (one returned, the other stolen) and noisily demanded that Cesar have M. Forrest ready to hit the campaign trail first thing in the morning. Tired as he already was, Cesar winced at the prospect of another all-nighter, but promised to do his best.

"Come back at 7 A.M.," he told Hayes.

Next thing he knew, Hayes was rushing off with Tuuve in tow, as if sucked away by a hurricane.

"I'll be back," Tuuve hollered from the entrance hall.

"What are you going to do about my car?" Spoon had called after them.

After the door snapped shut, Witherspoon kibitzed while Cesar installed the new MOP. "Can anything else go wrong tonight?" Spoon gave a wry grin.

Cesar didn't respond as he gingerly pried open the damaged rail and slid the board tightly into its slot just below M. Forrest's knee.

"Anything else I can do to help?" Witherspoon yawned.

"Nope. I've got a long night of data crunching, but that's a one man show. Go grab some z's."

Spoon left to sack out on a gurney in the assembly room near his two anesthetized guinea pigs, and Cesar was left alone feeling disquieted. He kept imagining he heard thumps of robot limbs against the outside walls. His heart raced, his head swam. He fought off fatigue with caffeine, slaps to his face and deep breathing.

After returning from the kitchen, he sipped the black mud they called coffee in this place and started the first round of memory tests, watching bleary-eyed as the error log clicked up one missing file after another. . . . There were just too many of them.

He did a manual check to see how critical the missing gaps were. It was a task that required meticulous care. One miscalculation could cause the robot to freeze up at the most inopportune moment. But there simply wasn't time to do everything by the book, not with Hayes's morning deadline. With some care and some luck, perhaps Forrest could function as is for a day or two while he knit a replacement matrix.

Cesar tapped the appropriate code to locate the first gap. Here he got the first of a series of surprises. For most humanoid robots, the earliest file records covered their first awakening in the lab. Subsequent files documented each day of training and the orientation exercises that continued for a month or so until the robot was capable of functioning in human society. There should have been thirty to fifty files to cover M. Forrest's training period.

But when the screen displayed the file directory, the listing filled screen after screen. Starting with 15 MARCH 2098, there was a file for every day of Forrest's thirty-two years. The damaged gap popped in sometime during Forrest's third year of life and lasted almost three and a half months, but there were still over 10,000 intact daily memory files. It would take a team of experts thousands of hours to transfer that much memory from the human Forrest to M. Forrest. It made little sense. Who would bother? No human remembers every detail of every day of their childhood anyway.

Page after page of the long list scrolled past. Suddenly the list halted at the date before the second gap. It was less than a year old, 31 OCTOBER 2129. Cesar's weary eyes brightened. The screen flashed with a system error message:

File Not Found: IDENTITY_TRANSFER_ B2C_00334_F········_N······

# USHERING OUT FORREST NEWCOMB

**C**esar tapped his teeth excitedly. Could this have been a record of the day when the robot Forrest stepped into the human Forrest's shoes—began to sleep in his bed, drive his car, hang out with his friends, take over his life? Cesar had long known that Forrest, son of the famous senator, had been replaced by this look-alike robot prior to the start of the mayoral campaign, but he had not really thought through the details of the swap. Now he wondered why he'd never wondered about it before. How had the swap been arranged? Of course, there must have been a specific time and place when the machine took over. How strange to imagine yourself perhaps sitting in a chair alone at home, then have a robot that is an exact duplicate of you stroll into the room, offer the robot your chair and walk away from your life, leaving behind your home, your car, your family and friends, every aspect of your present and past, creating a void for the robot to fill.

Intensely curious, Cesar clicked open the file registry. The computer beeped. "Target file deleted."

. . . . . . . . . . . . . . . . . . . . . .

"Tell me something I don't already know," he muttered.

After a bit of guesswork, Cesar was able to locate most of the file remnants still intact on the hard disk. After a bit of tinkering, he reassembled the blocks into something close to their original order. After a bit of byte manipulation, he was able to get the partially corrupted video clip to play.

The opening scene showed a bright room, its white walls covered with unframed sketches of robots, old and new, from the earliest fantasies to the latest prototypes, indeed of every type of robot that had ever been imagined, from the simplest to the most complicated, the most frightening to the most endearing: Tobor, HAL, R2D2 and C3PO, Cybot1, down to L-3 and beyond.

Seated around a long, bronze-colored table was the Futurist Governing Council. All the usual suspects were there: Malcato, Hayes, Sincardo, Sugimoto.

Optima Sincardo looked bored and distracted as she doodled on a scratch pad. When the roll call vote was taken, her name was called three times before she responded. Nevertheless, the decision was unanimous. M. Forrest Newcomb would be the Futurist Party candidate for mayor of Lake Worth.

The meeting was chaired by a metalloid robot, one Cesar hadn't seen before. Sugimoto stood and spoke. She noted the historic nature of the occasion—the first Futurist board meeting presided over by a robot had selected the first robot to run for office in Florida. She lamented that the candidate's robot identity was to be hidden from the public, to say nothing of the illegality of what they were doing. Still it was a start. Soon enough all would be out in the open, and the bright day of Futurism would dawn in the sunny Republic of Florida.

When the meeting adjourned, Optima chummed up to Sugimoto. She gave Sugimoto a sly smile. "I liked what you said. Could you stop by my office for a few minutes? I've got something quite novel to show you."

Sugi looked surprised. It was unusual for Optima to make friendly overtures. The two women had very different personalities and seldom got along. Sugi was optimistic, upbeat, easy going. Opti was sour and grumpy and bristly. She had repeatedly made it clear that Sugi's perky demeanor irritated her. Nevertheless Sugimoto, after a chary blink, quickly accepted. "Sure, Opti, I'd be happy to. Just give me half a sec, I'll be right down." Optima hated to be called Opti, but she let it go, gave a taut smile and turned to leave.

The scene shifted to Optima's office. The two women hovered over the computer monitor. Optima pointed to the screen as she launched into a detailed explanation of some kind. Sugi looked impressed if a little puzzled, her eyes wide in wonder. But Cesar couldn't hear what was being said. The audio wasn't working.

Cesar fiddled with the settings, trying to get the sound to work. He paused the replay and checked the file parameters. Sure enough, an audio fragment had not been restored in the undelete process. And this wasn't the only missing data block either. The file was replete with audio and video gaps. Nevertheless, he assembled as much as he could, leaned forward in his chair, his nose inches from the screen, and resumed replay.

The scene shifted to a residential backyard. It was a bright, clear day under a deep blue sky. The yard was enclosed on three sides by a high wall displaying a video mural of a deep forest scene. Snow flurries drifted softly to earth. Leafless, gnarled oaks and tall hickory trees blanketed the craggy ground, wind swaying leaf and limb. A few winter birds hopped from branch to branch, picking late fall seeds and berries, undisturbed by the movement of their perches. Over the wall, neighboring roofs and the tops of palm trees seemed to float in mid-air, suspended above the wintry woodland, creating a strange incongruity.

Stranger still were the people depicted walking through the virtual trees. Apparently, it was Halloween. Everyone was in mask and costume, mostly of the horror film variety: Dracula, Frankenstein, Glenda the Ghost. They walked to and fro, heads down, mumbling in undertones, reading from books held at their waists. Snow powdered their heads and shoulders.

At the far end of the yard stood a typical Palm Beach manse, two-story, stucco, dolled up with a sea-view tower and widow's walk. A hand-lettered cardboard sign over the entrance read, "MONSTER MASH."

Near the backdoor stretched a long table, cluttered with finger food and cold drinks. Forrest Newcomb sat on the open lawn, rocking in a swivel chair. A pretty thirtysomething woman dressed in jean short-shorts and a bikini top sat beside him, chatting gaily.

As the image drew nearer, Cesar recognized the woman as Optima Sincardo. She was talking to Forrest, acting unusually friendly, even flirtatious. "Forrest, you look wonderful today." "Forrest, let me try on your sun-lenses." "Forrest, where did you get these lenses. They are beyond cool."

*Opti, laying it on with a trowel?* Cesar thought as he watched. *This is getting interesting.*

Another thing about the video struck Cesar as strange: the camera work. Memory files, by definition, take the point of view of the subject and are unedited. He'd expected the scene to be shown through Forrest's eyes. But this clip seemed to have been shot by a third party, maybe by an incognito robot without the subjects' knowledge.

An older, tweedy man and a woman dressed in black sauntered over, carrying two drinks apiece. Optima introduced them to Forrest as "Dr. and Mrs. Pike, from Transylvania." On hearing that, they laughed and corrected her. "From Pennsylvania." In welcome, they handed the extra drinks to Forrest and Optima, who accepted the cold glasses with smiles; each took a sip.

"We're so glad you could join us today," the woman said, continuing to stand. "We usually have a big party for Halloween, but this year we didn't get back from Pittsburgh until mid-October and didn't have time to plan much. Optima was such a doll to invite you."

The man grasped Forrest's empty hand and took his turn to offer a greeting. "No, please, don't get up. Yes, I'm afraid our party is rather small this year, just Stan, our butler over there, and the four of us. Instead of our usual guests, I've created this animated scene in your honor."

"Thank you. How v-very nice," Forrest said, trying to control his stutter and looking puzzled.

"Oh, I get it!" Optima said, with shrill laughter. "It's your name, honey. We're in a virtual *forest*."

Newcomb forced a respectful laugh. "Wow! That's in-ingenious," he said, and he drained his glass.

The woman stepped forward, taking the empty glass from him, and looked him in the eye. "Without further ado, let me say, 'Forrest, you've been recalled.'"

Forrest again looked puzzled. "Did a phone ring?"

Optima's smile, as false as her flirting, froze, and she gave the strangers an awkward glance.

The man stared intently at Forrest and enunciated, "Forrest Newcomb, you have been recalled."

All at once, the swivel chair rocked back. Forrest's arms drooped to the ground. His face went ashen, his eyes bugged with stiff surprise, his jaw hung loose.

Optima's cheeks brightened; her lips drooped into their more usual, petulant smirk. Relieved, she asked, "Why didn't it work the first time?"

The woman winked at her husband. "I didn't say the trigger exactly right, did I, dear?" The man smiled, embarrassed. "Yes, I forgot to tell her to use his full name."

"That's all right," the woman replied. "Let's get him down to the laboratory. We have work to do."

The man leaned over Forrest's body, still limp in the chair, and made eye contact. "Forrest, come!" he commanded. With slow, lumbering movements, a granite-footed Forrest got up and followed the threesome across the yard into the gray mansion.

The video screen flickered and went black as the playback hit one of the unrecoverable data blocks.

Cesar rubbed his weary eyes, struggled to make sense out of what he was seeing. What a creepy scene! The Halloween party seemed like a ruse to get Forrest into the house. Why would they need a deadening verbal trigger? Why not simply invite him inside? Dios, how utterly weird!

The screen flickered back to life, filled with distorted, half-formed images. For the next several minutes, disjointed fragments of scenes flashed across the screen. Cesar could make out a descending staircase, open overhead beams, some electronic equipment, a glimpse of Optima, but couldn't tell what was going on. The file was corrupt at a critical spot. After several minutes of indecipherable moving images, the continuity gradually improved and he began to make out bits of scenes. There was a gurney. No, two gurneys. Forrest lay on one of them, gagged, his hands and feet strapped to the side rails with tourniquet-like restraints. His body jerked wildly against the bonds, his pained eyes vainly pleading for mercy. The man from the previous scene injected his arm with a syringe. Within a few seconds, Forrest passed out.

The man patted Forrest's chest with mock sympathy, then began implanting needle-like electrodes into the recumbent figure's sagging face. The veins in Forrest's neck bulged blue. The needle points oozed blood.

Optima and the woman stood nearby, unfazed, laughing lightly. They chatted. They pointed. They giggled. The more needles stuck out of Forrest's skin, the giddier they got. Cesar watched, biting his lower lip, appalled. The man removed the gag and started pouring a thick, green chemical over Forrest's face. The liquid covered the electrodes, flooded his eyes and nostrils, dribbling into his mouth. Wires were attached . . . . Without warning the video screen again went blank.

Cesar sat in front of his monitor, in a mild state of shock. His mind replayed what he had just seen: Forrest taken against his will, tied up, poked, prodded, pierced, slavered in harsh-looking chemicals. It was ghastly. Optima seemed to be thoroughly enjoying herself, even seemed to be showing off for the other woman. He couldn't imagine any purpose other than pure, maniacal sadism.

After another gap, the replay resumed. A stiff, lifeless figure lay on the second gurney, directly adjacent to Forrest. The man peeled away the now hardened liquid from Forrest's face, carefully lifting the newly formed mask from the electrodes. He took his time meticulously cleaning vestiges of green gunk from the ends of the electrodes. The mask was then transferred to the second face, and a new set of needles were embedded in the old holes. Wires were clipped from each needle to a corresponding needle on the other gurney. When the process was complete, dozens of wires draped to the floor.

With a cool frown, Optima inspected the wires. When assured all was in order, the threesome stepped behind a screen. A control lever was pulled. Sparks danced off the victim's face, igniting the mask and filling the room with caustic smoke.

Cesar felt a wave of nausea grab him in the stomach and ascend his chest, but he couldn't pull himself away from the screen.

Before the smoke had completely dissipated, the man emerged and lifted the mask; beneath it, a face appeared, exactly like Forrest's, so similar that if the gurneys had been switched, it would have been impossible to tell which of the two was real.

Just then, Cesar's screen again flickered and went dark. He jiggled the connecting cables in vain, knowing they were not the problem, then grit his teeth to stifle a curse. The lost data infuriated Cesar, adding to his outrage over the mistreatment of Forrest. He breathed through flared nostrils for several minutes of blank screen until "End of File Marker" appeared.

Cesar grumbled in frustration. During the indoor scenes he had heard no sound, no voices, which only added to the horror of what he had witnessed. Somehow the sound tracks had separated from the video. Cesar replayed the scene several times, amplifying, filtering, recalibrating. But he was unable to make any progress until a loud buzz erupted from the computer's speakers. Cesar clicked down the volume. The monitor flashed with a reference to a detached video clip. He manually repaired the clip's scrambled file header and hit play. Distorted images of the figures on the gurneys could be seen amidst the garbled pixels onscreen. Finally the distortion cleared.

On the left lay Forrest Newcomb, unconscious though still tied to the bed, an overhead instrument panel displaying his vital signs. On the right was the robot version of Forrest Newcomb, with his chest and belly cavity and both upper thighs opened to reveal his electronic interior. The man inserted tubes of memory chips in either leg, cabled them up, reassembling the chest, belly and legs, then closed up the outer layers of fake skin. He turned to the two women, who had been standing with their backs to him.

"You may turn around now, ladies," he said. "Voila!"

He made a flourish to the two identical figures lying at the feet of the three humans.

"Please feel free to study these two gentlemen. Can you tell one from the other?"

Optima walked up to the gurneys and swept her eyes up and down the two figures. She bent close and examined the hands, necks, heads—details of fingernails, lines on their palms, the shapes of the earlobes—and lastly the immobile faces of the two silent forms. "My congratulations. A perfect match."

Cesar paused the playback and examined the two faces.

The side-by-side comparison allowed him to see a slight difference between them. Even in this recorded image, the robot's jaw radiated with a sharp infrared signature produced by its synth-muscle, easily distinguished from the more diffuse pattern emitted by the human jaw. His cyberyes gave him an advantage he hadn't realized before. Cesar carefully studied other muscle groupings, and now that he knew what to look for, the signs, though subtle, were clear. He sat back and restarted the playback.

The woman followed, using a handheld magnifier, examining one head, then the other, comparing eyes to eyes, lashes to lashes, nostrils to nostrils. She poked the cheeks to check texture and resilience, felt the pulses of the two figures, took their skin temperatures. When she was satisfied, she looked over at Optima. "Your team's done a great job. And Pike not the least," the woman boasted.

The man shrugged off the compliment, though his pleasure was evident.

A white, five-gallon bucket had been placed on the floor alongside the gurney on which the living Forrest lay. The man untied Forrest's hand and dangled the limp arm over the edge of the bed, directly above the bucket. As the man held Forrest's arm, Optima took a surgical razor and slit Forrest's wrist as nonchalantly as if she were buttering a piece of bread. The blood made a soft swishing sound as it pooled on the plastic bottom and gradually began filling the bucket.

Optima began to chuckle. "See that the body is cut into morsels and fed to the sharks."

"Our pleasure," said the woman.

Within minutes, the bucket was over half full, and the flow slowed to a trickle. Forrest's face had turned white as a ghost. The man threw a sheet over the lifeless body, then turned his attention to the robot. He conducted one final inspection of the heel port, then rotated the head, arms and legs and switched the robot on.

M. Forrest rolled out of bed and stretched, as if arising from a refreshing night's rest. Without batting an eye he asked, "Where's the party?"

"Follow me," Optima said as she led him up the basement stairs and out into the sunlight. They strolled across the yard as if nothing extraordinary had happened. The new Forrest filled a plate with food, grabbed a beer and returned to his rocker under the tree. Optima sat down next to him and began flirtatiously pilfering tidbits from his plate. The older man and the woman in black poured themselves stiff drinks, giggling at each other's jokes and at one point bopping each other over the head with seat cushions like a couple of Punch and Judy puppets.

"We're crazy like catnip," the woman cackled. "Look what horrible things we did today!"

The screen flickered and went blank. Sugimoto's voice could be heard over the plop of pillows. "Do you really find this funny?" she asked in an appalled tone.

"Don't get all prissy on me, sugar." Optima answered with more than a touch of saccharine sarcasm. "The job had to be done, so why not have a little fun with it?"

## NARRATIVE PAUSE 007

JURAT SCRATCHED his head. By rights, he should get a warrant for the arrest of Optima Sincardo, track down the two Transylvanians and charge all of them with murder, but (there were so many buts) he didn't have a corpse, he didn't have a murder weapon, he didn't even have an eyewitness he could use. All he had was the fragmented remnants of a deleted memory file. What's more, he had promised Justice Pawl; no arrests, yet.

The Inspector hit the pause key, stood and stretched. How badly he needed a break. Maybe Alice would agree to go to lunch. He looked at his watch. Gads, the hours were slipping away. Tomorrow's Pawl's deadline and today's half gone. Better eat in.

He sat back down, rubbed his eyes and mused about how nice a nap would be, but pinched himself instead.

From the food service menu, he ordered up a corned beef sandwich and an unprecedented second cup of coffee, double strong, no cream, no sweet, and slowly sipped on the thick black mud. It was bitter, but it did the trick.

# LIBERTY

**C**esar's hand trembled as he clicked off the video screen. He sat on the edge of the bed feeling shaken and despondent. Only a few minutes had passed since he'd discovered the truth about Forrest, but it felt like an eternity. His blood buzzed in his ears. He attempted to defrag his brain by slapping his face, but it didn't work. Splashing cold water on the same place might help. The bathroom was only twenty steps away, but putting one foot in front of the other was a physical challenge for his shaky legs. Reaching for the cold water faucet, he clobbered his elbow against the edge of the sink. Coño! He stood frustrated, frozen, staring at himself in the mirror, eye to eye with his reflection, trying to compose himself. He needed to clear his head, fast.

The water temperature dial read sixty degrees. He twisted it down to thirty-five. The icy flow swirled in the sink. He inserted first his elbow, then his head. Water splashed down his shirt, spraying on the mirror and over the floor. Heedless of the mess, he bobbed his head in and out of the full sink until the excess heat drained from his cheeks. When he turned the water off, his pants, even his socks, were drenched.

He heard something—a creak of floorboards—in the hallway. Could Hayes be back this soon? Turning quickly, he took an ill-placed step and slipped on the wet floor.

Lying twisted in a puddle of water, soaked from head to toe, dripping hair dangling in his eyes, Cesar realized groggily that he had imagined the sound. No one else was here in the house. His frazzled, paranoid head had been playing tricks on him . . . .

Then there came to him one of those rare moments of clarity, when a long incubating thought finally emerges.

Just as there must have been a specific day when the swap of identities between the human Forrest and the robot Forrest was made, there must also have been a plan to deal with the real Forrest Newcomb, make him disappear as long as the replacement robot was around.

Cesar had always assumed Forrest moved to a distant town, changed his identity, created a new life for himself, like someone in a witness protection program. Never in a million years, not in his worst nightmare, not in his most paranoid moment, would he have imagined what he'd just seen: a murder, with one of his Futurist associates draining the man's blood into a bucket.

This crap gives new meaning to the term "identity theft."

He shuddered.

The Party had long ago become as crooked the corrupt system it was supposed to be fighting. It had moved past legality with its moves into politics with the clandestine use of robots. Now it was going into murder.

One of Papi's favorite sayings popped into his mind: The road to hell is paved with good intentions. Cesar's intent was and always had been to do good in the world, but now he felt as if he had been hiking a hellbound road for some time, never noticing the constant downward slope or the growing sulfurous fumes. Then, moments ago, he rounded a bend and got his first whiff of the infernal place.

From the beginning, Cesar had fought off uneasiness about Remp's deceptions and rationalized what they were doing—this was politics, if you wanted to win, you had to do what you had to do, and if that required a certain amount of duplicity, so be it. But the decision to form an underground operation to pass off robots as humans had been a turning point, a shift from talking, advocating, petitioning, educating, persuading, convincing, to lying, deceiving, misinforming, manipulating, cheating—but he had talked himself into believing it was an unavoidable and necessary evil.

His next downward step had been the surreptitious conditioning of co-workers, using helmet programs—he remembered the doubts he had had when reprogramming Tuuve's mind just the day before—doubts he had ignored, denied.

There was a clear pattern in all of this, not just the occasional convenient falsehood, but a deliberate plan of deception and manipulation. And now murder. Forrest hadn't gone into some half-imagined pleasant exile in Tahiti. He'd been duplicated against his will, maybe dumped into the Atlantic for shark bait.

All for the sake of benefiting mankind? No: he saw it now. The Party had only one goal: power. Suddenly he could feel flames licking at his feet. He would not hold the course, not take another downward step. Yet turning around and climbing out of this pit would not be easy. The downward road had been smooth, easy to tread, but the upward path was already littered with obstacles. With that dogged reporter Reid camped out front and vulture Ragers ready to descend at any time, it was hard to imagine keeping Remp hidden much longer. The minute word got out there would be a colossal scandal. What would happen when the police found out about the disappearance of a famous senator's son? The murder would be discovered. Investigation would be followed by arrests. The trial would be a circus, with the media salivating over every gruesome detail. The images would provide fodder for an endless stream of reporters, commentators, piranha bloggers.

Cesar could picture the convicted conspirators, after the inevitable guilty verdict: Optima, as the mastermind, wired up to an electric chair, her red hair standing on end, ready to fry; the Pennsylvania couple standing in line, nervously waiting their turn. Reina, Braad and other accomplices from the Lab staff behind bars for years, decades.

And what about himself? Even if they couldn't pin the murder on him, there were numerous crimes he was guilty of, ranging from mutilation of Tuuve's mind and the minds of many others through helmet entrainment, to violations of electioneering laws, to innumer-

able breaches of robot limitation laws. Any exposure of
Remp would bring an avalanche that would bury him.

He was trapped. He couldn't go forward and he
couldn't go back. Fear of prison petrified him. Loyalty
had its place, but not when faced with such gross inhu-
manity. For too long he had turned a blind eye to the
betrayal and deceit that violated the beliefs Futurists
were supposed to be fighting for. The demise of his
dream shook the ground under him. Everything he had
dreamed . . . everything he had worked for . . . his whole
world was starting to crumble. Devastated and betrayed,
he felt the sense of loss sucking the life out of him.

He lay numb on the floor. Bit by bit, another haunting fear began to creep into Cesar's already overtaxed
mind. *What if they found out I reassembled the Forrest
snuff flick? What if, to cover their tracks, they tried to knock
me off and replace me with a robot version?*

He pictured his own face replacing Forrest's face on
the gurney. . . .

No, they'd never do that: the replacement of Forrest
had been necessary, according to the Party, for the robot
candidacy, but there was no reason to replace a tekkie
like himself. There was nothing to this, he was overtired
and paranoid. But Optima's creepy, inhuman disdain for
Forrest, the glee she showed at his suffering, was too
upsetting. And she couldn't have taken out Forrest on
her own without the support of the board. Now, if the
Party thought of robot candidates as an improvement
over human candidates, what about improving party
staff? Wouldn't Remp be better off if the entire team

was composed of unquestioning, loyal robots instead of someone like himself who was capable of seeing through their machinations? And of rebellion?

Cesar's gut cramped. He felt naked in the eye of a hurricane with the forces of chaos swirling around him, with only the thinnest of walls holding off the outer turbulence. To settle himself, he needed solid, real evidence that he was not being set up to be duplicated and replaced. He needed to know for sure, one way or the other.

He sat up and wiped the water from his face. His head felt like a steaming sauna stone as he tried to devise a way to test himself.

Bearing in mind that Forrest had been immobilized by a simple verbal command, was it possible that a helmet scan could locate a similar verbal trigger among the millions of neural patterns in his own brain? It was worth a try.

A definite idea and plan of action cleared his head and revived his self-control.

Rising to his feet, Cesar toweled himself off. His clothes were still soaking wet. Under the sink, he found an old-fashioned hair dryer and used it to dry out his pants and shirt.

Returning to the back room, where M. Forrest still lay stretched out on the bed, he sat down in front of the input screen. His fingers typed with a staccato rhythm as he hurriedly programmed his own DJ helmet to search his neural patterns. He was looking for a conditional cascade trigger containing the word "recall."

It was a simple task. Within a couple of minutes, it was ready to run. Cesar secured the chin strap with a tug so strong the strap dug deeply into his skin; his mind was too focused to register the discomfort. Once the procedure started, he sat quietly, breathing deeply, staring at the readout screen, waiting for the results to beep in. He could almost feel the hot spot of the search beam at work inside his skull, passing subliminally and systematically through axon, dendrite, synapse.

An uneventful ten minutes passed. Just when Cesar thought he might be clean, a chime went off, indicating that the search had found something suspicious. Sure enough, hidden in his corpus callosum, a region of the brain associated with attention and hypnosis, lay an artificial neuron pattern. Its precise symmetry marked it clearly. No organic nerve cell grew with such geometric perfection. Checking each tendril for the gateway, he found what he feared. Coño! Predictably enough, when decoded it read, "Cesar Komenen, you have been recalled." A verbal trigger sat in his brain like a time bomb. All someone had to do was utter the words, and he would become a zombie, alive, but unable to think for himself or control his own body.

No doubt Optima was behind this. She was the only one with both the technical skills and the scheming hard-heartedness to do this. And when? When had she had an opportunity to implant him? He'd forestalled any such potential during the Buddy Bot activation. The only occasion he could think of was during his initiation into Remp. Perhaps it was just a general precaution, taken for all operatives. It made no sense any other way.

Cesar felt his stomach sink with an overwhelming sense of betrayal.

Cesar was an idealist: he had joined Remp because he was willing to take risks for a virtuous cause, not to play trust-no-one games. As long as that hook lay lodged in his brain, he would be vulnerable. Anyone who recited the trigger phrase could reel him in like a flapping fish. The hook had to be cut out, ruthlessly if necessary. There was no way he could face the rest of his life, even the next day or hour, with the knowledge that his inner life could be stolen from him, leaving only an automaton, a shell.

And the corruption that had infected the Party: that too had to be cut out. Ruthlessly if necessary.

There was no way that he could carry on as before. Tomorrow would not be like yesterday. He found himself rehearsing, repeating, re-digesting, trying to absorb his new orientation into his old being.

The Futurists were supposed to be about freeing the people, empowering them to improve their own lives. But the Party was sinking into a depravity that seemed to have no limits. They intended to take over the lives of anyone who got near them. It had betrayed its basic principles. The evidence was blatant and damning.

Cesar felt his body stiffen. A surge of adrenaline pulsed through him, stuck halfway between fight and flight, threatening to immobilize him. He issued sharp orders to himself: *Focus on escape. Concentrate on things that need to be done.*

Zang! How could he get rid of that thing inside his head? The only thing to do was burn the offending plexus out of his brain. There was no time to calculate the odds of success, no time to access the risks or possible side effects. He'd have to live with the results, whatever they were.

He set the helmet to over-stimulate that treacherous cluster of nerve cells, using the narrowest laser beam possible. No sense killing more healthy cells than necessary. He put the helmet on, was just about ready to start the procedure, when an icy fear raised goose bumps on the back of his neck. Concerned that his mind had been wandering when he set the controls, he took the helmet off again, double-checked the inputs for errors. Relief replaced panic when he confirmed that the settings were correct. With the helmet back on, Cesar took a deep breath and fired a death ray at the evil implant within himself.

Sweat rolled down the back of his neck as he waited for the procedure to begin. Slowly, a spectral aura arose, like the beginning of a drugless hallucination, an anesthetic against the coming cellacide. He felt rather than saw a light, glowing around his scalp, an emanating rosy hue, shimmering, like the aurora borealis, into brilliant greens, blues and violets. If he hadn't been in the middle of the cell-burning procedure, he would have immediately taken the helmet off to check the drug simulation settings. The hallucinogenic effect shouldn't have been this intense or long lasting. But rather than interrupt the burn, he decided to sit back and take the trip.

It had been a long time since Cesar had used a DJ helmet as originally intended, to tap, like LSD, unconscious parts of the mind and bring them into awareness. In a way, he was glad for the distraction. The play of light and color was simple and soothing. As he watched one shapeless form melt into the next, a yellow crescent moon rose over a borderless horizon, curved upward, morphed into a cat's grin. Two widely spaced, lidless eyes, then furry ears, then a striped body and swishing tail emerged until a Cheshire Cat floated nose to nose with him.

Cocking its whiskered face, the cat spoke.

"Beware the jabber's wake," it said.

"What?" Cesar muttered.

The cat began to recite:

"Three Justices rowed out on an old worthy lake,
One Jewel, One Key and a Park.
But pirates plied paddlers in poor jabber's wake,
And no justice came home after dark."

"Is something going on with the Supreme Court Justices?" asked Cesar.

But the cat quickly faded away, leaving not a whisper behind.

Just as abruptly, the trip ended. Cesar blinked himself back to reality. He removed the helmet, scratched his scalp. From head to toe, he moved every muscle in his body to see if his motor functions were working, then quizzed himself to see how much damage the burn might have done to his mind. The unintelligible cat ditty notwithstanding, a loss of ordinary inhibitions was one possible side effect of corpus callosum injury.

He imagined himself in an array of embarrassing situations, wearing tattered clothes at a formal dinner, Jewel telling him he had bad breath, dancing naked in public. His abashed reactions indicated that his usual inhibitions were still intact. As far as he could tell, there were no noticeable side effects. There was no way to know if adverse effects would later appear. The best thing to do would be to go about his business: get on with reactivating M. Forrest, meanwhile monitoring himself to see what might arise.

Cesar glanced down at the prone, inactive robot. Now was the perfect time to take additional steps to protect himself. With a little reprogramming, the bot could be transformed from a potential adversary to an ally.

Rather than take control of the robot right away, he constructed a defang subroutine, parallel in function to the Forrest trigger. Upon utterance of a chosen phrase, the robot would be transformed into a loyal ally, ignoring commands to attack Cesar and disabling any would-be attacker. The entire database of Remp instructions would be flash deleted. Thereafter, the robot's functionality would be greatly diminished, retaining only speech, motor skills, the ability to follow direct commands—basic functions common to all robots. A security protocol sampled Cesar's voice and locked out all other command input sources, so the trigger could not be countermanded.

All he needed to do was select a phrase to trigger the cascade. It had to be something unique that could not, under any circumstances, be uttered inadvertently. The first thing that popped into his head was, "Hail, Forrest! Tamer of Tyrants!" It was too cheesy for anyone to say accidentally.

As a precaution, Cesar used a mem-sphere to make backups of all of the robot's files, just in case something essential was deleted inadvertently. As time permitted, he would sift through the Remp instructions, looking for clues as to who ordered the recall programs and what their ultimate purpose was. As a final step, Cesar rigged a booby trap so that any attempt to modify or delete his defang program would shut down the bot and fuse its neural pathways.

He triple-checked everything. The code sequence logic was tight. He moved a tertiary backup copy of the defang program to the Puppet Master. *Now encrypt, double-encrypt, and throw away the key.* If push came to shove in any recall attempt, there would be at least one ally he could count on.

He restarted the matrix writer, then lay down on the bed next to M. Forrest. At long last he could relax, maybe he could grab a few winks. The writer would run for at least another hour.

Cesar closed his eyes, nodded off for half a second. But, instead of falling asleep, his mind immediately honed in on the challenges ahead. If events unfolded as he feared they might, he might have to go into hiding. Perhaps leave the country, go to Cuba, as he'd often dreamed of doing? Maybe he'd take the converted M. Forrest and Buddy Bot with him. He could always find work for the bots cutting sugar cane in Cuba. But what a boring, unadventurous life that would be.

He had to remind himself of what he really wanted, more than anything else in the world—what had made him want to join the Futurist Party in the first place— and that was to see a real Robot Republic take hold in Florida. Once in Cuba, he could establish a sort of

Florida RR embassy in exile and perhaps little by little try to get control of the Florida Futurist movement.

Cesar felt his confidence begin to return. At least he had a glimmer of a plan. He stood and headed into the next room, where Buddy Bot stood staring at the security monitors. Witherspoon and the Ragers were still sacked out on their respective gurneys in the lab. Cesar motioned to Buddy to follow him into the back bedroom.

"How may I serve you, sir?" it asked.

"I need to check your systems," Cesar said as he cabled Buddy to the PM.

"I'm operating at optimal levels, sir, and am not due for service for another three . . ."

Cesar ignored the bot. Once the cable was in place he made the necessary modifications and transferred a copy of the defang program into Buddy, who would now become the second soldier of his growing army.

The robot swallowed hard, as if it were having difficulty ingesting the new command. Cesar thought that odd and scanned for anomalies. Since he first found Buddy standing in the Safe House kitchen, he had suspected Hayes might have a trick or two embedded in the bot. Nothing showed up on the scan so he dismissed his concerns and sent Buddy back to sentry duty. Mission accomplished. One ally just might suffice for what he needed to do right now. Cesar's tenseness began to dissipate. He could feel his muscles relax, his face soften.

On returning to the back room, he once again lay down next to M. Forrest. The two lay there, side by side, on their backs, like two corpses in a tomb. But as soon as he shut his eyes, another set of concerns began to rain down on him, swamping any attempt at sleep.

What if other staffers besides himself had been set up for recall? Who else was vulnerable? Surely he wasn't the only one. In an instant, his anger expanded like the hot spray of the Big Bang rushing to fill a universe of darkness. He had to expose and stop Remp's recall conspiracy, otherwise he'd be leaving friends and colleagues in jeopardy. It had to be halted, on all fronts.

But how? Seeking help from a Party insider was out. There was no insider he could completely trust. Going to the police was out. The police were notoriously robophobic and would treat all Futurists, himself included, as equally suspect. Besides, a police investigation would drag on for months.

What about the press? A media exposé would have an immediate effect. And Pete Reid at the *Web-Times* lived for exposés. The man had the patience of a spider, but once the fly was in the web, acted decisively and above all quickly.

It was an idea. Cesar would have to be careful how he approached him. He didn't want to come off sounding zaggy crazy. Perhaps he could give Reid a copy of the recall video clip or a scan of M. Forrest's mechanical guts, or better yet let him watch as Forrest was opened up or dismantled.

He suddenly felt dizzy at the possibilities that were opening up on all sides.

Zeet! These thoughts—these plans—he was starting to scare himself. Was he really so angry at the Party that he was ready to destroy it? Even if they deserved it, did he have the courage to go through with it? Was he really prepared to leave all this: his job, friends, hopes? He had worked so hard building the name of the Futurist organization. Now was he really ready to undermine his own hard work?

A wave of nausea came over him.

He stared up at the ceiling forcing himself to focus on his immediate physical sensations. He felt the pressure of the bed, the slight cooling of air in his nostrils, the blink of his eyes. Unhurriedly he used his cybereyes to examine the imperfections of the wavy edge where the wood wall paneling met the white-tiled ceiling.

He lay there, sweating, swept up in his internal chaos, like a newborn infant thrust into a strange, cold world. Above all he couldn't permit himself to panic. *Zig out, man*, he told himself. He pictured Jewel sitting cross-legged, doing her breath work. "Breath control," she explained, "quiets the monkey mind." He commanded himself, "Breathe now, think later. Deep breaths. Easy. Easy. Slow, calm. Focus on the breath. In, out, in and out." He stared at the profile of the emotionless white face of the deactivated robot, wishing there was a button on the bottom of his own foot so he could turn off his out-of-control thoughts just as easily.

He needed to stop thinking too far ahead and focus on the present. A façade of normalcy was essential until he had a chance to talk to Jewel, arrange for sanctuary in the Robot Republic, make his plans for action.

The memory recalibration beeped itself to completeness. Cesar forced himself up to a sitting position and studied the error log. There were still fourteen damaged files, corresponding to fourteen random days of M. Forrest's personal history; none of them seemed important except for the abduction file he had already partially reconstructed.

He examined the open leg, trying to think of details he'd forgotten to attend to. The damaged parts had been replaced and the memory contents reconfirmed. No, that should be it. He saw no reason the bot shouldn't be able to go back to the campaign trail. It was time to finish up and close this tin can.

Methodically, Cesar selected a series of clamps and with trembling hands struggled to pinch together the two edges of the crack in the shin casing. He kept repositioning the clamps, wiggling and squeezing until the gap closed, then used a hand-held laser to weld the crack shut. The result was hardly a work of art. The seam looked like it had been stitched together by a drunk. Nevertheless, the crack would be hidden under M. Forrest's trousers and hold until a new one could be fabricated. As a final step, Cesar reattached the ankle.

He still had a way to go to fully regain his composure. Sitting down on the edge of the bed, he grabbed the Drugless Joy helmet and dialed a fantasy program, set the timer for a three-minute session and firmly pulled the helmet over his head. Vibrant images flashed in rapid sequence. The colors, smells, sounds grabbed his senses more intensely than reality: salt air, hot sand, breaking surf, rustling palms, sips of fruit-garnished drinks in tall, icy glasses. Almost instantly, he began to feel like himself again.

# BEGIN FILE 026, SOURCE CK:

# A MORE PERFECT UNION

A figure stood at the door, watching Cesar's eyelids flutter under the helmet. Startled, Cesar snapped out of his helmet euphoria and stared bleary-eyed, unable at first to identify the intruder in the doorway.

"Didn't mean to disturb you." It was Spoon. "Can we talk later?"

"No!" Cesar said, startled for a moment. "No, come in." After his first surprise, his voice became uncharacteristically flat, without enthusiasm.

"You okay?" Spoon asked, giving him a careful look.

"Yeah, sure," Cesar said unconvincingly, "just taking a little break in drugless land."

"I just wanted to tell you about the Pink."

"You tested it on our two Rager friends—and?" Cesar asked while fidgeting with his fingernails.

"Not only do our formerly wild Ragers now obey without hesitation, but they're as happy as puppies and as eager to please."

"Unquestioning, loyal subjects. Now we can control the masses with an air freshener." Half-heartedly, Cesar held up his hand for a high five. "Congratulations are in order."

"Not so fast," interrupted Spoon as he gave Cesar's outstretched palm a perfunctory tap. He hesitated. "These are my first human subjects—up till now, it's just been a few rabbits and a spider monkey."

Still absorbed in worries of betrayal and recall, Cesar only half listened to what his friend was saying. Then it dawned on him how this new tool might help him out of his predicament. "Your mixture worked as you thought it would?"

"It's too early to tell what all the side effects might be, but I used a minimal dose, and the stuff is too effective, if anything. When Tex regained consciousness, he acted manic, he spoke too fast, his speech was silly, disconnected. I was the first person he saw, and he bonded to me, followed me around like a dog, did whatever I told him."

The smallest edge of a smile emerged on Cesar's face: *too effective* would not be a problem. "Why don't you make him clean those disgusting stickers off his van?" It was the first display of emotion from him since Spoon had entered the room.

"I'm sure he'd lick them off if I ordered him to. I had him crawl on all fours, bark, sniff around the room with his nose to the floor, then I had him shine my shoes with that lacey shirt of his." Spoon looked down at his shiny shoes with an embarrassed grin.

Cesar looked at his old friend with disbelief. "And the point of humiliating him was . . . ?"

"I know how juvenile it sounds. But I wanted to test him breaking a social taboo, shaming himself. Problem was, he wasn't the least bit humiliated."

Cesar giggled in spite of himself. "Okay, at least your shoes'll be spit and polished. How about Tony?"

Spoon rolled his eyes. "He's as bad as Tex. Those two ex-Ragers are now full-monty do-bees. If we told them to strip naked and turn somersaults down the centerline of Dixie Highway, they'd do it. If we told them to jump off the roof of the Citrus Tower, boom! There they are, two smashed melons on the sidewalk. No hesitation. Done!"

A skeptical look crept across Cesar's face.

"You think they wouldn't? They'll do whatever we ask. I even had them kill two lizards with their bare hands."

"Not the ones that live in the locked closet," Cesar lamented.

"Afraid so. Sorry. They happened to be on hand, trapped placidly inside the L-3s."

Cesar stiffened. "It wasn't much of a test. Those Ragers would have killed a couple of cute critters for sport with or without Pink."

"Okay, bad idea. I should have told Tex to stab a knife into his own arm and drink the blood." Spoon threw back his head and laughed.

"Did you get any solid numbers on our guinea pigs?"

"I tested their IQs and they came out in the low 60s. I gave them an ethics exam, and they scored a flat zero. This is Malcato's dream potion. Pinkees will lie, cheat, steal, maybe even murder, without a question, protest or hesitation."

"I suppose that's good news." Cesar paused. "As long as we're the only ones who have the stuff, right?"

Witherspoon's face had grown long and tight; his shoulders drooped.

"Look," he said. His tone was serious, almost grim. "From the start, my purpose has been to find a way to overcome prejudices against robots, to block irrational anxieties, to eliminate the power of fear-mongering politicians—to make people smarter, able to see through attempts to manipulate them and so be more in control of their lives. But over time, and with constant pushing from the higher-ups, what I came up with is just the opposite: a substance that makes people dumber, destroys their conscience, makes them pliable, easier to indoctrinate. It seems all we do is create one mind-control method after another, Puppet Master, Pink—" he shook his head despondently.

"And indoctrinating helmet programs," Cesar added warily.

"And corrupting robot politicians with MOPs. That wasn't exactly our original purpose," Spoon scoffed disappointedly at himself.

The two men stared at each other with long hard looks, searching for assurance that they could trust each other, that their confidences would be kept, that they were not stepping into a quagmire of self-incrimination by sharing their inner doubts.

Spoon was first to break the silence. "I'm afraid of what would happen if the formula fell into the wrong hands, such as . . ." He held his words, studied Cesar's eyes, smiled, then resumed. "I'm specifically concerned about Malcato," he said exhaling slowly "We need to make sure she doesn't get hold of the Pink. Better yet, pink *her!*" Witherspoon looked at Cesar inquisitively to see if he had made a mistake mentioning Malcato.

Cesar sighed with a deep sense of relief. Spoon's mind had been tracking his own doubts closer then he could have hoped for. But then, why should he feel so surprised? This was hardly the first time they'd been on the same frequency.

"I couldn't agree with you more, Spoon. Listen: I'm no longer comfortable with all this Remp skullduggery either. Malcato—and Sincardo too, they're two iron-fisted peas in a pod, no heart or compassion, just power-hungry, trample-everyone fanatics. After what I've seen, nothing would give me more pleasure than converting them into a pair of eager do-bees."

Witherspoon stretched his neck left and right. "I've been thinking seriously about getting out of this whole thing, leaving my job, leaving Remp, going back to non-political work, like maybe teaching at PBU."

"Do you think they would let you walk out the door so easily?"

Witherspoon gave Cesar a bewildered look.

"What do you mean?"

"I made a troubling discovery just now. I found yet another mind-control scheme, devised no doubt by our Two Peas. It involves a signal planted in my brain, completely without my knowledge or consent." Cesar continued, more somberly, "Would you let me helmet scan you?"

"What kind of signal exactly?" Witherspoon's eyes deepened with consternation.

"There's probably nothing."

Witherspoon didn't like the sound of his old friend's vague reassurances. "Can't you tell me what you're looking for?"

"It would be better to run the test and then explain." Cesar's eyes pleaded for trust more clearly than with his voice. "The explanation would bias the test results."

His old friend reluctantly assented, scowling as Cesar picked up the helmet.

"Spoon, look. We've known each other all our lives, going back to grade school, right? Have I ever lied to you?"

Witherspoon's face softened a bit. "I could always trust you in a tight spot."

"Then believe me when I tell you the scan needs to be done without prejudicing the test. Okay?"

The last of Spoon's resistance melted away. He took the helmet and strapped it on himself.

"Fire away."

Cesar patted him on the back, then tapped the keys on the controller panel, activating the brain search program he had used on himself, searching for the trigger code.

As the procedure started, Witherspoon squirmed on the edge of the bed. The two old friends stared blankly at the wall as they awaited the results.

After an interminable couple of minutes, the helmet beeped a high-pitched warning. Cesar studied the readout on the control panel with a concerned look.

"It found something, didn't it?" Witherspoon asked.

"It did. It found the same verbal trigger I found lodged in my head. Now be extremely careful: I'll show you the trigger, but the words you see must not be uttered out loud under any circumstances. They are capable of starting a synapse cascade in your brain."

Witherspoon face went flat.

Cesar turned the helmet so he could see the read-out. In baby blue letters the message said, "Charles Witherspoon, you have been recalled."

"I had the same thing, with my name instead."

"What the hell is it supposed to mean?" Witherspoon raised his hands to his ears, having no idea what his friend was trying to get at, frightened by what he might hear next.

Cesar sat next to his taller companion. "About an hour ago, I discovered that the human Forrest Newcomb had been abducted, duplicated and murdered. You heard right: murdered," he repeated at Witherspoon's astonished look. "He didn't volunteer to have a robot double made or offer his identity to the Party to become our robot candidate. They kidnapped him, killed him and replaced him with a duplicate."

Cesar looked over at M. Forrest lying immobile on the bed. He gave Spoon a few seconds to digest the implications.

Spoon said nothing but stared at him skeptically.

Cesar keyed a few commands into the terminal.

"Let me show you something."

The two friends sat side by side, watching the recon-structed clip; the picnic scene, the entrance of the peculiar European couple, the zombification of Forrest, the dungeon-like basement where the green goop was poured over Forrest's face, then the silent splash of Forrest's life blood as it drained into the bucket. When the clip finished, Witherspoon's face was slick with sweat.

"These people are sick," he said. "Malcato must be in on it with Sincardo."

"Right," Cesar agreed. "Sincardo has the technical skills, but only Malcato has access to the Lab and resources needed to build duplicates."

Spoon began to rock back and forth as if he'd been kicked in the gut.

"To think all this time I've been used by those two damn . . ."

"Yeah," Cesar said with pursed lips. His friend was going through the same sense of disillusion and betrayal he had just gone through not an hour ago. "We've dedicated every waking moment to this movement," Cesar said with quiet anger, "and now these two have taken over. Our downhill slide began when Remp was designed as a secret organization. We lost our commitment to transparency, honesty. I haven't heard any talk about open program code in years."

"We're just as corrupt as the corruption we intended to fight."

"So what should we do? Jump ship?"

"Well, I'm ready," Spoon said. "I'm more than ready."

"It won't be easy. Remp hooks are buried deep in each of us." Cesar went on to explain what he'd done to burn the recall trigger from his own brain. He explained the risks and asked if Charley was willing to chance possible damage to his brain.

After a brief, stern-eyed pause, Witherspoon consented. He sat wordlessly as Cesar strapped the helmet back on his head, set the inputs and started the search for the trigger's synapse pattern. His scalp tingled, and he imagined a sizzling worm creep through his skull, burning away pieces of his mind. After a couple of ageless minutes, he saw Cesar smile and lean forward to remove the helmet.

"Done?" asked Spoon, relieved. There had been neither sizzling nor burning.

"Done. The trigger's gone. No reason why I can't say 'Charley Witherspoon, you have been recalled.'"

Spoon froze, a vacant smile on his face as he stared at Cesar.

"Spoon?" Cesar asked his old friend, laughing uneasily.

Spoon didn't move.

"Come on, don't kid around," Cesar said, his mouth suddenly dry. "Spoon?" His old friend stared at him with a blank, dry-eyed expression. Had he made a mistake? Had he zapped the wrong cells? "Spoon!" Had he been such a damned fool . . .? "Spoon! *Spoon!*"

Spoon's mouth opened mechanically.

"M. Charley Witherspoon to you, buddy."

"Quit it!" Cesar cried out with a gasping laugh.

"Quit it, yourself," Spoon retorted, "*master*."

The two friends melted in howls of relieved laughter.

"Seriously, how do you feel?"

"Unaltered. I feel like Charley Witherspoon, human."

"Good. No cats dancing in your head?"

"What?"

"Under the influence of the helmet, I had a hallucination of a cat warning me—something about the Supreme Court. You experienced nothing similar?"

"Don't we have more important matters to discuss than interpretations of hallucinations?" Questions poured from Witherspoon like fizz from a well-shaken Champagne bottle. "Number one. How are we going to keep the Pink from Malcato? She wants the formula, and she's already made threats if I don't give it to her. I can't sidestep the issue much longer. If I resist—" He hissed through his teeth. "You know how dogged she is. She'll try another recall, a kidnapping, some new hypnotic indoctrination technique, on and on, one mind-control gimmick after the other until she makes me her puppet."

Cesar nodded.

"So—is packing up and leaving town the answer? Where would I go? How would I live, work, eat? Are you ready to go away with me, live on the lam? Even if we flee, how do we stop Malcato from tracking us down?"

Cesar held a finger to his lips. Without a word he crept to the door and peeked around the corner again. "I thought I heard Tuuve coming back," he whispered. "We can't let him hear anything about any of this."

"Why not feel him out? He might want to join us."

"Not a chance," Cesar lamented. "I used a helmet brain-mole program on him. He's conditioned for loyalty to the Party. He can't be trusted."

Witherspoon chuckled dryly. "Too loyal to be trusted," he said.

"And too buddy-buddy with Hayes."

Witherspoon squirmed. "We've got to get away and take as much of the puppet technology with us as we can. Helmets, PM, Pink, all of it."

Cesar nodded pensively. "What about heading back to Cuba? They have a genuine robot republic that serves the people without all these puppet games. I know people there. We could borrow a boat—with Jewel's connections at Lantana Sea Farms, we can get a shrimper to take us all the way to Havana if we wanted. We can make arrangements in a couple of days."

Spoon smiled skeptically at his friend's usual getting way ahead of himself. "It's an idea . . ."

"In the meantime we lie low. Go about our business as if nothing has happened." Cesar looked at his doubtful friend. "Come on, Spoon! We can do this."

The wood floor in the salon creaked. Cesar jumped up and walked softly from the room to check.

Poking his head back into the room, "It's just Buddy, eyeing the security monitors," Cesar said. "Tuuve's back, sacked out on a gurney beside the two Ragers. We should call it a night. Go home and get some rest. I'm beat. I'd like to run over to my place and snatch a couple hours of sack time. Then we'll come back in time to reactivate Forrest before Hayes arrives."

"You go on," Witherspoon gestured. "I should keep an eye on my Ragers. And while I'm here, I can see what I can do to repair more of Forrest's damaged files. Recall, I did the original work on those files."

"Oh, yes, I do indeed recall," Cesar said with a nervous smirk. He didn't know if he'd ever be able to say that particular word with a straight face again.

# ONE IF BY LAND

**H**ayes' phone rang. "Who is it and what do you want?" he demanded groggily.

"It's Tuuve. We've got a problem."

"Explain!"

"Actually, two problems."

# LEX BURNING

The hulking body of Reverend Rebolt backed Jewel into the corner. She was glad she was wearing her pajamas rather than the thin negligee she normally wore on hot nights. Rebolt's bulging eyes were inches from her face. "So where are they?"

"Where are who, reverend?"

"Don't play innocent with me. You know who I mean!"

Despite her fury at the reverend's insinuation—she knew precisely who he meant, the terrorists, including Ahmed Rajul Khalid, he'd been looking for at the Cloister the night before, but she wasn't going to give the satisfaction of saying so—Jewel could think of nothing more insulting to do than laugh.

"Before you continue making false accusations, my dear Reverend, do you mind if I get dressed?" Since he was supposed to be such a righteous man, an appeal to modesty seemed a reasonably safe thing to do.

"Make it snappy," he barked.

She slid into the closet, firmly closing the door behind her, and slipped on her work clothes from the day before, a pair of jeans and a loose fitting T-shirt. From the other room, she heard Mama shouting, "You call yourself a Christian, barging into our home in the middle of the night. Go! Go! Leave us alone."

There was a thud. Jewel rushed into the salon to see Mama kneeling on the floor, clutching the picture of Einalli to her chest. Three oversized thugs stood over her. "Get up, lady," Rebolt called from across the room. "Give me that abomination."

One of the thugs ripped the picture from Mama's grasp and handed it to Rebolt. The Reverend held the image up to the light, deep disgust contorting his face.

"Cross and crescent." He spat out the words. "The two are eternal enemies. If you cling to the crescent, you dishonor the cross. Won't you repent?"

Everything about this pretentious, self-righteous, patronizing, chauvinistic bully antagonized Jewel.

Mama pointed to the serene face of the guru's photo. "He has a peace in Christ that a bully like you will never know."

"I'll show you peace. Here's a piece of my mind." He kicked the kneeling woman in the gut, gloating with triumph as she doubled over with a cry. Jewel's three sisters appeared huddled in the doorway, staring at their mother curled up on the carpet and sobbing in terror. Turning to his men, Rebolt ordered, "Get 'em all dressed and take them outside."

Mama, Jewel and her three terrified sisters were hustled down the nineteen flights of stairs. The men followed a few steps behind, carrying the Einalli photo and arm-loads of books. Without a pause, the materials were piled on the sidewalk at the building's entrance, doused with kerosene and burned. The fire leapt up, bindings crackling in the flames, bits of charred paper floating on the night breeze, glowing red around the edges. A big galoot of a man casually tossed Jewel's cherished copy of *Universal Skills* into the flames. Jewel stood by passively at the edge of the fire, squeezing her feet tightly together, watching the flames consume the sacred words, her jaw trembling with rage.

# CONCORD

The sky was midnight dark as Cesar hurried north on M Street. A half dozen night vultures swirled above the lampposts, casting elongated shadows on the shining black pavement. His syncopated steps echoed across the empty street. He was headed back to his room, too tired to care if anyone followed. Desperate for sleep, but with a huge caffeine head buzz, the thought of tossing in bed, tangled in the sheets, fretting about escape plans and transportation and Jewel and Spoon and sanctuary and Malcato's pursuit—bed was the last place he wanted to be right now.

Where could he go at this hour to soothe his exhausted soul? Ah for the sea, waves softly lapping over his feet. A walk on the sand was just what he needed to ease his monkey mind. He'd pick up his hover-car, now parked at the Hummingbird, grab a pair of sandals and head for the beach for an evening stroll, clean air and clear think time.

As he approached the corner, a sudden flash startled him. A pair of disembodied woman's lips filled the front yard of the corner house, glowing brighter as he watched them curl into a wicked smile. How could he have forgotten? This was the famous Malevolent Mouth of M Street, an animatron composed entirely of light. Giant chocolate-stained fangs nibbled the head off human-shaped morsels. A forked tongue emerged, undulating menacingly at passers-by, then licked its chops with an exaggerated "Mmmm."

Azziga McMow lived in that house, an artist with a distinctly perverse sense of humor. Cesar wondered how the neighbors put up with the perpetual sound of smacking lips.

After crossing Fifth Avenue, he passed at least a dozen more animatron figures. Many of them were newly installed. This area was becoming an artists' enclave. In the 400 block, a house was covered with video skin, transforming the house into the spire of a derelict, off-kilter Empire State Building. An oversized, if predictable, King Kong raged on the roof thumping its chest. Fortunately the gorilla's antics were performed in silence. The display was tacky enough without a sound track.

A few paces further down the block, the image of a mother and baby manatee swam through the air to the edge of the sidewalk and watched him walk past with enormous, curious eyes. Jewel would flip over their cute, quizzical expressions. With all the changes looming in their lives, he doubted if he would ever get a chance to bring his sweetheart by.

A block ahead, Cesar could see the big antique clock in Cultural Plaza just as it struck ten o'clock. A smattering of young couples milled around, listening to a Tibetan monk play sync-drums under the glow of the Justice Ball, a blue and green globe of the world, three stories high, that over-shadowed the plaza. As the gigantic globe rotated, pictures of human rights leaders lasered in and out within a frame outlining the continent of Antarctica: Gandhi, Martin Luther King, Pablo St. Cardo Cabal, Seminole Chief Amachatchee. The monument was silent most of the time, but on special occasions he had witnessed video dramatizations of the accomplishments of each leader. Cesar hoped one day to see Futurist Party founder Meeka Makrai Paz up there. She had been an honest champion of the people. The current Remp fiasco could not be laid at her feet.

At the end of the plaza, Cesar turned left into the commercial district on Lucerne Avenue. Due to the late hour, the scoot-sidewalks were turned off and unlit. Cesar's lightened mood suddenly vanished. There were too many shadowy places for punks to hide. Overhead, a flock of the mutant night vultures landed on the roof of the three-story *Web-Times* building. A rustling noise at his feet startled him. The side yard was lined with a row of tall hibiscus bushes, the color of their drooping blossoms indistinguishable in the dim light.

One of the vultures leaned forward, intently eyeing something moving across the uncut lawn. Suddenly, it lifted off and dove toward the foot of the hedgerow. There was a thump and a whine as the raptor found its target. A wounded housecat darted from under the hedge, dashing back and forth across the yard, trying to find a place of concealment. The vulture twisted around and lunged again. The subsequent shrieks were unnerving. The bird stood atop the stricken body, its head bobbing up and down as it tried to peck out its victim's eyes.

Cesar darted diagonally across the lawn, shouting, "Shoo, you monster, shoo!" Nonchalantly the bird lumbered off, as if it could care less whether it ate the cat or not. Lazily, it stretched its wings to rejoin its companions on the rooftop. With a wary eye on Cesar, the cat managed to limp off into a side yard to lick its wounds.

"What a stupid thing to do," Cesar scolded himself. It had been foolish to draw attention to himself in that way in the empty street, all for the sake of a feral cat. But the attack on the poor creature's eyes had struck a deep cord, irresistibly rousing him to action.

Cesar ducked into a shadowy side yard, surveying the street to see who might have noticed the noisy encounter. The space was narrow. With outstretched arms, he touched the walls of the adjacent buildings. Their cold surfaces grounded him, providing a moment of rest. Gradually, his heart rate slowed and his breath calmed. The wounded cat emerged from the tall grass and purred at Cesar's feet. If Jewel had been here to witness the cat's rescue, she would have heartily approved.

Cesar peered out through the bushes. An older man, apparently homeless, limped down the opposite side of the street. He stopped and turned. Despite the distance, the man seemed to be staring right at him. That face, rising like an apparition, felt oddly familiar and intimidating. He could only make out a silhouette, but for an instant, he saw the stern, unsmiling face of his grandfather.

Papi Paati had disapproved of Cesar's Futurist job; he had called it "foolhardy and disreputable." If he had

seen Cesar at this moment, creeping about past midnight, he would have scowled mightily. Papi was big on
respectability. The risks he was taking this dark evening,
in fact the entire direction of his life, had grown partly
out of resentment of—and rebellion against—Papi's
hard-edged brow and penetrating scowl.

He felt almost out-of-body as he watched the old
man arthritically descend the curb and cross the street
toward his hiding place. Suddenly, in a blur, the face
yelled at him: "Be careful, boy! Politics will make you a
liar, it'll turn your friends into enemies, maybe even get
you killed," but there were no words. The voice was in
his mind, and he scolded himself, "Be careful, boy! Keep
your head."

Cesar waited until the man evaporated into the
night, then continued toward the Hummingbird and his
parked hover car.

The one-seater was dark green, with dark-tinted
windows, wheel-less, designed to float on air. When he
climbed in and shut the door behind him, he found the
still silence of the confined space restful. He sat momentarily looking out at the dark street, and his eyelids grew
heavy.

Cesar found himself draped in a Roman robe, a
green laurel circlet on his brow, wandering aimlessly
through a maze of dark, dungeon-like tunnels. Up
ahead, the flicker of firelight and echoing voices beck-
oned. Stepping over fallen rocks and around the bodies
of scores of dead cats, he came to a chamber where a
bonfire blazed in the middle of the stone-paved floor.
Optima Sincardo welcomed him. "Join our feast on the

Ides of July, a feast dedicated to you, Julius, our Most Imperial Majesty. Hail, Caesar!" Malcato and Hayes ignored his entry but stood tearing little bits of paper and tossing them into the fire. Tuuve was off to one side, hunched over a mountain of metalloid arms, legs and heads, busily reassembling a dismembered robot.

Tomato #7 emerged, smiling demurely and said, "Hungry? Have a bite." Cesar blinked as she splattered his forehead with an unripe tomato. The she-bot laughed heartily as the green pulp spread over his eyes and nose. Unable to see, he wiped the gunk from his eyes. Soon, Optima, Reina and Braadrik joined in laughing and pelting him with green, then blood-red orbs.

Tuuve turned around from his work and scowled. "Is this any way to greet our guest of honor?" he protested.

Hayes put his arm around the newbee. "Aw, we're just giving him his just deserts," holding out a bushel basket full of spotted rotten tomatoes. "Now it's your turn to join the fun."

They all laughed and egged Tuuve on. "Go ahead!" "Blast him." "Don't you realize what he did to you. Let your vengeance fly!" Tuuve's countenance went scarlet as he rubbed his head with both hands, realizing for the first time how Cesar and the helmet had messed with his mind. The newbee dug his hand into Hayes's basket and began hurling the sloppy missiles at his tormentor. The tomatoes tore through Cesar's white robes, burned his flesh.

In pain, Cesar protested, "Et tu, Tuuve?"

"Yes, me too! Most of all, me!" came the reply accompanied by a storm of flying fruit that piled around him, reached his head and buried Cesar in darkness.

He woke in a cold sweat, confused in that fuzzy-headed moment before realizing he had been dreaming. Breathing heavily, staring up at the car's furry roof-liner, he sat trying to collect his thoughts. What a crazy dream! Fears of betrayal were stewing in the back of his mind. The longer he sat there gazing at the empty street, the more vulnerable he felt.

Starting the engine resulted in a sharp jerk as the vehicle lifted vertically several inches from the smooth black pavement. With his left hand, Cesar fisted the steering wheel at nine o'clock. The vehicle pulled squarely into the traffic lane. His right hand moved to twelve o'clock, and the vehicle glided forward. A left turn placed him eastbound on Lake Avenue, heading toward the Lake Worth beach.

A wave of nausea rose from the pit of his stomach. Speeding random thoughts bombarded his system, making it tough to think. Cesar yearned for a moment of clarity, hoping the sea breeze would be more effective than the helmet at grounding his spinning mind.

As soon as his bare feet pressed into the wet sand at the water's edge, Cesar's spinning head began to decelerate. The rhythm of his steps unconsciously synchronized with the rhythm of the surf. His brainwave patterns shifted dramatically from beta to theta. Over in the west, the constellation Leo stood aloft above Venus as they moved together toward the rooftop horizon.

If Jewel had been there to interpret the signs, she would have retold the story of the Great Cat King in a white, winged chariot pursuing the Goddess of Love across the Great Eastern Desert. After growing weary, weak and foot-sore, she loses hope of escape and out of desperation throws herself into the burning aura of the Sun, there to become Venus, the bright Morning Star.

But tranquilized by fatigue and the waves' cadence, Cesar walked with his face bent forward, watching the rhythm of his footfalls, lost in a fog, oblivious to both the beauty and the significance of the cosmic drama above.

Cesar reached the inlet and gazed across at the inflowing tide. There had been no inlet here fifty years ago, just the landlocked Lake Worth Lagoon, muddy, algae-chocked, a catch-basin for urban runoff. Then Hurricane Zeta hit Palm Beach Island, washed away a mile of dunes and connected the sea to the long-polluted lagoon, finally cleaning its waters. Cesar felt an affinity with the old lagoon; locked up, stagnant, filthy with secrecy and political tricks, badly in need of a storm that would force it open and flush out its filth.

He could not simply leave Remp, like a phantom, and evaporate into the night. Someone else would just step in and continue the program. Malcato and company had to be dealt with. The doors of secrecy had to be flung open and the sunlight allowed to shine on the ugly truth. He dug his heels into the sand as he walked.

Maybe after all he should expose robotic Forrest to the press. It would be catnip to Reid. Reid was well-connected, liked to play up his independent image. Further, he was cozy with Senator Newcomb and the Alliance. He'd be thrilled to dish up dirt on the Futurist opposition. All he had to do was invite Reid inside the SH for a little show-and-tell. Reid would then tell the nation, within hours; with a single blow Cesar would knock the legs out from under Remp's secret campaign.

The second option was more daring. Rather than simply expose Remp, which would leave the local Party in disarray, he could try to save the Party from itself, infiltrate the board somehow, close Remp down, clean out Malcato, Sincardo and Co. and get the Futurist movement back on track. With Spoon's help, he could pink Hayes, Malcato, Sincardo and as many voting members of the board as was necessary to take over the board. They'd elect someone to the executive who shared their vision for the Party. He should sound out Sugi. Whose side would she be on anyway? She'd been opposed to Remp from the start, but what if she'd been triggered like Forrest?

His two choices were the old standards: flight or fight. Sneaking info to the press meant more cloak-and-dagger games. He'd had his bellyful of deception. And running away to Cuba was close to giving up. Staying here and reclaiming the party apparatus was the hard choice but maybe the right one. They could clean house, disinfect it, then, building on previous efforts before the corruption had set in (surely it wasn't too late for that—there must be more like himself), carry on the struggle. It was a tall order. And there was no way he could take on such a huge task alone. He'd need allies. The first order of business was to get Spoon on board for this new plan—Cuba could wait. . .

Cesar's body felt light. Soon he could return to being an honest guy, the ideals of his youth restored. He virtually floated over the sand. Much uncertainty lay ahead, but now, at least, he had some sense of what he wanted, what he would do, where he was headed and what to prepare for.

He strolled along the shoreline, pressing his feet into the sand, enjoying a sense of boyhood freedom under the night stars as he sauntered back toward his parked hover-car. The storms would come, storms he chose to face. His mental churning would undoubtedly return, but for these few minutes, there was calm, a carved-out moment of grace.

His stomach grumbled. He hadn't eaten since noon. The Lake Worth Pier was just ahead, lined with food-pits and sidewalk cafes. It was the weekend; the eateries would be open all night. As he approached, Cesar could already make out the brightly lit Benny's Beach Buffet sign. The deck was crowded with well-dressed couples and circles of young singles dancing to the hot Latin beat coming from Johnny Gyro's.

If he were free from this crazy Remp intrigue, with the stars, the water, the music it would be a perfect party night. He would give Jewel a call. She'd come out, dressed to the nines. After a couple of vigorous dances he'd lose himself in the music and movement.

But such good times would have to wait. Someday they'd build themselves a sweet, carefree life, whittled down to a twenty-hour work week, have plenty of laze-at-the-beach theta time. He and Jewel would go out dancing often, a lot more often. After he'd dealt with Remp. And rebuilt the Party.

A wooden flight of stairs led from the sand to the pier deck, the railing wobbling as he climbed. Just as

Circles of singles dance to the hot, Latin beat
coming from Johnny Gyro's.

Cesar reached the top step, a tread broke free, clattering to the sand below. He fell forward, smacking his forearms against the deck. His left leg twisted awkwardly beneath him and slipped through the gap. For an instant he thought he would fall straight down, like Alice down the rabbit hole, but he caught himself at the last moment and pulled himself up.

Safe and unhurt, Cesar stood at the head of the stairs looking back down. *Funny thing if I ended up breaking my leg just as I'm about to save the planet*, he thought, with an inward chuckle at his own grandiosity. An incongruous image popped into Cesar's mind: he and Forrest swapping legs, exchanging a flaccid robot leg for his broken, mangled human one. The parallel created in him a strange sense of kinship with the robot. He saw M. Forrest as a kind of evil twin, a kind of archetypal partner in a mythic dance, man versus machine. Cesar's practical side laughed at his melodramatic, flighty side. *Where do these weird ideas come from?*

In front of the café entrance three teenage girls stood huddled, talking, dressed to kindle. The leader was tall, a bit too bony, with blunt elbows and knees. Her purple body suit shimmered with the illusion of fish scales.

Clinging to shimmer girl's side was the youngest, most likely carrying a fake ID; she was googly-eyed and hung on shimmer girl's every word, trying to prove how grown up she was, wearing a loose-fitting reptile skin that broadcast to the world she was mature enough to shed.

The third stood a few feet away, staring blankly at the dark ocean, radiating cool aloofness. She wore a simple lacy white top with leopard-spot bellbottoms.

They looked barely twenty, on the prowl and smoking the new health cigarettes that smelled like jasmine and claimed to improve lung capacity. Clubbers who rarely got any physical exercise needed a little help to dance through the night. Jasmine smoke was the chic new stim-u-drug. The girls had planned on a long evening and stood around puffing, chatting, on display, waiting for the boy bees to come to the honey.

Cesar had to brush past the three girls to enter the café. The large room inside was brightly lit and crowded with empty tables, not an employee in sight. He grabbed a Snook Island Sandwich off the shelf. As he exited, he pressed his thumb on the door-mounted pay pad and strolled out to a table on the deck facing the water.

Not two bites into the sandwich at the table where he'd taken a seat, he found himself surrounded by the girls, batting their lashes. Without invitation, the three sat down, crowding close and cooed over him.

"You're cute," said googly-eyes.

"I saw him first," countered shimmer girl.

"Come on, Twaila, there's enough of him to go around," said the third.

Cesar sucked the air in through his teeth, thought of Jewel and shook his head. "Sorry, ladies, I'm feeling kinda indivisible tonight."

Twaila leaned across the table so that her nose almost touched Cesar's. "Hey, big boy. Afraid you can't handle all three of us?" Her smirk was a dare.

Cesar rolled his eyes and looked away. "You girls need to find school boys in your own grade."

Twaila took a deep drag from her cigarette and exhaled directly in his face. "We've got enough jaz-z-z-mine to keep you going all night." The "z" reverberated like a provocative growl in her throat.

Cesar yawned, hoping his blank stare conveyed his lack of interest.

Just then he heard Georgia Sugimoto's rescuing voice. "Hey, Komenen! Can we join you?" "Hi," Cesar said, a little cagily. What was Sugimoto, of all people, doing here? Cesar didn't think of her as a party kitten, and he certainly didn't expect her to be out on a Friday night prowl.

The three girls whooped in chorus.

"Wow! Did we get lucky or what?" said shimmer girl. "Twins!"

Two perfectly identical men were standing next to Sugi. They indeed looked identical, they were even dressed identically, but Cesar found something odd about them. The one on the left looked like he had drunk himself into mild painlessness. But the one on the right . . .

"Ladies, would you care to introduce yourselves?" Sugi suggested.

"I'm Twaila. My name means two girls for every boy!"

"Hi, I'm Gary," said the guy on the left.

"Hi, I'm Larry," said the guy on the right, with almost exactly the same intonation, if less drunk.

The guys exchanged looks. "Now, this could get interesting!" said the guy on the right with an unconvincing leer.

Cesar adjusted his cyber-eyes: the guy on the right had perfectly symmetrical eyes and mouth, whereas the other's eyes and mouth were slightly off center. It was a little hard to tell because the guy on the left wouldn't stop moving. But then Cesar was certain: the infrared began to glow from rightie's chin. Rightie wasn't human, he was leftie's robot twin. Hm, they had to work on his drunk-and-making-a-pass programming.

The girls now had more receptive targets to flirt with: it would almost be worthwhile to stay and see what happened when they finally figured out what they were dealing with. But Cesar had business to attend to.

At the first opportunity Cesar slipped away and headed for the parking lot. Strange about Sugi. He didn't fully comprehend what was going on. Not that it mattered. They could do as they pleased. What would shimmer girl do when she found out her boyfriend for the evening had more metal in him than she could dress herself with? Just before he reached his car, he felt a hand on his shoulder. It was Sugi. "Could you do me a favor?" she asked.

"Sure," he said after a moment, with a shrug he hoped seemed relaxed. He gave her a keen look. Was she pinked, or was she not pinked? That was the question. Unfortunately cybereyes couldn't read minds. Yet. "What can I do for you?"

"I know it's late, but . . ." She gave him her most gracious smile. It looked real enough. "Would you run to my office and bring back another DJ helmet? We brought two, but now I need three. I can't go myself right now. The third girl might wander off."

Cesar looked at her incredulously. "You figure those girls need artificial encouragement?"

"No, well . . . I'm doing a social survey on dating behavior. I use the helmets to monitor people's reactions," Sugi explained as she handed him her office thumb key.

"Sure. Nothing like a party hat to complete the party."

"Thanks." She smiled perkily. "I owe you one!"

*Not really*, Cesar thought. *It looks like I owe you one.*

This was some luck. He had lacked a plan for getting to Malcato and Sincardo to pink them, as he had mentioned to Spoon. Now an opportunity had fallen into his lap. He wouldn't need to hack the Lab's security or make up an excuse for being in the building at some crazy hour. It wouldn't take him long to rig an L-3 with Pink, hide it under Malcato's desk, set it to trigger sometime when she was alone in her office. Ditto Sincardo. This was working out better than his wildest dreams. Things were starting to move almost too fast.

"I'll be back in an hour with the helmet," he said, "Meet you inside the club."

Sugi gave him a final smile.

He hesitated: didn't it look just a little . . . unreal?

Cesar shook off his suspicion and headed for his hover-car.

# SMILES OF AFFIBILITY

Witherspoon sat on the edge of his chair absent-mindedly staring at M. Forrest's prone form, still lying inactive on the bed. He could not stop brooding about the mistreatment of its human prototype.

A short musical beep signaled that the memory analysis was finally done. No remnants of the thirteen missing files were found, but neither were there missing cross links. Cesar was right: M. Forrest would function fine as is.

Witherspoon yawned, then checked the time. It was just past 1:30 A.M. Plenty of time before Hayes would return. Plenty of time to run M. Forrest through its paces to be sure the repaired components, and especially the MOP, were working correctly. And besides, he'd like to perform a little experimenting of his own. What would the bot do if caught in a lie?

Witherspoon walked through the various steps of the activation procedure. M. Forrest stood up, shook its legs, dropped its pants briefly to inspect the seam and ran a self-diagnostic. Moments later, the robot gave a thumbs up. "How would you like to join the main-tenance team under my administration? You do nice work."

"Thank you, sir. But I only backed up Cesar on your memory recalibration. I believe Tuuve did the joint and muscle repair. Maybe you'd want to offer him the job? As you know, I'm a researcher, not a botchanic."

"Too bad." The bot shrugged disappointedly.

Spoon couldn't help marveling at the engineering, the genuineness of its reaction. It was impossible to act toward the robot as toward a mere machine. "I need to make sure the memory recalibration worked. May I ask you some questions?"

The bot paused, as if considering something. "My security list gives you complete clearance," it piped up cheerfully. "Fire away!"

"First off, you know you're a robot, right?"

"Of course."

"And you know that I know you're a robot."

"Yes."

"Were you always a robot?"

"No, sir. I was once human, just like yourself." He smiled a little condescendingly.

"What's your occupation?"

"I'm an economist working for the Futurist Party of Florida, currently running for mayor of Lake Worth. Before that, when I was human, I worked for my dad, in his Tallahassee office."

"You're a robot but you say you have a dad. Isn't that a contradiction?"

"Not really. I was once a boy and then I became a

teenager and then a man. And now I am a robot. Does that mean I'm no longer myself?"

Witherspoon paused thoughtfully. The robot's logic was both strange and compelling, pricking at the edge of his mind like a taunt. He'd have to let it go for now: this was no time to speculate on the metaphysics of consciousness and identity.

"Is this the first time you've run for office?"

"Yes."

"Since your 'dad' is a higher up in the Alliance Group, what does he think of you running as a Futurist?"

"Well, he certainly doesn't agree with me on many policy matters, but I think he wants me to win. Call it family pride."

"Do you get along with him well, even after leaving his employ?"

"Oh, yes. Definitely."

"Does he know you're a robot?"

The bot looked at Spoon with deep, sad eyes. "I certainly hope not. But he never approved of me as a human. I wasn't ambitious enough for him. Since I became a robot I have become smarter, more articulate, more self-confident—now he'll like me a lot better, as long as he thinks I'm still human."

Witherspoon paused. "You could certainly fool me. The humanity of your reactions is very impressive."

"That's Ms. Sugi's work. She's the best," the bot said with warmth as if the engineer were a lifelong friend.

Or his mother, Witherspoon thought sardonically. "May I continue with what may seem like a trick question? I'm still checking functionality."

"Please continue."

"What would you say if Senator Newcomb or Pete Reid or a voter asked you if you were a robot?"

"I would have to deny it."

"And if they confronted you, opened an access port and discovered your mechanical insides, what would you say?"

"I'd refer them to Hayes. I am not authorized to disclose our little secret to anyone except a short list of cleared maintenance personnel."

"And who's on the list?"

"Hayes, Komenen, Robinson, Sincardo, Sugimoto, Witherspoon."

"Who's Robinson?" Witherspoon asked with a puzzled look.

"Your predecessor."

"Malcato's not on the list?"

"Reina Malcato? No."

*Now we're getting somewhere*, Witherspoon thought. "And who's authorized to change the list? Add or delete names? Or change any of your programming?"

"Only the six," it stated matter-of-factly.

Spoon hesitated for a moment, realizing he needed to be careful here.

"Delete Robinson."

"Robinson deleted. Five security names remain."

Spoon took a breath, scratched his ear. "Report subsequent actions, logs, notifications, backup lists."

"Two log entries in the last twenty-four hours. Most recent: Robinson access rights deleted, authorization Witherspoon. Wireless notice of deletion sent to Optima Sincardo."

He whistled under his breath. He'd been tempted to delete Sincardo but not willing to let her know. Good thing he'd done a test on Robinson.

"What about the earlier log entry?"

"Prior entry, wireless notice of VMP malfunction sent to the Minister of External Affairs, Cienfuegos, Cuba."

"What the blazes does that mean?" Witherspoon muttered to himself.

The robot answered anyway. "There's an embedded subroutine in the VMP that generates notices of malfunction. Notice sent, Friday, July 14, 2130, at 11:45 P.M. Usually such notices go to the manufacturer, but due to the politically sensitive nature of exporting humanoid components to Florida, Cuba was involved. I have no further information on the nature of their monitoring. Sorry, boss."

*The moment of the accident at the school*, Spoon thought. *Cuba! Why in heck would they want to know? Better tell Komenen.*

Witherspoon sat quietly for a moment, contemplating actions and consequences. "Is your VMP identifying any issues at this time?"

"You mean is my VMP making me feel guilty about anything?" the robot said.

"Feeling guilty? That's a rather human way to put it—but yes."

"No issues at the present. No guilt."

Relieved, Witherspoon nodded and thought about what other repaired functions he needed to check. "Tell me, what's an MOP?"

"MOP? I have no record of an MOP."

Spoon worded his next question carefully. "We activated you a couple of hours ago for testing. Can you remember what was said?"

"Komenen performed some tests on my interpretive speech processors. Everything was working properly."

"You don't recall saying anything during the verbal test?"

"I do not have any record of words spoken."

*That was a lucky break,* Witherspoon thought. M. Forrest's angry outburst had been cleared out in the recalibration. Its loud shouting of "You made a liar out of me!" gone without a trace.

A wrist phone beeped. It was Cesar. Spoon tapped the monitor to deactivate M. Newcomb before answering; as jittery as he felt, he was not inclined to allow the bot to overhear this conversation.

"There are a couple of L-3's in the assembly room," Cesar asked breathlessly. "in the cabinets on the outside wall. Could you load them with vials of Pink? Then set a wireless signal to break the vials and release the Pink by remote command. Okay? I'd like them tonight, as soon as possible."

"Right," Witherspoon said, then told him about the robot communication with Cuba.

"What?" Cesar gasped on the other end. "It was from the school? Not during the repair?"

"Yeah. Just a bare bones notice. No details provided."

"And nothing after that, such as during the liar incident?"

"That's it, there's no other record."

"Well," said Cesar, "as far as they know, the VMP broke. If they inquire, we tell them about the leg damage and tell them we fixed it. They have no reason to suspect anything about the existence of the MOP override—not that I can see."

"I thought I should mention it. You still want the Pink?"

"Yeah."

"There's one problem. Tuuve's asleep in the room with my equipment. We don't want him to know about these pinked-up L-3's, do we?"

"Wake him up and send him home."

"Right."

"How long will this take?"

"If all goes well, fifteen minutes. The Pink is already mixed."

"Fine, I'll be there in thirty. Thanks, dude."

# TWO IF BY C

As Cesar drove his hover-car west over New Harbor Bridge, Dr. Malcato was home, in bed, reading an urgent text from Braadrik. The man loved high-priority messages, but he'd never before roused her in the middle of the night.

No emotion showed on her stern face as she rolled a thumb over the security entry on her z-pad. Her lips pursed as she read the message. *Could things really have unraveled so quickly?* She laid the pad down on her coverlet, humphed once at the last vestige of disbelief, then forwarded an urgent copy of Hayes's message to Optima. When prompted, she clicked Awaken Recipient and Confirm Receipt. Her instructions were simple: "Take care of situation immediately." Optima was bright. She would know exactly what to do.

# LA LUNA LIBRE

**C**esar passed two cars on the right, then got stuck at the K Street light in front of the Hummingbird. A pair of dome-shaped L-3's sat lifelessly beside him on the passenger's seat. On the opposite sidewalk, a group of Guatemalan sea-farm workers lined up to board their work bus.

How strange and out of character for Sugimoto to send him on an errand. She wasn't one to ask for favors. A tingling anxiety stung the back of his neck, began to rise toward the top of his head. After learning about Malcato and Hayes's tricks, it was easy to become suspicious of everyone. But Sugi was not in their inner circle. *Zag! You're just being paranoid.* It wasn't unheard of in his case. Paranoia was one of his better skills, second only to conjuring night phantoms. And he laughed out loud.

It felt good to laugh, even at himself.

Adopting one of Jewel's techniques for dealing with baseless suspicion, he began to enumerate the facts about Sugimoto, as he knew them. She was sweet, perky and unguarded, not suited for membership in the Reina and Optima Cat Club, not by a long shot, and more often than not at odds with their schemes. She was a solid scientist who didn't have the taste or hubris for such games. She'd gained an international reputation for groundbreaking work on robot humor. (Curiously, she didn't have much of a sense of humor herself, sweet people rarely did.) During innumerable forays to comedy clubs, she'd gathered reams of data on how human comedians made people laugh. Body language, intonation, timing, physical and verbal tricks were recorded with meticulous attention to detail. The nuts and bolts of humor proved to be surprisingly complex. From the raw data, she'd identified thirty-seven distinct families of sequential laugh triggers. Once translated into robot code, her mechanical comedians became hysterically funny, fully capable of standing toe to toe with anyone in the business. If not for the Limitation Laws, robots would by now have taken over the field of stand-up comedy and Sugi would be enormously rich.

Having mastered humor, Sugimoto had turned her attention to robotic dating, where she quickly advanced to the field-work stage. She needed data on social interaction, as distinct from physical sex. Sex was a no-brainer. The physiological stimulus-response pairs were well known. Dating was a subtler art and a more challenging topic for study.

He could picture the doctor, sitting at this very moment in a quiet corner of the club, clip-pad in hand, observing how the girls reacted to the behavior of their respective dates. Each girl would wear a Drugless Joy helmet while Sugimoto watched the helmet readouts and adjusted the robot's behaviors to mimic the human's.

She would carefully tweak the variables, experimenting with joke-telling, body language, attentiveness, teasing, the provocation of jealousy, subtle flirtations buried in smiles and glances, all to match the human model. The robot would be entrained to evoke in his partner the exact same neural responses as the model had produced.

He had not thought much of it at the time, but some weeks ago, Sugimoto and Cesar had been talking with a couple of female assistants down at the lab when one matronly gal proclaimed, "Robots can't be sexy."

"Oh, no?" Sugi came back at her. "One day you'll see. You'll tear your clothes off when my robot walks into the room."

"You're missing the point. Listen up. A robot can never love me. Heartlessness is the ultimate turnoff. You may be able to program in all the right moves," she said, "a charming smile, a great come-on line, bedroom eyes, muscles reeking of pheromones to high heaven, but in the end a robot is nothing more than clockwork. It executes a program dictated by a distant clinician in a white lab coat. It is incapable of feeling or returning my love. Love is what it's all about. Love, sister, love. And a robot is just not up to the job."

Sugi's response had been a shrug. "Love? That's not a measurable result. I'm a scientist and I'm focused on concrete goals. What I'd like to see is a robot able to lure you ladies into bed, with a sexiness so enticing that no one could resist. Think what we'll learn about erotic behavior in the process."

At the time, Cesar had brushed aside the conversation as speculative banter. But apparently there actually was a dating research project underway and Sugimoto was leading it. Cesar disapproved. There were higher priorities right now than perfecting robotic playboys. Besides, men didn't need the competition.

As he hovered around the A Street circle and headed south toward the Palm Beach University—Medical Campus, he rolled down the window and turned on his Music Pump. The lyrics pounded out into the night air, a hip mix of Spanish and English:

> Recall the night con la luna brillante.
> An eternal night bathed in moonlight.
> Fortuna's shadow graced our steps.
> Recall la noche of the brilliant luna.
> Eternal love soared among the stars.
> We walked on the moon,
> Went right to the edge,
> Two hearts forever one,
> Immortal, unafraid of falling.
> Life was full,
> Like the full-faced moon,
> Full to the brim.
> Life smiled at us,
> Like the upturned horns of the crescent moon,
> Like the glowing grin of the invisible cat.
> We were alive, really alive.
> Recall the night.
> Recall the night.
> Recall the night con la luna brillante.
> Recall the night.

Cesar quietly sang along. Time and space stood still. Idealism, beauty, daring, taking charge of life, saving his beloved Futurism from the wiles of the heartless . . . Yes, there were still danger and doubt lurking ahead—a long night before the coming dawn—but he felt hopeful and happy.

When he reached the campus, Cesar parked, then methodically activated the L-3s he had picked up from Spoon, programmed his wrist phone to receive their output audio and set up the trigger for releasing the Pink on his command. When done, he stuffed the minibots into a sack, stepped out onto the pavement, quietly slid the hover-car door closed behind him and hopped onto the sidewalk scooter.

While riding toward the Futurist Lab building, he noticed from afar that the third floor lights were still on. The data masters were pulling an all-nighter. Not surprising, with the election only days away.

At the lab entrance, he hopped off the scooter, entered the glass security checkpoint and pressed Sugimoto's thumb key into the door pad. The entrance lobby was hexagon shaped; there was an archway in each of the six walls, each arch inscribed with a Futurist slogan: "No Worker Left Behind," "Robots Are Our Future," and the like.

Cesar entered under "Leisure and Retraining" and rode the quantum lift to the fifth floor. Hardly waiting for the lift doors to open, he hurried to the supply room at the end of the hall. A set of shelves in the far corner held the building's lost and found, a collection of forgotten, unwanted and disowned items, anyone's for the taking. Cesar dug through a box of surplus DJ helmets, finally selecting one inlaid with neon squiggles: it looked like a party hat and should nicely fit Sugimoto's needs.

The hallway was absolutely quiet. He stuffed the helmet into the sack on top of the L-3s and briskly walked to Optima's office around the corner. As he flipped her wall switch, a dozen cockroaches scurried from used coffee cups and wax bags of half-eaten jelly donuts. Papers and trash were everywhere. Cesar tiptoed around the litter and placed the first L-3 under Optima's computer desk. The device automatically extended its legs, clinging upside down to the smooth underside of the pencil drawer, when Cesar heard a strange scratching sound, like tearing paper. He laid himself face up on the floor and scooted in to have a look. An unsealed envelope was taped to the underside of the desk. While perching itself, the L-3 had mangled the paper edge of the flap with one of its clawed feet. Cesar reached inside the envelope and pulled out a handwritten note. It read, "Opti, good job! Your funds are in Sudbury Bank of the Caymans, account number #39–347. Memorize and destroy immediately. –D'Camp"

Cesar shook his head as he reread the note. Optima in cahoots with the LPers? On the take and compromising the Futurist cause? In typical fashion, Optima, who'd never been one for following instructions, chose to keep, rather than destroy, D'Camp's message. Hurriedly, Cesar tapped the account number into his wrist phone, replaced the note in its envelope, stood up, turned off the overhead light and quietly left, hardly breathing as his head swirled with the implications of Sincardo's betrayal.

He was careful to leave the office door half-open, as he had found it, then darted across the hall into Malcato's office. This was neat as a pin, desk surfaces clear of files and paper, trash can empty, desk chair inserted fully under her desk. Cesar slipped the second L-3 under the desk, beside the chair without touching it, and felt its legs grab onto the rear wall.

As he was about to reopen Malcato's office door, he heard footsteps reverberating down the hall. It didn't sound like either Malcato or Sincardo, the pace was too clipped, like a short-legged woman in heels. Cesar stopped breathing. He quickly hid the sack under the desk and looked around for something to write on. Not that it really mattered if she, whoever she was, saw him here. He had Sugi's alibi and could believably say he was leaving Malcato a thank-you note for the quick job she'd done on the MOP—or some such; nevertheless, he'd feel more comfortable slipping out unnoticed.

No such luck tonight. The door swung open. Standing in the doorway was young, petite Guatemalan woman of twenty-three or -four, curvaceously dressed in a security guard's uniform, female version: a tight navy-blue skirt, platform heels, a white, platinum-studded blouse, her ample breasts stretching the top buttons, her long, black hair directing attention to a pair of pistols strapped to her Barbie-doll waist.

"I thought I heard someone opening doors up here," she said pleasantly. "Can I do something for you?"

She was pure embra, projecting an unspoken ooh-baby-I've-got-it-but-I'm-here-on-business-so-don't-get-any-ideas. Clearly, her getup was designed to distract and disarm male intruders; Cesar had to struggle to avoid gawking.

He had the presence of mind to flash his ID, slow enough for her to see the Lab's security hologram but too fast to read his name. "I'm just leaving Chairwoman Malcato a note. I'll be outta here in two minutes."

"Okay, Cesar Komenen, Robot Repair Technician, First Class—as long as it's a quickie," she said with a devilish grin.

Cesar's neck snapped and she laughed with a sly wink. As she laughed, her lower jaw glowed in servo-motor infrared.

"Are you an M?" he asked. Evidently Sugi had been working on programming female sensual behavior as well as male.

"Would that make me more or less tolerant of your dilly-dallying?" As she continued to smile, her upper lip stiffened.

While the robot embra held a watchful eye on him, Cesar hurriedly penciled six words on a memo pad and leaned it against Malcato's monitor stand. As he kneeled to retrieve the hidden sack, he glanced under the desk and was relieved that the L-3 had positioned itself out of sight. He stood, held the sack to his chest and sheepishly smiled. "A little gift for Georgia Sugimoto."

"Show me what you've got."

He removed the helmet, let her inspect it inside and out, and turned the bag upside down to demonstrate it was now empty.

"No problem," the guard said matter-of-factly. "You've got top clearance, but it's my job to record everything that happens on my watch."

He put the helmet back into the sack and quickly slipped past her into the hall, avoiding eye contact. She closed and locked Malcato's previously unlocked office door with a key card, closed and locked Optima's door as well and silently escorted Cesar to the building's exit.

"I'll let Georgia know you're on your way back with her helmet," the she-bot said as she showed Cesar out. "Nice of you to pick it up for her."

As he drove away, a sense of relief descended like a cool shower. The bot had obviously been in contact with Sugi, who had cleared him. More importantly, no one had seen him plant the L-3s. Zig! He'd had a narrow escape. If she had come into Malcato's office just a minute earlier, while the bot-let was still in the bag, he would have been in scalding hot water. His luck was still holding.

Cesar was in such a pent-up mood he felt like speeding. *Now . . . watch your step*, he ordered himself. *You've got a lot yet to do tonight. Take it a step at a time. Return to the pier, drop off the helmet, go back to the Safe House, coordinate with Spoon on the next steps. Don't get ahead of yourself*. Attentively, he succeeded in keeping the needle at one m.p.h. below the speed limit.

Before returning Sugi's office key, Cesar wiped the thumb key clean of skin oils. *Just in case*, he thought.

The place was dark and loud when Cesar re-entered the dance club. A purple-fishy girl danced alone in the middle of the floor under a spotlight, gyrating wildly. Other dancers kept their distance. One dressed-to-the-nines couple enacted a mating rite in slow motion, the peacock strutting to allure his aloof partner. Hips and hands pleaded for her attention while only the occasional disapproving glance penetrated her cloud of pretend indifference. They were extraordinarily sexy, young and attractive. Behind them, a cluster of older women paired off and stomped out a traditional tango.

Cesar enjoyed the incongruity. Despite differences in tempo and style, everyone managed to sync with the same salsa beat. Freedom lives on the dance floor. Colored lights flashed around the room. Several patrons wore Drugless Joy helmets, most with the faceplate open so they could see the other dancers. The latest rage was to run a virtual light show in the helmet while dancing. It would play in the mind's eye and create a double layer over the external scene—stim upon stim—so the partiers could drown in sensations.

Cesar finally spotted Sugimoto seated in a far corner, clip-pad in hand as he had imagined. He started to walk her way when fishy girl ran to intercept him. "Dance?" she said, reaching for his hand.

He waved a finger. "Save it for me, fishling. I'll be back later."

The girl grabbed the helmet from his hand, punched in a code and snugged it to her scalp. Sugi's robot—Larry—appeared, grabbed the girl around the waist and led her spinning away. A conga rhythm split the air as the dance floor was quickly mobbed. Waves of red and yellow light caught the beat, turning the floor into a hot sea of pulsating bodies. Cesar managed to worm his way over to Sugi, who was now standing on a chair, struggling to catch sight of her subjects in the undulating throng. The loud music made speech impossible. Cesar handed her the keys, gestured that fishy girl had taken the helmet and signaled good night.

As he pushed through the swaying bodies toward the exit, a helmet-topped couple collided with him from behind. Papi would have been both pleased and alarmed if he'd seen how ubiquitous his invention had become.

Once outside, Cesar felt relieved to be away from the crowd and noise. Light from business signs cast deep yellow shadows that illuminated the shoreline and played on the long, parallel waves of rolling surf. Rhythms from the dance hall floated on the gentle southeast breeze, lending the night a slow-paced island ambiance. Cesar sauntered along the planked pier, pensive, savoring the brief respite. He needed to get through one more night without the Rempers catching on. What if they already suspected something? He remembered the lights on the third floor at the Lab: as if they were monitoring a mission—maybe his own.

The tempo accelerated the moment his feet hit solid pavement. In front of the café a pill punk was hustling the passing crowd. How unusual to see a punk working alone. Cesar suddenly had a thought. He walked up to the loner. "Where can I snag a buzzer?" he asked.

"Your lady need a little encouragement?" The punk smirked. Buzz guns had a reputation as a date-rape weapon. A five-second blast would render a victim limp and unconscious, awakening half an hour later to an endorphin euphoria and only a slight headache. The punk was not what you'd call a smooth salesman. How stupid to make a crack like that. What Cesar needed was a non-lethal weapon that would work on both humans and bots.

Cesar gave the kid an impatient look. "Do you have one for sale or not?"

"For you, only the best." He reached down and pulled a narrow, pinky-sized tube from his boot. At the press of a button it expanded into an intimidating and scary-looking weapon. "Prince of Darkness model," he explained. "Adjustable knockout duration, too. Use this dial to choose from five to forty-five minutes."

Cesar took the weapon in hand and looked it over. It was a bit bulky and crude, but looked reliable and had the advantage of being just small enough, when reduced, to fit in a pocket. "How much?"

"For you, sir, a bargain price, three fat Charleys."

Cesar walked over to the thumb pad at the café exit, entered his code for cash out and received three newly minted, hundred-palm-dollar coins. He was paying twice the going rate but was in no mood to dicker.

Before leaving, he set the gun's inputs to five minutes, and, after looking around to be sure no one was watching, swiped the kid with a quick pass of red laser light across both knees. The kid's smile went sour as he fell back against the wall. His body slowly slumped to the ground. *Hmmm,* Cesar thought. *Maybe I should have tested a lower setting first.*

Trusting the punk would snap to shortly, he strode across the parking lot. Unfortunately, he couldn't figure out how to close the gun or shrink it back to its original size. *Zang! Why had he knocked the punk out.* He pushed every button, twisted the barrel, poked and prodded, but without success. As it was, the thing was much too large to fit in Cesar's pocket; wouldn't have fit in his boot even if he had been wearing any. Not knowing exactly what else to do, he laid the weapon on the car seat beside him, started the engine and headed out the parking lot.

The circular beach drive was lined with cops sitting in their cars, sipping coffee and watching for intoxicated patrons leaving the club. Cesar motored slowly past, accelerating modestly as he crossed the coastal highway and headed over the New Harbor Bridge. Left on Golfview, passing Bryant Pavilion and Newell Marina on his left, he found himself at a stop sign in front of the Cloister Temple.

After taking a right on Sixth Avenue, passing through Palmway Garden and hanging a left on M Street, Cesar glided his hover-car into an open parking space at the end of the block. He switched the motor off and sat in the dark, thinking. A lot could go wrong. What if the Pink he'd just planted at the Lab got only one of his targets: Malcato and not Optima, or vice-versa? Whichever of them got away would be sure to suspect Spoon as supplier and himself as planter. He fiddled with the buzz gun.

The sidewalk was still dark and empty. He walked the half-block to the Safe House, awkwardly holding the gun against his right leg. As soon as he got inside, he'd stash the gun in an inconspicuous place, then act as if everything were normal. It was getting late. Hayes should be back soon.

As Cesar keyed the entrance door, he sensed a distinct presence behind him. Startled, he turned; there was no one. Exhaustion had made his paranoia worse. With soft finger tips he tried to soothe his throbbing temples. He chided himself for being so erratic, exuberant one moment, depressed the next. Did he have the presence of mind to deal with Hayes, hide his anger and his intentions? He took a deep breath and stepped inside.

The soundproofing dampened his footsteps as he ducked into the seldom-used recharging room, where he found an old, dirty towel and wrapped up the gun, making an ad-hoc safety lock by cramming folds of cloth behind the trigger. Suddenly, unexpectedly, the gun shrunk down to original size. He unwrapped the gun and reproduced the maneuver. Evidently pressing and holding the trigger forward did the trick. He opened and closed the gun several times to be sure he had the hang of it and stuffed it in his right-hand trouser pocket. Feeling more secure with the tiny weapon on his person, Cesar went out into the hall.

The air was deadly still except for a muted conversation taking place in the back bedroom. Tuuve said something and a second, unfamiliar voice answered. Cesar froze to listen. The voice didn't belong to anyone he knew. The voices were coming from behind the closed bedroom door.

He walked through the vacant salon, then stepped into the bathroom. As he closed the door behind him, he heard the bedroom door open. Footsteps ran across the wooden salon floor, waited a minute and ran back. Cesar relieved himself, washed his face and stood staring at himself in the mirror. In the last twenty-four hours, how many mistakes had he made? How many quick decisions might he later regret? He gave himself a pep talk, telling himself to keep courage. All he needed to do was to get Spoon aside. Together they'd figure out how many doses of Pink they'd need to take over the Remp board. After administering a few shots in a few well-deserving faces, they'd have a beachhead from which to carry an honest campaign to the people.

Cesar emerged from the bathroom. Except for an occasional word, the conversation behind the bedroom door was still undecipherable. Curious and cautious, Cesar gently pressed his ear to the door.

In shrill tones, the second voice crooned, "Za-ang, ma-an!"

The Tuuve voice responded, "Lower and less sing-song. Make the 'a' in 'man' a little flatter."

"Zang, maan!" came the second try.

Cesar, once again, felt incredibly foolish. Paranoia was making him crazy. It was just M. Forrest getting a voice lesson. Apparently, the robot's voice had been thrown off kilter by its injury and Tuuve was retraining it to match the original.

He had to take control of himself; his mood was shifting from super-charged to scared stiff every few seconds. Time was short. Hayes would be here any minute.

Cesar knocked on the door, intent on finding out where Spoon had gone off to.

The bedroom door creaked open. Tuuve turned to the intruder and smiled. Cesar had been wrong about the bearer of the second voice. Although the infrared signature of the jaw muscle was clearly robotic, it wasn't M. Forrest. The face looked familiar, but it didn't belong on a robot. It spoke softly with a slight Spanish accent. "Zang, man! There you are. We've been expecting you."

Cesar gave it a puzzled look.

"Let's have a seat in the salon," it said with a kindly gesture. "I'll explain everything."

Cesar held his ground. "Zag! What the hell is going on?"

"Zig! If you want it straight, I'll give it to you straight. Cesar Komenen, you have been recalled. I'm your replacement."

The face was the same one he'd just been staring at in the mirror—the one he'd been staring at all his life. The face was his own.

# BUNKER HELL

Cesar's face stared back at him with a patient, solicitous look as it waited for its human avatar to collapse into submission. The human Cesar's ears pulsed, his eyes glazed, his mind deadened. Wave after wave of dread washed over him though he had foreseen this very threat. Squared off with his imitation self, he knew he had a plan but struggled to retrieve it from the January-thick molasses of his mind.

Over the robot's shoulder, he saw M. Forrest sitting on the edge of the bed. Bits and pieces of his plan began to surface. All he had to do was issue the correct command and Forrest would come to his aid. But when he tried to open his mouth, all that came out was a raspy exhalation. He couldn't find his voice.

Cesar's momentary paralysis was a perfect imitation of what the trigger in his brain was supposed to do: create an appearance of complete submission to the robot's command. The robot smiled with satisfaction.

With a jolt, Cesar managed to open his mouth and shout the words, in a strangled voice, "Forrest, help—"

The plea was interrupted by a sharp right-hook to the jaw. The robot then kicked Cesar's ankle out from under him, driving him backwards into the salon. Twisting around, Cesar tried to get his arms out in front of him to break his fall but succeeded only in flailing. As he tumbled down, his forehead hit the sharp edge of a table lamp, which went crashing to the floor, shattering into hundreds of shards. Cesar staggered to his knees, almost regained his footing, then went sprawling face-first on the floor. Dozens of small splinters stung the side of his face like a swarm of angry bees. Cesar rolled on his back. His hand groped for his pocket. He shouted, "Hold it!" as he pulled out the buzz gun. But he'd spoken too soon. It took a second to locate the expander button and before he could press it, the dupe booted the weapon from his hand. The gun clattered across the floor, landing with a thump on the opposite side of the room.

Cesar scrambled on all fours in the direction of the thump, but the bot blocked his way. He looked up to find his stern-faced self towering over him. The robot leaned down, grabbed Cesar firmly by the ears, stared into his eyes and pulled his face close to its own. In flat tones, the robot stated, "Cesar Komenen, you have been recalled. You have been recalled."

Cesar gritted his teeth and slammed his forehead into the bot's hardened face. The robot retaliated by grabbing Cesar's head and squeezing it between the flats of its palms. Cesar yowled in pain. "Hail, Forrest, Tamer of Tyrants," Cesar cried in a breathless falsetto. But his voice was too soft. He repeated his panicked plea again and again, a little louder each time, slamming the back of his head against the floor to energize himself. "Hail, Forrest," then "Spoon, Tuuve, Buddy, anyone, help!" he shouted. But there was no response. Where was Spoon? Why didn't his buddy robot, dedicated to his protection, respond—had Hayes instructed it to leave him in the lurch just when he needed it? What about Tuuve? Why didn't he show his face? Most bewildering was M. Forrest. The bot was certainly able to hear this ruckus from its spot in the nearby room. Why wasn't it responding? Had something gone wrong with the cascade program? Maybe it hadn't clearly heard all the words of the command. If only Cesar could get to the back room to issue the order directly.

The rest of the house was eerily quiet. Still supine on the floor, panting and frightened, he stared up at the replica of his face, framed in a circle of stringy, long hair that dangled straight down at him. A bizarrely irrelevant thought stuck him: If that's what he looked like in long hair, he'd run to the barber shop first chance he'd get—if he ever got out of this jam. "Hail, Forrest," he shouted again in desperation.

"You have been recalled," Robot Cesar retorted. It looked surprised, baffled. The robot repeated: "You have been recalled. You have been recalled." Its baffled look deepened.

The robot seemed stymied. Apparently it hadn't been programmed with a plan B but like a broken record kept going back to a plan that wasn't working. Its hold on Cesar was weakening.

Careful to make no sudden moves the robot might interpret as a preparation for attack, he slowly got up

It took every ounce of Cesar's strength to keep the
gun from slipping from his grasp.

from his prone position, first to his knees, then back to his feet. The bedroom door wasn't ten steps away. If he could get there first, he could close the door and lock the robot out long enough to rouse M. Forrest.

He suddenly sprinted through the door, slamming it shut behind him. He stood panting, his body weight holding it closed. He could hear his robot dupe clawing at the door, on the other side, trying to get through.

Tuuve sat in one corner, looking sullen. "I don't want any part of this," the newbee said. "Please leave me alone."

A muffled cry came from the opposite corner. When he turned his eyes, Cesar saw Witherspoon stretched out on the bed, tied hand and foot, gagged, his eyes bulging with fear.

Cesar had no chance to untie his friend. Pressure against the door grew steadily as hammering blows struck one after the other. The robot's strength was too much. Slowly it forced the door open and M. Cesar stepped in, gloating triumphantly. Just behind stood M. Forrest, holding the buzz gun waist high, aimed at Cesar's head.

Cesar cried out, "Hail, Forrest, Tamer of Tyrants!"

The robot froze, staring at Cesar.

"Throw me the gun," Cesar shouted. M. Forrest tossed the weapon to him over Robot Cesar's shoulder, who had stopped, briefly confused. Just as Cesar caught the buzzer, the robot dupe charged, grabbed Cesar by both wrists and dragged him toward the doorway. It took every ounce of strength for Cesar to keep the gun from slipping from his grasp. The robot held his hands in an excruciating pincer grip, but he endured the pain; at last maneuvered a finger around what he hoped was the trigger and managed to get off a shot. A bright line of red laser light flashed as the shot drew a glowing stripe on the reflective ceiling. The robot retaliated with a kick to the gut. Cesar tried to lower his aim, but the bot's grip was too strong. Cesar's shoes skidded on the polished wood floor as he was dragged back, irresistibly, into the salon.

"Forrest, help!" Cesar shouted.

The robot dupe slapped a hand over Cesar's mouth, loosening its grip on his wrist. Cesar twisted around and thrust the gun barrel into the robot's ribs. "Freeze," Cesar bellowed, "Or I'll turn you into a pile of silica."

The robot pushed the barrel aside with a cool karate-like chop, and the two Cesars, struggling to control the weapon, caromed around the room, knocking over another lamp and an end table, tipping over the salon's lone armchair. A panel on the robot's arm popped open, revealing a mass of wires and mechanical parts. Cesar grabbed for the opening, but the robot pulled the human's arm out of reach. Cesar couldn't hold his own for long against the robot's superior strength.

M. Forrest entered the salon, its movements slow and cumbersome. The cascade had apparently worked, emptying the robot's database of Remp commands, granting Cesar full control, but it had left the bot disoriented and witless. It would have to be told what to do each step of the way. "Forrest, grab the robot that looks like me and get it off me!"

M. Forrest lumbered forward and, without a moment's hesitation over which of the twin figures was human and which was not, seized the dupe by the neck, causing M. Cesar to go limp, with a dazed, far-away look, like a kitten being held by the scruff of the neck by its mother.

Cesar was just about to wiggle free when Tuuve rushed in. It took Tuuve somewhat longer than the robot to figure out which of the struggling twins was which. Then, with all his strength, Tuuve hit the real Cesar in the gut with a monster punch.

Cesar doubled over. "Tuuve!" he groaned. "I thought you wanted no part of this."

"Traitor!" the newbee yelled, hitting him again and snatching the gun from his hand.

Cesar raised both hands in a gesture of surrender.

Waving the gun, Tuuve ordered Cesar to right the upturned chair and take a seat. Instead, Cesar staggered to his feet, holding his bruised head. It was a long shot to reason with a brainwashed human, but it was either that or try recapture the gun: a suicide mission. "Tuuve, stop, listen!" Pointing at the robot copy of himself, "Who's the traitor here?" he demanded. "Remp betrayed me, it betrayed all of us."

The newbee stood motionless. Cesar continued, "I twisted your brain with DJ programs. You aren't yourself. I programmed you for unquestioning loyalty to the Party. I'm sorry, Tuuve. This Party is not the idealistic crusade we signed up for. It's manipulating all of us like puppets. It's lost its way. Remp betrayed us."

There was a loud bang. Witherspoon, still bound hand and foot, had managed to pull himself into a sitting position and use his bound feet to pull himself across the floor.

"Who betrayed who?" Cesar shouted. "Who tied him up?"

Tuuve grinned broadly. "I did," he shouted. "You are the traitors! Contemptible traitors, both of you."

Darting his eyes at Tuuve and cocking his head, Spoon gave Cesar a let's-take-this-guy-out sign.

As if on cue Spoon quietly leaned back, spun on his butt, and drove his feet into the back of Tuuve's knees. Cesar, instantly grasping Spoon's strategy, shoved the newbee in the chest. Tuuve lost his balance and with a wail fell backwards, firing a wild shot as he fell. The gun slipped from his startled grip and clattered noisily on the floor. Cesar grabbed the barrel and cradled the weapon to his chest. He'd hang on to it this time.

Cesar helped remove the restraints from Spoon, then Spoon transferred them to Tuuve, who was soon gagged and bound hand and foot to the upholstered chair. The newbee looked stunned in disbelief that the situation could turn against him so swiftly.

Cesar instructed M. Forrest to remove M. Cesar's shoe and sock and deactivate his dupe. M. Cesar slumped lifelessly into a heap onto the floor, amidst the glass shards and overturned furniture. Cesar looked warily at his duplicate lying limply on the floor at the feet of M. Forrest. It looked asleep. It was eerie: he wondered if that was how he, too, looked when he was sleeping.

"You're not going to get away with anything," Tuuve muttered. "Hayes, Malcato, Sincardo, they'll learn about this. You're done."

"Put a sock in it," Cesar shouted.

M. Forrest took one of the dupe's socks and stuffed it into Tuuve's gaping mouth. It had taken Cesar's words as a literal command.

Cesar and Spoon broke into wild laughter. It was laughter of relief.

Once they regained their composure, Cesar wanted to know what had happened in his absence. "How did you get tied up in the first place?" Cesar asked Spoon.

"Follow me, I'll show you."

Cesar instructed Forrest to keep an eye on Tuuve. "Keep him tied up here. If he tries anything, break his neck." Not that Tuuve was in shape to do much of anything at this point. But at Cesar's words, certain to be interpreted literally by the humorless bot, Tuuve's eyes turned into glassy spheres of terror.

Cesar still had dried blood on his lips and nostrils from the fight. He rubbed the blood off, then left with Spoon.

Witherspoon led Cesar to the robot assembly room. Buddy was lying on one of the gurneys, immobilized; they untied him and let the metalloid struggle to its feet.

In the corner, the closet door—the door Cesar had not been able to open on his first investigation of the Safe House, and where the two synth-hemoglobin-eating lizards had lived—was now ajar. Witherspoon turned on the light and gestured for Cesar to look inside. The narrow closet was lined with duplicate robots. There were six against one wall, six against the other. Two, carrying the faces of Witherspoon and Hayes, were instantly recognizable. The other ten were unknown.

"Sincardo's been busy," Spoon said grimly.

"You sure Optima could pull this off?"

"Who else has the know-how or the warped ambition?"

"With Malcato's support."

"Of course."

At 5:20 A.M., ever-eager Hayes strode through the front door, earlier than planned. He was standing in the assembly room before realizing anything was amiss, startled to see Tuuve stretched out in the gurney, gagged and kicking. Next to him were two grubby, sleeping guys he didn't recognize. The door to the security closet was wide open.

"What the hell," Hayes said, in a loud whisper, not to awaken the strangers, as he hurriedly untied Tuuve's gag. As soon as Tuuve's mouth was free to speak, the newbee shouted, "Watch out!" But it was too late: before Hayes knew what had hit him, Buddy and Forrest had jumped him from behind, then twisted his arms behind his back and pulled him down to the fourth gurney, to which they lashed him. Cesar and Witherspoon emerged from the closet and exchanged smirks.

"You won't get away with this, Cesar." Hayes yelled. "You can't conquer the whole world by yourself."

"Right you are," said Cesar, dryly. "That's why I use robots."

Hayes looked like he'd burst a gasket.

Cesar looked to Tuuve and the converted bots.

"Traitor!" Tuuve shrieked. "You'll pay for this, you traitor!"

"Sedate them both," Cesar ordered. Forrest rummaged through cabinets, looking for injectable meds. Cesar was relieved to see the bot functioning at level 3, *with the capacity to formulate and execute a plan of action.* A couple of minutes later, the yeller and the shrieker were resting quietly.

"You know," Cesar said as he slapped Spoon on the back, "you and I make a great team. With Pink and Puppet Master, we could conquer the world."

He was only half kidding.

"I like the way you think," Witherspoon answered with the same sarcastic lilt. "But we need to conquer Lake Worth first," he continued with a glint in his eye. "And to do that, for starters I'd like to Pink up those two," gesturing toward Hayes and the newbee.

They spent the next half hour restructuring the minds of the two former Remp loyalists. Spoon was getting better at it; it took less time than expected.

"I'm almost going to miss," Witherspoon said wistfully, as he completed the reprog, "their old obnoxious personalities, their wiles, their chicanery, their deviousness."

"No, you're not," Cesar said with a grin.

When Hayes was untied, he stood, bright-eyed and bushy tailed, waiting for his first command.

Witherspoon matter-of-factly led him back to the salon. Debris from the fight still littered the floor. "Clean this mess up," he commanded.

Hayes jumped into action, sweeping up the shards, straightening the tables, wiping blood from the floor. He found the buzz gun lodged in the corner and handed it to Spoon. "U da man!" he panted.

"Now, how did you know that?" Spoon asked with a smile.

Spoon fiddled with the barrel for a few seconds, the gun shrunk to banana size, and he stuffed it in his baggy pants pocket.

With Witherspoon in charge of the cleanup, Cesar headed to the back bedroom to nap. "I had barely a wink all night," he griped.

Cesar had just managed to close his eyes when his wrist phone buzzed. There was no one at the other end. Once he was able to focus, he recognized the call as the audio alert he'd set in Sincardo's office. *How nice of her to come in at six on a Sunday morning.* He yawned and tuned in the video from the L-3 cam. It showed a pair of legs crossed in summer white slacks, the tie-less running shoes kicked off.

A second pair of legs in gray slacks and black dress shoes came up from behind. "You're fooling. You didn't really lose contact with M. Cesar, did you?" It was Reina Malcato's impatient voice.

"It stopped transmitting a couple of hours ago," the voice of Optima answered, the legs on the screen uncrossing and re-crossing.

"And we can't reach Braadrik or Tuuve?" Malcato added incredulously.

The left leg started tapping its big toe. "Any idea what's going on over there?"

This was too good: Cesar couldn't have dreamed up a better plan.

He switched over to the L-3's command mode and sent the signal to release the Pink. He heard a soft hiss as the liquid in the vial began to vaporize. Then he saw Reina's hand reach down under the desk, grab the L-3 and rip it from its perch under the desk.

"Don't breathe!" she shouted.

All four legs disappeared and the office door slammed.

Cesar wasn't breathing either. If they had breathed in merely a whiff of Pink, they were goners, but they wouldn't be able to hear Cesar's commands, transmitted via the L-3, that would claim mastership over them. On the other hand, if they'd heard the hiss and left in time, they would be unaffected—and soon guessing who was responsible. Damn! How could he find out what was going on over there?

He switched the video to the L-3 sitting under Malcato's desk. His luck was holding: Optima was on the floor on all fours, staring blankly into the cam. Cesar pressed a button: a small pink cloud appeared on the monitor screen, just beneath Opti's nose.

Malcato's voice echoed in the background. "Witherspoon," she yelled at the top of her lungs. "I'll kill you for this!"

Malcato flopped down on the floor, slid over to Optima's side and put a limp arm around her vanquished companion. Both were staring weakly at the cam.

"Me-ow," Cesar said as he pressed the button again, and another small, pink cloud appeared on the screen. "Zing, zang!" Cesar gave a shout.

Pressing another button, to activate the two-way audio, he spoke commandingly. "Lock the door. Stay right there. We're on our way."

Optima nodded.

"I will obey," Malcato flatly replied.

Cesar gave out a celebratory whoop. Spoon hurried in.

"We've snared both in one trap," Cesar said with a chortle, explaining how he'd hidden the L-3s in Sincardo's and Malcato's offices. "Look!" His joy was boundless. "The Party is ours."

"One step at a time," said Spoon. "It's a little early to count our chickens. Let's get over there and make sure we've got the ladies under control. Then we can consider our next step: how to take over the Lab with a tekkie, a research nerd, a couple of robots and a motley crew of obedient Pinkees."

Cesar vigorously rubbed his hands together. "Zing! Us in control of the two pompous peas. What a beautiful thing. Want to hop over there in my hover-car?"

"No. It's a one-seater. It would be best for us to stay together. Let's march over to the Lab with the entire troop."

"I guess you're right," Cesar bit his lip. "It should be safe for Buddy on the street with the troop on guard. Ragers won't tangle with a group this big."

"Who knows? Maybe with a show of force we'll be able to convince a building full of robot geeks to join our revolution."

"Now, that *would* be zaggy!" Cesar beamed. "Change this fight into a cake walk."

Before leaving, they collected anything that might be of use—several folded DJ helmets, a fistful of Pink vaporizers along with a supply of antidote, even a bag of energy bars. Cesar gave himself another protective dose of the antidote, just in case, and stuffed the equipment into his black case. Witherspoon loaded his own briefcase with Pink components and the moebius equipment.

Cesar's nascent army lined up two abreast in the salon. Tuuve and Hayes were in front, followed by Tex and Tony, M. Forrest and M. Cesar, Spoon and Buddy with Witherspoon bringing up the rear, a platoon of ten.

Cesar addressed the three bots. "Deactivate locator sensors. Delete all Remp addresses and access codes." Then moving to the head of his little band and facing them all, he gave the command: "One and all, follow me."

Cesar and Witherspoon, the links to their underground past broken, were giddy from a mixture of exhaustion and euphoria at their roll of good luck—a roll that couldn't last forever. But Cesar was beyond caring: he marched out the front door of the Safe House, imagining himself the head of the newly formed Army of the Robot Republic of Florida. Unlike his Roman namesake, Cesar carried his own baggage. It was the egalitarian thing to do. Viva la Robot Army!

Viva la Robot Army

# SUNSHINE SOLDIERS

**T**he red glow of dawn filtered through the palms as Cesar's army set out on foot for the campus Lab. The day promised to turn hot and muggy, a typical Florida midsummer day. Yet at this early hour, the morning breeze still offered a breath of cool, light air. A flock of large-beaked pelicans soared overhead in a V-formation, skimming silently across the sky as they headed seaward to feed.

Across the street, the reporter's van was back. Reid sat in the front seat eating an apple, watching with amusement as the troop lined up on the stretch of sidewalk. Cesar walked over and motioned for the reporter to lower his window.

The glass barrier came down, wiping off hundreds of heavy dew drops, which streamed down the driver side door and puddled on the pavement at Cesar's feet. Without preliminaries, Cesar reached up and offered Reid a handshake. The reporter hesitated for a second and then leaned forward to reach for the outstretched hand. His trust was rewarded with a shot of pink spray square in his face. The pungent solvent burned his nostrils. He opened his mouth to speak. Nothing came out but a raspy groan. With clenched teeth, he flung the last of the apple at Cesar and started to zip up the window. But before the glass reached the top, his scowl had melted into a silly, mindless grin.

Cesar yelled though the open window crack, "I will give you orders from now on. You will do as I say without question. Understood?"

Reid nodded.

"Lower the window."

The glass slowly rolled back down. The reporter's eyes glazed with awestruck reverence. "I'm yours to command," he said with complete sincerity.

"Don't look at me with that goofy grin. Anyone who looks at you would know you aren't yourself. Keep your transformation secret. This is just between us. We mustn't let on that you've been recruited into my service. Is that clear?"

The reporter instantly slouched back in his seat, and his face regained its previous devil-may-care nonchalance.

"Much better," Cesar said. "Now I want you to endorse Forrest Newcomb for mayor. Can you do that without giving yourself away?"

"Sure, I'm cool," he said with a blasé shrug.

"Go back to your office," he said. "Write a glowing report on the robot rally at the school last Friday. Tell your readers you've been investigating the Futurist movement and are now convinced that robots are our future. Call for the repeal of the robot limitation laws. Is that clear?"

"Got it, chief. Robots create leisure. To own a worker-bee is the ultimate freedom. I'll get an editorial on the morning newscast. In the old days, advocating for one political party over another would've gotten me fired. But nowadays, he'd fire me if I didn't take sides. People don't want just the news anymore—they want to be told who's right and who's wrong."

Cesar gave Reid a big thumbs up.

As Reid drove off, Cesar strode up to his troop, took their lead and resumed the march to the Lab. They moved at a quick, synchronized cadence, except for M. Forrest, who limped on his partially repaired knee.

As the troop headed north on Dixie Highway, a white sedan heading south abruptly crossed six traffic lanes, made a U-turn, crept past them heading north and then awkwardly parked fifty meters ahead with its front wheel on the curb. A bald, paunchy middle-aged man in a long-sleeved white shirt and skinny green tie slid over into the passenger seat and pressed his nose to the glass, watching the troop go by. If Cesar had looked closely, he might have recognized the make and model of an unmarked squad car. At that moment, Cesar had too much on his mind to pay attention other than noticing the man's slightly odd behavior and slack jowls.

It was early Sunday morning. The few shops that weren't permanently boarded up were closed. There were few cars on the road. A single mutant vulture took off from its lamppost perch and began circling overhead, eyeing the troop's militant presence, hopeful for some fresh carrion.

A neighbor lady, oblivious at first to the unusual troop marching down her street, came out of a well-kept house in the middle of the block, carrying a bowl of cat food. The cat, startled at first, scampered across the sidewalk, yowling as it ran between M. Forrest's legs, and hid under a parked hover-car. The woman dropped her bowl, splattering brown pellets on her front steps as she jumped back behind her door. As the troop ran past, Cesar attempted to flash her a reassuring smile, but she was gone too quickly.

Cesar's wrist phone buzzed. It was Jewel.

"How's Clunk?" he asked without breaking stride, assuming she had called about her dog.

Jewel had bigger troubles. "Naabilat vigilantes are on a rampage. They came to our apartment in the middle of the night. They dragged us out of bed and started firing questions at Mama and me. They're psycho-nuts, they think we're hiding terrorists!"

"What? Wait! Slow down! Who did what? Are you okay? Are you hurt? If anyone touches you, I'll mangle 'em!" There was a sound of commotion in the background. "Where are you? It sounds like Friday night football," Cesar joked nervously.

"At the Cloister. The Naabi thugs forced us to run all the way here, down the middle of the street, pushing us and jabbing us with hammers and crow bars. Mama and I are locked in the john. They won't let anyone make calls, so we slipped in here."

Cesar could hear repeated pounding, like the thud of hammers. A muffled baritone yelled. "Everyone into the abomination room. Quick, quick, quick. Get moving!"

"What the hell was that?" Cesar demanded.

"They're corralling everyone into the Mecca Room, they're turning it upside down and destroying the Kaaba mural, prying it off the wall, smashing it. They're gathering all the friends, barking at us to renounce Islam, threatening to demolish the building brick by brick unless we do. They still claim they're searching for Rajul Khalid but it's just a ruse. It's like the ransacking of the Sixth Avenue Mosque all over again. . . ."

Jewel was interrupted by a series of loud crashes. It sounded like a herd of elephants stampeding through a forest.

"Cesar, I'm going to hang up and call the police."

"No! Jewel, sweetie, please. Do you really think they'll defend you against a bunch of raving Christian fanatics? They'll just make things worse."

Jewel's voice grew increasingly desperate. "Don't argue with me. I've got to at least try. Who else can stop them?"

Cesar turned to look at the troop and waved for them to halt. "Something better than the cops. Babe, keep your head down. I'll get there faster than a speeding bullet. . . ."

Witherspoon came up to the front of the line. "What's up? Why did we stop?"

Cesar quickly explained Jewel's predicament. They looked at the motley crew and then each other, their expressions suggesting they'd come up with the same idea. "I'd better get over to the Lab and see to the ladies," Spoon smiled. The buzz gun came out, and he offered it to Cesar.

"Yeah, I'll need that," said Cesar. He stuffed the gun in his pocket with his other hand; the wrist phone was still open to Jewel. "And you'll be needing these." He tossed his car keys in the air. Spoon caught the keys and gestured with his chin. "Wish me luck," he said as he hustled off back toward M Street.

"About face," Cesar ordered his little army. "Now, double time!" He raised his wrist phone back to his mouth. "Jewellie, you still there?"

"Still here."

"I'm bringing help. Stay on the line till I get there. Tell me what to expect."

"There are about a dozen young burly guys here with that Reverend Rebolt. They're on a rampage, destroying everything Muslim."

A door slammed on Jewel's end as her sister, Emerald, entered the washroom. "They've finished demolishing 'Mecca,'" she rasped in a weak, breathless voice. "Now they're combing through the library, tearing books off the shelves, ordering everyone to gather on the lawn for another book burning."

"Cesar, get here quick," Jewel pleaded.

"And that's not the worst of it." Emerald paused to catch her breath. "This other guy, the same guy who came to the house with the vet, says, 'Too many heretic books scattered all over the place, it'll take too long to sort through this crap. Burn the place top to bottom.' That's what he said."

A look of dread and fear came over Cesar's face. "Jewel, get out of the Cloister. Don't fool around."

Over the phone, Cesar heard a loud metallic pounding on the door and the same baritone voice. "You ladies, how long does it take to pee? Come out of the can immediately or I'll rip this door off its hinges."

"Cesar, Cesar," she pleaded, "Hurry!"

Cesar looked over his shoulder at the line of his marching troop. "Baby, don't worry. Open the door. Don't fight them. Leave the brutes to me. I'm on my way and I'm bringing my army."

"What army? You don't have . . ."

There was a deafening clamor as the door gave way.

A gruff roar exploded. "Get off that phone, bitch, or I'll tear your arm off, phone and all."

"I've got my rights, this is still a free country!" Jewel shouted futilely.

Cesar grimaced and broke into a trot, waving for the others to follow. He wished to God she would take her own advice for once and stop arguing.

Cesar heard amusement in the quick retort. "Right, lady, you have rights, plenty of rights," it laughed. "You've got every right to watch us burn this hellhole down."

Then the beating started.

Whack.

Whack.

Whack.

Scream.

Jewel's shrill cries reverberated in the small bathroom as Cesar heard her being struck with what sounded like a club or baton. He went half wild. "Hold on, baby . . ." he shouted.

"Your conspiracy with that heretic Einalli—" Whack. "Your weak-kneed sympathy for terrorists . . ." Whack. "Did you think we'd let you get away with giving comfort to our enemies?" Whack. "Your boyfriend can't save you." Whack. "I am the fist of God. I am the future." Whack.

"Future" was the last word Cesar heard. Then the phone went dead.

# WAR

**A** plume of dark gray smoke tilted west across the crystal blue, early morning sky as Cesar's troop neared the Cloister. A high hedge, broken in the middle by a narrow, arched gate, concealed the lower level of the building as well as the garden and grounds. Except for a large passenger van parked in front, there was no sign of activity, no squad car, no fire truck, no curious spectators. Cesar ordered his men and the three robots to circle around to the east side of the compound. A thick row of sea grape trees near the water's edge provided good cover and gave him a chance to assess the situation. Stealthily they stepped though the sandy soil, avoiding the brittle fallen leaves.

Peering across the east lawn, Cesar saw a half-dozen young men standing in a circle, taking turns throwing books onto a bonfire. They wore headbands that covered their eyes and masked their faces. Jewel, Suyapa and several other Cloister sisters Cesar knew only by sight were lashed to the trunks of a long line of royal palms that lined the garden walk. The women watched with horror-stricken faces as a crowd of Naabi thugs, mostly young but several middle-aged and one with a shock of white hair, hustled in and out of the building in grim silence, carrying boxes of papers and photos and relics of various kinds and displaying them to Rebolt for his instant judgment.

The bulky frame of the reverend stood with crossed arms, supervising, approving each find with a frown and a grunt, simultaneously engaged in animated discussion with a slender-framed uniformed policewoman. From a hundred meters away, Cesar recognized the mechanical heat pattern in both of their jaws. Stunned and dizzy, his mind tried to digest the implications. He hadn't realized there were robo-plants outside of Remp. But then he'd known nothing about his own robot dupe either. "Did you know Rebolt and Braxil are both robots?" Cesar whispered to Hayes who had walked up to him with his serene smile.

"Now you force the revelation of my deepest, darkest secret," Hayes chuckled with total compliance. "Yeah, I knew, but Optima swore me to silence."

"Tzz, she single-handedly built and maintains them both?"

"She had help, experts up from the Cuban RR. For months she used the Safe House as her private domain. She's building more dupe bots all the time. But I—" Hayes thumped himself in the chest. "I told her I couldn't run Forrest's campaign out of the Lab any longer. It's too visible, too public. So she had to make room for me on M Street."

"And she's behind Rebolt? That's weird. Why is she using a Futurist bot to promote his cult?"

"I dunno the answer to that, but I do know one thing—that reverend's not a dupe," he said with a grin, as if he'd just let the cat out of the bag. "That one was a robot from the start."

Things were getting stranger by the minute. There were so many unanswered questions: Why would Optima plant a robot preacher and police chief? What was their mission? And how many other personal robot toys did she have running around Lake Worth—and elsewhere?

A yell from the Cloister yanked Cesar back to the present.

Quickly Cesar gave assignments to his men. On signal, they charged from their hiding place into the open of the garden. Buddy and Cesar caught the robot Sheriff Braxil off guard, stuffed a handkerchief into its mouth to silence its startled screams and dragged it to a royal palm down the line from the Cloister women. There they pulled its arms around the trunk and used its own handcuffs to shackle it to the tree. The robot's eyes bulged with perfectly programmed fury and hate at its two grinning assailants.

Cesar gave Buddy a high five.

Reverend Rebolt, however, was not so easily subdued. When M. Forrest and M. Cesar tried to tackle the bulky reverend bot, it turned the tables on them, tossed M. Forrest into the chipped mulch of a flower bed, then threw M. Cesar against a jasmine bush, covered with thorns. Two alone were no match for the big robot.

They didn't make that mistake again. On the second attempt, Tuuve and Buddy joined in. The robot reverend roared and writhed like a wounded gator against the combined strength of its assailants as the four attackers grabbed its massive limbs. On a word of command from Cesar, they dragged Rebolt to the nearest palm where Cesar lashed its arms and legs to the trunk. The robot's face turned beet red. Its face puffed; its mouth foamed—impressively human, Cesar thought, even when portraying the most extreme emotions.

Jewel, still tied to a nearby tree, broke through her boyfriend's reverie with a shout. "Honey cakes, are you going to leave us here indefinitely?" she asked sarcastically.

"Sorry, sorry," muttered Cesar as he untied the cords binding her hands. Once set free, she wrapped him in a passionate kiss. "You're the most romantic creature on the planet," she cooed, "the sexiest stud since Robin Hood rescued Maid Marian."

"You say the hottest things in the coolest ways," he said with a blush.

Then she kissed him again with a quick dart of her tongue on his. "Danger is such an aphrodisiac," she purred.

Cesar forced his libido to subside. "Hold on, foxy," he panted. "We've got work to do."

Now it was Jewel's turn to blush. Her arms dropped disappointedly from Cesar's neck as she turned away and began untying the other women.

Half a dozen Naabi thugs appeared, hurrying through the garden into the building carrying red overflowing cans. The liquid splashed the gray pebbled walkways with dark, greasy-looking spots. A random breeze brought a sharp, sweet chemical smell to Cesar's nostrils. In a flash he realized what it was: an ancient, highly volatile fuel that had been banned for decades—he only recognized it from a chemistry class he'd had many years before. Kerosene.

Cesar tore through the garden, re-gathering his troop of robots and Pinkees. Without plan or forethought they rushed into the temple, searching for the kerosene carriers. Four of them were splashing the volatile fluid against the Cloister's wood-paneled inside walls when they were caught from behind and dragged out of the now fume-filled building. Cesar ran through the darkened sanctuaries searching frantically for the two missing arsonists.

In a connecting corridor, he found evidence that they'd passed through just moments before. A trail of kerosene had been left along the floorboards. His nose burned with the vapors. He dared not turn on the lights for fear a spark from the switch might ignite the fumes.

Fortunately, Cesar's cyberyes served him well in the darkness of the windowless worship rooms. A quick glance told him the Mecca Room was empty, its floor littered with bits of the damaged Kaaba mural. Halfway through the City of Peace, the kerosene flashed. Flames erupted on his right and behind him. The heat and smoke were intense, blocking his exit. He jumped up on a desk and tried to hurl himself out a window, but the thick, hurricane-proof glass did not yield. He fell bruised to the floor, his shirt absorbing fuel that had puddled on the hard surface.

Now half-drenched in kerosene, with orange flames starting to lick up all around him and smoke choking him, he became desperate. Near him stood a small stone statue of St. Therese of Lisieux; he seized it and began hammering its haloed head against the window pane. After the third blow, the window shattered into pea-size bits. He kissed the saint's head with a "Mil gracias, Santa Teresa!" before dropping it to the ground and, with a diving leap, hurled himself through the jagged opening and landed face down on the lawn. As he staggered to his feet, he felt someone give him a heavy push from behind. He stumbled forward, lost his footing and fell face first into the bonfire of books. He covered his face with his hands as his shirt burst into flames. Cesar let out a bloodcurdling shriek, not of pain, but anger. "Hijo de perro!" Scrambling atop the burning pile, he tried to get his legs back under him but succeeded only in kicking flaming volumes onto the lawn.

From across the garden, Jewel had little time to react. She had been talking with Suyapa when the sound of crashing glass snapped her neck around. She turned just in time to see Cesar fling himself through the flame-ringed window. Momentary relief flooded over her when Cesar, apparently unhurt, stood and brushed himself off. Then she saw a young Naabi thug with a vicious grin rush up behind Cesar and give him that hateful push. She watched helplessly as Cesar landed in the fire.

She screamed as she rushed with Suyapa to the fire. They grabbed him by the legs and dragged him from the blaze, then started pounding the flames on his chest. Soon his shirt was charred tatters, leaving exposed sections of his chest red and soot-smeared.

Half in shock, Cesar looked down at his shirt. Whiffs of smoke drifted out from under its charred fragments.

"Roll," Jewel shouted. "Roll!"

Still in a daze, Cesar rolled back and forth on the ground through the flower beds lining the Cloister's outside walls. The plants were still wet from the morning dew and the fire soon hissed out, leaving behind a smell of peat moss, crushed grass and burnt polyester. He lay winded, stunned but now alert in the cool grass. Yellow lantana blossoms were pressed flat over his skin and clothes.

Jewel couldn't believe her eyes. "You okay?" she asked, bringing her face close to his. "I was so afraid your face—" she said with a moan.

Cesar popped open an eye.

"Afraid your pretty boy toy might not be so pretty anymore?" "You naughty boy!" Jewel slapped him lightly on the cheek. Then she jumped on top of him and began kissing his blackened but uninjured face. "But you're still beautiful. My beautiful hero." she repeated over and over. "My beautiful hero!"

"What I really need" Cesar cracked, surveying his tatters, "is a clean shirt."

The firefighters arrived with an EMT van in tow. A crowd began to gather as they quickly set up a perimeter and began pumping water into the burning structure. The southern wing blazed into the morning sky. Cesar could see the worship rooms and their ritual murals framed in fire, collapsing one by one into the inferno. The wall with the Kaaba covered in black jute and surrounded by worshipping throngs appeared, half destroyed by the thugs, slowly eaten by the writhing, dancing fire. There was no chance the rooms or murals could be saved.

The Cloister faithful stood around in small groups. Some discussed their fate. Where would they go? What would they do? Could they ever raise funds for a restoration of what they had lost? Some stood quietly weeping. Many just stared blankly at the devastation.

Cesar and Jewel stood in the garden, their hands tightly clasped, surrounded by blossoming orange trees, and watched the firemen's frantic efforts. Hose after hose was dragged from the truck, pouring thick streams of water onto the building. Although she put on a stony face, he knew Jewel was feeling overwhelmed by the sudden destruction of her spiritual home. A hot gust of wind blew their way, carrying pungent smoke that stung their eyes.

Cesar slid up to her, wrapped his arms around her waist and pulled her close to him. "You can rebuild," he said.

She nuzzled the back of her head against his shoulder. "Yeah," she replied sarcastically. "Like the Sixth Avenue mosque was rebuilt."

Her cheeks streamed with tears.

# FOREIGN ENTANGLEMENTS

"The Einalli crowd is plenty resourceful," Cesar reassured Jewel. "You'll find a way to carry on."

Jewel perked up at the name of her guru. "Did you know he's here?" she said excitedly.

"Who?"

"The Master." She looked through the faces in the crowd, trying to locate the guru. "He's looking for you."

"What does he want with me? And how did he get here so fast?" Cesar glanced at his watch. "It's barely seven in the morning."

Jewel ignored his questions, her face radiating an ethereal glow as if it were obvious he would know of their troubles. "I want you to meet him."

She spotted the guru fifty meters away, speaking earnestly with Suyapa, who waved, motioning for them to come over.

Jewel tugged on Cesar's sleeve as she led him to Einalli.

"Ah, the swan and the raven," the guru said as they approached.

Cesar didn't know quite what to make of that comment. *Was Jewel the swan, pure and beautiful? And what was he supposed to be? A raven, omen of gloom and doom?*

"Swan and raven?" he said, expecting an explanation, but Einalli simply embraced them both.

"Welcome," he said with a pained smile. He turned to Jewel, who stared up at him with wide, hopeful eyes. "It is terrible what has happened to your temple, my child. I feel for the loss to our local members, and even more for the awful price the lost souls who caused this to happen will pay in karmic suffering. Still, we must always remember that all things pass but what we know in our hearts. It is the faithful who make up our true Temple. For the future there is always hope."

Jewel smiled, glowing with gratefulness for his kind, wise words.

Einalli paused with his eyes bent to the ground, in respect for his young follower. Then he turned to Cesar. "Come sit in my vehicle away from this commotion. I have some information you may find helpful."

He bowed graciously to Jewel and left her, a beatific look on her face, sitting cross-legged on a flat slab of rock in the garden as the two men climbed into the back of the guru's Habi-Van. From the outside, the van looked gray and ordinary, like any one of hundreds of similar vehicles on South Florida roads, but inside it was an entry portal to inner space, a meditation center on wheels, a small, secluded cubical cosmically detached from the outside world. The fluid inner surface morphed as they entered, forming a temporary portal and resealing itself behind them. Three-D black walls engulfed the space, stretching off infinitely through myriads of softly humming stars, scattered with nebulae and wispy proto-stellar clouds, glowing pale red, waiting to give birth. The illusion was masterful, and Cesar gazed in astonishment.

Two auto-form chairs emerged in diagonal corners of the cube. Einalli and Cesar sat down and exchanged pleasantries. The guru held out his heavily veined hand, offering Cesar a ruby-colored chip. "Here's a message for you from the Minister of External Affairs at the Cuban RR. He's willing to grant you political asylum from the renegade Florida Futurists until your trouble subsides."

Cesar looked at the chip but hesitated to take it. "Renegade Florida Futurists?"

"The minister's term, not mine. The EA gave financial aid to your Florida unit, considerable sums, but now regrets it, and, if you ask me, for good reason, seeing how they've violated so many core principles, doing irreparable damage to our common cause, in his words."

Cesar thoughts turned to Jewel, waiting for him in the garden and then to Spoon, wondering how his encounter with Malcato and Sincardo was going. He scratched his head and sighed. "I'm feeling the same betrayal as the EA, but frankly I don't see how this has anything to do with my current situation. We're at a critical point in our efforts to get the Party back on track. There are things I need to attend to. With all due respect, I can't really talk for long." Cesar bowed from the waist in a reverential gesture to the guru.

"Certainly, I'll get directly to the points I need to make. Number one, the EA's sent you an official hovercraft. It's waiting in Lantana Harbor, ready to take you to Cienfuegos. He wants to support your reform effort but knows your life is in grave danger. The hovercraft will be at your disposal should you decide to take up the EA's asylum offer and come to Cuba."

Cesar's eyes deepened in their sockets. He gazed past Einalli's face at the starbursts on the wall behind him. "He—and you—seem to know an awful lot about my business," he gruffed.

"Perhaps there's an explanation on the chip," the guru suggested.

Cesar shook his head, impressed and curious about the extent of the EA and Einalli's knowledge, and how they had obtained it.

"Number two," Einalli continued, "the minister requests that you give me a list of all the persons treated with your pink gas. And further, and this is not nego-tiable—he insists you forego its further use, as a condi-tion of asylum."

The blood rushed to Cesar's face. He slipped his hand into his pocket and felt the cylinders of Pink roll against his leg. His plan called for using Pink to take control of the Remp board. With Malcato and Sincardo now, presumably, neutralized, he only needed to "per-suade" one or two additional voting members. Now was not the time to set aside the Pink. That would feel like snatching defeat from the jaws of victory.

"What does any of this have to do with you?" Cesar challenged. "Why do you want such a list?"

Einalli gave him a warm smile. "Don't you want all these mind games to end?"

Cesar exhaled.

Einalli continued to plead. "All I have to do is look at the vacant eyes of those pinked men to see what's been done to them: their brains have been severed from their souls. I'm involved because we believe my time chamber may be able to heal the damage done to Pink victims. You do know about the mental health applications of my time loop techniques, right?"

"Not much."

"Briefly, your pink vapor interferes with the time loop that creates self-awareness. The result, at its strongest, is robot-like behavior, unthinking, unfeeling and blindly obedient. My machine reinitiates the temporal dimensional moebius, restores personhood. GEMS, my colony in Cuba, provided technical help to your Dr. Witherspoon to develop Pink. I, like the EA, have regrets. We feel responsible to fix the results that were unfortunate."

Cesar took the slender chip from the guru's heavily creased hand, slipped it into his wrist implant, said a hurried good-bye and opened the van door. "I'll be back with you."

Heavy hands reached inside the vehicle, took firm hold of Cesar's collar and heaved him into the street. Vainly, Cesar tried to wriggle from their grasp, but four police officers combined to knock him to the ground, push his head against the pavement and quickly handcuff him.

Einalli stepped out of the van, saw the prostrate Cesar and started to protest. "This man came here in peace. Leave him in—"

Before he could finish his sentence, the officers forced the guru back into his vehicle and slammed the door.

After confiscating Cesar's buzz gun, two officers dragged him face to face with the chief. Standing behind her, with a look of enormous satisfaction on his face, was the jowly U-turn man who had spotted Cesar's troop on Dixie Highway. M. Braxil stood looking Cesar over with an equally satisfied grin, rubbing her wrists. "You're under arrest," she said through a broad smile of robot-patterned infrared.

Tex and Tony were also in custody, handcuffed and sullen. Buddy stood beside Cesar in the grasp of a two stern-faced policeman and bound with so many ropes he looked like a mummy. Ten or eleven officers huddled around the group in a circle.

Cesar looked over toward the trees where, minutes before, Braxil and Rebolt had been tied. A set of cut rope ends lay at the base of a tree. Firemen were still in the process of releasing Rebolt.

"Arrested? On what charge?"

"For multiple violations of the Robot Limitation Laws," M. Braxil said. "This robot of yours is not licensed for public exhibition or to appear on the street at any time. It assaulted the reverend. And it assaulted an officer of the law: me."

Cesar laughed out loud. The officers plainly thought he was loony, but he couldn't help himself. Despite his predicament, the irony of an illegal robot arresting him for possession of an illegal robot that had attacked another illegal bot was just too funny.

## NARRATIVE PAUSE 008

FULLY ALERT, Jurat reversed the narration and studied the emulation image of himself. He'd never realized how jowly his face had become or how much flab had accumulated around his waist. Resolutely, he promised himself he'd lay off the conch fritters for a while.

Shrugging away his vain introspection, he stepped through the narration in slow motion, looking for a clear image of Sheriff Braxil. There "she" stood, on the curb, giving orders, indistinguishable from the real Sheriff. He moaned in disgust. He'd been on the scene at the Cloister fire—he'd even ID'd Komenen to her—and he'd had no idea she was a machine. It was only the Komenen brain scan, which gave him access to the kid's inner thoughts, that had opened his eyes. Astonishing. He'd worked with Braxil on nearly a daily basis for fifteen years.

Not the easiest boss, but fair, in her own head anyway. Apparently the robot Chief had been on duty for less than a month. He went back over the last few weeks in his mind trying to figure out when the swap might have occurred. He hadn't noticed any change, really. Norma seemed perfectly normal—maybe a little less intense, more inclined to crack a joke, but he'd figured maybe she'd changed her PMS medication. All the more credit to the skill of those Futurist roboticists—pulling off a stunt like that. Just to be sure he hadn't misinterpreted anything, Jurat searched the mind scan file and located the spot where Cesar saw the heat patterns of Braxil's robot anatomy. Although Jurat didn't have cybereyes, he was learning to use Cesar's acuity, as recorded on the scanned images, to distinguish human from robot patterns. Sure enough, the evidence was there, plain as day.

With a quick tap of his index finger, he paged the on-duty officer at the jail. "This is Inspector Jurat. Can you get me an examination room? . . . Soon as possible. . . . Cesar Komenen. . . . I'll be down in ten . . . Thanks."

The Palm Beach County PD didn't have the sort of advanced mind-scanning equipment that the Futurists enjoyed. Instead of a soft, comfortable helmet, Jurat lowered a large metal dome down onto Cesar's head. A spiral track circled the dome's lower perimeter and spiraled its way up to a knobby peak. A caterpillar sensing-wand rode along the track, jogging back and forth, systematically scanning the gray matter beneath the helmet.

Jurat got right to the point: "Your cybereyes can detect robots on sight, right? You can walk into a room and immediately tell if there are robots present masquerading as human?"

Cesar sat unresponsive, saying nothing. Jurat slowly and deliberately repeated the question. The awkward silence was palpable.

Cesar just sat there without moving. Finally he said, "You're asking the wrong question."

"How many duplicate robots are roaming around our community?"

Cesar gestured futilely. "You mean besides Braxil, Rebolt, Forrest and me? None as far as I know. I'm as much in the dark as you are."

Jurat had only half heard the response; he was staring at the brain wave monitor, which was behaving strangely. It remained blank, showing no mental activity. He checked connectors and wiggled wires without benefit. Feeling completely foolish, he turned to Cesar.

"Do you know what's wrong with this thing?"

"Why, nothing at all. It's functioning perfectly."

"What do you mean?" Jurat said, pointing at the blank screen. "Look, no wave patterns!"

"The logical explanation, the simple explanation and the correct explanation, my friend, is that there is no mental activity."

"Huh?"

"There's no neural activity because there's no brain in my head. I'm a robot."

Jurat stared, dumbfounded, at the figure sitting across from him.

"Would it help if I showed you?" M. Cesar offered. He pushed his stool back into the corner and abruptly stuck out his leg. He proceeded to remove his shoe and sock, and with firm pressure, popped open the data port in his heel. "Cable me up," it declared. "Boss has a message for you."

# FIRST PETITION TO JURAT

The island sun was just beginning its late afternoon descent to the sea. Cesar stretched out poolside at the Hotel Cy-Bar, wearing a blue-flowered shirt and swimming briefs, looking as relaxed as if he'd been on vacation for a month. Robot attendants roamed from guest to guest, offering towels, suntan lotion, massage. Across the water, a marimba band played a hot, Afro-Cuban number. A bikini-clad Jewel walked up carrying two mint mojitos, handed one to Cesar and stretched out next to him. He leaned over to kiss her, took a sip of his drink, smiled into the video camera and began.

"Inspector Jurat, as you have probably guessed I am now far outside your jurisdiction, free, here in Cuba. With all due respect, sir, I don't really owe you anything. But I'd like to see the situation with the Futurists resolved quickly and fairly. First off, I need to tell you about Forrest Newcomb—the real human variety."

On cue, a large, awkward figure strolled into the frame and sat down at the foot of Cesar's lounger. He gave the camera a red-faced cringe. "Inspector Jurat, I—I—don't th-think we've had the p-pleasure of meeting," Forrest stuttered. "But let me take this op-portu-nity to introduce myself." The human Forrest looked over his shoulder at Cesar, who signaled encourage-ment. Forrest turned back to the camera.

"Don't be nervous, Forrest. Take your time," Jewel reassured him.

"I—I—I've been here for a few months. Cesar thought I was murdered, but as you see, it ain't neces-sarily so." His eyes widened. "Fact is, I wasn't kidnapped either. I came here of my own free will. Hayes paid me eleven million Cuban pesetas. He had me s-sign all the candidate p-petitions filed with the S-Supervisor of Elections office before I left. I sold him the legal rights to my identity, got a new face, a complete new look and agreed to stay in Cuba, never to return to Florida. I was rich and ready to have a good time. At first, it was like being on permanent vacation. The nightlife here is zazz hot. Parties went on night after night. But over time, the fun wore off. Beaches, rum and bikinis only go so far." Forrest shook his head with regret. "After a while, I wanted my old life and my old face back. I called Hayes and he hit the roof, shouting at me I was endangering his whole operation. Then I got Pinked, dose after dose. Of course, I didn't know anything about Pink at the time, but I guess Malcato stole it from Witherspoon's research lab. I totally lost track of days and weeks, didn't know who I was or where I'd come from. These guys found me and restored my mind and face. Now I'm trying to sort out the rest of my life."

Forrest hesitated. "One thing you should know. One decision I've made is that I intend to stay in the race. There's a week left before Election Tuesday. You cannot legally r-remove my n-name from the ballot. All the papers were properly signed and filed before I left Florida. My attorney's petitioned the court for an injunction in case there's any dispute. I want to be Lake W-Worth's next mayor. If elected, I will s-serve."

Forrest again glanced at Cesar. "That's all I w-wanted to say."

Cesar nodded. "You don't need my permission."

The camera zoomed in for a tighter shot on Cesar and Jewel.

"Jurat, we'd like to cut a deal. I—We"—He pointed to Jewel.—"would like to return to Lake Worth, but we need immunity from prosecution. What can I offer you in exchange?"

Cesar's delivery was slow and unhurried. He had a lot to say and wanted to let each point to settle in before proceeding. He took a sip from his drink, stirred it and took another.

"I may be able to help you in several ways, especially with regard to Sheriff Norma Braxil. Under an immunity agreement, we're also willing to share additional information about robot stand-ins for other prominent Floridians."

Cesar gave his last comment time to sink in. "Yes, we know that robot duplicates have replaced two other highly placed officials." He paused again, looked at Jewel, as if to ask her if she wanted to add anything. She declined, and Cesar continued to sip on his mojito.

"M. Cesar will serve as our communications link. You can also upload messages to the robot, and it will forward them to me, here in Cuba. Just as you obtained this file by accessing the data port in the robot's heel, you will be able to acquire my future transmissions in the same way. Soon you'll be receiving additional files. They provide the background so you can understand my motives. Hopefully, if you know all that, you'll feel you can trust me.

"As a courtesy to you, I'm also sending an explanation of how I escaped your jail and made my way to Cuba.

"More importantly, you will find a copy of a revelation vision given to me by Professor Einalli. It demonstrates the critical choices you and I now face. In view of the irresistible power I now command," Cesar said with light irony, "my recommendation is: Let's make a deal.

"After considering my proposal, give your response to M. Cesar so it will be conveyed here to me. That's all for now."

Jewel looked puzzled. "Don't you want to tell him about the Un-Pink Procedure?"

Cesar shrugged.

"At least tell him that Braxil is okay. That she's been mistreated but you had no part in it, that Einalli's time chamber restored her to her former self and mended her mind completely. Now she's as good as new."

Cesar smiled broadly at his eager, ever-earnest Jewel. "I think you just did."

## NARRATIVE PAUSE 009

RELIEF WASHED over the Inspector like a storm surge. "The chief's not dead after all," he muttered, thinking of the sharp, diminutive matron who constantly clucked over everyone in the department like a brooding hen. It might have been his imagination, but the robot version didn't seem to hover around her reports quite so much. Imagine what it would be like having two such hens clucking around. He shuddered. No! No one in the department would stand for that.

"Braxil is alive," he muttered again. "And so is Newcomb." But that surprising discovery raised more questions than it answered. He'd seen the record of Newcomb's demise with his own eyes, as a prelude to the activation of the robot duplicate. And he'd naturally assumed Braxil had suffered the same fate.

It didn't take long for Jurat to figure out how to step backwards though the files and locate the Newcomb clip. He watched in reverse as the scene unfolded; the robot Forrest exiting the basement, the human and robot pair laying side by side on matching gurneys, Optima draining the human's blood, the making of the green transfer mask, the insertion of needles in Forrest's face, the odd man and woman "from Transylvania," the backyard picnic, the horror costumes, then Sugimoto watching the clip in Optima's office, then finally Cesar pulling together fragments of the clip. The file date flashed on the screen: 31

October 2129. He paused the replay and stared at the date. October 31: Halloween. Of course! The costumes—he should have thought of this before. What if the clip were nothing more than a Halloween gag, shown to Sugi to freak out the perky little sweetheart?

Jurat scanned back to the spot where Sugi visited Optima in her office. He froze the frame at the exact place where Optima pointed something out on the computer screen. It was hard to see what she was pointing to, but the screen format looked suspiciously like the emulation software.

Following a hunch, he recorded a still of the image and magnified the radio button portion of the screen. Sure enough: "Fiction mode—1950's horror style" was checked. Optima had created the clip through the emulator for amusement. The clip was pure self-indulgent fantasy.

Just at that moment, Alice's kitten, which had walked silently into Jurat's office and skittered under his desk, now jumped into his lap and started purring. Lost in thought, the Inspector stroked it behind the ears. Next thing he knew, his neck snapped. "I must have dozed off," he thought. And in the twilight space between waking and sleep, he could swear he'd seen that kitten smile at him. Gads, he was tired. Fortunately, it was late, time to get home, curl up without any reading material whatsoever and get a good night's rest. He'd be able to get through the rest of Cesar's material in the morning, then call Pawl by noon as promised. Yawn. Now that was the best future plan Jurat had heard in ages.

# PRISONER SWAP

"I'm still worried about the mask," Jewel said. "Put the sunglasses back on and let's have a look at you."

M. Cesar showed no sign of impatience. For a third time, he slipped the paper-thin mask over his synth-skin face, bristly with several days of synthetic unshaved beard, looked in the mirror, then added the almost black, tinted glasses. The mask gave him Jewel's jaw line, nose and thin lips. "I'll pass for your brother, no problem," he said.

"Until you try to talk," Jewel said skeptically. "The lips and jaw don't move properly. You look like a marionette, with your lower lip snapping up and down on a string."

"A string puppet? You think so?" he said, with an almost human twinkle in his eye. *They sure caught Cesar's humor,* Jewel thought as she looked at him. "I think I look more like a cat."

"Hm," Jewel said thoughtfully. "Maybe you do."

"Just call me Leo, the lion among the stars." And he gave her a smile that made her nerves tingle as she remembered her vision on the beach.

Witherspoon was too busy refilling spray tubes to look up. "I can physically deactivate its speech subroutines if that would make you feel better. Less chance of a slip-up."

"There's no need," said Jewel turning to Spoon. "If a robot can't obey orders to keep quiet, nobody can."

Witherspoon finished the final tube, washed his hands and turned his attention to M. Cesar's appearance. Running his finger down the side of the robot's cheek, he said, "A perfect fit, I can't even find the edge of the mask. The sunglasses are okay; just take them off once we're inside."

Just yesterday afternoon, Jewel and Spoon had both been in holding cells at the Lake Worth lockup, waiting their turn for helmet interrogation. Fortunately, it had taken only a few hours for Jewel to be cleared. Witherspoon had been charged with conspiracy to violate the Robot Limitation Laws along with Malcato and company. By early evening, they'd all been released on bail except for Cesar, who was being held on felony charges of assault and battery against a police officer.

Cesar was facing a possible five-year prison term, and considering the fact that the "officer" in question was a fake—well, the injustice of it appalled both Jewel and Spoon.

From the moment of their release, they had been working on a plan. It was risky. A lot could go wrong.

Now the moment of truth had come. Either the plan would work, or it wouldn't.

They headed out the door of Spoon's apartment with M. Cesar in tow. Spoon slipped eye shades on, as did Jewel. The midday sun was startlingly bright, even for Florida in July. Even though they got stuck at stop lights on both Federal and Dixie, the drive to the G Street jailhouse took only seven minutes.

Inside a thick glass enclosure, a female officer sat at the entry desk, absorbed in a word puzzle, absent-mindedly tapping out the Florida National Anthem with her fingernails on the desktop. The lockup was small, clearly intended for short-term use, with one narrow hallway and no more than a half dozen cramped cells, all clearly visible from the entrance. The security cameras in the corners and the black-and-white security monitors on each wall seemed redundant, as did the multiple glass walls and see-through electronic barriers separating the prisoners from freedom. Jewel rapped twice, softly on the pane, so as not to startle the officer.

When the woman noticed the visitors, she greeted them warmly through a fuzzy intercom. "Are you the ones who called about seeing Komenen?"

"That's right," Jewel said.

She buzzed them in. From the street lobby they passed through a glass door in a glass wall into a chairless holding area. "I'll have to search you. Please go into the inspection chamber."

One by one, they took turns in the clear plasticene box that stood in the corner like an upright coffin. Spoon went in first, then Jewel. When M. Cesar's turn came, instead of simply turning the door knob and entering, the bot ripped the knob from the door.

"The door's stuck," he shouted. "I can't get in."

The officer came out of her desk enclosure, reinserted the knob and tried to open the chamber door. At first it seemed stuck, but with a firm tug it came flying open. From behind, Jewel pushed her into the chamber. Before the officer could call for help or utter a sound, M. Cesar slapped a hand over her mouth, and Spoon hit her square in the face with a blast of Pink. Her eyes glared as she elbowed M. Cesar in the ribs, to no effect.

After a minute, her eyes softened as the drug took effect.

"I am your commander now," Spoon whispered. "You will do what I say and only what I say."

With downcast eyes, she nodded.

M. Cesar released his hand from her mouth.

"Tell me, quickly. How many officers are on duty in the jail?"

"Three besides myself. One is seated at the end of the hall watching the cells. The chief and a third officer are having a chat in cubicle two. That's it."

Jewel looked at Spoon quizzically. This was a chilling turn of events. As a robot, the Chief was immune to Pink. And her cooperation with the escape was hardly to be counted on. *Why was she down here instead of upstairs in her office?*

"No sweat," Spoon said. "We'll be in and out before they know what's happening." He had the reception officer buzz the watch officer and ask him to come to the front. The stuck-door trick worked on him as well. They pinked him, imprinted him and gave orders to lower the laser bars on Cesar's cell. Without fanfare, M. Cesar walked stealthily alone down the dank, tiled corridor, treading as lightly as possible. Spoon and Jewel waited at the entrance, where they could see the entire floor, their eyes trained on the steel door with the large number 2, fearful it might spring open at any moment.

The real Cesar stuck his head out of his cell and stared, confused. He wasn't in on the plan and didn't recognize the masked robot coming towards him. M. Cesar lifted the mask, showing his dupe's face, which only added to Cesar's bewilderment. Jewel, watching Cesar's reaction, and not knowing what he might do, decided to take a chance. She stepped out in the hall and vigorously motioned him back into his cell. A spark of understanding finally hit him, and he snapped back inside.

M. Cesar stepped into the cell, gave Cesar the face mask and sunglasses and then sat down placidly on the narrow cot riveted to the wall next to the cell toilet. Cesar was impressed: they had even remembered to "forget" to shave his beard.

"Jailbreak time," M. Cesar said placidly, as if he were announcing teatime.

Cesar slipped on the mask. "Have a pleasant stay," he whispered to his double as he retraced the robot's steps. Luckily, door number 2 remained closed the entire time.

As they exited the jail, Jewel managed to restrain her joy as the threesome hustled out of the building.

Once in the getaway car, Spoon drove while Jewel jumped into Cesar's lap, squeezed his hand, kissed him. The two Cesars had looked, acted, felt identical. They were even dressed alike.

A wave of doubt suddenly passed over her. . . . What if, by a horrible mistake the swap hadn't taken place as planned, and instead she was riding next to . . . ?

Without warning, she dug her teeth hard into Cesar's neck.

"Madre de Dios!" he cried out, turning to her with a look of hurt and shock. "Hey, babe, why'd you do *that?*"

She laughed, relieved. Her bite had raised a large purple hickey just under Cesar's ear lobe.

Jewel kissed his lips, eyes, cheeks, forehead. "I need to see you bleed," she said.

# SALARIUM OR SOLARIUM

One minute he was starting to snooze, stretched out in a lounger on the aft deck of the *Gato del Mar*, the boat Einalli had told Cesar would be put at his disposal; leaving Lantana Harbor, feeling the boat's wake plow rhythmically through the three-foot swells of the inlet and starting to snooze, and the next minute he was startled by a DJ helmet tossed into his lap.

"Can't you give a guy a moment's rest?" he chided as Jewel hovered over him, her long hair billowing in the sea breeze.

"You're the one who asked for the helmet," she flirted.

"You know, you get prettier every day."

"Save the flattery," she turned to go. "You have work to do."

He sighed, inserted Einalli's ruby chip in the DJ and strapped it to his head.

Even before he had time to reach for the activation button, there was a shift of blue light. Wet spray slapped his face. Seated in an open-cockpit aircraft, floating in warm, tropical waters that lapped softly at the underside of the fuselage, silently, without the roar of an engine, its single boomerang-shaped wing lifted into the balmy air.

Physically Cesar was still sailing for Cuba, but every sense told him, with stunning realism, that he was airborne. The horizon receded as the plane ascended. Emptiness grabbed the pit of his stomach. Wind pressed back his eyelids. Saltiness crept into his tongue. The kickback of acceleration locked his chest, making it hard to breathe. He zoomed high over the Caribbean, barreling through one cloud bank after another. Cesar clamped his eyes shut to block out the dizzying strobe effect. His white knuckles frantically gripped the sides of his seat as the wing banked south. The G-force seemed to last forever.

When the aircraft finally leveled off, Cesar reopened his eyes. The wing was perhaps twenty feet long, made of a transparent bioplastic that allowed him an unobstructed view of the ocean below. It nosed gracefully through the fluffy white clouds with no indication of where it was headed.

"Two roads diverge in a yellow wood," a disembodied voice said. Einalli's frosty detached baritone was unmistakable. *There are no woods here, green or yellow,* Cesar thought.

As if it could read his thoughts, the voice explained, "In the woods, your vision of what lies ahead is blocked by trees. My friend, you have wandered about in a forest-like terrain, carrying the future of the humanity in your hands, blinded to the consequences of your actions. Up here, in the vast open air, I shall make all things clear to you."

Cesar slapped his forehead in self-deprecation. Of course, the program could read his thoughts.

The voice belly-laughed.

From horizon to horizon, Cesar felt awash in azure; endless turquoise waters below, misty pale sky above. Freedom from the confines of gravity was exhilarating, even if an illusion. "Where are you taking me?" Cesar asked.

In a teasing tone the voice responded, "Do you want an answer now?"

"Yes, immediately, without a second's delay."

"My, we are impatient," the voice scolded playfully.

The plane lurched suddenly forward with a force that pinned Cesar back in his seat. A jolt split the sky, searing the world into two separate universes, contorting the sky, bending it to the breaking point, reforming its sharp-edged fragments into two blue domes, right and left. Land rose from the depths of the sea, two identically formed islands, one under each dome, each surrounded by a ring of golden sand, blanketed by swaying palms, bejeweled by a single hilltop city, glistening in the tropical sun. From this distance there was only one difference between the two islands. An enormous pink cloud floated above the one on the right; the other offered clear skies. The color of the cloud made Cesar wonder.

"Oh, son of double vision. You stand at the cusp of history. Choose a future. The one you choose shall become the world."

The wing lurched as it hit an air pocket. From that point on, Cesar was in control of the aircraft. If he leaned right or left, the plane followed. Playfully, he zig-zagged back and forth, banking until the G-force pinned him against the seat as he thrilled to the motion.

The islands approached. Cesar knew he'd soon have to decide which island to explore first. After a few more zig-zags, he reached the point where procrastination was no longer possible. Choosing to find out what this vision was supposed to be about, he headed toward the pink cloud, aiming for a water landing just off the beach. As he splashed down, the cloud followed close behind, darkening, threatening, descending just offshore, looking like a giant pile of flashing mauve neon sparks.

Cesar quickly dragged the wing onto the sand and ran for shelter in a line of trees a hundred meters from the water's edge. The trees parted, revealing a well-worn path leading up toward a city. A bolt of lightning landed a few steps behind him. Thunder shook the plethora of orchids hanging in the trees, radiating blue in the odd electric light. As he hurried along, one bolt after another stalked behind, forcing him to quicken his pace. The jungle trail rose strenuously uphill, working its way around craggy outcroppings and giant banyan trees. Cesar began to pant but did not allow himself to slacken his pace, worried that the lightning would catch him if he slowed.

Exhausted, he reached the outskirts of the city and stopped. The jungle receded as the meandering trail turned into an arrow-straight street. The street ran smoothly uphill, past homes, shops and a series of public squares up to the central palace. Its slender white spires towered upward like an army of queens on a chess board.

The lightning ceased. Cesar stood at the edge of the city, hands on knees, listening to the chatter of civilization. People were going about their daily business, apparently oblivious to the looming storm; buying, selling, digging ditches, walking their dogs, erecting walls, chatting with neighbors.

Suddenly, just as Cesar's feet were about to cross the threshold to the city, the storm cloud came down, enveloping the city. A thick, light-obscuring dust began to fall, a snowstorm of angel breath that invaded every street, tinted the atmosphere cherry pink, penetrated every wall and window, wormed its way into home and office, transmuted the air into a volatile ether, penetrated every nostril. The sidewalks looked pink, the towers looked pink, the faces looked pink; every leaf on every tree looked pink.

With the first inhalation of dust, the inhabitants stopped whatever they were doing. Eyes glazed over, chatter ceased, activity ground to a halt. Not one cough, sneeze or wheeze erupted from protesting lungs. Blood began to drip from ears, nose and eyes as the life drained out of every brain. Bodies stood passive, immobile, patiently awaiting initiation into a new mode of life.

All eyes turned and fixed upon Cesar's statuesque form. A voice from the cloud thundered, "Behold your king!" A crowd of countless men and women, young and old, children and youth, rich and poor, healthy and sick, even animals, cats and dogs and birds—seagulls and swallows and falcons and doves—the mosquito with its sting and the snake with its poison, all moved in a great mass uphill toward him, with the sound of a great clamoring, some in the lead shouting, "Hail! Hail! Hail, Cesar! Our victorious king has returned."

Again the clouds flared with lightning and thunder rolled across the city. Rain began falling in a torrent of gallon-sized raindrops that quickly grew to a flood. Ten-pound hailstones battered the streets, yet the people kept coming. Nothing slowed their passion. Some were engulfed by the flash flood or struck by hail and washed away, but others immediately took their place in the surging crowd. None would be denied access to his royal majesty.

Continual lightning scorched the earth, killing scores more. People gave no heed to the danger. The crowds kept coming, wading through the putrid, rising water, cheering, oblivious to the bodies floating past all around. "We love our king, we serve our king, we obey our king!" chanted the crowds.

As the water reached chest high, they lifted Cesar on their shoulders, carrying him toward the palace at the city's center. The flood turned pink, then deep blood-red as it rose above the heads of the throng, now numbering in the tens of thousands. One after another, Cesar's worshipful supporters, blissful and enraptured in pure joy, drowned and were washed away. And an endless supply of willing hands were available, eager to rush in and take the place of fallen comrades.

The torrent of blood surged higher and was soon too strong and deep for even the self-sacrificing mob to manage. A team of horses pulling a gilded litter fringed with purple velvet tassels waded in until the putrid liquid reached the top of its gargantuan wheels. Cesar clambered onto the litter, with its throne of gold and silver and ivory, and seated himself and was carried, to the joyous cries of the crowd, on toward the palace gate. The blood rose higher still, reaching the bridles of the horses.

While bedlam raged outside, Cesar cocooned himself in the mobile sanctuary of his throne. He found himself transformed as his superior destiny and rightful leadership were about become a reality. Everyday clothes miraculously changed to flowing silk robes of the purest white. Jeweled rings appeared on each of his fingers. Upon his head rose a triple-tiered crown emblazoned around with long-winged flamingoes in flight. At the gate the litter stopped. His shoeless feet grew mercury wings, lifting the throne from the litter and up to a balcony where it hovered, clean and dry, above the blood-soaked heads.

"Hear this, eternally loyal citizens of this Great Empire. Today is the most important day in the history of the world. Today we put an end to all conflict and strife, to violence and anger and combat and war. Today we all become sisters and brothers in loyalty and love, faithful and true, in harmony with each other, with ourselves, with our world, now and forevermore. Today we begin anew. Today we create the Robot Imperium."

At that word, the flood waters drained away. Ocean breezes cleared the clouds from the sky. Sunshine emerged. A host of buddy robots marched in, rank upon rank, file upon file. With swinging mops, they cleaned the blood stains from the streets and buildings. Each citizen was assigned a buddy as a servant, worker and life-long companion. Busily the robots cleaned the clothes of their new owners while still on their backs; they brushed and groomed, straightened and fussed until not a spot or wrinkle could be found. The crowd cheered. "Viva our Cesar! Long live the Robot Imperium!"

Cesar smiled upon his subjects, a gracious, reassuring, fatherly smile. "Today leisure is proclaimed the law of the land. Today justice is established. Freedom from toil is yours. The robot paradise has come! From this moment forward, I declare you shall be happy."

Cesar entered the palace. As the throne room doors flung open, Sir Charles Witherspoon greeted him. "Your Majesty." Spoon bowed with regal formality. "Here is your sword, which I have guarded until this moment of your happy return."

The pink-alloyed blade shone brightly. Cesar grasped the hilt and spun the sword on the tip of his finger. The sword multiplied into ten spinning swords. Ten robots appeared, each grabbed a sword. They lined up facing one another, forming two lines, marking a path to the throne. With the slightest effort of his heel wings, Cesar floated up the steps to the dais and enthroned himself. Swords and guards continued to present themselves for his service. They multiplied endlessly. Hundreds became thousands. The robot faces cheered nonstop as the throne room expanded to accommodate the growing army of swordsmen. Thousands became tens of thousands, then millions. The outer walls of the throne room could no longer be seen. All the world was filled with mindless robots shouting their undying devotion.

"All hail our Emperor, a leader worthy of his salt," they thundered in unison. "All that we have is rightfully yours! All hail Cesar!"

Cesar stared at the adoring masses with wonder. He wondered at the enormous numbers of beings, both living and machine, all honoring him. He wondered if, in the real world, outside of Einalli's vision, if Pink really gave him the power to forge this world. He wondered if he would really enjoy being Emperor of the Universe. Above all he wondered, after having created utopia, what could he do then, and how would he avoid growing frustrated, like Alexander lamenting at having no new worlds to conquer, or bored, like Solomon, confined in his very splendor and glory?

Dimly he remembered an episode many years before in Cuba, with Chat and the wrist gauge that measured happiness: what would his wrist gauge say at this moment? Wasn't this a little like jumping the line everywhere, at all times, now and forever? Wasn't there something terribly wrong about being the permanent center of everyone's attention? Even if they seemed to want it—wasn't it perhaps something they should not have? Both for their sake—and for his?

The throng kept cheering and cheering and cheering.

*But it feels . . . so good. . . .*

A disembodied voice whispered in his ear, "Have you had enough, my friend?"

Cesar thought for a long, hard moment. Finally, after what felt like an eternity to the young man, he spoke. Even if he liked it, even if he loved it, maybe it was not something that he, or anyone, should ever have.

"Yes," he said, almost sadly. "I've had enough."

In a flash, the hall emptied and grew dim. It took several minutes for the din to clear out of Cesar's ears. He stood breathless and exhausted and subdued.

"Can the pink do all that?" he asked the air.

The question resounded as if echoing through a hundred empty chambers.

"All that adulation can be yours—if you want it," said the voice, replying in a whisper.

Witherspoon climbed out of the darkness and joined Cesar on the dais. He sat down on the over-sized arm of the throne. The two grinned at each other. Overwhelmed with accomplishment, tipsy with celebrity, they knew there were no limits to their power. But simultaneously they both shook their heads.

"There has to be more to life than vanity," Spoon said, giving his friend a significant look.

"There has to be more to a world than one ego ruling all," Cesar agreed, a little ruefully.

The wind again roared in Cesar's ears. Spoon was gone. He found himself back at the point of the vision where the two worlds split apart. This time he veered to the left. As he approached the island of that universe, he could once again make out a bright city set atop a cultivated hill, its white buildings gleaming like tall, alabaster chess pieces in the sunlight. Paired teams of human and robot were busily gardening, building, washing, buying, selling. Everyone stopped what they were doing and waved as the wing circled the city's clear skies. The roadways and even the alleys glistened, clean and crystalline, in the morning light.

The major thoroughfares of the White City were laid out in concentric circles around an enormous plaza, an open expanse lined with white-columned buildings. A series of circular classical fountains of swans and dolphins ran around the perimeter of the plaza, the pools here and there catching the reflections of the surrounding columns amid the fountain spray.

At the northern end stood a Romanesque, larger-than-life, statue of Lady Liberty carved in white marble, extended her blessings over the happy inhabitants of the city; her head crowned with a victory wreath, her noble form, tall, dignified, promising equality and justice for all. She stood facing rows of Florida Republic flags, waving in the breeze, marking the path to the seat of government, a transparent glass dome containing a robot congress, much like the RR congress Cesar had seen in Cuba as a kid. Atop the furthest flagpole was a golden ball, which grew into a globe representing the world and casting a shadow over the entire plaza.

The wing circled the plaza several times. Cesar took in the grandeur, knowing that in this place he would have no special standing but would just be an ordinary citizen living among his peers. The wing next headed to the southern edge of the city and there landed on a lawn at the entrance to Cyber-Bot's main factory. Lifted out of its seat, Cesar's body flew unaided. He had to duck to avoid bumping his head on the low doorway. On the factory floor an assembly line, manned by human-robot teams, assembled metal-faced bots, all looking like Buddy.

The next thing he knew, Cesar was dumped unceremoniously at the foot of a lab-coated inspector. The man was tall, ruddy skinned, with a clipboard in hand. Cesar picked himself off the floor; dusting himself off, he muttered, "Pleasure to be here."

Without looking up from his pencil work, the inspector asked, "Do you know why you've been brought here?"

Cesar shook his head.

The man led him over to a large screen. It contained page after page of robot code. "Your job is to verify the Veracity Monitors," the man replied. "Our robots must be true and honest in all things, at all times, completely trustworthy, squeaky clean."

Cesar nodded in agreement.

"If you need a permanent job, we're looking for an expert roboticist to devise a foolproof method so that the VMP cannot be tampered with again. We understand you have some unprecedented experience in that area." The man smiled knowingly.

Cesar raised his eyebrows. *Quite a demotion*, he thought, *from king of the world to robot hack prevention.*

Spoon popped out of nowhere and stood by Cesar's side, listening.

"As you know," the man went on, "it's an ongoing assignment. There are some pretty smart guys out there always looking for a way to cheat the system, trying to get more than their fair share."

Pointing at Witherspoon, Cesar asked, "Do you have a job for my colleague?"

"Sure, there's a position over in bio research that would be perfect. We're designing a VMP for humans."

Witherspoon stepped closer. "A veracity monitor for people?" He looked puzzled.

"Exactly, to help people who want to be honest," the inspector explained. "It would be an implant with a system of internal sensors. It will set off an internal bell when people lie to themselves, when they are in denial, when they should know better but don't put two and two together. The idea is not to forcibly stop people from lying, if they so choose, but to make sure they know they're lying and not living in the shadows of self-deception."

"Sounds intriguing," Witherspoon nodded.

"Is this project already underway?" Cesar asked.

"Just getting started. You would be the project leader."

Spoon and Cesar looked at each other, eye to eye, recalling how much satisfaction there was in working for a cause they could truly believe in. The sunlight crested over a window ledge and lit an oblong patch of floor at their feet.

"Yes, I'll take it," they said simultaneously. Then they looked at each other and broke out laughing.

The next minute Cesar was alone, transported back to his lounger. The sudden change, coupled with the sea swell, made him dizzy. He removed the helmet, but his head felt just as heavy, thinking about the decision he had to make. The trip to Cuba had been imaginary, an excellent job of multi-sensory simulation. But he was in fact en route to Cuba where the same two life options confronted him—to be Big Cesar or Little Cesar.

Cesar lay still on his lounger for a long time, mesmerized by the rhythmic waves, trying to decide if the choices before him were as stark as Einalli had presented.

# SECOND PETITION TO JURAT

**C**ool piano jazz replaced the earlier, livelier marimba rhythms. Jewel, stretched out in a flowered, terrycloth cover-up, cuddled in a poolside lounge with Cesar, while Buddy busied himself ferrying drinks and endless trays of sushi. For the last hour, they'd watched the moon's shrinking reflection in the glimmering water.

"There's something special about a lunar eclipse," Jewel purred. "It makes everything magical."

Cesar rubbed her neck behind the ears. "Um-hm," he agreed lazily.

As the moon shriveled to a bare crescent, Buddy set flickering bamboo torches around the deck. "It's time to record the message," Buddy reminded them. "The equipment is set up, ready to go."

"Okay," groaned Cesar as he forced himself to a sitting position.

Back in the shadow stood a line of three silhouettes, standing upright, their faces unrecognizable in the dim torchlight.

Cesar wasted no time. Addressing the camera, he said, "Jurat, listen. It's been a long day sending messages back and forth. I'm tired, you're tired. You're on a tight deadline. So without delay, let me share my three surprises with you."

The leftmost silhouette stepped forward. A spotlight illuminated her face with such sudden brightness that she recoiled and held up a hand to shield her eyes.

"Here's your missing Sheriff. RR investigators found Chief Braxil, along with these others, in a flea-bitten Havana hotel. Their faces had been altered and their brains wiped clean. They had no idea who they were. When we found the Chief, she didn't even know her own name, but she did know how to drink rum coladas. Fortunately, with the help of Einalli and some very talented RR docs, we were able to restore the chief's brilliant mind and good looks."

Braxil laughed nervously. "But, yes, I was, we all were, rather scruffy. We're still hopeful we can keep this embarrassing incident quiet, off the webcasts."

Norma paused to check herself in a hand mirror and readjusted her studded earrings. "As I was leaving for work, almost a month ago, just a few days before our big Independence Day celebration, early one morning, I was waylaid on the sidewalk in front of my home and sprayed with a pink chemical. Without explanation of reason or motive, I was brought to Cuba. I was in a drugged state without the power or will to resist. Every few hours they sprayed me again. I became more and more disoriented, eventually forgetting who I was. They used some kind of slimy gunk, pressed against my face, to alter my looks and make me unrecognizable. They gave me a new name, a new personality, new childhood memories, a whole new life. I was encoded to believe I was Lola, a morning drunk, Havana barfly straight out of a B-movie melodrama. Admittedly, my hair was pimped." She stylishly brushed the side of her head. "And I've had two or three very wild and memorable evenings!" she cooed. Then she blushed. "But at this point, it's straight up embarrassing for a gal of my age and sterling public image."

"With that drug in your system, no one is going to hold you responsible," Jewel reassured. "What happens in Havana, stays in Havana."

Norma blushed again, buried her face in her hands for a moment, then continued her story. "Apparently Reina Malcato was behind my abduction. She left a robot in my place. Apparently, no one on my staff noticed that the real me was gone." She glared playfully. "But in view of my extraordinary competence, it's a bit hard to fathom a robot ever doing my job."

Pointing at Jewel and Cesar, she said, "Now, thanks to these fine people who did notice that I was not myself," she smiled, "my face and memory are restored. I've begun to mend. My one complaint is that my face is exceedingly puffy and sore from its second gooping in little more than a week. But I've had a chance to rest a bit here, as a guest of the Robot Republic, being pampered by robotic servants from morning to night." Her eyes were cast downward. "It's been a rough week, and that's all I have to say right now."

Cesar rose from his lounge, put his arms around her and gave her a reassuring hug. "Here's to your courage and resilience," he was about to say when the camera lights went out, leaving the group in total darkness. Cesar yelled across to the unseen camera crew: "Hey, guys, get on the ball! Bring us some light."

"Sure thing, boss. Two spots coming right up."

Cesar went back to his seat, popping his lips in impatience. Jewel reached over from her lounger and took his hand in a calming gesture. He smiled back at her but continued to click his tongue in exasperation.

When the lights came up, they were focused on the two remaining faces in the back row. "Now here's the grand surprise." He whistled. "These two were rescued along with Braxil and Newcomb. You may think this is some kind of a trick, but I assure you it's on the square. Please hold on for a second." Cesar allowed time for dramatic effect. Nothing happened for what seemed like an inordinate length of time. Finally, the moment Cesar had been waiting for arrived. The moon disappeared as the eclipse entered its umbral phase. "Let me present Justices Ramsey Thomas and Clint Geoff of the Florida Supreme Court."

SUSPEND PLAYBACK

---

## NARRATIVE PAUSE 010

JURAT FROZE in his seat. He couldn't believe what his eyes and ears were telling him. How was it possible that this affair had reached the highest corridors of power? Then again, it certainly would explain Justice Pawl's interest in the case. No sense procrastinating any longer. Now's as good a time as any to call the Justice back as promised. At least he had something noteworthy to report. Jurat took a deep breath and picked up the phone.

"Justice Pawl?"

"Yes?" The voice was the same dry, slightly impatient one he had heard a few days before.

'This is Inspector Jurat. There are unconfirmed reports that your benchmates, Justices Thomas and Geoff, have been kidnapped to Cuba."

There was a long pause at the other end. "That would be odd, Inspector. Especially as I just spoke with them on a conference call not an hour ago."

"Well, sir," Jurat continued, with a gulp. "The justices you spoke with were . . ."

"Were what, Inspector?"

"They were . . . with all due respect, sir . . . robots."

There was a dead silence at the other end of the line.

Jurat went on with nervous haste. "My source tells me the justices have now been freed, though still in Cuba. If these reports are true, for obvious reasons we want to keep the matter hush-hush. I recommend that you locate the robot dupes, find a quiet, private place to swap them back and keep the matter off the web."

"Indeed."

"Sorry, but Cuba is outside my jurisdiction. I'm not in any position to help the Justices. All I have is a video clip purporting to show Thomas and Geoff alive and well."

"Who are your contacts on this matter?"

"Cesar Komenen, at the Hotel Cy-Bar in Cienfuegos—he's my only contact."

"And you believe the justices are to be found at the same place?"

"As of this moment, yes, along with Palm Beach County Sheriff Braxil and Lake Worth mayoral candidate Forrest Newcomb, the real Newcomb. You know he's decided to stay in the race."

"The boy wants to run?" Pawl's voice squeaked with surprise.

"Right. We're told he signed the original documents to enter the race. We were surprised to learn, there was no legal fraud."

There was another long silence on the other end. Jurat got up to stretch. He hit the speaker phone switch, held on to the back of his chair and began to stretch his calves.

Jurat could hear Pawl clear his throat on the other end of the line. "Is that the end of your surprises, inspector?"

Jurat swallowed hard. "There's the matter of Reverend Rebolt. Of course, the Reverend is in a separate category, a robot with a fictional persona, not a duplicate of a real human. Did I tell you?" Jurat's voice quivered before continuing. "Now the Rebolt robot has gone missing."

The office door creaked open. "Mew!" Alice's kitten stood on the threshold, licking its little chops. Half a step behind stood a Cheshire-grinning Peter Reid, dressed in a sheriff deputy's uniform, shoes, cap and all.

Jurat nearly jumped out of his skin, hurriedly signed off with the Justice, clicked the phone off, faced the reporter and bellowed. "How the hell did you get in here?"

The reporter just smiled back. "So what's the real story on Rebolt's disappearance? Where is the good Reverend?" he asked casually, as if for the time of day.

The inspector glared at his feet. He could have kicked himself for using the speaker phone and allowing the reporter to overhear. Damn. He reached for the intercom button. "Am I going to have to arrest you to prevent the dissemination of unfounded rumors? Impersonating an officer will do for starters."

"What, me?" said Reid, unfazed. He raised his wrist to his mouth and spoke: "Prominent South Florida clergyman Reverend Rebolt has gone missing. The Reverend, suspected in fact of being a ro- . . ."

"Reid, you've pushed me once too often! You're under arrest."

Jurat stepped forward, slapped down the reporter's wrist and whirled him around, using his great girth to pin the reporter's slender chest against the steel door. The reporter yelped and tried to lift his phone to his mouth; Jurat grabbed the arm, stretched it out straight and repeatedly pounded his wrist against the door jam. Small broken fragments of the implant rained down on the floor, leaving the wrist bloody.

Seconds later, a couple of officers, responding to the racket, forced the door open. They quickly handcuffed the reporter and started to lead him away.

"You're making a big mistake," Reid cried out. "My people have already been alerted. The story about Rebolt is already on the web."

Jurat tapped his foot on the floor, knowing he had to make a quick decision with lasting consequences. To his men he said, "Leave him here! Just post a guard at the door."

When the two were alone again, Jurat motioned for Reid to sit down. "Okay, explain. What's out on the web?"

The reporter silently took his z-pad out of his pocket and rapidly tapped.

"Preacher Found Dead," Reid began to read from the screen. "The mangled body of Reverend Reginald Rebolt was found early this morning behind the altar of First Savior Community Church. According to Inspector Solomon Jurat, of the Palm Beach County sheriff's department, Rebolt had a heart attack, passed out and fell from the choir balcony. No foul play is suspected in the death. Rebolt had a history of coronary disease. Arrangements for funeral services to be announced. . . ." He lowered the pad.

Jurat pounced. "Who made up that fairy tale?"

"My editor, of course," smirked the reporter.

"That fox. I heard what you called in. You told him practically nothing less than two minutes ago. How can you call yourself a journalist when you're a party to such bare-faced lies?"

"Oh, my dear inspector," the reporter chided, "grow up. This is the news-tainment business, we need only a glimmer of the facts. Everything else is for amusement. The today's news is fast, virtually fact-free and creative. Rush, rush, rush."

Again it was decision time. Damn, Jurat hated being put on the spot. "The story is a complete fabrication."

"And there's plenty more where that come from. My boss will be pretty pissed if you hold me."

Jurat felt his jaw tighten as he held his tongue. He'd promised Pawl minimal publicity. The last thing he needed was a hostile press. "Scram before I change my mind." He shooed Reid away. "But watch yourself or next time I'll put you in the clinker for so long you won't know sunup from sundown. Now would you please get out of here? I have work to do."

Reid turned to go, but paused in the doorway. "You know, Solomon," he said, with mocking familiarity. "If you had tested out my story, looked it up on your computer, you'd have discovered I was bluffing. The story of Rebolt's death was never issued."

"Gads!" He wanted to spit in the reporter's face. "Get out of here!"

Reid closed the door gently behind him.

The inspector counted to ten, got up, peeked down the hall to make sure the so-called reporter was gone, then paced around his office, longing for a view of the water to gaze at. Damn, why was this case so funky frustrating? He yearned for some relief. Better than a water view would be a chair on the beach, ankle-deep in lapping waves, toes in the sand.

But allowing himself to daydream only made matters worse. Sighing deeply, he sat back down, dug his elbows into his desktop, propped his chin against both hands, exhaled, phew!, and got back to work.

## RESUME PLAYBACK

Justice Geoff spoke. "We don't want to risk a panic by having robot replicas of ourselves publicly exposed."

Justice Thomas chimed in. "I agree fully with my esteemed colleague. Can you imagine the chaos, the hysteria? Our robot replacements must be quietly captured and removed from public view before we can return. The same is true for the Braxil robot. This operation must be handled on the QT. No press. No arrests. No panic. We are counting on you to handle this immediately, tonight if possible, tomorrow morning at the latest, and inform us immediately once the task is done. As soon as we hear from you, we'll head back home."

"One more detail," Cesar stated for Jurat's benefit. "Please make arrangements to send the two pinked employees from city jail down here to Einalli for rehab. Chairwoman Sugimoto promises the Party will cover all their medical and travel expenses. It's our way of saying thanks for your grant of immunity."

Cesar rose and shook the justices' hands, thanking them profusely. A festive joy hovered like jasmine in the fragrant night air as the crescent moon reemerged. They all felt lighthearted, victorious, united, as if they'd weathered a great storm together. A hostess came over and positioned the group for a final photo. Gathered around the pool, they looked like a typical group of American tourists on holiday except for Buddy's metallic face shining from gear to gear.

CLOSE ALL FILES
END EMULATION

## NARRATIVE PAUSE 011

IT WAS SUNDAY, park Sunday, jazz Sunday. With his portable hammock slung over a shoulder, Jurat crossed the
open lawn to a cool, shady spot where the band shell didn't
block the sea breeze. The sun, the music, the fresh, salty
air were delightful. Like a yawning cat, he stretched out
in the hammock. Every muscle in his body turned into
seedless jelly. How different from one week ago, when his
investigation of the robot affair was just getting started.
Confused and frustrated, he'd been stuck at the office
trying to make sense of the Futurist machinations.

The hammock swung gently in the breeze as the
inspector mused with satisfaction on the success of the
past week. He now was a player on the political scene
and had the respect of justices of the Supreme Court.
The County Sheriff owed him, big time. And there was the
exciting prospect of his first date with Alice Blain. She'd
run to Too Jay's for sandwiches and a bottle of zinfandel
and should be along any minute.

Jurat scanned the crowd from his comfortable perch.
Open Grass, a well-known local band, was playing an energetic funky number and hordes of fans were packed, elbow
to elbow, tromp-dancing and enjoying themselves. To the
left of the band shell, near the water's edge, stood a tall,
oddly-shaped object draped in a silvery sheet: its unveiling
was to be part of today's festivities.

Not far away from his hammock, Jewel was sitting under a tree gold-edged book in hand, engrossed in reading, apparently deaf to the crowd and the music. Cesar Komenen stood next to her, snapping his fingers to the beat. When he caught Jurat's gaze, he leaned over and whispered into Jewel's ear. She gently closed her book, kissed its cover, stood up and dusted off her jeans. The name of the volume was just visible under Jewel's slim arm: Universal Skills of the Spirit. The two of them strolled hand in hand toward the inspector's hammock.

"Inspector," Cesar said, "we'll be ready for the unveiling as soon as the band takes its next break."

Jurat nodded. "Mr. Komenen, do you mind if I ask the lady a question? I'm just curious about a little something."

Cesar looked back at the stage. The musicians were going strong. "It looks like we've got a few minutes," he said with a shrug.

The inspector pulled himself up, swinging his legs over the hammock's side. He turned to Jewel and tapped his fingers against his open palm. "I couldn't help but notice how you treasure that particular volume you're holding. How did you manage to save it from the fire?"

Jewel shook her head. "What are you talking about?"

"The bonfire of books outside your apartment building during the Naabi raid, didn't you lose all your books? And wasn't that particular volume tossed on the fire that night?"

Jewel's incredulity deepened. "I'm aware of no book burning, certainly not in front of my building."

Jurat shook his head in disbelief. "No?" he pressed. "And wasn't there a second book bonfire on the Cloister lawn just a few hours later?"

"Not that I know anything about," Jewel assured. "Certainly this book was never touched."

Jurat threw back his head and laughed. "Are you telling me you didn't witness any kind of bonfire of books at either place?"

Cesar and Jewel looked at each other and simultaneously shook their heads. "No, nothing like that," they insisted, almost in unison.

"Ray Bradbury!" Jurat said through an awkward laugh. "A take-off on *Fahrenheit 451*."

"Am I—supposed to know—this Ray Berry?" Cesar sputtered, as confused as ever.

Jurat wrinkled his brow as he began to piece things together. "Bradbury, the science fiction writer, you never heard of him? *Fahrenheit 451*, it's his best known novel, a story about book burning by one of the most famous authors of the twentieth century."

"Never heard of him," Cesar shrugged.

Jurat cursed under his breath. "That damn emulation program!" He locked eyes with Komenen. "You know that fantasy file? The one that showed the Frankenstein-like scene and the murder of Forrest Newcomb in the castle basement?"

Cesar bit his lip.

"That scene turned out to be pure make-believe, generated by storytelling software: an Optima fantasy interwoven with elements of Edgar Allan Poe stories."

Cesar nodded affirmatively. "Eventually I too figured out it that the file was fiction."

"Well, that same software added bits and pieces of Bradbury stories to my investigation, especially confusing were the inserts from 'Usher II'; rich patrons killed and replaced with robots." He pointed toward Cesar. "You know for a while, I suspected that you and your Futurist friends were guilty of Newcomb's murder." Jewel's felt a lump rise in her throat. "I'm totally confused. You use fiction software to investigate your cases? And it made false accusations?"

Jurat smiled. "No, fortunately things never went that far. The emulation was used on an experimental basis only, never relied upon for evidence." He equivocated, trying to reassure her.

"Whew," she exhaled with relief.

"We all like to be constantly entertained," he added with a touch of embarrassment. "Look how news, even weather reports, are sensationalized. Unless the facts are dramatized, spiffed up, injected with humor, we quickly lose interest. Say, why don't the two of you come by my office on Monday morning, and I'll show you some amazing, though apparently buggy, program code."

"Thank God you never thought my Cesar was an assassin." Jewel seemed deeply grateful. "And thank you, inspector, for our little deal, for trusting us. . . ." Jewel cast her gaze reverently up at the clear, blue sky. "Things have worked out amazingly well, amazingly fast," she mused. "Don't you wonder if there's more to our good fortune than luck?"

Cesar jumped in. "By the way, you may be interested to know that Peter Reid and Tuuve D'Camp completed their Einalli cures today and are already on their way home to Florida. Hayes, Malcato and Sincardo likewise have been depinked but are being admitted to the Cienfuegos penal colony for rehab. Just wanted to let you know we're holding up our end of the bargain."

The music stopped as the band's final crescendo melted into applause.

"We're up next," Cesar said urgently, extending a hand to help Jurat out of his hammock. But Jurat ignored the hand and instead eased back into his favorite position: supine.

"I'm much too comfortable here." He gave the hammock a steady swing. "Let Justice Pawl give his speech. He's the one with the startling announcement."

A half dozen camera men from various web news outlets wormed through the crowd, stationing themselves around the band shell. Something big was afoot. The three Supreme Court justices stood side by side onstage, their long black robes swirling in the salt breeze. Justice Pawl spoke. "Ladies and gentlemen, your Supreme Court has reached a decision with broad implications for all of us. We're delighted to let the citizens of Lake Worth be the first to know." He paused. "By virtue of the power vested in us by the Republic of Florida, section 23 of the Robot Limitation Laws is hereby ruled unconstitutional."

Scattered applause ran through the crowd, but most were unmoved, not yet realizing the changes that were about to erupt into their lives. "From now on, each of you will be entitled to own a robot twin. Under the constitution, you cannot be denied the right to make a copy of anything you own. Since we each own ourselves, including our personalities, our voice, our fingerprints, our facial appearance, we also have the right to make copies of ourselves. The court has let stand the labor-sharing clause of section 22. This limits each of us to one gainfully employed robot apiece, so that no one is deprived of a job."

"That's an odd twist," Jewel whispered to Cesar. "Does that mean that humanoid dupes are legal but buddy bots are still illegal?"

"That's exactly what it means," Cesar said excitedly. "It sounds like a very smart ruling."

"And it's good for law enforcement," Jurat added. "Say a guy owns a dupe. It'll have his brain, his personality, his behavioral patterns, and he'll be responsible for its actions, including any crimes it may commit. Since the bot looks exactly like its owner, identification of the responsible party will be simple."

"Brilliant." Cesar grinned. "It also means that for now individuals, not corporations, will control the expanded work force." He looked askance at the Inspector. "But what if a rich guy sues for the right to employ ten thousand copies of himself and fire all his employees?"

Jurat blinked. "Man, you're already fighting the next war."

"That's why we call ourselves Futurists," Cesar rejoined. "We're always looking ahead."

"Ladies and gentlemen of Lake Worth," Pawl continued, "your election for mayor is only two days away. On Tuesday, you will have a chance to decide on the role of robots in our society. Please listen carefully to both sides of the issue."

The justices took their seats at the rear of the platform, and Forrest Newcomb approached the mic. "Thank you, Justice Pawl," the would-be mayor began with minimal stuttering. "My friends, you may have heard reports that I withdrew, but I'm here to tell you that I'm v-very much in this race. If I am elected, we here in Lake Worth will be quick to educate the public on how to take advantage of the court's ruling on robot ownership. I want to ask you for your v-vote this coming Tuesday. A new day is about to dawn in our new Republic. From that day forward, robots will make your lives easier. They will work beside you on the job, increase your income and your leisure. Your robots will perform the drudgery, the dull r-repetitive tasks, the hazardous jobs. We no longer need poor people to provide cheap labor. Robots will do the d-dirty work. From that day forward, it'll be possible for everyone to become rich. The benefits of t-technology shall go to all the people."

Cesar and Jewel began applauding enthusiastically. Others, recognizable from the South Grade Robot Show, rose to their feet and joined in waving and cheering. Soon the lawn was filled with hundreds shouting, "For-rest! For-rest! For-rest!"

When the excitement subsided enough to be heard, Newcomb went on. "Next, I'd like to introduce my robot assistant, who will act as my personal aide during my tenure as mayor. Gentlemen and ladies, here he comes: M. Forrest Newcomb."

M. Forrest walked over and took his position beside the mayor. The two of them clasped hands, danced in a tight circle, spinning around several times until it was impossible to tell which was which, then straightened to face the crowd.

"Who's the real Forrest?" they challenged the crowd.

The audience pointed, guessing and laughing as the twins continued their banter.

"Do these look like robot eyes?" said the one, leaning over the edge of the stage so those in the front could get a good look.

"Does this look like robot hair?" rejoined the other.

Jurat slipped on a pair of glasses. "These spectacles see in infrared. The one on the left is the bot," he proclaimed.

"Oh! You heard about the jaw trick," Cesar said, surprised. "You must have plucked it right out of my thoughts."

"Right you are. Your brain scans were most helpful," the Inspector agreed. "And I'm gonna make a fortune on these glasses. Everyone will want to know real from robot."

"I am a real robot," M. Forrest shouted.

"And I'm r-really human." Forrest bowed.

"Together, we will do great things!" they cried together.

The cheering resumed as the pair was lifted onto the shoulders of Futurist partisans and paraded around the park, finally depositing them at the edge of the sea wall in preparation for the unveiling.

Forrest took a moment to catch his breath. This reception was completely unexpected for the ne'er-do-well son of the famous senator.

Pawl slipped off the stage while the politicians continued to prattle on. He walked up to Jurat with a determined-looking scowl.

"I have a bone to pick with you."

The inspector climbed out of his hammock, looked the justice in the eye and waited for the blow to fall.

Pawl squared off with Jurat and pointed a finger at Cesar's face. "I understand you granted Komenen here immunity from prosecution. Isn't that just a little above your pay grade?"

Jurat, completely taken aback, glanced toward the two justices on stage. "Didn't you just rescind the laws he broke? And didn't he save your associates, sir?"

Pawl leaned forward. "Don't change the subject. You should have consulted me first."

Jurat recoiled. "I accept full responsibility, sir."

A voice boomed from the stage. "May I have your attention, please. A lost tabby cat with a pink collar and dragging a leather leash has been brought to the stage. Will the owner please come up and claim it?" The master-of-ceremonies held the cat aloft.

"A cat again?" Jurat muttered. "What is Lady Luck up to now?"

Scared, the cat jumped out of the announcer's arms and scampered through the audience, causing laughter and futile attempts to grab it. The poor animal finally managed to escape its pursuers by climbing on the roof of the stage, where it sat cross-legged on the edge, serenely looking down at the people, who pointed and joked cheerfully.

Pawl broke into a belly laugh. "Listen, I'm kidding, just giving you and robot-boy over here a hard time. You did an outstanding job, Inspector Jurat. I'm in such a good mood, I don't think I'll ever vote to convict anyone ever again."

Jewel looked up at the cat pensively. Something about it reminded her of something she had once seen in a vision. It was night and Venus was being chased to the horizon by the constellation Leo, and the moon drew down close to her and spoke: "Look for the Cat the Cat the Cat. When the time arrives, your destiny will be made known. Watch and wait for the Cat. All will be well."

Once the crowd settled down, the MC made one final announcement. "To commemorate this day, your sister city of Cienfuegos, Cuba, is presenting the City of Lake Worth with a symbol of the economic and political freedoms that the legalization of robots will bring to our country. My esteemed friend Cesar Komenen will now unveil this gift from the people of the Robot Republic."

Cesar stood at the ready. The band broke into a triumphant strain of "Happy Days Are Here Again." He walked up to the tall covered object and, with a quick jerk, pulled the broad silvery sheet to the ground. A collective gasp rose from the crowd.

A twenty-five-foot statue of Lady Liberty stood majestically atop the sea wall, dominating the sky, her metallic, robot face smiling at the crowd, her stony white robes glistening brightly in the midday sun.

"Wow!" Jurat said. "That's impressive."

Alice, who had snuck up as Pawl melted back into the crowd, smiled and handed him a cool glass of zin. "That makes the two of you, Solly."

Jurat laughed in surprise. He could get used to being thought of as impressive. And he loved being called Solly. It had a pleasant, sunny sound.

"Alice, did I ever tell you? You have the prettiest smile I ever did see." She beamed.

Cesar slipped away as the people continued to celebrate. He felt happy and satisfied. Standing behind the band shell, looking over the water to the bridge beyond, watching the normal, everyday traffic, folks going out to the beach for a day of sand and sun—after the intense excitement of the Remp underground, he wondered if he could be satisfied with a "normal life." He tried to picture himself married with children, going off to work at 8:15 each morning.

Jewel came up from behind and kissed him. "The lady is beautiful," she said. "Congratulations!"

"Ah, yes," he replied, pounding his chest with both fists. "I certainly did great things this last week. I could have been emperor of the world, but I'm such a great guy, I gave up wealth and fame for the good of all the little people." A sarcastic smirk stretched from ear to ear.

"Oh yes, so good, so self-sacrificing, so concerned for the well-being of society." She shoved him playfully. He momentarily lost his balance, tottering at the sea wall's edge. Jewel couldn't resist the opportunity. He was just about to regain his footing when she pushed him again. This time he knew he couldn't catch himself and was going into the water. Just at the last moment, he reached out, caught Jewel's hand and pulled her in after him. The two floundering bodies made an awkward splash as they hit the dazzling blue tropical waters.

Bystanders gathered at the sea wall looking down. They shaded their eyes, squinting into the midday glare, wondering what the commotion was about. As their two heads surfaced, Cesar and Jewel laughed. Bobbing gently, their lips met in a long, lingering kiss to the applause of the crowd. They floated effortlessly, leisurely in the bath-warm water, the rhythms of steel drums filling the air. They waved to the crowd, beckoning watchers to join them. On a carefree whim, one couple, then others started leaping, fully clothed, from the sea wall into the water. The moment felt free, weightless, unencumbered. Everyone was splashing and laughing, immersed in the moment. Sunshine glistened, strong and hopeful, off a sea of smiling, wet faces. It was a time to frolic.

# GLOSSARY OF

# SUNSHINE REPUBLIC
# TECHNICAL TERMS AND SLANG

**Alliance Group**—Business-oriented political movement responsible for the breakup of the United States into a loose alliance of small independent countries. Supports the right of local governments to retain, repeal or modify Robot Limitation Laws.

**bot**—Abbreviation for robot.

**dupe**—Abbreviation for duplicate.

**embra**—Latino slang for a young, respectable woman who is, or pretends to be, unaware of how sexy she is.

**First Wave / Second Wave**—Successive tsunamis that hit South Florida during the third quarter of the twenty-first century, originating from ocean quakes on the newly active Mid-Caribbean Fault.

**Futurist Party**—Populist movement seeking to combine the best features of capitalism and socialism; advocates restoring universal education and promotes economic justice in a free-market framework. Promotes equal distribution of robot technology between employers and

......................

employees through its No Worker Left Behind program (see entry below).

**garch**—Slang; abbreviation of "oligarch." A member of the moneyed class that controls the vast majority of the nation's wealth and dominates its political and social institutions.

**Habi-Van**—Automobile designed to be used as living quarters, manufactured by Halliburton of Najaf.

**humanoid robot**—A robot with a human-like physical form and personality functions. Usually surfaced with synth-skin. Prevalent in Cuba. Illegal in the former US, where robots were required to have metal-surfaced heads and hands.

**M.**—Abbreviation of "machine." Title for a humanoid robot, used in place of Mr. or Ms.

**metalloid robot**—A robot with a human form and metal-surfaced head and hands.

**Micro-Government Party**—Libertarian-oriented political movement that favors the abolition of all laws except those immediately concerned with protection of life, liberty and property. Advocates sale of public roads, schools, parks, sanitation facilities and fire departments to private interests. Known informally as the MGPers, jocularly as the Micro-Brewers and derisively as the Microbes.

**More Options Protocol (MOP)**—Set of rules governing robot behavior that allow dishonesty and deception. An invention of the Florida Futurist Party to override Veracity Monitoring (see entry below).

**Naabilat Creed**—2120 Declaration of the Inseparability of Religion and Politics, promulgated by the Naabilat Patriots Church of America (see next entry), calling for "a sacred crusade against Robots, Islam and Liberal Terrorists."

**Naabilat Patriots Church of America**—A nationalist movement that seeks to reserve Floridian citizenship for native, born-again Christians who adhere to the Naabilat Creed of 2120, Idaho Interpretation.

**No Worker Left Behind**—Legislative policy proposed by the Futurist Party to end the corporate monopoly on robot ownership and to assist each adult citizen in obtaining a personal worker-bee robot (see entry below).

**Rager**—A member of a loosely-organized direct-action movement advocating vigilante destruction of metalloid and humanoid robots.

**Robot Limitation Laws**—Laws that restrict ownership of robots to licensed industrial corporations and restrict usage of robots to dangerous tasks, such as nuclear reactor repair.

**synth**—Any synthetic materials, such as synth-skin, synth-muscle, synth-tendons and synth-hemoglobin used in the production of robots, or substances such as placticene or skinicon.

**Tekkie**—Slang job title for robot engineer.

**texas mutant night vulture (also mutant night vulture; night vulture)**—Species of urban night-hunting vultures that first appeared after the Dallas Dirty Bomb of 2119 and are widely assumed to be mutants of irradiated lineage.

**Veracity Monitored Protocol (VMP)**—Set of ethical rules governing robot behavior, hardwired into central circuitry, that makes honesty the highest priority.

**worker-bee robot**—A rudimentary metalloid robot designed for labor, lacking in personality and other high-level humanoid functions.

**zag / zaggy**—Socially unacceptable; synonym for uncool, behind the times, out of it, weird.

**zig / ziggy**—Synonym for cool, off-beat, unique.